The Battle for Darracia

Books I - II - III

Michael Phillip Cash

Disclaimer

The characters and events portrayed in this book are fictitious. Any resemblance to real persons, living or dead, on Earth or Darracia, is coincidental and not intended by the author.

No part of this book may be reproduced, or stored in a retrieval system, or transmitted in any form or by any means, electronic or mechanical, including photocopying, recording, or otherwise, without the express written permission of the publisher.

Schism

Book I

Michael Phillip Cash

OTHER BOOKS BY MICHAEL PHILLIP CASH

Brood X: A Firsthand Account of the Great Cicada Invasion

Stillwell: A Haunting on Long Island

The Hanging Tree: A Novella

The Flip

The After House

Witches Protection Program

Pokergeist

Life is either a great big adventure or nothing.

—Helen Keller

I

"PAY ATTENTION, YOUR Highness," the navigator implored the disinterested young man who gazed through the wall of windows. "Prince V'sair, please. Your father demanded…" The teacher pointed to the mathematical problem that hung in midair, ignored and unsolved. He raised his arm reluctantly, and the numbers dissolved, instantly to be replaced by a history lesson. The lad loved that subject; surely he would finish something today!

The teen turned, his blazing-white hair a nimbus around his lean, wolflike face. A pale, thin braid trailed down his strong back. Only males in the royal family wore them. He was a handsome boy, whipcord lean, with a high forehead and bright-blue eyes that studied his tutor with growing disdain.

"Emmicus, my head aches with your numbers and

sums. I know the speed of time inside and out. I can calculate the distance to travel to Fon Reni, get our mid-meal, and be home in time for chay with my mother. I am weary of this." The older man approached his young charge with sympathy in his rheumy eyes. "Yes, yes, I know, Your Highness. Your wit is brighter than our own Rast." He bowed his head reverently and watched the boy do the same as they repeated together, "Great Sradda, giver of all life and love, we commend ourselves to thee."

Together they made an arc with their forefingers that touched their breastbones. There was a minute of silence, so thick that the air vibrated, and the tutor, lost in prayer, failed to see the younger man look up and through the giant clear wall again. He heard the sigh and climbed out of his peaceful state. The boy was not himself today; the pained look was on his face yet again. Emmicus loved this man-child as if he had sprung from his own loins; the boy had been under his tutelage from the time he had left his mother's womb. Emmicus had taught V'sair to dress, read, fight, and ride the wild stalliuses that had been tamed for only the noble class and royalty. He had taught him to wipe his own ass, and then his nose, making sure he didn't contaminate either.

Gently Emmicus tried again. "V'sair, what is it, my son?" he asked kindly, moving close to him for privacy. Though they were alone in the room, their voices some-times carried throughout the great auditorium.

The prince looked at his elderly teacher. How to say it without hurting him? Emmicus protected him from his father's wrath when he failed to do his work and hid him when his uncle played his dirty power games.

V'sair was a half-breed, the only one in the kingdom of Darracia. Was it his fault his father, King Drakko, had traveled to Planta as a young man and married the first female he had seen there? His father had defied his tribe, cast aside his betrothed, and taken for a wife the orange-tattooed daughter of his grandfather's greatest enemy. He had found her on a mission to Planta, a world where many Darracian warriors had met watery deaths in its boundless ocean. Drakko had fought and won the heart of Reminda, princess of Adon, the lush island surrounded by a great green sea. He had stolen her away, fighting her father, then his own, to be with her. It was his greatest battle, and Reminda was his favorite prize of war.

V'sair knew others considered him to be a freak. While his father had the pebbled gray skin of the Darracian race, his skin was tan, with a hint of blue to match the silvery-blue eyes he'd inherited from his mother. Built like Reminda, he was long limbed and graceful looking, not nearly as tall as the rest of the male Darracians. His skin was smooth and hairless, making him feel like a pet rather than an offspring. He knew his father loved him as fiercely as he loved his mother, but did he trust him? Did he have faith in his abilities? A boy—nay, a man—of his age already should have learned the secrets of the Sradda. The ceremony was long overdue and did not look like it ever would occur. V'sair was older than many of his cousins, yet he hadn't received the Fireblade or spent the night locked with the elders, learning the lesson that would turn him into a warrior. It was a rite of passage that marked a Darracian male's journey to adulthood. It was as if a club had been created in which he was not allowed membership. He was no better than the Quyroos, imprisoned on the Desa, left to live in the treetops to hunt and forage for food many miles from his kingdom.

"I might as well color my skin red and wear long braids," he muttered angrily.

"Nonsense, young sir! Nonsense." The older man placed a warm hand on his shoulder. "You are royal born!" He caught V'sair's angry glare. "No one can take that away from you. You are a descendant of the most high Darracian, Carnor the First. His life force strums in your veins."

"Pah. I am equally the product of my mother's clan."

"Less so, V'sair! You have been brought up here among wealth and knowledge. You have studied hard and know the Sradda Doctriness better than anyone. You are as brave as you are smart. I am proud to have you as a pupil."

"Only you see it, Emmicus. The secrets—I want to take part in the ceremony. I fear the elders will never let me take up the Fireblade. I am being left behind. They are going to make me a…a navigator." His face blushed blue when he realized he had insulted his best ally. "I mean…there's nothing wrong with being a navigator. It's an important job, Emmicus…"

"V'sair, V'sair, stop. I know you are not meant to

be a scholar." He turned the younger man to face him. "You are a warrior, with a warrior's life force, great Sradda willing." They both bowed their heads respectfully. "Your time will come, I know. But for now, how about we recite the Sradda? If you won't do my lessons, give your old navigator some pleasure and tell me about the creation."

V'sair looked at the hope that lit up his teacher's face. The Sradda Doctrines was just a jumble of words to him. He had prayed for years and had been denied the one thing he wanted more than anything else. He'd rather be out, riding Hother, the purebred stallius his mother had presented him last year. He loved to bury his face in the white velvet neck, then take off and glide through the atmosphere, holding on for dear life. Hother could fly above the treetops, her hooves sparking with energy when they landed.

He thought he should abdicate so his older half brother eventually could take the throne. If only they would let him. Zayden was full-blooded Darracian and one of the best warriors in the army. Anyone would be happy to follow Zayden as their leader, but the plain fact of his illegitimacy made this impossible. V'sair was destined to be the future king whether or not he wanted it. He opened his mouth to complain, but when he saw Emmicus's eager face, he began the first calls to the Sradda Doctrines, hoping the melodious cadence of the tale of his ancestors, his birthright, would calm his aching heart.

He walked around the vast chamber, his booted

feet making scuffing sounds on the polished floor. It was a huge room, and he moved to position himself so his voice would echo off the vaulted ceiling. He knew this room inside and out, as he had studied there with Emmicus almost every day of his nineteen years. He was way past the age for a schoolroom; most of his boyhood friends and cousins already had taken their places in the army. He frowned, knowing he rode better than any of them, his lithe frame making him agile and fast, their Darracian bulk weighing them down. He touched his braid thoughtfully and opened his mouth, but instead of the first prayer, he continued his argument as if they hadn't stopped their discussion.

"I disagree with my father, Emmicus. You know I could hold my own against any of my cousins. *I* know I could," V'sair implored his tutor.

Emmicus bowed his craggy head. "It is true. You have Plantan agility. You are fleet of foot." He moved close to V'sair and tapped the boy's smooth forehead with his wrinkled finger. "It's what is here that is important, V'sair. You must be able to outwit your enemy." V'sair pulled away angrily; Emmicus moved his finger to the boy's heaving chest and gently touched the area over his heart. "You must use tools other than brawn to lead. Your father and I have discussed this. If you are to command, you must do it with your heart, soul, and mind. Anyone can fight, V'sair! The trinity of the Elements alone will make you a leader—the greatest in the history of Darracia. Now, if you please… 'The Song of Sradda.'"

V'sair looked up at the ceiling, unsure whether his

voice would crack with emotion. He was frustrated with Emmicus, his father, and the entire planet. He tossed his braid behind him, then placed his hand on the cold pane of glass that overlooked Cloud City and began, his voice a whisper, "The three Elements were designed by the Creator. Molding them from ether, he grew them from the nothingness of space, to pulse with the knowledge of the ages to bring life to all our worlds. Lovingly formed, with noble intention, they were dispatched by the Creator."

V'sair bowed his head as he was taught to do, making the arc of life from his fingers to his breastbone, his voice growing stronger, more confident, the words vibrating through his heart, his mouth reciting the words. But his thoughts were on the elusive Fireblade. Emmicus watchfully mirrored his motions.

"The one who created our living universe." A five-millisecond pause, and V'sair began again. "It was up to these three Elements to leave behind a universe of order. While they were created for the good of all-kind, one must earn it, work for it, for the Creator brings the spark only to those who deserve it. These are the tools, the conduit, and I shall name them…'Ozre.'"

Emmicus chanted after him, "Ozre, Ozre, light the path."

V'sair continued, "Ozre, Ozre, light the path. Ozre, oh, great Element of earth. Ozre who swirled the dust in its path, and with this the rocks were created. The rocks were heated into stars, and the stars gave birth to planets. Joining like particles of life in the air, they began their orbit, and Ozre was happy. Ozre's joy begat Ereth, giver of life."

Again the older man repeated the refrain, his eyes an odd glow of one wrapped in prayer, lost in the moment of deep thought. V'sair noted it with a smile and continued the ritual, knowing he was well trained, and his voice filled the room. He was a good yeoman, a born speaker who could call people to prayer and make the unbelievers holy once more— if only it would work for him.

"Ereth, the Element of water, giver of oceans and lakes and rivers to divide the lands. To make the Desa grow. To create the waters for the spark of life to grow. And Ereth's joy begat Ine."

"Ozre begat Ereth; Ereth begat Ine; Ine, mother of life…"

Emmicus was swaying, his body vibrating, lost in the pleasure of prayer.

"Ine, the Element of life, giver of the planets their seed of life. The first breath of existence as we know it. Creator to Ozre to Ereth to Ine—one is powerless without the other. Each is connected with the spirit of life. One without the other is not whole. The Trivium is whole. The Elements are whole."

V'sair's voice soared to the corners of the great ceiling, his bell-like tenor filling the chamber with the music of the Darracian soul. Detached, he watched Emmicus, his tutor's face rapt with the music of the words, knowing he affected the older man deeply. He wished the words could do the same for him. While he recited with all the passion that the navigator had immersed into him, the prayers meant nothing to him. He longed to understand what others felt, wondering whether his tainted blood played a role in his detachment. Though his voice was rich, he felt empty. Perhaps he was not really Darracian.

He continued softly, "And the Creator left behind his most important gift, the Trivium, our Elements. Though he is all knowing, he left these sentinels to guide us, watch us, empower us. As they move around the stars and sprinkle the seeds of life, they bathe us with their light, each with its own color of light from the spectrum of the all knowing. A shining orb of red, glowing hot, for the birth of strength; blue, ice-cold, for the reason of justice; and green, for the freedom of choice. The Creator left behind these three spirits for us, only us, so we could grow, learn, and be dominant. They are the universal subconscious. They are the all-powerful.

Without them we are nothing."

V'sair just wished he could believe they were really there.

II

THE DOOR OPENED, and his mother, Reminda, entered in a flurry of flowing robes and the flowery scent she liked to wear. Her skin also was dusted blue, but she was darker than her son, and circular orange tattoos swirled over her high cheekbones. She turned her iridescent silver-blue eyes on him. They were alight with mirth when they touched gently upon her son's face.

"Your Highness." Emmicus bowed his shaggy head, not making eye contact with the king's wife.

"Arise, Navigator." She touched the top of his forehead, and he dipped in respect. "Leave us. I have need of my son." She had a musical voice that captivated one and all.

The older man bowed once again and said, "I will see you after your visit, Your Highness, Great Sradda willing." His heels clicked loudly on the polished stone floor.

"Walk with me, V'sair. Come watch the setting suns."

"As you wish, Your Highness."

She paused and looked at his face, her eyes caressing his smooth skin. "What nonsense is this, Vsos?" she chided him affectionately. "You used to call me 'Mo'mo.'"

"I was young, Mother." He gave in halfway, still refusing to call her by his childhood name for her.

"You are angry, Vsos. Tell me what's wrong."

They stepped toward the glass wall, and as they approached, a portal opened, allowing them to step onto one of the parapets of the vast castle. Their fortress floated above the purple clouds of the planet Darracia. Two bold suns— one fiery red, named Rast; the other a dull orange, called Nost—hung low on the horizon, glowing hotly in the pewter sky. Their home was made of the red rocks of the planet, so dense and thick that it could be polished to a metallic shine and as solid as it was impenetrable. The sky around them was filled with buildings, all polished to a high gloss with red glass made from the ochre sands of the Plains of Dawid. The city was vast, the buildings tall, spread out as far as the eye could see.

Slowly small colored lights popped on, defining the city skyscape, as the day was waning. Only the castle used white lights. Randam crystals kept the city a mile above the red planet and separated from its less civilized inhabitants below. These small crystals, a gift from the Elements, powered the entire Cloud City. They were mined from the trees on the planet by the Quyroos. Darracians led the world, and the Quyroos, the people of the trees, did the labor. Cloud City was a busy metropolis, a great financial hub. V'sair saw vehicles move from port to port, taking Darracians from work to home. In the distance the residential area floated in clusters over the great Sea of Darracia. Air buses moved the Quyroos back to the planet after a weary workday. They couldn't travel back unless Darracians powered the shuttles. This system kept the two societies separate and subjugated the Quyroos to the will of the Darracians.

The Quyroos were divided into two distinct groups, Tree Dwellers and Bottom Dwellers. The Tree Dwellers lived in the tall branches of the Desa Forest and used all the resources the planet had to offer. Whatever they mined was controlled by a Quyroo league that traded only with Darracians, who then controlled all prices. The Bottom Dwellers often were outcasts, thrown from their clans to live on the floor of the forest, eating only what they could forage.

The Darracians had built a complex city here in the clouds, with its many-storied buildings floating over the mountaintops and its vast ocean, never to be touched by the unpredictability of the land.

In the distance, Aqin, the giant dormant volcano, smoked sulkily. It had erupted eons ago, long before the Darracians had seized control of the planet. Small illegal Quyroo villages dotted its craggy red hills, stubbornly clinging to their rocky walls. The Quyroos were forbidden to build on the sacred land of the great volcano, but many of the Bottom Dwellers persisted in breaking the law and tested the limits of Darracian patience and strength.

The Darracians were a prosperous people, wily as they were smart, and ruled the planet with their wits as well as their brawn, though many claimed it was only by the grace of the Elements alone. They had been the dominant force for more than a thousand years, when V'sair's long-ago ancestor Carnor the First had harnessed the power of the Elements to overcome the civil wars that were destroying Darracia.

V'sair took in the might of his father's army and smiled, knowing the Elements were not always on the side of the righteous so much as on the side with the greatest warriors. Whatever his beliefs, without the support of his kingdom, a hollow crown would rest upon his head. Without the test of the Fireblade, he may not be considered mighty enough to lead these people. His parents never had even let him hold a Fireblade, even if he knew he had the strength to light it with his warrior's heart. A heaviness rested in his chest. Darracians respected might and despised weakness.

He looked at the army of guards that surrounded the many towers, their granite faces all the same dark gray of his father. The Darracians' tough pebbled skin and huge mass made them formidable enemies. He wondered whether they would put their faith in him when the time came. Sradda willing, he thought automatically, his father should live another two hundred years, but when the time came for him to be crowned, would he have the support of these beings? They were a cold people; it was strange that his sire had taken his mother, the peaceable and pliant Plantan woman, as his mate.

Reading his thoughts, Reminda smiled and said, "You're wondering how your father chose me?" Her forked tongue touched the tips of her full lips. V'sair had the thick, solid tongue of his Darracian ancestors and had loved trying to catch his mother's serpent-like appendage when he was a child. She smiled, and her cheeks dimpled.

"It's not fair that you know all my thoughts." He had the grace to blush the palest blue. The darkening shadows, however, painted his face violet.

"Even if I were not Plantan, I would know your every thought, Vsos. You are my son." She pressed her smooth forehead against his. "Tell me of the storms that are brewing behind your fine eyes."

V'sair ducked his head away, embarrassed that the guards might have seen his mother's affection. "Stop. I told you I am not a child. Am I not allowed a modicum of privacy?" He stalked down the wide terrace, feeling the heat of the two setting suns on his face, even at this distance. If he wasn't careful, he would burn, as both he and his mother could not withstand the strong rays of both suns.

"You cannot compete with the strength of the Darracians. They will destroy you," his mother said as she calmly followed him.

"Please lower your voice." He turned to her, wanting to keep their discussion private. "How am I to be accepted as a leader if you won't let me take part in the Fireblade?"

"Son." She nodded with great understanding. "You

worry about the Fireblade. You have no need of that. You are Drakko's son, descendant of the mighty Carnor. You are an heir to the Elements. You have no need to prove yourself with the Fireblade."

"Oh no, Mo'mo." In a rush of emotion, he stopped her, and she smiled at his slip from manhood. "Don't you understand? I have to take my place beside my cousins. If I don't, they never will respect me. Aside from that, Zayden is equally the heir to the Elements. People would rush to his banner."

"Nonsense, V'sair. I adore Zayden, but he is just your father's by-blow. He is a fine warrior and will make an able counselor to aide you, but the stain of his bastardy never will allow him kingship. What talk is this? The Darracians *must* respect you. You are going to be their anointed king," she chided him.

V'sair leaned against the balustrade of the terrace and gazed at the whole of Cloud City spread out before him. One by one more lights from the buildings flickered on, and the city in the clouds looked like diamonds strewn across purple velvet. "I am not Darracian," he said.

"Oh, Vsos, of course—"

"Hear me out, please, Mo'mo."

He stopped her, and she came up to stand next to him, her slim body buffeted by the hot winds. Shading her sensitive eyes from the blazing sunset with the delicate webbing between her fingers, she shook her head. "Go on." She scanned the deepening sky, the orange flames of the two suns giving way to a mauve twilight.

"I am not like them." He gestured to the hulking

guard standing nearby, his dark gaze intent on the vista before them. "They don't understand my intellect. I am a hybrid. I am not a Plantan like you either." He showed her the corded muscles of his arm, then flexed his individual digits, finally making a fist. He watched a smile light up her face, then turned to look up at the dull sky and gestured toward the descending suns. "Look, Mo'mo. The two suns of our planet. Rast, rich with energy—its strength puts the weak shine of Nost to shame. Zayden and my cousins are Rast."

He hung his head, and she wanted to stroke his ivory-haired pate.

"I am the weakling. I am Nost. I am not even like the Quyroos."

"Thank the Elements for that, my son!" Reminda said with a tinkling laugh. "Who would want to spend their days swinging from tree to tree, living in their limited world?"

"Don't you see? I am a nobody. I am not acceptable for any of our species. I am an anomaly."

"You are the best of every world, a combination of all that's the finest of what we each have to offer. Your father and I have discussed this from the day you were born. You cannot compete with the Darracian might, so we have developed your intellect." She looked at him sideways, her eyes glittering. "Emmicus had retired, and Dado brought him back just for you. You know he tutored your father and uncle. You are the new Darracia. You will change this world with your will and fine mind. You will bring it into the present. The Quyroos want to move into the new century as equals, and they need a perceptive leader to ease the entire planet forward. Just think of what you could accomplish when all the species work together. Think of the medicine and science, and the trade that will open up with other planets. We can't be taken seriously in the galaxy as long as some of our inhabitants are oppressed. You are special. I have known that from the moment they put you in my arms. I have worked so hard for this, and things are finally changing here…" She twirled a long strand of her white hair until it curled charmingly around her triangular face. They stood in silence for a bit, watching the many stars begin to dot the blackness of the sky. She smoothed back her hair, taking it out of the ribbon that secured it at the base of her delicate neck so that it fell like a cloak around her. "It's your universe."

V'sair stared out into the horizon, knowing his mother had brought the first breath of change to his land in ten thousand years. Society had fractured here, and the two species had separated—one the oppressor, the other the oppressed. There never had been a thought for change until Reminda gently introduced ideas of enlightenment in her salons. Many a noble had sat at her table, and with good food, drink, and conversation, she was able to slowly urge prejudice and intolerance to give way to acceptance. She had rocked this planet to its foundation. V'sair looked at her serene face; he loved her with all of his being.

Reminda turned to face him, a gentle smile on her lips, her elegant hand caressing his forearm. "Your suns are burning me, Vsos. I cannot stay out any longer."

III

V'SAIR WALKED BEFORE his mother and, waving his hand, reopened the portal so they once again found themselves in the cooler confines of the castle. They walked a small distance, making an attractive couple. One might almost think them brother and sister. They had entered the vast throne room. A fire blazed in the hearth that spanned an entire wall. Drakko had installed it for his wife, who found the cold Darracia nights intolerable. V'sair looked longingly at the roaring flames but knew it would be rude to walk away from his mother.

A group of musicians played softly in the corner, and Darracians wandered from group to group. The court was full today. V'sair knew they were to have important visitors, and his parents had demanded every general and all the important noble families to be there tonight. The room buzzed with conversation. Quyroo servants with trays of food and steaming drinks mingled among the crowds. It was an elegant court—his mother had made it so—with beautiful women dressed in an array of colors, fanning themselves with the fashionable handheld disks they used to keep cool. Three Darracian females danced in a section of the room, their bodies swaying to the gentle music Reminda had chosen. A Quyroo handmaid stood just beside the arch of the doorway and held out a small jar filled with a glistening liquid. V'sair recognized her and nodded to the girl who was never far from his mother's side.

"Ah, Tulani, you read my thoughts." Reminda smiled at her.

The girl ducked her head, her auburn braids bobbing around her wiry body. She was red skinned and had the black star-shaped eyes of her people. She was dressed in servant garb, a white one-shouldered draped toga, and looked as out of place as V'sair. The prince stared at her, his blue gaze intense. He watched how she moved, his interested eyes following her lithe figure.

Reminda stopped to observe her handmaid and her son. There was an energy there; she felt it pulse along her spine, and not for the first time. The room crackled with it. Though Tulani stood with her head bowed, Reminda watched with amusement as the girl stole a glance at her son, appraising his fine form. His muscular chest looked well defined under his blue tunic, which set off his dusky skin.

As always, V'sair was oblivious to any interest in him. He was completely without guile, a rare find on

Darracia. He brushed back his shaggy white mane unselfconsciously, unaware that the girl was watching him almost breathlessly. He was handsome by any planet's standards—this his mother knew. *Ah, look, but don't touch, Tulani*, the queen thought. *I have plans for you yet.*

"Tulani!" she called out sharply. "Attend to me."

The servant didn't answer Reminda but obediently went to her side, her eyes downcast. She held the glass jar in the palm of her small hand, a cloth in the other, her face impassive. Reminda dipped her fingertips into the fluid and wiped them down her face, bringing relief to its heated surface. Her orange tattoos stood out starkly, irritated by the heat. She offered the jar to her son, who declined the cooling salve with a shake of his head.

"I'll never understand why anyone would want to burn themselves red," she said with a sniff. She glanced sideways at her handmaid and her son, a smile once again on her lips. She watched Tulani bristle, knowing she was baiting her and enjoying every minute of it. She liked her and recently had watched her perk up when V'sair entered a room. The girl vibrated with desire; she was beautiful and smart.

When Reminda had taken Tulani under her wing so many years ago, she hadn't expected to love her as she did. She had brought her up as if she were her daughter, which had angered many of her husband's people. She wondered whether V'sair had really noticed her as a female yet. Certainly tonight was the first time she had seen his attraction to her.

Tall, with the long legs of her people, Tulani had a

slim torso and small rounded breasts that were bound by her dress—just as an appropriate Darracian handmaid should appear. Reminda knew these clothes were uncomfortable for the Quyroos. They were used to wearing narrow fiber strips that covered only their loins. The girl was bright; that's why Reminda had succored her fifteen years ago. Her parents had been starving, desperate, thrown from their clan to roam the forest floor, becoming Bottom Dwellers, the lowest caste on the planet. Mori, the girl's father, was a corrupt, lazy chieftain, despised by many. He had cheated his village, and they had lost a valuable hunting domain. Tulani's grandmother, the high priestess Bobbien, maintained her rank, but barely, and served Reminda in many ways. When Bobbien feared Mori intended to sell the girl, she brought her to the castle and asked Reminda to hide her. The queen was beholden to the witch woman and took Tulani as a personal servant. While they both knew the task was beneath the girl's noble background, the role protected her from the dangers of the Desa Forest, and she grew educated in court life. Reminda never had regretted her decision; the girl proved to be an able maid as well as a trusted confidant.

She watched Tulani from under her long lashes. While the girl's head was demurely bowed, her eyes stole glimpses of V'sair. She would be good for him. He had not been initiated yet; Drakko had spoken of it but had done nothing, and that old fool Emmicus cared only for learning. It was time for her son to become a man, and while he could be injured competing in the Fireblade against an oversize monkey of a Darracian, he certainly could increase his confidence with her handmaid. Who knew where it might go from there?

It was late already; evening was descending. Reminda knew what she had to do. She worried her bottom lip; she'd never sent him to the planet below without a full complement of guards, but the queen accepted that the time had come, and timing was everything. She warred inside her mind as she thought about letting V'sair go to the Desa, but looking at Tulani gave her peace. Sometimes things just fell into place. An idea formed in her head; perhaps she had a new way to work out the restlessness from her child and appease Tulani's curiosity as well.

"V'sair," she commanded, "I have need of more Glacien ointment. It is running low."

Tulani looked up, her dark eyes wide in her face. What Reminda had said was untrue, but when she caught her queen's dancing eyes, she stilled her tongue.

"Take my girl," Reminda told her son. "Yes, go with Tulani, and bring me some from the Deep Fells."

"The Deep Fells? It's past sunset. Surely one of your—"

She turned an angry face to V'sair. "What? Does a mother ask too much from a son?" she demanded loudly, and the music stopped. She then lowered her voice. "Are you afraid to go to the planet's surface?".

V'sair's pale skin turned a darker shade of blue. Clearly embarrassed by her question, he shook his head. She shot a fierce glare at the bandleader and nodded regally for him to resume. He hurriedly motioned for the group to again play the gentle wind instruments.

The door opened, and King Drakko, his son Zayden, and two high-level Petrion guards flanking them entered the room, bringing a draft of cool air that always seemed to envelop the king. V'sair saw Drakko's eyes light up upon spying Reminda. His half brother was much older than he and a perfect specimen of Darracian manhood. Tall and imposing, he smiled at V'sair, his amber eyes twinkling. Zayden looked so much like the king that from a distance they could be confused. Drakko had allowed him a royal braid, and he wore it proudly. V'sair saw Zayden scan the room, knowing he was looking for someone, and registered surprise when his half brother's eyes rested on the welldressed back of a female. V'sair couldn't make out who it was at this distance.

He watched his mother shiver with delight. Her eyes glowed when they settled on her husband's broad chest. Drakko was a mountain of a man, with shoulders so wide that V'sair used to pretend he was swinging from one tree-top to another, just like a Quyroo, when he was a young-ster. He wore his pitch-black hair in a thick royal braid that reached the middle of his wide back. Of late V'sair had noticed a few silver stands entwined in the dark locks.

A strict, firm disciplinarian, his father demanded loyalty, bravery, and hard work from everyone in his charge. The only individual who openly defied Drakko was his twin brother, Staf Nuen, the grand mestor. He was V'sair's uncle and a heartbeat away from being the heir—V'sair's heartbeat.

Tulani dropped to her knees, but both Reminda and V'sair dipped one knee only.

"Reminda, my lovely." The king guided his wife up, taking her elegant webbed hand and kissing it. Drakko was almost twice her size, and V'sair felt dwarfed by him. While V'sair was tall and slim, the Darracians were huge, with beefy chests that filled their armor. They had thick legs and short, muscular tails that could be deadly in a fight. "V'sair." His father nodded, allowing him to stand straight. "Where is your navigator?"

"My lady mother dismissed him for the day."

As Reminda rested her thin arm on the ropy surface of his, Drakko headed to the audience hall, the rest of the group following silently. Together they looked like platinum and gold. Drakko's armor glittered in the light of the room, and Reminda's dress sparkled as her many jewels reflected the light. The whiteness of her hair was the perfect foil to his father's jet-black mane. The king acknowledged many of the clusters of men, while his mother proudly held her head high and smiled serenely. Here and there they stopped to speak with a group, laughter floating among the many diverse conversations. The music changed, becoming martial, a favorite of his father's. It served to drown out the echoes of the booted footsteps of the Darracian guards marching in the adjacent hallways. Noble ladies walked in small groups, nodding demure greetings. V'sair spied his aunt, Countess Beatha, strolling with a small entourage, his four female cousins trailing dutifully behind her. There was bad blood between his mother and aunt, but V'sair didn't know the source of it. Beatha was a cold woman and barely acknowledged him, bordering disrespect; V'sair never liked her. He caught his youngest cousin, Hilde, peeking up, her gaze resting on Zayden, who returned her look with a strange intensity. *Oh ho*, he thought with amusement, *so that's the way the wind is blowing.* V'sair smirked, knowing tonight he finally had a formidable weapon to tease his impervious, perfect sibling.

Hilde let loose a nervous giggle that floated in the air. Only the countess's baleful expression quieted her laugh. V'sair noticed Emmicus's entry to the room, but when he thought to approach him, his tutor turned to discuss something with one of his father's many generals. He walked over to his half brother with a smile playing on his thin lips.

"Is something going on with Hilde?" he asked innocently.

Zayden rested his hand on the young prince's shoulder. "Hilde? No. How goes your lessons?"

"I'd rather be out with you."

"Father will not allow it. He doesn't want you polluted by the rabble I ride with." Zayden smiled, a dimple appearing in his cheek.

"I probably would learn more about leadership with your rabble than I do being stuck in a classroom with Emmicus."

Zayden shrugged. "Someday you will long for lazy school days and miss the droning of history lessons."

They walked together toward the roaring wall of fire. Zayden took two glasses from a passing servant and handed one to V'sair. "Hide behind that pole, and drink it fast. Do not let the king see it." He smiled at his younger brother's eager face. "Do it quickly, V'sair.

If I get caught, Father will send me to watch over the shuttles for the rest of the year."

V'sair glanced at his parents, who were walking around the perimeter of the room, smirked, and gulped the fiery liquid in one shot. His eyes opened wide as he wheezed, his breath caught between his gullet and his chest.

Zayden laughed as he thumped him mightily on the back. "Not that fast, you keewalla. Don't blame me if you start weaving around the room!"

♦

"Reminda," the king admonished his wife, still not finished discussing his son's tutor, "you indulge him. He must continue his studies. If he is not to be a warrior, he must be able to lead with his mind." He guided her toward the golden throne that sat on a dais under a blue-starred awning. The firelight illuminated her beautiful face, and Drakko's breath caught in his throat. She was as lovely today as she was when he had stolen her from her watery home fifty years ago.

"Tosh, tosh," she said, dismissing Drakko's guards. "He is the child of your noble loins, my liege. He can outwit the fiercest monster. He has my tensile strength just waiting to be unleashed." Reminda smiled knowingly and swayed closer to him, her hair catching on the foil of his cloak. "It is time for him to go on an errand," she confided softly.

Drakko paused and raised one dark eyebrow, his eyes

warm on her face. "An errand, my love? You would make our son and heir a servant?"

"Hardly." She teased him with the dual points of her tongue, her smile wide and inviting.

"I am sending him with Tulani." She nooded knowingly. "Not all lessons should be learned in the schoolroom. I will give her special instructions," she added coyly.

"It is late." Drakko searched Reminda's face. "Do you think this wise?"

"I am not happy about sending him to the Desa at this hour, but he is restless, Drakko. If we don't allow him some freedoms…Oh, look!" Her eyes caught V'sair and Zayden on the edge of the room. "If V'sair gets too drunk to ride, I will strangle Zayden."

Drakko's eyes followed hers and rested on the antics of his sons. He sighed. "I see what you are saying."

"Sometimes we must let nature do what it must." Reminda faced him. "It is not easy, but we must let him find himself."

"He is young. I thought sometime next year." Drakko frowned. "Should I send a detail to follow him?"

Reminda raised her finely arched brows. "If he sees them, Tulani will never have a chance. V'sair is exceedingly private." She saw her husband's dark lips purse. He was struggling with the whole idea. "He wants to learn the Fireblade," Reminda told him in a soft voice. "It will kill him."

"I agree, but he does not feel like a man."

Drakko grunted. "I was afraid of this. I cannot let him do it, Reminda. He is your only son. There are many who would take this opportunity—"

"Tosh, tosh, my husband. You have made the king-dom safe. You have set the stage for a great future. V'sair will bring in a new age to this planet—one of peace and unity. Quyroos, Darracians, and Plantans will have an equal say in the Moon Council."

"In that order, my love?" he asked her with a charming smile. He was so rakishly handsome that her eyes never tired of drinking in his strength and masculine beauty.

Drakko held her hands in his giant ones. "You are cold?" His face appeared concerned. He looked up and called to one of the many attendants, "A wrap for my lady!" Then he looked at the two Quyroos who fed the constant fire in the enormous fireplace. "Build up the fire!"

They turned the lever that added fuel, and he watched the flames roar, the heat bathing Reminda's face. Many of the Darracians hurriedly moved away from the warmth; Countess Beatha scowled and tossed off one of her jackets. She snapped for a servant to bring her fan, opened it, and made a great display of her growing discomfort with the heat. Drakko smirked and told the servants to make it hotter. He motioned for an attendant to bring a steaming cup of chay for his wife. When it was delivered to her, she sipped it with a satisfied smile.

Reminda had worked hard to tame this wild race. Darracian men were quick to temper, and Drakko's father had ruled this planet with an iron fist. Though she came from another world, Darracians did not take well to any-one who looked different. It was only after the birth of their child that she had seen a change in her husband. A smile touched her lips when she thought of the first time she had placed the soft, mewing newborn into his ironlike embrace. The steel had melted, replaced with a bond of love. That day the great warrior king had changed forever.

Drakko threw back his great head and roared with laughter. "So it is finally time?" he asked Reminda, his face full of mirth. "You know I would have arranged it." He looked at the servant girl appreciatively. "It is late for him to be traveling to the Desa."

"I know, but we have to let him do something...Oh, I can't believe this!"

"What?" Drakko started to turn.

"No, no. Don't look at them." She pulled his arm so that he faced her. "Zayden has just given him another a drink." She laughed lightly. "Poor V'sair. He has such a stupid look on his face."

Drakko smiled. "Should I call Zayden?"

"I need to speak to Tulani. He should be fine by then. Make sure this is his last one."

"Of course. Do you need me to talk to V'sair?"

"There is no need. Mo'mo has it all handled. One moment, m'aore," she said affectionately as she caressed his rugged face. Reminda held up an elegant finger and motioned for Tulani to follow her to an alcove in the room.

◆

V'sair stood in the center of the room, nodding to various guests. He spied a group of unmarried daughters of noble birth gathered close to a water-filled structure with fish from around the planet. It was a globe, with colorful deep-sea specimens. Hands behind his back, he wandered over, looking to engage in conversation, but their remarks froze him in his tracks.

"So, if you marry him, there's a chance his mother's fishy toes will grace your children's feet."

"That white hair, even if it has a royal braid, is hard to stomach," another said with a giggle.

"I don't mind Zayden."

"Your father would kill you and probably betroth you to Pacuto."

"Did you see how small Zayden's tail is?"

"At least he has one!" came an amused reply.

V'sair stalked off, disgusted with the conversation. He despised them and wondered whether he would have to stomach one of them as a wife one day.

IV

V'SAIR WANDERED OVER to his father and dipped a knee.

"Sire."

"Son." Drakko looked at his V'sair's flushed face and put his arm around the boy's narrow shoulders. They were strong, he knew, but could they hold the weight of their world on them? He smiled conspiratorially at his older son and nodded toward a group of officers who were arguing in the corner. Zayden understood immediately, leaving to represent his father in the discussion. Drakko was proud of Zayden; he was a strong warrior, loyal, and one day would serve V'sair very well. He looked down at the frowning face of his younger son. This one had a special place in his formerly cold Darracian heart. He hadn't known he was capable of that kind of feeling until Reminda entered his life. It was so simple but also so complicated now. He loved the boy, but would his people follow him?

After so many years of strife, Drakko had forged a tentative peace that the citizens of the planet hadn't shared for eons. Great Sradda willing, V'sair would be able to take Drakko's foundation into the next generation. Their planet had been so close to total annihilation, with species killing species; it had been a brutal time. But the Elements had reached Drakko through his love for Reminda, and he had been able to turn the might of his armies to bring reason to all the warring factions. It was as difficult as riding a wild stallius. Although it was sometimes a thankless job, his work had paid off, and for the first time in many millennia, Darracia was enjoying a new awakening, and he was the driving force. Though many had tried to sabotage his plans, the planet was moving toward unity. Small outbreaks of violence still erupted, but he was working very closely with the Quyroos to bring about peace. Would V'sair be able to complete what Drakko had begun? He snapped to a servant to bring a drink to water down the liquor in his son's stomach.

V'sair took in the lowered brows of his father and asked, "Something troubles you, sire?"

"Just the usual. How go the studies, my son?"

V'sair declined the glass, but his father insisted. "Drink it, V'sair."

He did so with little grace, feeling it wash away the dreaminess of the drinks Zayden had shared with him. He liked those better, he wanted to tell his father, but chose not to. Instead, feeling courageous, he decided to broach the subject that stood between them.

"Father..." V'sair turned to look as his father. "When can I...I mean...studies are fine, but I must be tested by the Fireblade."

Drakko turned away abruptly. "No. You are not built for the Fireblade, V'sair. We will not discuss it."

"But Dado," V'sair complained, "how can your people respect me if I don't accept the challenge? I must. It's a rite of passage. How can I lead if I cannot set an example?"

"They are your people too, V'sair. Respect will come from what you do, not how you fight."

"You have held this land together with force."

"Only to bring peace." He took his son by the arm and walked through the great room, waving away his guards. He nodded to Emmicus but did not call him over. "Those were different times. I have only you, V'sair. Things are changing. The Quyroos will not continue as they have before. I brought back Emmicus to ensure you had the best education. You are the future of this world."

"But the customs--" V'sair implored him.

"We will circumvent this custom."

"Circumvent!" V'sair was shocked. "You cannot. Every king, every soldier, everyone—even Emmicus— has been tested by the Fireblade."

"I can circumvent whatever I want. I am the king!" His father pumped his gloved fist into the air, his voice booming.

The room quieted, the music stopped, and V'sair noticed that everyone stared at them. His father glowered at the crowd and waved off the musicians, who gathered up their instruments and left. He stalked to the other side of the room, and V'sair knew the subject was closed. A cluster of advisors and top generals surrounded Drakko, and V'sair angrily stopped himself from following. Emmicus wandered over to the group, his shaggy gray head deep in thought.

Night was falling, and the great hall was illuminated by bright lights that reflected off the polished red walls. Screens hung from four posts; the nightly news was on. A female Darracian newscaster was speaking, the image of a raging fire behind her. Concerned Darracians surrounded the screens, murmuring softly, watching the news unfold. Drakko was deep in discussion with several council members. One of them appeared quite angry; General Swart was arguing fiercely with the king. He was one of the older officers and was walking a fine line. V'sair wondered whether his father would erupt during General Swart's tirade. The prince wandered over to one of the screens and caught only that the fires were in the eastern provinces, where lately there had been Quyroo unrest.

"These are troubling times, Your Highness." V'sair knew Emmicus was standing next to him before he spoke.

"Why do they build on Aqin? It is foolhardy as well as against the law. That land is considered sacred."

"Think, sire. Why would the Bottom Dwellers tempt Darracian wrath?"

"I don't understand," V'sair said. "The Quyroos finally desire peace. My father has met with them."

"Yes…"

"The settlements only put off the peace talks. How can my father trust them if they can't control their own…Oh, Emmicus! I understand!" Light dawned on V'sair's face. "It's a power play to keep the accord from happening."

"Just so, young master." Emmicus beamed. "Our lesson continues after all. As long as the Bottom Dwellers continue to settle on the forbidden lands of Aqin, there will be no peace accord. Should their tampering with the holy land of Aqin awaken the wrath of the volcano, the whole of Darracia will be in danger. Just look at those fires," Emmicus noted, clicking his tongue. The reporter on the giant screen continued to speak of a growing rebellion in the eastern provinces.

The newscast suddenly was drowned out by the blare of trumpets announcing V'sair's uncle.

Staf Nuen entered the room, his son—V'sair's cousin Pacuto—walking purposefully next to him. They wore flowing black capes, and the red dust of their planet covered their boots. They must have just come from the outdoors. They wore full armor, and while Staf's braid was wound tightly, Pacuto's looked slightly disheveled. Staf wore a neatly manicured beard that covered his pitted face. He was battle scarred and a pale imitation of his handsome twin brother. Staf brushed past V'sair without even a nod and approached the king, dipping his knee ever so slightly, almost an insult.

His father never seemed to mind, but it bothered V'sair. His cousin, as usual, ignored him.

"Highness," Staf growled in a raspy, powdery baritone, rudely interrupting General Swart.

Drakko inclined his head as he smiled benignly. "Staf. I can see by your impatience that you have news for me," he added indulgently.

Staf bristled, and Pacuto's face was an impassive mask.

V'sair wandered over to find out what was going on, but the group blatantly ignored his presence.

"The Quyroos in the eastern quadrant have dammed the river Stevin. Our supplies are at the halfway point. They demand a seat in the Darracian Moon Council."

"Childish pranks that were put down by General Swart before dusk," the king answered curtly, his gray face impassive. General Swart bowed deeply, a smirk on his granite face.

Staf was outraged. "I saw the fires!"

"A diversion. The supplies were released, the youngsters sent on their way," General Swart responded smugly. He hated Staf Nuen, thought him a bully. Even though Swart argued with the king, he was loyal unto death and never would let Staf know he disagreed with any of Drakko's policies. He had wanted to destroy the Quyroo village. It was his suggestion that they torch the settlement to teach them a lesson, but this new era of peace and understanding was interfering. Swart stared hard at the crown prince and fervently prayed for the good health of the king, Great Sradda willing.

What would happen if the boy reigned? He shuddered with distaste. World order was in jeopardy; the entire planet was upside down. Bottom Dwellers were building on the sides of the great volcano, tempting the Elements. Quyroos considered themselves equal to the population of the clouds. They wanted to control the export of the randam crystals. In his 150 years, Swart never thought he'd see such nonsense. Yet the king refused to act as his father had before him. The Plantan woman had made him soft, he thought with disgust. But Swart was the king's liege and knew his duty. Staf Nuen's roar interrupted his thoughts.

"Sent on their way!" Staf exploded. "This is how you treat rebellion? Will you invite them to dinner as well?"

General Vekin, Drakko's most powerful commander, bristled at Staf's insulting tone, and his broad face darkened with anger. He was about to answer, when the king broke the tension with a chuckle.

"How did you know?" Drakko laughed. "The most high lord, Jonis, leader of the Quyroos, is on his way for our evening meal. He brings his female—a lovely girl, I've heard." There was a challenge in Drakko's softly spoken words.

"The times are changing, Brother. A new dawn has come."

"The evening has just started," Staf said. "Dawn has much to bring."

"The Quyroos merely want a spot on the council. It is hardly the end of the world. We need the randam crystals. They have them. It's simple politics."

"We don't need their permission to take the crystals. We never did."

Drakko considered this for a moment, thinking how best to answer his brother. "Well, yes, this is true, but what has it gotten us? The Elements tell us to work together."

"*Darracians.* The Elements were given to the Darracians." Pacuto couldn't help himself and burst into the conversation. Everyone stared at him, appalled at his rudeness.

Zayden rested his hand on the pommel of his sword, his face contemptuous, his stance threatening.

General Swart glared at the young man, his eyes two shards of glass. "In my day," he began in a withering voice, "we threw hotheads off the balconies."

The king stayed his old general with a hand, but Staf Nuen was livid. Embarrassed and furious, he wanted to teach the old Darracian a lesson but instead took out his anger on Pacuto.

Staf turned angrily on his son. "Quiet, young fool! Go stand by your mother," he growled.

"I was only stating the obvious!" Pacuto replied defensively.

"Go stand with the women. Now!" Staf commanded him, his voice a menacing hiss.

Pacuto hesitated, his face suffused with a dark grayness. Drakko held up a finger and urged him to come closer. The king narrowed his gaze at his nephew. The boy was big, almost twice the size of V'sair. He had lead-colored skin and small glittering eyes. He was dull and good for his army, nothing more. He never would rise past captaincy; he was too stupid to be trusted, the king thought. He wondered briefly whether he should award him a governorship on one of the isolated planets located thousands of miles away, just to separate him from his father. Drakko saw trouble brewing behind those angry eyes.

"The Elements were given to the Darracians to guard

for the well-being of all the species on the planet. The Quyroos have evolved. They have schools and hospitals. They are building cities now. They are no longer primitive, and"— Drakko's face was inches from his nephew's, his voice menacing but quiet—"they share our planet. They should have a say in the Moon Council."

The Darracian Moon Council met during the moon's third phase in order to discuss planetary events. Both Quyroo groups, the Tree Dwellers and Bottom Dwellers, had long been excluded from any decisions. Of late the Tree Dwellers had made strong overtures to work constructively with the Darracians. They controlled the sap from the cathedral-like forests, which dripped from the trees and eventually formed the randam crystals. These minerals powered the fuel that kept the Darracians' floating city airborne. The Tree Dwellers knew the ancient techniques to gather the sap, and the secret formula to transform it into valuable fuel. In exchange for the crystals, they wanted a say in the government of the planet. It had been a hot topic, with the entire population divided. Drakko was leaning toward allowing them a seat on the council.

It's an abomination, Staf thought angrily. Darracians had ruled the planet for eternity. The Quyroos were tree people, incapable of rational discourse. They were beneath the Darracians on every count, subpar, barely coherent, and now his own brother was entertaining allowing them a say in the council. *What next?* His thoughts raced through his head. *Perhaps he'll appoint one of them as a grand mestor.*

"And…?" the king asked, noting Staf was bristling with anger.

"And," Staf responded, flustered, "I told you last month that we should have destroyed the eastern provinces when they first rebelled." He punched a gloved hand into his large fist.

"Appealed, applied, asked…" Drakko corrected. "They have used legal channels to ask for a voice."

"It smacks of revolution, Your Highness. Rebellion must be rooted out. We cannot let them attend. Next they'll demand a vote."

"Who knows?" the king said with a laugh. "They may share our city in the clouds one day."

"You are soft, Brother," Staf whispered fiercely.

"You are hard. Soft bends and is resilient; hard breaks. Hard cannot bend. Times are changing, Staf. The winds of the spirits have brought change."

"You speak like a Plantan." V'sair felt the heat of his uncle's narrowed gaze. "You must root out insubordination. That has always been the Darracian way."

"Who knows, Staf? Perhaps your son will marry a Quyroo," the king said with a grin as he turned his back on his brother to join V'sair.

V

REMINDA STOOD IN the alcove with the red-skinned girl, appraising her. "You held your tongue." She smiled with approval.

Tulani dipped her head and replied softly, "I know Your Highness is well aware of how much salve she has." She was rewarded by the queen's musical laugh.

Reminda saw the smile in the girl's eyes. "You like my son?" she slyly asked.

"Who does not admire Prince V'sair?" she answered coolly.

She was a smooth one, Reminda observed. She had seen the attraction, had watched those dark star-shaped eyes soften when the prince entered the room.

While the girl was young, Reminda knew instinct drove her. Of all her servants, Tulani was her favorite—strong, smart, and the granddaughter of the Quyroo priestess, Bobbien. She had yet to come into her own.

"You know what is expected of you?" the queen asked.

Tulani licked her generous lips. "I have an idea."

"I am sure you do." Reminda grinned. "You will be rewarded."

"The reward is in the trust Your Majesty has given me." She bowed her head respectfully, but Reminda saw something fierce in her eyes.

"My precious jewel." Reminda looked out a large window to the velvet skies. "V'sair is my precious jewel. This may be your destiny."

The girl looked up proudly. "I know," she said simply.

"You'll do." The queen's cool fingers touched the girl's forehead. Something tingled between them; an understanding was exchanged, words unnecessary. "You'll go to your lady grandmother." Bobbien would watch out for them and keep them safe, the queen knew.

"I had thought of another place."

"Ah?" The queen tilted her elegant head.

"He will want privacy, I think."

"But is it safe?"

"I feel safe." Tulani shrugged in typical Quyroo fashion.

"Just so. Where?"

"I know of a place."

"Stay away from the eastern provinces," the queen told her and glanced up to watch her husband and his brother argue. She thought to add, "And Staf Nuen."

They walked to the center of the room, Reminda's eyes searching for her son. She glided away from Tulani and over to her husband, who opened his wide embrace and enfolded her in the security of his arms.

"You have spoken to the girl?" he asked, dismissing General Swart and the others. He was done with his brother and his tiresome temper.

Without a backward glance, Staf walked away. Reminda watched her brother-in-law's face turn a violent shade of purple.

The king kissed her hand and rubbed it against his face.

"You give me great pleasure."

"No regrets for mating an outsider?" she asked, flirting with him. Though they were in a room filled with people, the entire court surrounding them, they felt as if they were alone.

"Never." He picked her up, oblivious to the crowd, and carried her toward their chamber. Before he left he turned to his openmouthed son. "What are you waiting for? Your lady mother gave you an errand." Then he left them all, his laughter bouncing off the stone walls long after he disappeared.

VI

STAF NUEN TAPPED his gloved hand impatiently against his enormous palm. His eyes narrowed with hatred at his nephew. He watched General Swart leave the hall and wondered what was bothering the older man. The king's bastard followed him out like an obedient puppy. Though Staf was often at odds with the general, perhaps there was room for discussion now. Swart was a hard-liner, fighting the coming peace talks, but his unwavering loyalty to Drakko was legendary. Perhaps if he could get him alone, they could reach an agreement. As far as General Vekin was concerned— well, he was an insect, and Staf couldn't wait to crush him into a pulp.

"What errand does he attend to?" Pacuto growled rudely.

Pacuto would make any Darracian father proud. Tall as his father, with a devious mind, he was a bold warrior who never played by the rules. He was known for his tryath, a curved dagger he had mastered. He could carve a man's head from his body, and the victim wouldn't even realize it until it had landed in his lap. His single brow gave him a perpetual scowl, and his bad temper made him one of the most feared army captains. He hated the king's sons. Though Zayden was no threat to the succession of the throne, he longed to kill the smug bastard. His fisted hand itched to grab the royal braid and lop off his insolent head. It was an abomination that the king insisted he be treated equally as those born of noble birth. He despised his sickly looking, blue-tinged cousin, the prince, with equal intensity. He was barely a Darracian. Pacuto sneered as he watched the Quyroo girl follow his regal cousin toward the door.

Where is he going, and why with that servant? Pacuto wondered. He stopped a servant and took a steaming drink, gulping it with satisfaction. Watching her swaying behind, he smiled, baring his pointed teeth. He had a Quyroo servant girl at home too and licked his lips as he thought of her. She was waiting for him in his chambers, chained to his bed. It was forbidden to keep servants chained, but Pacuto used his position to do as he pleased. Who would be stupid enough to report him anyway? He had left her early this morning, after having used her all night. She wasn't as pretty as the queen's girl, though. He'd like to wipe the smile off that one's face. She was always at Reminda's side. No one could get to the queen without first speaking to that Quyroo. He saw her superior attitude when his sisters served the queen. He would have to see if he could get her alone. Yes, he'd ruin that condescending smirk, he thought, fingering his dagger.

Pacuto grabbed another glass, but when he raised his hand to drink it, Staf stayed his arm. "I need you to be alert tonight."

"What?" Pacuto held up the light-green drink. "I can drink ten of them and be alert!" he boasted. His eyes followed the queen's servant, and he sneered.

"Humor me." Staf observed his son with detached amusement. "Tomorrow you can drink yourself to hell, and I won't say anything. You can get drunk with that one chained to your bed." Staf gestured toward Tulani. "To your reward," he said as he tossed back the liquor.

"That was mine," Pacuto complained.

"We need V'sair to remain here," his father said gruffly, his narrowed gaze following the prince.

"What will you do?"

"This will delay things." He walked to the throne and placed a hand on its golden arm. "A delay!" he cursed under his breath.

Countess Beatha glided over to her husband and son. Sensing discord, she placed her fingers on his arm, stopping him. "Something is wrong?" She had slits for eyes, her mouth a purple rictus of hate. She was older than her husband, a general's daughter, as well as his cousin. Originally betrothed to his brother, the king, he was forced to marry her when Drakko had wed the Plantan female. Though he never had wanted her, her dowry had included all of her father's lands. When the old man died, she inherited so many men of arms that

Staf became the most powerful general on all of Darracia. She had given him only one son, Pacuto, but also four daughters, who would bring him good alliances. Staf and Beatha had groomed Pacuto his whole life. He was the greatest warrior on the planet and had achieved the highest level when he had taken his Fireblade. It was still talked about three years later. Their combined lust for power had created a super Darracian, one who would be worthy of leadership, Sradda willing.

"She sent the boy on an errand," Staf told Beatha.

"This complicates things. Will you put it off?" she demanded.

He turned to her, his eyes glittering like obsidian. "I cannot. Everyone is in place. Every commander has been ordered to the palace tonight to welcome the Quyroo delegation. We'll never have another chance like this. We go tonight." His eyes blazed with an inner fire.

"My father always said, 'Divide and conquer.' Send Pacuto to follow him. He can dispose of them both by himself."

"I cannot take a chance that V'sair might escape," Staf responded, his voice curt.

"Pacuto will make sure he doesn't."

"He is my second-in-command. He should be here by my side," Staf murmured. "He is my heir."

"*Our* heir. I will be here to take my place at your side; he can join us later," Beatha continued, her voice filled with venom. "This is to be my victory too. I should be queen."

It was a long-standing feud; her resentment at Drakko

still simmered. When he stubbornly had taken the Plantan woman as his wife, then had the audacity to crown her as queen, Beatha's cold heart had turned to stone.

Staf grunted in assent and motioned his son closer.

Pacuto ambled over, confident and excited about tonight's plan.

"Follow V'sair."

"But Father, I need to be here." His reptilian eyes flashed with anger.

This earned him an angry glare. Blood rushed to Staf's face as resentment filled his chest. "Enough!" he ordered. "Follow the prince and kill him."

"I can do that and be back in time for the coup."

"I expect no less from you. Take two guards. Remember, he has Hother." The stallius was the fastest mount in Darracia.

"Pah. Winata can beat him any day," his son boasted. "I'll be back before you even begin, with his head on my belt to show his parents when you destroy them."

VII

V'SAIR STORMED THROUGH the castle to the stables, angry at his parents, furious to have Tulani as company. She was Quyroo, red skinned with thick mud-col-
ored braids that came down to her slender hips. Every
so often he caught her black starshaped eyes watching
him. It was forbidden for her to make eye contact with a
royal, and her boldness astounded him.

"I can't keep up with Your Highness," she called out
to him, her long dress hampering her from keeping up
with his wide-legged stride.

He stopped, yanking her hand and pulling her along
with him. The drinks he'd had with Zayden made him
feel reckless. Their palms fit strangely together, and he
felt the warmth of her blood pulse under her skin. He
wanted to disengage his hand from hers but also wanted

to hold it tighter. He didn't know what he wanted and felt mightily uncomfortable.

"Highness, please," she pleaded. "Go slower. Surely your lady mother does not expect us to run the whole way."

V'sair turned on her, his eyes blazing. "You dare to imply that you know what my mother, the queen, is thinking?"

Tulani wasn't afraid of him, and squaring her shoulders, she looked up to him boldly and shrugged. "Certainly you realize I know your mother better than anyone here. She took me from the treetops of Desa fifteen years ago and has kept me at her side ever since."

V'sair was breathing hard, his chest moving quickly. "I didn't ask for you to come. You will only slow me down," he said haughtily. He was smarting that for his first trip to the Desa alone, they had saddled him with a baby-sitter, not only younger than him but also female.

"Oh, you think so?" she challenged him, standing firm. "You will never find my family's encampment without me. You are a Darracian. You don't understand the Desa," she finished acidly.

She had hit a nerve, and V'sair's voice grew thunderous. A vein bulged on his forehead, pulsing with anger. "I could have you arrested." He met her eyes with a steely gaze.

"Ah, but I am your mother's favorite. She sent me with you for a reason."

"Why?" he demanded.

Two guards marched past them, and V'sair pushed Tulani into a small corridor. She was openly defiant, and for some reason, V'sair didn't want anyone else to see it.

She nettled him; he turned to find her face inches from his own. Instinctively they held their breaths until the echoes of the booted feet receded. In close confines they stared at each other, her moist eyes watching him with amusement.

"I know not the queen's mind, do I, Prince?" she asked him. Though her voice was a subservient whisper, it bordered on sarcasm.

The corridor was quiet; only water dripping from a high ceiling broke the silence. He had known this girl his whole life but never really had noticed her before. Her unwavering gaze irritated him, and he wondered whether she would act this way if the queen were present.

V'sair turned to stare out the panoramic windows that ran along the red rock walls. Lights shimmered in the distance; ships zipped through the air; and the ever-present Petrion guards, riding inky-colored stalliuses, pranced through the night sky.

Despair overwhelmed him. "I am not even Darracian," he muttered to himself. "Not Darracian, not Plantan, not Quyroo. A freak," he whispered under his breath.

Tulani moved closer, feeling his sadness, sorry she had appeared defiant. Sometimes she couldn't help herself. "Your Highness?" She touched his shoulder, and a current sparked between them.

He spun suddenly, surprise on his face. Coloring, he turned back to the window, ignoring her. His whole body was tense, and he felt threatened by the strange feeling coursing through his body when he looked at her. His lungs were robbed of breath, and he averted his eyes so she wouldn't catch them roaming her lithe frame.

She stood silently beside him, drinking in his presence, hoping she had calmed the raging tornado she sensed in him.

She had a light scent that teased the prince's nose. He let his breathing return to normal, and when he felt ready to speak, he asked her softly, "Why? Why did she take you from here?" Tulani represented all that he was, an outsider, an outcast never to be accepted.

"I'm sorry…What?"

"Why did my mother take you from the Desa?"

"Who knows? I only know she took me when I was young and has trained me to fulfill her every need. You may not want to hear this, but I do know what she is thinking all—well, most—of the time," she finished with a gentle smile.

V'sair looked at her for the first time really, trying to disengage this new, unwanted attraction. She was pretty; he noticed she wore her makeup similar to his mother's. She clearly was not Darracian but of the conquered Quyroos, the treetop people. She was tall but delicate, perfectly formed, with the delineated muscles of her species.

"Do you miss your family?" he asked her.

The girl shrugged. "I hardly know them. The queen sends me home every quarter moon to reacquaint myself, but they are angry."

"Why?"

"I cannot be mated with one of my tribe. I have lost my chance. There was a dispute many years ago. My grandmother took control of the family, and it has brought more shame to my father. My parents have lost their fortune. They are aging and have no one to defend them. They have become Bottom Dwellers."

V'sair nodded, understanding this was not a good thing. Bottom Dwellers roamed the planet's surface, banished from the treetops, where most of the food could be found. Instead they foraged on the forest floor, eating what refuse they could find. They were the lowest life-forms on the planet. They didn't fit in, and this was a feeling with which he was familiar.

He looked at the girl and asked, "Does my mother know this?"

"You mother knows everything. It's whether she cares or not that matters."

"Then does she care?" he asked carefully.

"She sends me home with supplies. She allows my family to make Glacien ointment."

"From the Deep Fells?"

The girl smiled, her small, feral teeth bright in her face. "If she chooses to believe that." "Do…do you like it here?"

Tulani looked up at the soaring ceilings. Her words were trapped in her throat, held captive until the right moment. How could she explain what she felt? He had her heart; must he rip apart her soul as well?

"'Like' is subjective," she told him simply. Living here was torture, knowing he would be taken from her when a political marriage would have to be made. Yet staying near and waiting for a chance like this was worth everything. If they had only a short time together, it must last a lifetime for her.

V'sair smiled, his thin mouth revealing perfect white teeth. She amused him. "Subjective how?"

Tulani thought and finally answered, choosing her words with extreme care. "Your mother shows a great preference for me. Sometimes it creates tension in our court."

"Yes?"

"Well…"

She bit her top lip, and V'sair thought her endearing, her arms folded defensively across her chest. *You are not so bold as you want others to believe*, he thought, a smile tugging at his lips.

"Sometimes others make those from the Desa feel unwelcome. It can be…disheartening."

"Do you share this information with my lady mother?"

Tulani walked over to the window and took in the boundless night sky. There were so many things she wanted to say to V'sair. She didn't like the way the Darracians treated her. They could be mean and cruel. Sometimes being a favorite was not a good thing, but she would endure all that and more just for a glimpse of his noble face.

"She has enough to worry about, don't you think?"

"Do you like my mother?" he asked her.

"She can be…"

"Hard?" V'sair supplied and felt his spirits lift when Tulani laughed. It came from deep in her belly—a rich, dark laugh as lush as the Desa itself—and he warmed to her.

"When someone gives you high expectations, it causes you to strive to be the best you can be. You should know that, Your Highness. The entire court talks of your devotion to the Sradda." He nodded, and she finished. "I love and admire your mother, more than my own. If not for her, I would be tethered to the ground and not flying among angels in the sky."

"Ha!" He laughed with pleasure. "Now I know you are roasting me. Darracians and angels, an unlikely match."

Tulani raised a delicate brow, her red face alight with laughter, her eyes drinking in his ethereal beauty. "I could name a few."

They walked through the hallways of the castle, toward the stables, more as equals now. V'sair had a newfound respect for the girl. She was not a bowing toady, looking to ingratiate herself with him to achieve her ends. He liked her, he realized with surprise. She listened to him, her face totally engaged when he spoke to her. She was authentic, and as they walked, a feeling of peace enveloped him. She didn't seem to mind his lack of a tail or his colorless hair. Even from here they heard the hustle of the busy area. Soldiers were coming in, their clothes dusty from the red soil of the Desa. In groups they entered, talking and bowing slightly to the young prince.

Two Quyroo stable masters jumped as he entered, rushing to ready his mount.

There was nothing V'sair loved more on this planet than Hother. A giant among the other stalliuses, she stood meters over most of the others and snorted softly as she sensed his approach.

"Hother awaits. Let's be off."

Hother was beautiful, with her huge muscles under a

white coat and giant white-feathered wings spanning six feet on either side of her heaving sides.

"He matches you perfectly." The stunning creature awed Tulani. She was blindingly white, the same color as V'sair's bleached mane. The servant girl reached out to stroke the stallius's side.

"*She*," he corrected her.

He patted her neck affectionately, and Tulani thought he was so very handsome when he wasn't scowling. Holding her halter, he blew gently on his mount's nose. The stallius snuffled, then pushed her head against his gentle hands. V'sair reached into his pocket and pulled out a fruit that was grabbed by large teeth.

"Forgive me, Highness. She is splendid, a rare beauty."

As if to agree, Hother snorted, her fierce nostrils flaring, her enormous hooves sparking against the cobbled floor of the stables.

In one fluid motion, V'sair lifted himself easily onto his stallius's back, then held out a hand for the elfin servant girl. "Have you ever ridden a stallius?"

The two attendants wrapped thick lines around their forearms in order to keep the restless animal captive. The gates to the sky yawned before them.

V'sair expertly handled his mount. Holding out his hand impatiently, he motioned for Tulani to take it, and she braced a small foot against the creature's side. She never had been this close to one, and worry must have shown on her face, because she felt the prince take her gently, tugging her up, and reassuringly give her leg a pat as she landed behind him. A current passed between them everywhere their bodies touched.

"Hold on," he told her, his eyes crinkling with laughter.

Wrapping her arms around his lean waist, she inched closer, feeling his breathing hitch. She pushed up against him, knowing her breasts were pressed intimately against his back. All sound receded, and Tulani closed her eyes, lost in the sensation of the powerful beast beneath her and the vitality of the youthful prince before her.

"Release!" the prince commanded, and urged his stallius through the towering gates that led toward the sky. Hother backed up, her muscles tensing beneath them, her vast wings gracefully gathering power as they pulsed with movement. The creature built speed, and Tulani jerked as Hother took off, leaping into the heavens, to hang suspended over the planet.

The stars littered the heavens like the sparkling bubbles that aerated the water. The four moons hung low on the horizon but lit the ground with their lambent glow. Red treetops beckoned, and Tulani gasped with delight as they floated above the land, which was now a speck in the night sky. It was as though they flew above a red-colored bowl. The sea roared to their left, and the cliffs of the Desa turned a deep burgundy in the darkness of the night. The moons illuminated the forest treetops, and she heard the rustle of the wind as it buffeted their bodies. A flock of gresh flew below them, and she giggled as they cawed.

"Is it not beautiful?" She heard V'sair's voice. Their

faces were close—so close that she could touch his cheek with her own.

"I've never seen the likes of it. Looking out from the portal does not do it justice."

"This is only the beginning." V'sair laughed as they took off like a rocket to dance among the red cliffs of Darracia.

The air was cooler, and for a moment, Tulani regretted not taking a wrap. She had gotten soft living in the clouds, but she knew she would adapt quickly to the climate change.

They hovered over the Desa Forest, the dense foliage whispering in the darkness. In the distance the castle rode on its cloud home as ships came and went from the two entrances. Here and there Tulani could make out Petrion guards riding black stalliuses on patrol, their expertise in the air as fun to watch as a magician's show. V'sair responded as they waved to them, acknowledging their presence in the dark skies.

"You ride very well, Highness."

V'sair shifted in his seat. The girl was pressed tightly against him, making him uncomfortably aware of every cell in his body. He cleared his throat, feeling her small hands caress his torso, which made him squirm.

"I...I...have ridden my whole life."

Tulani laid her cheek against his shoulder. He smelled like home, the rich scent of the forest, the fresh, clean smell of the needles of the trees. She knew the laundress at the castle used a mixture her grandmother made. *This is fun*, she thought with a smile. V'sair was still as innocent as she, and perhaps that was a good thing. She moved her hands up the front of his tunic, stroking his chest, and when he gasped, the winged creature dipped dangerously. Tulani screamed as he gained control of the beast.

"What are you—" he yelled.

"Tulani." Her mouth was close to his ear.

"What?"

"My name. It's Tulani. Say it."

"Tulani…" It rolled off his tongue as sweat dotted his forehead. V'sair was finding it difficult to think.

"I like the way you say it." She paused, then whispered, "V'sair."

The last was said in a puff of air that caressed his earlobe. *Could that be her tongue?* V'sair thought wildly as he felt it touch the outer shell of his ear. He shifted and realized it was indeed, and a smile graced his handsome face. He flexed his arms and pulled his mount with newfound urgency, heading south into the Deep Fells. In the distance the great shadow of Aqin blocked the night sky, its belly ominously belching a swirling dark mist.

VIII

PACUTO, FLANKED BY his guards, impatiently walked the stable yard, looking for V'sair's grooms. Slapping his quirt against his powerful leg, he looked for the Quyroos who worked exclusively for the prince. He found them cleaning a large stall.

"Where did the prince go?" he demanded.

Known for their closemouthed sullenness, they gave him a disrespectful shrug. His own guards bristled at this breach of etiquette. Pacuto swiftly lashed out with his quirt, slicing the red cheek of the groom. All action stopped, and the stable became so quiet that the only sounds were Pacuto's voice and the harsh breathing of the injured Quyroo.

"Do you know who I am?" he shouted, his teeth bared.

"I may know who you are, but that doesn't mean I

can give you information I don't have, my lord Pacuto," the Quyroo said disrespectfully.

"Insolence!" Pacuto shouted, his face flushed with anger.

The quirt slashed again, this time the other cheek. Red droplets sprayed across the immaculate tiles. This time the Quyroo was hurt; he huddled in the corner.

"I know not, my lord," he said with a quiver.

"Prince V'sair does not think a servant important enough to give him his itinerary," the second Quyroo sneered from behind Pacuto.

Pacuto bunched his bulky shoulders and swung his short tail mightily, impaling the startled Quyroo. Shaking him, he roared with laughter at the shocked look in the servant's dying eyes. He felt his tail slicing organs as the Quyroo slid into a bloody heap on the floor.

He took out his tryath and neatly severed the quaking Quyroo's head while saying, "If you are so unimportant to the prince, then you are equally useless to me." He tossed the head into a corner, laughing as it rolled to a stop in a pile of excrement. He turned to his guards. "Saddle Winata. Now!" He stomped out, leaving a trail of bloody footprints.

The stable, usually a hub of activity, became as still as a tomb, the Quyroos who worked there ducking behind the stall walls.

◆

V'sair and Tulani glided over the landscape in hushed silence, breathless with anticipation. The wind ruffled

Tulani's braids, and she released them, letting her tresses tangle with V'sair's white locks. They skirted the rocky crags of Aqin and felt the rumble from its deep recesses.

"Aqin is angry," Tulani whispered.

"Nonsense. It's a volcano that may or may not erupt. It has no personality," V'sair retorted smugly.

"Did the Elements tell you that?" she challenged him.

"I base my answers on science. What proof do we have that the Elements exist?"

"That's blasphemy." Tulani's voice was hushed, the wind buffering all other sound.

"I cannot accept everything my tutor tells me," V'sair said impatiently. "If the Elements truly exist, tell me why we have war and inequality." He turned his face to see her for a moment, then returned to watching the skyscape. "How can I accept something I can't see?"

"We don't see air, yet we know it is there," Tulani responded. "The Elements are the Trivium. They make up the substance of life. Without them we are nothing!"

"Words. Merely words." V'sair closed his mouth, at a loss to explain his feelings. "I don't know what I believe in anymore."

Tulani's hair tickled his nose, and V'sair brushed her curls from his face.

"I can't see. Tie your hair back," he said.

"It feels good when it touches you, no?" Tulani asked seductively, her clasped hands resting intimately against his lower belly.

Gracefully they descended to the forest floor, coming to rest on a bed of red clover and lichen-covered rocks. They heard the call of wild birds and the keewalla monkeys that roamed the glades. A waterfall cascaded over the high rocks, and the gentle creatures of the night called to them.

"Deep Fells," V'sair said with wonder. His skin prickled, and he was acutely aware of the female behind him. His urges made his fingers tingle; his lips ached to touch hers.

"Part of them. It is my family's home."

In the distance the castle floated, its many turrets outlined by the gleam of its white lights. The other buildings used different-colored lighting, so the city in the sky looked like a brightly colored constellation. V'sair rarely had seen his home from a distance. Once, Zayden had stolen him away without his parents knowing to see the city from the ground. It was as exhilarating then as it was now.

"Waaw!" V'sair's eyes took in the lush gardens, bathed in the moonlight of the four moons. Overhead he heard the leathery wings of the herns, along with their screeching call for the mates they chose for life. He looked up to see a flock of them flying in their strange formation. He never had been so close to one, except in the museum, of course. He couldn't believe his mother had let him fly here without a detail and in the evening. He knew he should return by daybreak, and that was a good thirty-four hours away. He glanced at the herns and followed their flight. They were predatory, he knew, but never attacked in the evenings.

V'sair dismounted, then lifted his arms to help Tulani as she slid off Hother. He heard her breath catch in her throat as his hands spanned her tiny waist. She rested her hands lightly on his shoulders, and the world narrowed to just the two of them. She was light as a feather, her legs sliding down his body, her full lips finding his own. He was acutely aware that nearly every part of his body touched hers, and his skin burned through his clothes.

V'sair slanted down, taking her mouth, kissing her tentatively, then opening his mouth and letting their tongues touch. Sparks flared between them, and Tulani felt V'sair's chest expand with the same excitement she felt. She reached behind him to pull his tunic free, and his hands skimmed down her body, coming to rest on a firm breast. She sighed with pleasure into his mouth, and V'sair deepened his kiss.

A burst of fireworks exploded in the night sky, and for a scant minute, V'sair thought their kiss had caused it. A great cackle split the silence.

"What do they do here?" It was a gravelly voice, as if from a rusty barrel.

"Bobbien…" Tulani closed her eyes. She thought they would have some time before her grandmother showed herself. "You are far from home."

"I am a wanderer, always wandering, don't you know?" She paused and pursed her wrinkled lips. "A maid, a man…" the voice continued, "what mischief is this?"

"No mischief, Greanam. It is Tulani…and Prince V'sair."

The prince bowed deeply, his face blushing blue with embarrassment as he tucked in the errant tails of his tunic.

"The prince…Prince V'sair…son of Queen Reminda, my good friend?"

The old Quyroo stomped out of the shadows. Her breasts hung flat and long; her belly was big, covered loosely with a brown loincloth. Her red braids reached the forest floor, dragging all kinds of feathers, leaves, and twigs in the knotted mess. She held a tall stick with a length of hemp attached to it.

V'sair bowed deeply, "At your service, my lady."

"My lady," the Quyroo cackled back, revealing broken yellow teeth before curtsying. "My good prince, you call a Quyroo 'my lady'?"

"Be she Quyroo or Darracian, any friend of my mother, the queen, is my lady."

"Oh, oh, oh. You are a good un." She laughed. "Tulani, he is a good un."

Tulani smiled at her grandmother. "He is the prince, Greanam. Prince V'sair, this is my grandmother Bobbien, who should never travel this deep into the Fells." Tulani frowned; she had thought she would be alone with the prince here.

V'sair moved forward, taking the old woman's hand and kissing her wrist gallantly.

"Does the young meat taste as good as the old one?" the woman asked coyly.

"Greanam," Tulani hissed, to which her grandmother laughed heartily, her great belly shaking up and down.

V'sair watched in silent fascination. He had many Quyroo servants, and had met both male and female

Quyroos, but never had seen one as old or heavy as Tulani's grandmother.

"Tulani, what brings you out to this part of the Fells in the darkness?" She turned a gimlet eye on her granddaughter. "You are too close to the eastern provinces. Fly at night, the wysbies do. Danger for you young uns!"

"I could say the same to you, Greanam," Tulani retorted, wondering what the old besom was up to. She was a canny old thing, with roots and plants dangling from her belt, her bright eyes missing nothing.

"My mother, the queen, has need of more ointment—Glacien ointment. Do you have any?" V'sair volunteered.

Bobbien looked at her granddaughter's full lips and the boy's flushed face. Oh, she had interrupted something here, for sure, but what could her good friend be about? Tulani was not to be used like a slattern woman. Though their fortunes had changed, she was in the line of the Nost women, the women of the sun. Tulani was a treasure and had been hidden by both the queen and Bobbien many years ago; she could not be thrown away as a pawn. The girl was as royal as the prince. She narrowed her gaze at her defiant granddaughter, who boldly stared back.

"Yes, she has need of your salve. She sent me on a mission." Tulani thrust out her bottom lip, just on the edge of disrespect.

She has been away too long, the older Quyroo thought.

She is forgetting herself and behaving without Quyroo dignity.

"A mission?" Bobbien raised her eyebrow.

"Yes, Greanam." She paused, then continued, "A mission with the prince."

The air was thick, and V'sair felt as though he had missed a part of the conversation. He watched the power struggle and felt the tension between the two women.

"A mission with the prince," Bobbien repeated slowly, absorbing the idea. "I must think on this a bit. Beware the eastern provinces and the wysbies," she warned as she scratched her matted head and, with a speed that belied her age, threw the hemp from her staff toward a branch and swung out of their view instantly.

"That was strange," V'sair stated, looking at the empty spot. "What are the wysbies she spoke of?"

"You know not of wysbies?" Tulani asked suspiciously.

"I rarely come to the Desa. Who are they?"

"Demons disguised as insects. They can be annoying. They sting, nothing more."

"She left because she's afraid of them?"

"Bobbien is afraid of nothing. She left to contact your lady mother. She doesn't believe us."

"What? Believe me? I am the prince," V'sair replied incredulously.

Tulani laughed, her face shining in the light of the many moons. "I think here you are just V'sair. Are you hungry?"

V'sair thought about that. He hungered. He had hungered to test the Fireblade for so long; now he felt the stirrings of a new hunger.

He took her hand and whispered, "Yes, Tulani. I hunger."

IX

BOBBIEN MOVED WITH agility through the branches despite her advanced age. She came to a stop where her hut rested in the cradle of two trees. Inside, her worthless son-in-law lay swinging in his hammock, while her daughter pounded epocks, sweet roots, for their dinner.

"Tulani has come," she stated coldly and turned to her communication device. "Mori, leave. I have need of privacy."

"I am comfortable, Bobbien. Go outside. My head aches," Mori whined back.

"I said Tulani has come. Don't you want to see her?"

"She behaved disrespectfully the last time she was here. I have nothing to say."

"Eeeehai," she scoffed. "She only asked for you to help me." She turned to her daughter, who was pounding the root, ignoring the conversation, a sullen look on her face.

"He won't leave, Mo'mo. Take your business outside," her daughter told her and went back to the monotonous pounding.

The older Quyroo eyed the younger one, wondering what kept him glued to his hammock. Oh, he was lazy, but he knew the value of the queen to their small clan. They needed the funds and supplies she gave them in exchange for Tulani's service as well as Bobbien's spells. He was hiding something; that was for sure. Mori, with a smug look on his puffy face, looked excited. Bobbien gazed again at her daughter, who turned her back, lest she give something away, but a furtive glance at a sack near the stove caught her eye.

"What have you there?" the old woman demanded, stomping over to it.

Mori jumped out of the hammock with a speed she had never seen. Her daughter dropped the epock root on the dirt floor, rendering it inedible, and stood before the bulging sack.

Though she was old, Bobbien had continued to swing from the treetops and had a powerful upper torso. She shoved her daughter and Mori away with muscled arms, snarling at their Bottom Dweller weakness.

"Crystals!" she cried. After sticking a hand into the bag to find it filled with sticky, newly formed randam, she pulled a handful out. "Fools! You want to get caught?"

The randam crystals were controlled by the Quyroo League for trade. It was illegal for Bottom Dwellers to even be near them.

"They will send you to the caves," she said as she stared at her daughter with horror.

"You are a high priestess, a daughter of Nost. I will get a slap on the wrist," Mori said nonchalantly.

"They will condemn us all to the caves. I will never see Tulani again. Even the queen will not be able to save us." "Who cares about that one?" Mori responded hotly. "What has she ever brought us? The trees are here for all of us. Their bounty belongs to everyone, not a chosen few, Bobbien!" Mori's yellow eyes narrowed. "I've had enough of grubbing on the forest floor for a few tasteless roots." He kicked the epock root so that it hit the hut wall with a thud. "Like it or not, I refuse to live on the leavings of the royal family. We will go to join the settlement on Aqin."

"You will die there." Bobbien stood tall, her expression somber. "Think, Daughter, of what you are doing."

Her daughter shrugged indifferently, bent down, and pulled another epock from under the table to pound into a paste for dinner. Mori chuckled and slid back into his hammock.

Bobbien grabbed her communication instrument, the forbidden nevi, to contact the queen. Mori smirked and pointed at it. "I am not the only one hiding things from the league."

Bobbien turned her eyes on her son-in-law, who laughed, his mouth wide, his grin evil. He rose and moved toward her. "What know you?" she demanded.

"Enough," he said defensively. "I know you use a nevi to speak with the cloud people. I know you go where you are not allowed." His voice dripped with sweet nectar now. "Yes, Bobbien, I know where you disappear for days at a time, and I think you should share your secrets. The Elements do not—"

Bobbien stamped her staff, demanding silence. She leaned in close to his face, her eyes inches from his. "You will get us all killed with your recklessness, Mori. You know nothing. Say it! Say it!" She rattled her medicine bag, and for once her feckless son-in-law was frightened.

"Oh, have it your way, old woman. I know nothing." He smirked and flung himself back into the hammock, placing a straw hat over his face.

Bobbien stalked off from the hut to find a private spot, where she gingerly held the shell-like device to her ear. The Quyroos were not allowed to have communication tools. This one had been given to her by the queen. Only her family knew she had it, and her discussions with Reminda kept them all from starving. In exchange she had helped the queen with some spells and given her special herbs when she had fallen ill from the hot climate; Bobbien's potions had saved her. Lastly she had given her Tulani for protection for both of their houses.

Static burst in her ear, and the queen's familiar voice came to life. "Bobbien, has my son arrived?"

"Indeed he has, Your Highness. And may I add, he was sampling some of the delights of the Desa."

"So fast!" The queen chuckled. "I knew I could trust Tulani."

"Of that I am certain, Highness, but I need to know what you are about. Tulani is worth more than a slattern.

She is royal born as well."

"Bobbien! There is a big difference between Quyroo and Darracian royalty. Tulani knows what she is doing. I suggest you leave her to my business."

"Tulani shall not be a pawn," the older woman persisted.

"Do not defy me, Bobbien. There is much you don't understand," the queen said as the line went dead.

<h1 style="text-align:center">X</h1>

PACUTO AND HIS stallius took off from yet another spot in the Desa. He had lost Prince V'sair. In the heavens there were no trails to follow, just the direction from other Darracian guards patrolling the wide skies. The dark outline of Aqin blotted the skyscape. Pacuto looked at the villages that dotted the hills and shuddered. He didn't want to tempt the Elements and search on the volcano. Though the prince's stallius was well-known, her stark-white color a veritable beacon, there was no sign of them. They could have landed anywhere in the Desa. He stopped several guards who reported that they had seen nothing.

A sluggish transport with five cars filled with random crystals rode at a snaillike pace to the left of them. Pacuto kicked Winata to fly next to them. A Petrion guard sat at the helm and another in the rear. Each car had a Quyroo to help with the unloading.

"Have you seen the prince?" Pacuto demanded.

"What? The prince? Or do you mean Lincom? The queen would never let her boy out this late." He winked and gave a guttural laugh.

"He's out with a Quyroo slattern," Pacuto spat. "The queen's handmaid."

"'Bout time they made a man outta him," the guard at the end offered. "He must be having fun on the ground. I've seen him ride Hother. He's got a talent. If he's done showing off, my guess is he's well occupied, and you won't be hearing from him for some time. Them Quyroos can keep you real busy."

The Quyroo in the car stiffened but remained silent. The other balled his fist, and Pacuto smashed it with the hilt of his sword. The servant wailed and stuck his red knuckles into his mouth.

"If you see them, call and let me know."

"Will do. Are we done? I'm late with the transport, and I have to get this crew back before the wysbies come out. They like to feast on Quyroo flesh." The guard laughed. "My men will be no good for anyone if they get 'em."

"Perhaps they went to the eastern provinces?" one of Pacuto's own guards grunted.

"Prince V'sair is not a fool. He would stand out there like a blazing torch," Pacuto answered, resting his big hands on his pommel.

"From where does the servant girl hail?" This came from his squire, a young cousin he'd been training.

"Good thinking, Grodot. The girl. Call and find out her home." Kicking mightily, Pacuto urged Winata higher so he could scan the red treetops. He paused thoughtfully when he spotted the fires lighting the Quyroo camps.

◆

Tulani had removed her Darracian dress and felt free and comfortable in her loincloth. V'sair lay on the velvet ground, his jacket open, his face serene. Hother munched contentedly on a bush off to the side.

Tulani bent over and tickled V'sair's pale stomach, her braids caressing him. Pulling her forward, he kissed her again, her small moans inciting him with desire once again.

"V'sair..." She nipped his ear. "It is dangerous out here. We must go. The wysbies fly at night, and I don't have a mind to get stung."

V'sair looked at her shining black eyes, their star shape so feminine. He brushed grass from her cheek. "I don't know how I never saw you before," he said, filled with wonder.

"You saw me every day, sire." She laughed, her fingers playing with the fine skin that covered his ribs.

"A little while ago, you called me V'sair." He kissed her deeply. "You are always in my mother's shadow; I never really noticed you." He gently cupped her face. "You are beautiful."

"So are you." Tulani straddled him, their bare chests touching, setting off sparks wherever flesh touched flesh.

"I am an ugly mutant. At least you know what you are." He held her red-tinged arm against his own light-blue one. "You are born of the red soil of Desa; my father is the gray sky of Darracia; my mother is the orange sun of Planta. I am not any of those things. I am neither—not red or gray or orange. I am nothing."

"Don't talk like that." Tulani kissed his cheeks and eyelids. She pressed against him, wishing to be closer. Her skin prickled where it met his and made them aware of every part of their bodies. She ran her nimble fingers through his hair, and with delight, she watched his eyes close. "You are beautiful and strong and wise. I have always known it. V'sair, I have always loved you."

V'sair shook his head. "I am not worthy enough of the Fireblade."

"You *are* the Fireblade to me. My Fireblade." Tulani enveloped him with renewed passion and ignored the call of the keewalla monkeys, which signaled danger.

XI

STAF NUEN WAITED in his room, his wife, Beatha, pacing the floor. "General Xam has reneged." He crumpled a note from his former ally. "He has gone back to his holdings and refuses us his men."

They were in their royal apartments, where they stayed when they were away from home. The quarters were small, and Beatha had bristled when they had been assigned to them. Reminda took every opportunity to shove her status as the queen in their faces. The countess licked her lips, thinking of what she'd like to do to the Plantan woman.

"Why?" Beatha sneered. "Perhaps you were not persuasive enough?"

"He says a revolt will destroy our economy, and trade with the outer planets will be affected. The Treaty of 771 will be rescinded. He thinks V'sair has a bright intellect," he growled with disgust. "Oh, yes, my dear. He says that the Elements shine in V'sair's soul and that the prince is the anointed one."

"General Xam is an old woman," Beatha said, her voice filled with scorn. "My father hated him and never trusted him or Lord Wetham." She turned her beady gaze to him. "Have you heard from him yet?"

Staf didn't answer. Instead he stalked over to a decanter and poured himself a glass of purple liquid.

"Do you think that's wise, Husband?" Beatha asked with venom. "Does not krayum make your mind cloudy and your tongue heavy?" She paused with disgust. "I don't think it's prudent."

"No one asked you, hag."

Staf's nevi beeped with urgency, and he removed it from his belt to see who was calling and turned his back to respond.

Beatha watched through narrowed eyes, waiting breathlessly. As he shook his head and spun around, her breath caught in her throat.

After ending the call, he turned to his wife. "Generals Veril and Blyst are with us. They are sending a detail to take out General Vekin." His bright-white teeth gleamed against his gray skin.

"What of Swart?"

"I am convinced I can turn him. He hates the idea of the accord." He poured himself another glass of krayum, and it overfilled so that it puddled on the tray. Beatha eyed him with disdain.

"He is a king's man. I don't trust him. You must kill

him. If you don't act soon, the entire rebellion will fail." Beatha turned to look at Staf, his face a deeper gray than usual. "Do your nerves fail you, Husband?" she asked, her gaze steely.

"You dare question my honor?" Staf stood his full seven feet in order to menace his wife. "You dried-up piece of—"

Their youngest daughter, Hilde, interrupted them, breezing into the room without a care in the world. She was lovely, with long black hair; she had just learned to put it up with black ribbons. Staf and Beatha had introduced her to the court this year so she could make an alliance with one of the wealthy families that attended. It seemed like only yesterday when Staf had bounced this one on his knee. She was the last—and to his mind, the best—of his litter.

"Where is Pacuto?" she asked, eyeing her parents warily, knowing she had disturbed an argument. Hilde had an acute sense of smell and could detect the odor of krayum on her father when she pressed her face next to his hairy cheek. It was never a good thing when Dado drank. His temper could become uncertain.

"Never mind. You were told to return to the donjon and stay indoors. What brings you here, child?" Staf did have a soft spot for this child. She so reminded him of his own mother, dead these last hundred years. Hilde was brave and sweet, not like her sisters.

"The queen requested Pacuto. I was searching for him. I have called him, but he does not answer."

Beatha stiffened. "Does she think a prince from the house of Nuen is her errand boy?"

"Not now, Wife."

"Where is the queen now?" Beatha demanded.

"The Ambros room," Hilde told them with a smile.

The Ambros room was the queen's private room, where the females congregated. The uppity servant girl who was always at the queen's elbow had left, and Reminda had given her niece some much-needed attention. As the youngest of five, she rarely was noticed, with Pacuto soaking up most of her mother's praise. While she could wrap her father around her finger, she never saw him much. He was, after all, the king's brother and a great warrior, as well as the grand mestor.

"She is seeing guests now," Hilde said. "She needed Pacuto to escort the Quyroo leader to her room." She smiled gayly. "The Quyroo and his mate have come. Oh, she is so pretty. I wish I had those star-shaped eyes," she added, wistfully thinking maybe her cousin Zayden would notice her more if she did.

Beatha reached out and slapped her hard across the face. Hilde gasped, her eyes filling with tears. She slapped her again and would have struck her once more had not Staf stilled her violence.

"You dare to compare yourself to a Quyroo? I should send you to the Desa and leave you to deal with—"

"Enough!" Staf roared. "Leave us, child, and talk no more of Quyroos."

"They are like us!" rebellious Hilde responded. "They are nice. They want peace."

This time Staf slapped her. "I said enough. Go to your room and stay there until your lady mother can stomach you once again. Take your filthy mouth and leave!"

The room was silent as Hilde backed out. What they didn't see was her quick turn to the anteroom, where she crouched low inside a giant wardrobe. She wanted to know what made them this jumpy. She'd bet her new hair ribbon they were hiding something.

"I should give that one to Faetha," her mother spat.

Hilde cringed, thinking of the ancient man with his stooped shoulders and withered tail. She'd die first, she thought dramatically. Surely her mother wasn't serious. They knew she wanted Zayden; she had made no secret of that. Though her parents were unhappy about his illegitimacy, he was still a king's son.

"Faetha is old," Staf said grudgingly.

"I tire of her antics. She is a handful."

Staf laughed. "Not unlike her mother."

"I was obedient. I married you, didn't I?" she said craftily.

"You wanted me," Staf told her, "and my bloodlines."

"I wanted your brother," she said with a scowl. "I didn't want your temper." In a swish of shimmery fabric, Beatha turned to leave the room and thought that what she really wanted was to have the throne.

"Wait!" Staf called to her. "Where will you be when the action begins?"

The countess stilled her hand on the door. "I don't want to be caught in the violence."

Hilde's eyes opened wide, and she strained to hear

the muted conversation. *Violence?* she thought. *What kind of violence?*

"General Crafe is handling the center of the castle. He knows you. He will only go after the king and the consort." Though her father's voice was low, Hilde heard him, and terror seized her. "He will kill Drakko and the Plantan woman."

"What will you do about Zayden?" the countess asked.

Hilde's back went straight when she heard the name. Pressing her ear against the door, she strained to hear more. What were they planning to do to Zayden? Her pointed teeth worried her bottom lip.

"He is loyal to both the king and V'sair." Hilde heard her father pace the room. "He is a problem and could be used as a pretender to the throne against us."

"Then he must die," Beatha said simply. "What of Drakko's guards? They are the best fighters on the planet."

"There will be collateral damage." Staf shrugged his giant shoulders.

"Collateral damage." Beatha laughed. "Tomorrow I will drink a toast to Your Majesty."

Staf lifted his half-filled glass and nodded. "As I will drink to yours." He dipped his knee and finished, "Your Royal Highness."

Hilde shrank back into the recesses of the wardrobe, her heart pumping with fear. What was she to do? Zayden was in danger. Her parents—to whom she owed her loyalty— were planning regicide. This was treason. Her king and queen were in danger. *Oh,* she thought, *Great Sradda, tell me what to do. What should I do?*

Hilde stayed frozen in the wardrobe long after her parents had left their chambers, so nervous that she bit her fingernail to the quick. She counted to forty, then did it once more for good measure and slid out into the darkened room. After running straight to the krayum decanter, she uncorked the lid and drank deeply, letting the purple liquid give her false courage. Holding the bottle to the light, she measured how much liquid was left and finished it. *Great Sradda, tell me what to do,* she thought. The liquor worked quickly and relaxed her taut muscles, her brain feeling just on the edge of fuzzy.

Wiping her stained lips with her wrist, she walked just a bit unsteadily to the dimly lit corridor. Guards were everywhere! Her parents were crazy; the king and queen had too many supporters. It would be a bloodbath. She paused for a second, her cheek smarting where she'd been slapped. Drakko and Beatha would be terrible leaders—abusive, arrogant. Her father had no business trying to usurp the crown, yet, she thought for a moment, would that not make her a princess? Her back against the wall, Hilde dreamily pictured life as a royal—a real royal. There would be parties and balls, as well as suitors for her hand. She glanced down at her lumpy gray hand and heard her mother's words echo in her head. *Give me to Faetha indeed! I will see you in Aqin first, Mother,* she thought indignantly.

"Daydreaming, Cousin?"

Her eyes opened, and Zayden smiled down at her. Her tongue was thick in her mouth, and she stuttered a greeting. He was so impossibly handsome, and his warm eyes were caressing her.

"Is all well with you, Hilde? You look worried."

Oh, where to start? Where to start? If she protected Zayden and the king, she would betray her father and her house. Her family would be political and social outcasts. She stared back at him silently. His arm rested on the wall beside her head, his face close to her own. She closed her eyes, wishing he would kiss her, but instead she felt his fingers touch the ribbon in her thick black hair.

He released the bow slowly and held the ribbon as a trophy. Hilde's locks streamed around her face, and she watched his eyes assess her. She knew her hair was one of her best features. She reached for her ribbon, and Zayden held it high over her head, a teasing glint in his amber eyes.

"May I have this?" he inquired with a crooked smile.

Hilde loved the way one of his front teeth slightly overlapped the other. It made him endearingly imperfect and approachable. They had played together as children, and Zayden had been educated with the rest of them. Reminda had welcomed him and nurtured him, and he had a fondness for his younger brother as well as his pretty cousin.

"For what?" Hilde asked softly, her green eyes luminous.

"A favor. I will wear it on my arm tomorrow for the tournament."

Oh, what to do? What to do? Hilde thought wildly. A fat tear slid down her pebbled cheek, making a shiny path to her lips.

"What is it, Cousin? What disturbs you?"

Hilde threw herself into his strong arms. Placing her head on his chest, she heard the reassuring thump of his heart. Glancing up at him, she asked, "Where is your loyalty, Zayden? Is it to your father or your house?"

"What crazy talk is this?" He pushed up her pointy chin with the pad of his finger, then wiped the puddle of wetness from beneath her eyes. "My father *is* my house. Surely you know that."

"Does not it bother you that you are Darracian, firstborn, and yet V'sair will rule?"

"The Elements have made it so." He shrugged and pressed his shoulder against the wall. "I will serve my father unto death." He liked Hilde, thought her spirited, and recently had asked his father if there was a possibility of a marriage there. He was past the age and had longed for a family since his mother had died. The royal family usually married within the family; it just remained to be seen if Zayden was considered royal enough.

"Yes, yes, I know." She pulled away to look out at the night sky from the portal. The moons glowed back, illuminating the red trees of the Desa. "But who would you serve first, your father or your king?" she persisted.

"My father is the king. You know that."

Hilde sighed in resignation, wishing the entire situation to go away. Perhaps she had dreamed the whole thing up; her parents always complained that her imagination ran wild. She eyed Zayden once again and said, "Come escort me to the Ambros room. I have yet to see the Quyroo leader's woman."

Zayden inclined his handsome head and held out his beefy arm, allowing her to place her hand on top of it. His body heat warmed her chilled hands, and she sniffed loudly.

"Do you want to talk about it?" he asked, taking a cloth from a pocket in his tunic for her to wipe her eyes. He pressed it into Hilde's hands, and when she put it to her face, she inhaled his scent, which remained on the cloth. Hilde held her breath, then shook her head. They walked arm in arm to the queen's salon. In the distance an alarm sounded, and they paused; Zayden looked alert and watchful.

"What is it?" Hilde whispered.

"I'm not sure. Everyone is edgy with the Quyroo delegation coming here. I'm not exactly comfortable with the whole thing myself."

She stopped him and looked him full in the face, holding his hands. "You don't agree with your father's policies?" "It's not my place to agree or disagree. I follow his orders, and if he desires to change the social order, then by the grace of the Great Sradda, I will follow his command."

"What do think of Reminda? Do you believe she has tainted the king's thoughts?"

"Where is all this coming from?" Zayden asked her.

The alarm was more strident, and he saw several guards rush from one of the palace rooms. He called out to one of them, "What's going on?"

The guard glanced at Hilde and hesitated for an instant. "Go on!" Zayden ordered.

"Captain Pacuto has gone on a rampage and killed several Quyroos. The king has ordered his capture."

Hilde gasped in horror, her head feeling light, and she felt as if she were listening to the conversation from a distance. "It is true," she whispered as her eyes rolled, and she lost awareness of everything around her.

XII

TULANI PLUCKED A fruit from a low-hanging tree branch and handed the sweet offering to the prince. V'sair took a healthy bite, smiling as the juice ran down his chin, staining his skin a bright yellow.

"Delicious," he murmured, pulling her close once again to kiss her, the juice making her lips as succulent as the ripe fruit. "You are delicious and juicy and sweet." "Sire…"

"V'sair," he reminded her.

"V'sair, we must be off. It is not safe in the forest at night. My parents' lodge is just through these bushes." She gestured toward the dense foliage.

Hother walked behind them, her hooves muffled by the carpet of leaves on the ground. The silence of the brush was cut by a scream, so loud and heart wrenching that V'sair dropped Tulani's hand and raced toward the source. As he rounded a bend in the trees, the forest cleared, and he found himself looking at a hut engulfed by flames.

Tulani ran to the spot next to him and gasped, "Mo'mo!"

Her mother's body was sprawled on the steps in a pool of blood. Her father was dangling upside down from a branch as the Darracians used him for target practice.

V'sair stopped and grabbed her shoulders. "Stay back. Stay hidden in the shrubs," he whispered urgently.

"No. I have to go!"

He kissed her full on the lips. "Stay and wait for me. That's an order from your prince." He walked into the firelight, commanding, "What is this outrage?"

Pacuto stepped from the shadows, triumph written across his hostile features.

V'sair looked puzzled when his cousin appeared out of the darkness. "Pacuto?" he questioned.

An evil grin slowly spread across his cousin's face. Pacuto dropped the sack of randam crystals and shouted, "The devil comes to us! Great Sradda, deliver me!"

"What is the meaning of this?" V'sair demanded.

Pacuto and his men surrounded the prince, their long spears menacing him. He glanced back into the shadows, warning Tulani with his eyes not to follow him into the open.

"V'sair, V'sair…you have lead us on a merry chase. At last"—he motioned toward the bag—"a double victory. A fortune in crystals for me and my men, and a personal triumph for the house of Nuen." He spat close to V'sair's foot. "Where is the girl? Tell me where your little playmate is.

Didn't your mo'mo teach you to share?" he taunted, grinning triumphantly.

"This is crazy. What are you doing? You will jeopardize the accord!"

"The accord and your father's reign are finished! This the beginning of the end of your father's tyranny. The possibility of peace dies tonight with *you*!" Pacuto laughed. "But this is hardly a fair fight, is it, men? I can sweep off his royal head." He waved his tryath near the prince's face. "No, no, this will be too easy. You have begged for the chance to test your skills with the Fireblade. I will kill you as you mangle that chance. Then I will take the girl on your cold body!" He threw his tryath to the ground, then withdrew his Fireblade, which roared to life.

V'sair's breath caught with rage, his face suffused with blue. He nodded to one of his henchmen, who removed his sword from his belt and threw it to the prince.

It landed at his feet with a thud, and Pacuto continued, "Oh, this will be fun. Pick it up, V'sair. This is your opportunity to finally take the test of the Fireblade. Defend yourself!"

Without taking his eyes off his cousin, V'sair bent down to pick up the handle of the blade, but it was useless without the engagement of the soul of a warrior. He was not trained and never had held one, and for the moment, it was dead weight in his hand. He knew it took years to learn how to clear the brain to accept the Fireblade's power. He turned his burning eyes on his cousin.

"By now your lady mother has been spitted by my father's blade; your father, the king, will be looking for his head; and it is the dawn of *my house!*"

Waves of hatred unfurled throughout V'sair's body. He pulsed with anger, his eyes slits of hate. The tang of the blade hummed as the sword turned a faint red, vibrating with a force he barely noticed through the haze of pain that glazed his eyes. Pacuto watched with amusement and held up his sword, which blazed with the power of experience. It glowed red from top to bottom, and he thrust it for a killing shot; he was mildly surprised when V'sair deflected it.

The strength of Pacuto's strike resonated from his arm to his heart, the bruising force of his strength nearly incapacitating the prince. He caught a glimpse of Tulani and warned her shocked face, urging her silently to run to safety.

She stood frozen in horror, her hands cupped over her mouth in silent fright. She worried that she was distracting him, so she slid back into the safety of the foliage.

The two men circled each other, the crackling fire the only sound of the night. They moved to the ancient dance of death, testing each other with a flick here, a feint here, a parry there. Pacuto expertly flicked with deadly accuracy, opening small wounds along V'sair's torso. Stepping forward, Pacuto rushed in, his sword flashing before the prince's eyes, and he felt it push into the meat of his shoulder, to the bone. Shock warred with pain, and he pulled himself off the blade, hearing the sucking sound of his flesh as the sword slid free. "This is too, too easy, V'sair. And to think you had pretensions to the kingship. I am ashamed to call you my kinsman." Pacuto laughed, showing two rows of sharp teeth. "Then I will find that Quyroo slattern and sink my Fireblade into her."

V'sair's face turned blue with fury as he screamed and attacked Pacuto with a strength born of hatred. The Fireblade glowed with red intensity, burned with a hatred V'sair felt. The night air was filled with the clanging of metal against metal, and they fought in the open meadow, firelight illuminating the battle. Blood saturated V'sair's clothes from various slashes, and he felt himself fading. Pacuto neatly sliced here and there, and soon the prince was covered with blood from the numerous small cuts.

Dizziness overwhelmed him, his blood dripping quietly to be absorbed by the forest floor. The blade felt heavy in his hand, and he raised the tip with much effort. Their sword points met and electrified each other, the weapons screaming with the touch of the positive and negative forces colliding. Pacuto sliced again, opening V'sair's right side from armpit to hip. The prince was weakening, and when Hother sensed her master's trouble, she screamed.

Pacuto grinned. "Ah, Hother, your head will decorate my stable." Raising his weapon, he moved in the for kill.

V'sair watched with detached calm, knowing he was about to die, when he heard Tulani's cry rent the air.

"Noooooo!"

"Ah, Tulani, right? Let me finish with this boy, then show you a real man!" Pacuto grinned with malice. He laughed hard, and with his free hand, he reached for his tryath. Deftly he flicked his wrist, neatly severing the prince's royal blade. "My trophy!" Pacuto's eyes gleamed with triumph. "I will hang it from my sword handle, next to your father's!" He picked up the blade from the ground and tucked it into his belt.

V'sair's fury bubbled up through his veins like whitehot lava. Concentrating his waning strength, V'sair reached deep inside himself, feeling something light up like a sun. Filling with warmth, he watched his blade regenerate with power, from a dull red to a fierce and threatening violet. Its blaze lit the prince's face, and ignoring the fatigue, he visualized a ball of energy that embraced his every pore. He became the aggressor, going after Pacuto, who now backed away defensively. The sword had a life of its own, and he moved his hand to where it would have the best advantage.

Pacuto felt the steel bite the flesh of his arm, slicing deep. They fought like demons, the light from the fire painting their faces so that they glowed with sweat in the dark night. The battle raged, and Pacuto stopped his insults, working hard to keep his balance against his cousin's Fireblade.

I feel it. I am the Fireblade, V'sair thought with

wonder as his arm followed the command of the sword, his very soul engaged in the pursuit of victory.

Pacuto feigned right and thrust his Fireblade deeply into V'sair's shoulder. The prince fell to his knees, the blade stuck in the sinew of his body. Pacuto struggled to remove it for the last killing blow, when suddenly all hell broke loose, and an explosion lit the night, throwing Pacuto to the ground. He rose unsteadily, wavering on his feet, looking at his cousin, when another bomb blew shrapnel that peppered his body.

"Come!" he ordered his men, leaving his Fireblade stuck in his cousin's body. After grabbing the bag of randam crystals, he tethered Hother to his own stallius and leaped onto Winata. They raced to the sky, his ride rocked by sound wave after sound wave as explosions blasted around him.

XIII

STAF STRODE OUT of his room to the quarters of his men, where he had planned a meeting with his officers. If Pacuto did not hurry up and kill the prince, he would miss the take-over. The halls were deserted, as most of the guests had gone to Reminda's salon for dinner. He might be missed, but at this point, he didn't care.

Four of his staff waited for him, their faces bright with excitement. Maps were spread out on a large table, and he bent over one.

"General Blyst is in position. He is cutting off Vekin in the west wing. They will be trapped," his chief told him.

"What of escape? Can they get to their ships?"

"Not likely," a fresh-faced captain replied. "We'll be bombing the landing bays. No one in and no one out."

"Communications?"

"We are taking out the tower so they won't be able to

warn each other. Nothing will work, not the intercoms or the nevi service. It'll be like target practice."

"What of us?" Staf asked. "The landing bays may take months to repair. I don't like it. We'll need to be able to bring more troops in here."

"We have secured the service entrance," the captain said. "I have a detail there already. They are only waiting for us to start killing the kitchen staff."

"Who will cook for us?" Staf said with a laugh.

"We'll have to import new servants, Your Eminence." The captain bowed his head.

"'Your Highness' will do." Staf inclined his own head. "An honor, sir…Your Highness."

"What of my ship?" he questioned.

"Admiral Harn has it parked and ready, should you need to move out."

"You said communications will be down?"

"Yes, my lord." The captain reached behind himself and handed Staf an antique communication device. "It's old and barely works. We have only two, one for you and one for the ship."

Staf smiled. "I remember these from my grandfather's day."

"We went to a lot of trouble to find them. Had to travel to the outer reaches, but there you have it."

"You don't have any others?"

He shook his head. "We had to rig the power source. I'm not even sure of the range, but it's all we have."

"Then it will have to do, Captain." Staf pocketed the small rectangular box. He laughed long and hard, his great frame shaking with pleasure. "So it begins!" He raised his fist into the air. "Long live the house of Nuen!"

A cry went up, sounding like a thousand voices, and Staf thrilled to hear their battle cry: "Long live the house of Nuen!"

The carnage began, and there was no mercy. It was as if the doors of hell had opened, allowing a plague to come in to destroy all life—Staf Nuen's plague of an army. They showed no mercy, killing male and female alike. Brains were dashed, stomachs ripped open; the soldiers were as pitiless as they were merciless. Swiftly and efficiently they wiped out an entire squadron of sleeping guards who never knew what hit them. Both Darracians and Quyroos were cut down, their loyalty to the king and queen the only reason for their deaths. Soon the halls were slick with blood from the vicious attack, when peace was what they had prepared for; the assault had taken the castle unawares. It was a vast fortress, and though a battle was waged, most didn't hear it. In the queen's rooms, the party went on.

Staf's soldiers had done their research; every guard— from the balconies to the many corridors—was cut down swiftly and silently, with only the victims aware they had been slain before they even had a chance to fight back.

Soon Staf's men lined the halls, controlling everyone in them.

◆

Staf entered his brother's chambers to find the king and Quyroo leader, Jonis, in a friendly discussion.

"Staf." The king looked up, unalarmed. "You're supposed to be at the dinner in the queen's rooms."

"I don't think so, Brother." He pulled his sword from his belt.

"What is the meaning of this?" Drakko stood up, his chest puffed out.

"Is this how you treat an honored guest?" Jonis asked, breaking the tense silence.

Staf turned to look at him with contempt on his pitted face. "No," he addressed the Quyroo. "This is how we treat our guests from the Desa!" With a vicious swipe, he lobbed off Jonis's head, wiping out any chance of peace.

"Staf!" Drakko yelled.

Two soldiers grabbed his arms, and Staf circled him. "We will see how far soft bends now, Brother," he spoke through gritted teeth.

XIV

HILDE CAME TO awareness in a rush and gasped. She heard music and lifted her head, only to be assailed by dizziness. A gentle webbed hand rested against her shoulder, and she heard the muted whispers of the queen and Zayden.

"Ah, you have decided to join us." Reminda bent over and smiled into her niece's eyes.

Hilde felt Zayden's strong hands lift her, and a glass was held against her lips.

"I looked for your lady mother, but she cannot be found," Reminda continued. "Do you know where she is, child? All our nevis seem to be out."

"Must be a solar flare," Zayden said. "I think I remember reading about them earlier this week."

"More likely the smoke from the fires in the Desa," the queen retorted. "A minor inconvenience." She smiled. "I rather enjoy being cut off from the world for just a bit."

Raising a hand to her forehead, Hilde responded quietly that she had no idea where Beatha was. Though she felt Zayden's gaze on her, she kept her eyes averted. *Sweet Sradda,* she wondered, *what to do? What to do?*

"You gave me quite a scare," Zayden told her softly, doubling her misery.

"My brother?" she whispered back.

Zayden shook his head. "Moon madness? The king has sent out a patrol to bring him in."

"Perhaps you are hungry?" the queen inquired, and slipped her arm through Hilde's to help her walk into the Ambros room.

In the serenity of the queen's chambers, there was no sign of the guards rushing about. Gentle music filled the air. It was as it always was—peaceful—and Hilde wondered whether she had dreamed overhearing her parents' plot. A large buffet filled with Darracian and Quyroo delicacies was spread across the entire back of the room. Strange smells drifted through the air, and Hilde noticed a small group of Quyroos laughing nearby. The Darracian court was observing them, and her mother, Countess Beatha, was noticeably missing.

"Where is the prince?" Hilde asked the queen.

"Off with my handmaid in the Desa."

Hilde stiffened; Zayden felt her tension and said, "Your Highness, allow me a few minutes with Lady Hilde, please?"

Reminda nodded regally and went off to join the group of Quyroos.

Zayden escorted his cousin into a private room.

"You're jumpy today, little one." He pulled her near a divan and stroked her arm. "I doubt they will do much to Pacuto—perhaps a banishment."

He cupped her hands in his own; his sword had made his palms calloused, but to Hilde they felt reassuring and made her feel safe.

"It's not that," she whispered urgently. "It's—"

Zayden pressed his finger against her lips. "I have spoken to my father. I have asked for you. I know I should first speak to your father, but he doesn't acknowledge me. Dare I hope you will take me as your husband?"

Tears gathered in Hilde's eyes. This was everything she had dreamed of; Zayden was the answer to all her hopes. If she told him what she knew about her parents' impending coup, he would feel only disgust for her. But how would he ever trust her if she failed to tell him what she knew?

"I…There is something…"

"Hilde, don't say another word. I must be brave and face your father." He smiled, his skin wrinkling in the corners of his eyes.

Before she could answer, the sound of booted feet interrupted them, and the doors to the Ambros room burst open. Hilde shrank back into Zayden's embrace. They could see everything but remained hidden in the shadows of the retiring room. Staf Nuen stood boldly in the entrance, the severed head of the Quyroo leader in his fist. A trail of blood dripped onto the pristine floor.

There were screams, and Zayden reached for his Fireblade.

The Quyroo's mate wailed and pulled at her red braids. "This is how you give us Darracian hospitality?" she cried bitterly.

Reminda moved directly in front of Staf, her face filled with cold rage. "Where is my husband, the king?"

"I am here." Two guards pushed Drakko into the room, his hands tied behind his back with thick hemp. He was bleeding over his dark brow, and a tic pulsed under his eye. He scanned the room and located his older son just off to the side in an anteroom with his niece. He bore into his son's gaze with a wealth of meaning, hoping Zayden would understand what he wanted him to do. He needed him not to react but to keep a clear head. Staring at him hard, he moved his eyes to the back exit.

His meaning couldn't have been clearer. Zayden bristled. *He wants me to run?* he thought with rage, his hand on the hilt of his sword, his intent written in his hostile stance.

Drakko then looked at Hilde, his niece, and held his breath for a second, wondering which side had her loyalty. *Good girl,* he thought, watching her turn to whisper to his son, barely hiding his satisfaction as they slipped out the back door. Their exit was missed, as everyone in the Ambros room was riveted to the confrontation between Reminda and Staf.

"What is the meaning of this?" Reminda demanded.

"We will not stand for the peace accords!" Grabbing her by her thin arm, Staf pushed her out of the way. "We will not change our ways. Drakko's reign is over."

"Don't touch my wife!" the king sneered.

Staf laughed. "Why, Brother? What will you do about it? It's time to put this Plantan in her place." Ruthlessly he tossed Reminda to the center of the room, where she fell hard onto the floor. Staf walked toward her. He pushed his booted foot on her hip, his eyes never leaving his brother's furious face. He grinned as the king stiffened. "What's the matter, Brother? You are not laughing at me. Do you not find me amusing now?"

"I will kill you," Drakko shouted.

"I sincerely doubt that, Your Majesty," Staf said with a snicker.

"Long live the house of Nuen," Countess Beatha said in a spidery whisper as she entered the room and circled her husband. "Pacuto has killed V'sair. He is the new crown prince. Your days of lording over me and mine are over." She walked closer to Reminda, her eyes venomous black pits of hatred. "Kill them, Your Highness! Kill them now!" she commanded her husband.

XV

"HELP ME WITH his feet!" Bobbien demanded of her granddaughter. "Tulani," she urged, "he is bleeding to death!"

The fires lit Bobbien's face, and Tulani stared back in shock. Her grandmother had appeared out of nowhere, lobbing the percussive zandy grenades. They were small and homemade but packed a powerful punch.

"Tulani!" she shouted again as she bent down to examine the prone prince.

Pacuto's Fireblade pinned his shoulder, and he bled from a dozen wounds. Reaching into a pouch tied to her waist, Bobbien sorted through herbs and twine to subdue some of the bleeding.

Tulani knelt, her head bowed. "Tell me what to do."

Bobbien motioned to Mori, whose body hung upside down near the burning hut. "Untie him, and throw him into the house. Let the fire do its work. He is beyond help. Drag your mother in there too." The older woman tied a cloth around V'sair's shoulder as tears dripped down her wrinkled cheeks. "I don't want animals to get her. Let the house be their pyre."

Tulani got to work, and by the time she returned, Bobbien had withdrawn the Fireblade from V'sair's shoulder. "He lives," she told her granddaughter, "but just barely. We must get him to safety." She slid the two Fireblades into the back of her loincloth.

"I will take him home," Tulani said.

"Did not you hear Pacuto? The prince no longer has a home. We must hide him. Come. We will talk later," she told her urgently.

They lifted V'sair's nearly lifeless body and placed his arms over their shoulders to carry him together. He groaned, then fell silent, but Tulani was reassured by his ragged breathing. His head hung listlessly forward, his eyes crinkled with pain.

"Where, Greanam? Where will we go?"

Bobbien grabbed her staff and pointed it to the rumbling giant, Aqin. "Into the belly of the beast."

◆

It felt as though they had traveled through the Desa for days. Living in the clouds had made Tulani vulnerable. Her arms ached from helping to carry V'sair, and she was clumsy with the tree vines. Her grandmother finally lost patience with her and hefted the unconscious prince over her thick shoulders so they could make better time swinging from tree to tree. Tulani admired the old woman's stamina. Wiping sweat from her brow, she followed breathlessly, the calls of the night birds jogging memories of her youth.

It was a clear night, and the four moons lit their path. Twin explosions lit the sky at the two entrances of the castle. Sirens wailed, and she watched the Petrion guards head quickly to the fortress, their flying beasts cut down by a giant cruiser that had moved to the front of the castle. Tulani watched the brave warriors being picked off like harmless gresh, the spraying torpedoes creating a rainstorm of blood and guts that pounded the Desa floor. She turned to Bobbien, fear written across her face.

"Hurry we must, child!"

Every so often Tulani caught Bobbien's worried expression, but she was too busy trying to keep up to speak to her. As she reached for an elusive vine, her fingers slick with sweat, the first wysbie attacked. She heard the hum, and her stomach clenched with fear.

"Wysbies!" she cried out. It started with a sting on her shoulder. Cursing, she slapped the spot, and the electric zap bit into her hand; a shout of shock escaped her lips.

Bobbien turned around and yelled, "Faster, Tulani. They are right behind you!"

The wysbies, with their innocent, fey-looking wings and streaming tentacles that stung with the ferocity of a thousand needles, attacked in force. Tulani gasped from the pain, slapping at the demons with her free hand but refusing to let go of the vine with her other. The harsh hemp sliced into her fingers, drawing blood. Bobbien turned around, her powerful arm wrapped around a vine, V'sair balanced on her shoulder, and a sack gripped in her other hand. The two Fireblades hung from her sides, and if Tulani weren't so scared, she would have laughed. Her grandmother looked like a many-armed spider.

"Tulani!" she called out. "Catch!" She threw the sack, and Tulani reached out to grab it. Suddenly her hand was covered by a screaming wysbie, its long streamers wrapping around her forearm like a thick bandage. Tulani wailed, her fingers slippery with blood, watching as the sack fell through her powerless fingers toward the Desa floor.

"No!" Bobbien yelled. She draped the unconscious prince between two branches, used a vine to secure him, then nimbly leaped down into the gloom. "The dust," she called out breathlessly. "Gums the wings, it will."

Tulani tore at the wysbie, its pink eyes bulbous sacs of fluid. Her arm lost color as the creature squeezed it tighter. Her vision narrowed, and a strange buzzing that had nothing to do with the gigantic insects filled her ears. Her death grip on the vine slackened a bit, and for a minute, she lost awareness of everything around her.

She realized sluggishly that Bobbien was thrashing her way up the branches, the sack between her teeth. The old Quyroo was humming, trying to communicate with her granddaughter to keep her from fainting, because speech was beyond the girl. Tulani dangled from a limb, her fingers numb, ready to release. Glancing down, she saw her grandmother's bright eyes burn with purpose. A wysbie had attached itself to the old woman's back, but Bobbien hardly noticed. She reached their level, hauling herself up, then grabbing Tulani's wrist. Tulani felt herself being lifted and watched in a detached way as Bobbien reached into the sack and threw something at the buzzing furies behind them. The insects screamed as a dusty substance coated them, their wings becoming useless as the creatures dropped to the forest floor.

Tulani heard more of the whining sounds nearby and knew another group was on its way. She stared at the struggling insects; she had forgotten how viciously these creatures stung. Maybe she didn't miss the Desa so much after all.

"Hurry, girl!" Bobbien urged. "Others will come."

She stared stupidly at her grandmother, as if she spoke a foreign language.

Bobbien shook her. "Hurry we must. They will come. Look!"

She pointed in the distance, and Tulani's stomach clenched as the white wall of a swarm headed their way. Bobbien untied the prince, heaved him over her shoulder, and with a speed that belied her size, moved as if the devil were on her tail. Tulani stopped thinking and just moved, her breathing harsh in her ears, her heartbeat thumping a wild tattoo in her chest.

They reached a dense grouping of trees.

"Shh," Bobbien warned her granddaughter, a finger before her lips.

Tulani heard the sounds of the Bottom Dwellers' encampments nearby, the sad string instruments they strummed whining on the breeze from the ocean. They were near the base of the volcano; she smelled sulfur expulsions from Aqin, and the air was thick and humid. They must be near the forbidden Quyroo settlements, where the Bottom Dwellers rebelliously chose to make their homes illegally.

"Why are we here?" Tulani asked.

Bobbien's eyes widened with a warning. She leaped to a branch and parted a wall of ferns. Tulani squinted in the darkness, peering through the dense leaves to see that her grandmother was waving her staff at a rock wall. *It must be Aqin itself,* Tulani thought with a shudder. *This is madness, Great Sradda!* Suddenly a strange light lit the darkness, coupled with an odd hum, and for a second, Tulani thought the wysbies had returned, but instead the wall parted, and Bobbien turned her head and urged her granddaughter through the narrow opening.

It was a hollowed-out cavern, pitch-black. Bobbien tapped her staff twice on the stone floor, and the chamber lit with an odd pink glow. Tulani looked, but her grandmother shook her head, letting her know to stay silent. The doors slid shut, and all sound disappeared. It was ice-cold in the cavern, but Tulani was drenched with sweat and blood and couldn't help the shiver that ran through her body. The welts from the wysbies were painful, and she longed to wash their poison away. Bobbien motioned for her to follow, and Tulani moved close behind her, her eyes wary. She glanced at V'sair, who was slung over Bobbien's strong back, his head resting on her grandmother's shoulder blade. The old woman wasn't even breathing hard.

It felt like they'd walked for hours, but Tulani knew it had been barely minutes. At each intersection Bobbien stamped her staff, and a twilight glow of weak lighting appeared and illuminated their way. Their feet echoed in the caves, and Tulani noted that while the walls were made of rock, they clearly had the finish that could be accomplished only by machines. She looked but could not find the source of the lighting.

They entered a huge cavern with clear, polished stalactites dripping from the ceilings, illuminated with a soft glow that bathed the room with gentle light. Tulani saw a crude bed, a stove, and a small store of roots and berries along with a few cooking utensils.

"You come here often?" Her voice echoed in the room.

"When thinking must be done," her grandmother responded, lowering the prince, then removing the two Fireblades from her belt.

Tulani watched Bobbien lay the prince on the bed and fell to her knees beside them.

"Get some water." Bobbien gestured to a cistern with running water on the back wall. "Now, Tulani!"

Tulani jerked as if she had been shot, then picked up a bucket to get the water. When she returned, her grandmother had stripped the prince and wrapped him with crude fiber blankets. She stood behind her grandmother and saw where the wysbie had stung her shoulder. A large red welt covered most of it, the poison dotting the surface in small bubbles of liquid.

"Now light the stove and boil some of this." She handed her a heavy pouch filled with dried red leaves.

"The wysbies did not get V'sair?" Tulani asked.

"Darracian blood they do not find tasty. Perhaps they find them as sour as we do."

Tulani absently rubbed her arms, and Bobbien took out a brown cloth. Small blisters started to appear on the girl's smooth red flesh.

"When you have put up the tea, wash your skin with this rag. It will help."

"Should I brew all of this?" Tulani asked, holding up the pouch.

Bobbien cocked her head. "Yes, I think so. He is bleeding much."

Tulani busied herself steeping the tea, and when the smell of the wet leaves filled the air, she knew at once that they were from the hallis tree; it was caylet tea, a healing beverage. She held her tongue but stole glances at her grandmother, who was working on V'sair.

She wiped her stings with the brown cloth and was amazed at the instant relief. It was damp and smelled of the deep-red hallis leaves.

"What is this stuff?" she asked the old woman.

"A bit of magic. Wipe my back, please, child. The stings, they do burn." She winced.

Tulani vigorously wiped Bobbien's humped back while skeptically asking, "Magic?"

"What? I am a high priestess, am I not?" "Will he live?" the girl asked tentatively.

The old Quyroo shrugged.

Bobbien stood up at last, stretching her back. "I am too old for this," she said with a hearty sigh. "The time is for a young un to do this." She shot her granddaughter a meaningful glance. "Mind the tea, child. If you overcook the leaves, I will have to get more, and we don't have time to cure them."

Tulani dipped her finger into the liquid and tasted the bitterness of the brew, knowing it would be done shortly.

"Do you expect a fever?"

"He has lost much blood. There will be a fever for sure."

She nodded sagely. "Nasty is the wound in his shoulder, but I have something special for that. So, Tulani," she said with a smile, "you probably are dying to know where we are, I am thinking."

Tulani poured the tea into a large cup and brought the steaming liquid to her grandmother, who took a healthy gulp.

"I thought that was for the prince!"

"An old body it can't hurt! He'll be fine, I be thinking." She handed her the cup. "All right, all right, feed your prince the rest! In a few minutes, he'll be needing more."

Bobbien plucked an uncured randam crystal from her pouch, blew on it, and held it up to the light. "It is a darker one that is needed, but magic, I know, will do the trick." "More magic?" Tulani raised a delicate brow.

The old woman laughed. "You have much to learn, cloud child." She licked the crystal.

"What are you doing? That is poison!" Tulani tried to knock it out of her hand.

"Oh, child, you have much to relearn. Think back, Tulani. The crystals get their power from the women of the Nost." She pursed her lips and blew on the damp crystal again. Tulani saw that it brightened. "Do it, girl. Try…"

She held out the rock in her grubby hand and dropped it into Tulani's curled palm.

"Spit, yes, not much more than a wysbie, perhaps, but it will do. Gently blow on the crystal," she told her. Tulani put her lips close and felt them start to tingle. She blew softly, and Bobbien said, "Do not be afraid."

She gasped, then let out a quick breath.

"Rushy, rushy! Why the rush? Do it slow, like a lover's kiss."

Tulani blushed red but let the air whistle softly through her lips, amazed when it grew bright and hot in her palm.

"Quickly, child. Do not burn yourself. Place it in the wound on his shoulder."

The crystal singed her fingers, but she gingerly tapped it into the gaping hole left by Pacuto's Fireblade and stood back. V'sair arched his back as he cried out, his face wincing with pain.

Tears gathered in Tulani's eyes. "It hurts him, Greanam. It burns."

"And so it must to do its work. Healing, you are, my girl. Healing as we are supposed to do. How does it feel to you?" Bobbien poked her granddaughter's arm.

"I…I don't know." Tulani thought about it for a

minute. Her own shoulder tingled, as though ice had dripped on it. She touched it with wonder.

"Yes, yes, you feel it! I knew you to be a healer, Tulani!" her grandmother exclaimed proudly. "Watchy, watchy! Watch what we do." They bent forward to see the crystal sizzle in the wound and the flesh turn white as V'sair gasped, reaching for it. "Hold his hand, Tulani. He must not ruin it."

Tulani took V'sair's hand in hers and kissed his knuckles. "Be still, my love," she whispered. He pulled out of her grasp, his hand gripping the edge of the cot, his knuckles turning white.

Smoke filled the air, and she watched, terrified, as the crystal bubbled as if boiling. V'sair moaned deeply, reaching up with his other hand to grab his shoulder. Tulani took his free hand and clasped it, tears brimming in her eyes. The flesh of V'sair's shoulder softened, and the bleeding stopped. She bent forward, her eyes wide as new skin formed. Soft as a baby's, a pinkish blue, it pulsed with a slow throb and began to heal over the gaping hole in his shoulder.

"He will heal quickly now." Bobbien nodded, satisfied. "The crystals are our secret."

"Secret?"

"Yes, Tulani. When the time is right, we will let these barbarians know the power of the Quyroos and the randam crystals. They think they know everything. Ha! They will realize the value of allies rather than slaves. They think we Quyroos are only good for fuel. The women of Nost know better."

Tulani bent over and gently brushed V'sair's white, sweat-drenched hair from his forehead. She pulled the blanket over his bare chest.

"So, Tulani, I'm thinking you be wondering where we be," she said with a laugh.

"Yes, Greanam. I have a feeling we are in the volcano. But how could we be in a room in the middle of the volcano?"

The room went pitch black, and Tulani bit back a scream. Her grandmother laughed deeply from her belly and started to recite the prayer of the Sradda Doctrines.

"Ozre, Ozre, light the path…"

The room vibrated, and for a moment, Tulani felt as though the floor had slanted. She got down on all fours, her long braids pooling around her. Multicolored lights filled the room, and her grandmother's prayers grew louder and louder to match the hum of a thousand insects. *Could the wysbies be inside the volcano?* Tulani thought wildly as she threw her body over V'sair to protect him.

"Stop!" she shouted, but her voice was merely an echo in her head. She stole a peek at V'sair, who lay in bed, oblivious to the explosion of lights and sounds around them. Suddenly the noise quieted, and the room was bathed in a red glow. A deep voice filled the room, its sound vibrating through Tulani's body.

"Ozre hears the call of prayer; Ozre answers the call of prayer," a very male voice echoed throughout the cave. Tulani watched her grandmother kneel, her arms outstretched, her eyes closed, her face turned up to the ceiling in submission.

"Great Ozre, we need your help." Bobbien threw herself to the floor and lay prostrate. "Heal the boy; heal the hearts; finish the quest for peace, he must."

There was a long pause; Tulani watched the red light bathe her grandmother. Then she felt it envelop her own body, invade her. Slowly, compelled, she slid to the floor, then laid her head on the cold ground and outstretched her hands in submission.

"Oh, great Ozre," Tulani whispered, tears streaming from her eyes, "Great Sradda, giver of life and love, I commend myself to thee. Heal V'sair…"

The Elements are real, was her last rational thought before she lost track of awareness and time itself.

XVI

PACUTO AND WINATA rolled in the sky as shock wave after shock wave pulsed through them. He knew he had lost Hother; her tether had broken with the impact of the explosion. He had seen the old witch throwing zandy grenades but hadn't felt their impact. The next time he came to the Desa, he would put her head on a stick, but for now he wanted only to return to Cloud City and claim his place next to his father.

Flanked by his guards, Pacuto noticed that the sky was strangely empty of patrols; in fact, he saw no traffic whatsoever. He pulled out his nevi, but the signal was dead. All communications were out.

He approached the castle entrance, but it was deserted.

Suddenly a large battleship hovered in the distance. *Friend or foe?* he wondered. He could not make out the name stenciled on the side. Only time would tell.

He took in the blown landing bays, wondering how he and his men would get inside. Light poured out from the huge wall of windows. He guided Winata onto a deserted balcony and gave over the reins to his squire.

"Go to the house of Nuen. Wait until you hear from me."

"Please let me come with you," Grodot pleaded. He had yet to bloody his Fireblade.

"No!" Pacuto shouted as he held out his hand for the younger soldier's Fireblade. Grodot handed it over with a decided lack of grace that earned him a slap with the flat side of the blade. "If anything happens to Winata, your head will be on yonder pike." He pointed to a row of columns at the north face of the tower. Go." Pacuto struck the black back of the animal and watched them ride home.

XVII

ZAYDEN AND HILDE'S shoulders hugged the walls of the parapets outside the queen's quarters.

"I feel like a coward," he said.

"Your death will not help the king," Hilde told him. "You must get assistance."

He stopped and turned to face her, the question too difficult to even consider. He wondered whether she knew of her father's plans. Everyone was gone, although here and there they came along a dead guard. Hilde's sad eyes took in their blood-drenched bodies.

"This was well planned. He couldn't have done it without help."

Hilde bit her lip. "Four of the seven generals are involved."

"Swart?"

"I am not sure." She shook her head. "I don't think so."

"If General Swart is involved, my father is finished."

Zayden withdrew his Fireblade from his belt and felt his energy pulse it to life. Vibrating in his hand, it lit a path as they entered a darkened chamber. Their footsteps echoed off the walls, and he heard his own harsh breathing. He was in one of V'sair's rooms, the one where his brother studied with Emmicus. He heard Hilde start to say something, and he quieted her with a finger over his lips. He saw the whites of her eyes glow in the dark. There was a faint sound of something, or someone, almost a moan. Placing his blade before him, he concentrated, letting his will brighten a blue blaze to illuminate their path. In a dark corner, he saw a pair of splayed legs just at the edge of his lit circle. He let the light travel upward and saw an ever-widening pool of blood. Zayden let go of Hilde's hand and bent over the dying man. It was Emmicus. He felt for a pulse and recoiled; the hand was dry and cold. He had seen death many times in his military life, but it was never easy. Finally, moving higher up his wrist, he found a feeble beat.

"Oh, my lord captain…" The tutor's voice was a thready whisper. "You must save V'sair. He is the future." He coughed, and blood dripped from his slack lips.

Zayden bent down. "Emmicus, hold on, dear friend."

He opened the old man's tunic, but a weak hand stayed him. "It's too late for me. Save the boy. He has the light of the Elements to guide him. He is just coming…into his full…Lord Zayden, he will be a great man." He paused, then pulled Zayden closer. "You have a duty to V'sair."

"I will protect him with my life."

"Sradda willing, you will be an excellent grand mestor."

Zayden shook his head. "No, no, Navigator. I am illegitimate. It is not the custom."

"Circumvent the custom, as I taught your father before you…" His head rolled to rest against the wall, the life-force draining from his eyes.

Zayden sat back on his haunches, silent for several seconds. "Did you know?" he demanded without looking at Hilde.

She didn't answer, and that revealed the truth. He rose, his eyes lit with anger, and grabbed her hand. "Come on."

Hilde's gray face darkened with shame. "I wanted to say something—"

"But you didn't," Zayden said, cutting her off. He refused to make eye contact, and had their situation been less dire, he would have confronted her. As it was, he was running in the halls of the castle, not knowing friends from enemies, and that included the person dearest to his heart. He felt a brittle wall surround him, locking out any feeling. Darracian males were supposed to be impervious to warm emotions. Once one embraced the Fireblade, the first allegiance was to the principles of the Elements, those of honor, bravery, and sacrifice. There was no room for love, and now he understood that his father's love for his Plantan woman had put the entire planet in jeopardy. That emotion was for poets and yeomen, not warriors. He heard Hilde sniffle, but it no longer affected him, his thoughts only on finding out whom he could trust to help his father. When he touched his Fireblade, he noticed that the shade had changed from violet to orange, then to a glowing red, and for a second he considered what was causing this strange occurrence.

They both spun as the crack of breaking glass broke the silence of the night.

"Pacuto!" Hilde saw her brother storm into the room, his sword raised, followed by three guards.

Zayden drew his blade, but Hilde stilled his arm. "He has not seen us. You are outnumbered. He will kill me." He tugged his arm away from her. "Please!" she implored.

Zayden grabbed her hand and raced for the door. They heard a shout and knew at once they had been seen. Zayden ducked out of the doorway, pulling Hilde by the arm. He spotted the cutout of a servant door in the smooth walls of the corridor. He pressed a hidden panel, and an opening appeared; they slipped inside, stepping on something soft that hissed in pain.

Something grabbed his foot, and Zayden fell to the cold floor. The wind escaped him completely when Hilde fell on top of him. Turning sideways, he found himself eyeball to eyeball with a shivering Quyroo who backed up defensively against the wall as he shook his head.

Scuffles sounded outside, and Zayden whispered, "Shh." "Where did they go?" They heard Pacuto's harsh voice, followed by the sound of a hand slapping a face. "Idiot! How could you lose them?"

"They vanished."

"Into thin air?" He paused, then said, "Go that way!"

Footsteps ran up and down the hallway. Then they heard, "I said, let's go…"

Sirens were sounding in all the main sections of the castle, and Zayden and Hilde heard the thump of the hermetically sealed doors locking out intruders.

"Do you know where the king is?" he asked a servant, who shook his head. "Do you know where anyone is?"

"Many of the servants are hiding in these hallways," the Quyroo whispered, his eyes wide.

"Swart—do you know where General Swart is?"

"I think he is trapped in the landing bay at the main entrance."

"Have you tried to leave?"

"To go where? They are hunting us down and killing without question."

"Can I get there through here?"

"This corridor runs only from the kitchens to these quarters, my lord. Take the central course down the center of the castle, and then cut through those servant corridors to get there."

"Will you be all right?"

The servant shrugged. "I think I am safe, unless they burn down the palace."

"I will come back for you."

"Great Sradda guide your path, lord."

They left the servant corridors and chanced the main hallways, but they ran from one dead end to another. Hilde bent over, nursing a cramp in her side.

Zayden held on to her arm, pulling her close to him when they turned a corner. He knew they had been spotted, and he thrust her behind him as two soldiers advanced toward them.

"Stay back!" he ordered her as he engaged his Fireblade with both hands.

Two soldiers screamed as they ran to him, their swords clanging as they met. Clearly one was more experienced than the other, so Zayden concentrated on taking out the younger man so he could then focus on the older one. Crouching low, he spun, the impetuous guard running headlong into his blade, impaling himself and dying with a sigh. As Zayden withdrew his blade, he felt the ice of steel on his arm, coupled with Hilde's scream. With a grunt he shoved his shoulder into the other man's stomach, throwing him off-balance, then cleaving him where his neck met his chest. The man fell with a loud thud, and Zayden leaned heavily against the bloodstained walls, his breath coming in short pants.

Hilde was on her knees, ripping a strip from the hem of her gown. "It's hardly clean, but it will have to do," she told him as she neatly bound the gaping wound on his forearm.

He looked down on the top of her head as she worked, the curtain of her hair hiding her face, but he could tell from her thick voice that she was crying. With his finger he tilted her chin to look her full in the face, and they stood in silence until he said, "We have to get out of here."

"I am distracting you. You never would have been hurt if I weren't here. Leave me," she told him softly.

"Find General Swart. He always has been your father's most trusted ally."

"Not on your life." Briskly he grabbed Hilde's elbow and pulled her along, his Fireblade drawn and ready in his other hand.

Using the Quyroo's instructions, they skirted through several smaller corridors and made it to the other side of the palace. They ran down the main hallway in short spurts, hiding where it intersected with offshoots. Zayden found the invisible door, and they ran through the secret corridors to the docking port. Several times they came upon quaking Quyroo servants who were hiding from the devastation outside their haven.

"This is it," he told Hilde when they came to another exit. "The docking bay is on the other side."

"But what if my father's men are there? You can't fight them alone."

"I can't hide like a coward in the servant hallway while my family is being murdered."

He opened the door a fraction, letting butter-colored light seep into their gloom. "You stay here. Do you understand?" he whispered harshly.

Zayden poked his head through the doorway and noticed a group of guards on picket duty. He pulled back in and turned to Hilde.

"Listen, don't move. Stay in here." He pulled her so they were nose to nose and looked her full in the face in the darkness. "If something happens to me, find your mother and throw yourself on her mercy." He shook her, staring at her intently. "Do you hear me, Hilde? Stay here until I come for you. If I don't return, seek the countess."

She nodded, her face drained of color. "I wanted to tell you," she whispered.

"It's too late now," he said as he cupped her face and kissed her with an urgency he barely controlled. Her whimper made him pull away and look at her. "We will talk later." Making himself as small of a target as he could, he eased out of the doorway and stopped just short of the corner to see whether the men patrolling were Swart's or his uncle's.

"What are you doing, Smen?" One of the soldiers strolled over to the one closest to Zayden. "It's forbidden to smoke inside the castle."

The older man pulled a long drag on his pipe and shrugged. "Don't make much of a difference now."

"That may be so," the younger man whispered back, "but Swart will have your hide if he sees that. It's insubordination."

"For whom? Right now I don't even know if I serve a king or a devil." He spat on the ground, his aim close to Zayden's feet.

"My father, the king, does not tolerate his ranks to break laws." Zayden turned the corner to confront the two men.

The younger one fumbled with his Fireblade, but Zayden rested his sword across the soldier's knuckles. One flick of his wrist, and the man's fighting hand would be destroyed.

"Captain," the pipe-smoking guard said with a smile, "we've been waiting for some direction."

"I can see how you're waiting," Zayden drawled, and nodded to the pipe. "You know you're not supposed to do anything but guard your posts."

"Well, now I do. You looking for the general?" The older guard turned to his younger cohort. "You heard the captain. Straighten up, Bernwyn." He tapped his pipe against the muscles of his powerful tail, and they watched the falling cinders. "Follow me. General Swart is inside, trying to make some sense of this thing."

"One minute." Zayden left and returned for Hilde. He held her by the upper arm and escorted her into the docking bay.

"General," Zayden saluted the officer, who looked greatly relieved to see him.

"Welcome to hell, Captain."

XVIII

V'SAIR BECAME AWARE of the heat first; it burned like the dual suns of Darracia and scorched his bones so they felt dry and brittle. He thrashed as he tried to cool himself, throwing off the blankets that smothered him. In his mind he fought Pacuto, the Fireblade heavy in his hands, his feet sluggish. He thought he heard Tulani, and he attempted to lift his heavy lids, but his pain forced him to keep them closed. Sometimes there was chanting, and he could swear a rainbow of colors filled the room, but the darkness called to him, and he went down, down, down to escape the heat.

"When will he awaken, Greanam?" Tulani bathed V'sair's fevered head as she watched his face grow pale.

"Who's to say?" The old woman shrugged in a very Quyroo way. "Only the Elements know for sure."

Tulani and Bobbien had gotten closer as they

sat huddled together, so much more understanding between them since they'd arrived. The Elements had soothed Tulani. For the first time in her life, she felt at peace, as though she actually belonged somewhere. She didn't remember much, only feeling as though she had been plucked from the inside out, the great beam of light roaring through her every cell to know her true heart. She had awoken to confusion and Bobbien's smiling face.

"Takes time, don't you know"—her grandmother nodded knowingly—"to accept what the Elements are saying."

Tulani stared back in wonder, not understanding what had happened but knowing she never would be the same. She watched as the light bathed V'sair, enveloping him in its heat and warmth. It pulsed with a life of its own, and he seemed as remote as the stars in the sky. His shoulder wound was completely healed; only a bluish scar remained. The spent crystal had rolled onto the floor and turned to white powder.

"How do you know of this place?" she asked the older woman.

"I am Bobbien, the high priestess. You are next in line. Learn your role here; it is time. When you finally accept what the Elements are saying, I will have nothing left to teach you." She walked off and busied herself with piles of dusty-looking leaves. Soon Tulani heard her exit the cave, her voice calling back, "Do not leave. I am going for food. Three mouths I now have to feed."

"But Greanam, what of the wysbies?" Tulani called, fear making her breathless.

"Wysbies! Ha! Sweet meat they only want, not this old leather. Wysbies, she says." Tulani heard the echoes of her grandmother's laughter in the dank cavern.

V'sair seemed to rouse, his heavy hand brushing away the wet cloth over his eyes. He coughed once as he tried to rise. Tulani pushed him back gently and told him to wait.

"How long have I been here?" he asked. "An hour, maybe two. Oh, don't move, V'sair." He pushed up anyway.

"Slowly, V'sair. You have been very sick."

"Tulani?" He let his unfocused gaze come to rest on the girl. "Where are we?"

"It's a long story," she said with a smile.

"I think the one thing I can be sure of is that I have the time."

As Tulani served him more of the caylet tea, she related their escaped. V'sair was able to drink it himself from a mug as he lay propped up by a pile of blankets. "Then she parted the trees, and we were inside Aqin."

"The volcano? How is that possible?"

"I don't understand it myself, but here we are."

"I dreamed of strange pulsing lights," he told her, his eyes scanning the cave.

"Bobbien prayed, and then...well, it's hard to believe, but I think one of the Elements was here. I heard it, felt it..."

"Tulani, that's crazy. You don't really believe in all that nonsense, do you?"

She shrugged. "It was like nothing I'd ever felt. It surrounded you for a while. Did you not feel anything?"

"I dreamed of colors and the Fireblade. But I am always dreaming about the Fireblade. Where is Bobbien now?"

"Getting food and more herbs for your arm."

He rolled off the side of the bed and used Tulani's strength to stand. "I have to help my parents." The room dipped, and he swayed. He would have fallen if not for Tulani's support.

"You are in no condition to do anything."

"I don't have a choice." His eyes fell on the Fireblade he had used in his fight. He stumbled over to it and picked it up, watching as it pulsed weakly with a pale red. He turned it around, and with each rotation, a hum started, filling his head.

"V'sair, you will start to bleed again." Tulani moved closer, but he waved her off, feeling stronger, as though his power came from the glowing colors of the sword.

Could this be it? he thought excitedly. He had vague memories of his fight with Pacuto and knew that the strange sword had felt alive, as though a force had magnified its power. It vibrated within him, and for a minute, everything receded; he became aware of only the blade, his hand, and his heart. Suddenly a voice echoed; he thought it might just be in his head, but a glance at Tulani told him she heard it too. It called his name, and as if on cue, they both dropped to their knees.

Oh, Great Sradda, could this finally be happening to him?

The room darkened, then brightened, a rush of wind making them both shiver with cold and excitement. A voice filled the cavern, their skulls, their every fiber. It rushed through V'sair, and he teetered on the verge of something great. His vision went white, as if all sight was stolen, yet he saw everything with a clarity that didn't need eyesight.

"You thought yourself not good enough for the secrets?" the voice chided him with a chuckle. "You thought we did not love you, silly child?"

"Ozre?" V'sair whispered.

"I would say 'in the flesh,' but that would be a lie."

The words surrounded him, bathed him. "Yes, yes, it is Ozre. I could have a bone to pick with you, young sir, but I know you. The belief was buried deep inside you. Hidden away, like a treasure. You want to learn the secrets of the Fireblade?" the voice teased.

"If you are Ozre, then you know I do," V'sair said boldly.

The room filled with laughter that rolled over them like the crushing waves of the sea. "You played the game of a nonbeliever, but that was only because you doubted. You know what the problem was, where the problem was."

"I am half Plantan—"

"There is the nonsense you speak of!" the voice roared, stopping him midsentence. "Think, V'sair. Think."

"They say that I am not strong enough to learn the Fireblade, that I don't have Darracian strength."

"You believe all one needs is brawn? You think we would go to all the trouble and just rely on brute strength?" The voice was soft but ominous.

V'sair sat on his haunches, speechless. For his entire life, he had been excluded based on his physical appearance. Of course one needed Darracian bulk to wield the

Fireblade; otherwise all species would want to learn to use it.

"If you need more than Darracian strength, then I am doubly at a loss."

A great wind barreled through the chamber, lifting objects to crash against the stone walls. "You bore me!" The room flared red, then pulsated blue. "I thought you more capable than this!"

Out of a black vortex, a glowing orb appeared in one corner and grew into a small ball of white light that gathered momentum by spinning around the room. It grazed V'sair's head, and he ducked to avoid an impact. His skull felt detached from his body. The orb came at him again, and he jumped so high that it buzzed past him harmlessly. Panting, he watched it crash against a wall and come speeding back toward his face. He spun around, weaving drunkenly, bending backward, and felt it burn across his chest.

"Better and better!" the voice yelled. "Do you wish to try again?"

"Brawn," V'sair said carefully, "is an illusion?"

Tulani called out, "It is one's perception."

"Quiet, girl, lest we deposit you in the fires of Aqin!" The small orb of flame danced around her. "When we want to know something from you, we will ask." The ball spun over, coming face-to-face with the prince.

"V'sair?"

The orb hung suspended before him. The light was so bright that it should have hurt his eyes, but it didn't. V'sair saw straight through it, to the red core in its center.

"Brawn is a state of mind?"

"You question it?"

"It's a state of mind," V'sair said firmly.

"Why did you desire to take the Fireblade?"

"To prove that I am Darracian, that I can hold my own among them." He thought for a moment. "To prove that I can lead them. To be like the rest of them," he finished weakly.

"Silly child…" The orb moved away and bounced before him. "You were planned. For eons and eons, you were planned. Darracians, for all their brains, are filled with anger.

Two halves make one whole," the voice finished cryptically. "Two halves make one whole?"

"V'sair, V'sair…use that head." This time the orb clunked him mightily, and stars clouded his vision. "Sorry, but you are dense."

"He's recuperating!" Tulani wailed.

"Excuses." The ball of light pulsed, then laughed once again. "Try to think."

When V'sair sat in silence, the orb floated toward him tentatively. "There was peace in this place until they segregated. Do you understand? When Darracians mated only with Darracians, and Quyroos mated only with Quyroos, they grew dull. Society stagnated. There was no exchange of ideas. The Quyroos became stunted and allowed themselves to be oppressed. The Darracians chose to interpret everything—from the Fireblade to the holy Sradda—to their own advantage. This is a dark age. When we wall ourselves away and there is no exchange of ideas, we think we know everything. It is no coincidence your father found your mother. That was planned, for the offspring would have the best of both. Do you understand?"

"I am the combination of the two," V'sair said, "but what of the Fireblade?"

"Ah…" The voice laughed. "All you ever think of is the Fireblade. You still think it makes you special," it sneered. "That is a notion of the Darracians. They are convinced it makes them superior. Watch, Tulani." The orb spun to bathe the girl in blue light. The sword rolled over to rest at her feet. "Pick it up," Ozre commanded. Tulani bent and wrapped her tiny hands around the handle of the sword. It leaped to life before her astonished eyes. "Move!" the voice commanded.

As if she had practiced her entire life, Tulani waved the sword expertly; it glowed bluish white, with the vitality of a thousand suns. Empowered, she smiled as she sailed around the room, parrying with an expertise that bordered on genius.

"A perception?" V'sair asked.

"Perhaps a leap of faith?" Ozre countered.

"A test," V'sair confirmed. "A test of belief in…" He was about to say "the Elements" but was suddenly blinded by insight. "A test in belief in myself!" he shouted, jumping up. "The test is in oneself."

"Took you long enough, V'sair. You now possess the great secret of the Fireblade, a truth evident in its blue color, which represents justice. When one understands the meaning—"

"Or your intent?"

"What do you think is our intent?"

"It says in the Sradda Doctriness that you are the Element of strength and that Darracians are strong, the strongest."

"I would hit you on the head again, Prince, but I think Tulani will go after me." Ozre laughed. "Strength is not always about brawn. There are different strengths."

V'sair was quiet for a moment; then his eyes lit up. "Strength to know what to do and not give in to our base needs!"

"Excellent!"

"The others talk of great strength exclusive to Darracians," V'sair said. "They claim it comes from you and the communion with the Fireblade."

"A way to keep the weaker oppressed. That was not in our plan."

"Why didn't you stop it?" V'sair stood and confronted the orb. "You are the power of the Elements," he spouted, "a force of nature, the soul of our universe. Why didn't you stop it?"

"What!" The orb spun angrily. "What of free will? Oh, yes, it's easy to blame the Elements for everything. What a perfect excuse, scapegoat us so one can behave as badly as he chooses and pretend it's our will." Ozre paused and asked softly, "Will you never learn? We are here for your benefit, for you to realize your insights—not to be used as an excuse to torment others for a society's selfish needs."

"So," V'sair said, "what happened to all my father's

people when they believed themselves initiated by the Fireblade? What happened to them?"

The orb danced in the air. "Pick it up and see for yourself."

Tulani placed the Fireblade in V'sair's open palm. It strummed to life, changing from its previous orange color to a cold blue. Watching with fascination, they observed the color deepen with startling intensity.

"All the others are shades of red?" V'sair asked the orb. "Reckless red, angry red, ignorant red." "You are red," V'sair offered helpfully.

"I represent the humble red of the planet. I," Ozre told him patiently, as if talking to an idiot, "I'm not a Fireblade."

The orb started to spin. "Your blade is blue for a purpose."

"Peace?" Tulani asked as Ozre moved from side to side.

"Cold reason?" V'sair cocked his head thoughtfully.

"Why?" Ozre circled them.

"The Fireblade should be used for justice, not hate or oppression."

"Emmicus can rest easy. He has done a fine job," Ozre said sadly.

"Emmicus, my navigator?"

"He tried to teach both your father and your uncle. Between Reminda and Emmicus's lessons, Drakko has opened his mind. Staf Nuen and his ilk are stuck with antiquated notions of their own superiority. They have twisted our intent. The Fireblade was intended to prevent injustice, not promote it."

"Then there are no secrets?" Tulani came to stand next to V'sair as they listened intently to Ozre.

"They believed their own myths to make them

superior so they could continue to ravage the planet's most precious resource."

"Peace," V'sair said quietly.

"Yes," the orb said. "We come back to peace. The most precious gift we have given you, and it has been squandered."

"There are no secrets. I understand."

"Yes," it hissed, "but do you now know what to do?"

XIX

STAF NUEN SAT on the golden throne. Beatha stood behind him, her hand resting on the arm. Reminda was seated at his feet, his Fireblade resting on her shoulder, holding her still. Should she move an inch, it would slice into her delicate neck. Drakko had been locked in a supply room, the most demeaning way for his brother to show his contempt for his older sibling. The adjoining Ambros room was a scene of carnage, with Quyroos murdered then chopped up and left to rot as the evening wore on.

Reminda hung her head, disgusted with the violence; fear and worry for her family were etched in the new lines of her face. Her blue skin was dulled, and her hands shook, yet she remained defiant when Staf addressed her. Pacuto entered the room, boasting of his kill.

"Ah, Pacuto," Beatha purred, "you have returned."

She looked at Reminda with barely concealed hatred. "You are wounded."

"Trifles, Your Majesty. Minor discomforts that I would gladly suffer for your success."

"The prince?" Staf demanded.

"When you give me a mission, I commit it, Your Majesties," he boasted. He held up the white braid of Prince V'sair, shouting, "Behold what's left of the prince!" Reminda paled, the blood rushing from her head.

There was an outbreak of noise in the room.

Staf stood and yelled, "Silence!" then turned to his son. "You swore you would bring his head!" Staf could not hide his disappointment for not having another display of bloodlust to rouse his troops.

"I had to leave. The Quyroos retaliated. It was a bloodbath, rest assured. Sire, we left more dead than alive." He grinned devilishly, his pointy teeth bared.

Staf stood and walked down the dais. "Are you positive the prince is dead?" he insisted, making sure Reminda heard their exchange.

Pacuto slapped the braid into his father's hand. "You need more proof, sire?" he asked sarcastically. "I am more than sure, Father. We were vastly outnumbered," he lied. "I would have taken his head, but I longed to return to share your glory."

Staf grunted, then took his son's beefy arm and raised it high above his head. "Behold, Darracia! Behold your new crown prince. Long live Prince Pacuto!" He turned to his son. "Where is your Fireblade? This is your squire's."

"In Prince V'sair's body."

Staf roared with approval and motioned for his secon-din-command to hand over his Fireblade. "I will give you another, studded with crystals, once our victory is complete!"

There were cheers, and Reminda lowered her head, memorizing faces for revenge. She was sure her son still lived; she would know it if he did not. Feeling a gaze bore into her back, she turned to see the satisfied look on Beatha's face, the pitiless black eyes triumphant. She balled her fists to stop their shaking and swore to the Elements that she would kill Staf and his family if any harm came to her son.

XX

"WHAT YOU ARE telling me is that we are outnumbered and alone." Zayden spoke quietly with General Swart. They were in the landing bay at the south end of the castle. The automatic doors had been blasted and hung open. The fight was over, bodies had been carted away, and soldiers lounged in various corners of the room. Swart had ordered them to stand down, knowing they must be alert when the final battle arrived.

"They have killed Mecon, Grenci, and two others in the high command," Swart said. "Communications have been scrambled. I don't know where General Vekin is holed up. Last I heard he had been backed into the service area of the castle. There was some fierce fighting there."

"Survivors?"

General Swart shrugged. "Your guess is as good as mine."

"What of your men?" Zayden leaned against a table with a crude map of the castle on it.

"They are at my base." He gestured toward a group of about twenty. "We didn't come prepared for a coup."

"Any word regarding my father?"

A young guard stepped forward, his arm in a sling. "He's been taken to the lower levels."

Zayden nodded. "Go on."

"I think he's been locked in some sort of stock room."

"Below the kitchens?"

"Yes, I saw him being dragged there."

"I know the area well," Zayden stated.

"Captain, I cannot let you try to rescue him. You will be needed here. Your father would expect me to secure your safety."

Zayden smiled at the older man. "I appreciate your concern, General, but I am a commander second and a son first. No one will stop me from saving my father."

Swart looked at the ceiling, then agreed. "You will need help."

"I will go with you!" Hilde jumped up from her seat and gripped Zayden's arm. "We played there as children. The guards will think…The guards will listen to the daughter of Staf Nuen."

"No!" Zayden shouted.

"I don't think you have another choice, Zayden. Take the girl." Swart pointed to a group of his men and motioned for them to stand up. "I will give you these four."

"If we don't return within two hours," Zayden said,

"try to get out and see if you can mobilize troops from the outside."

"If you do not return, we won't need to," Swart replied grimly. "There will be nothing left to fight for."

"My brother?"

"Is missing and presumed dead."

Hilde gasped, and a sob escaped, but no one acknowledged it in the tense room.

"May the Elements guide the light of your Fireblade, and Sradda have mercy on our souls."

XXI

V'SAIR STRUGGLED WITH his tunic, his arm sore, blood staining his bandage. Sweat dotted his forehead, and his eyes shone with feverous intensity.

"Stop, V'sair! You cannot go anywhere," Tulani implored him.

"I have no choice. My parents are in danger." He continued to get dressed, his fingers clumsy.

Tulani placed her gentle hands on his and urged him again. "You surely will die. It's not safe."

"Then I will die," he responded simply. He took her hands in his own. "If I die, I only regret that we had so little time together, Tulani." He tenderly kissed her full lips. "I love you. I think I must have always loved you."

"You never even noticed me before last night!"

"I have known you in here." He pressed her hand against his thumping heart, and her legs became liquid.

Tears welled in her star-shaped eyes, and when they dripped, five silver runnels streamed down her cheeks.

"You don't even have a way to get back," she told him after a soft hiccup that he found endearing.

His thumbs caressed the softness of her face, and he rested his forehead against hers. "I will come back for you." He kissed her again deeply, their tongues entwining.

Tulani pressed her body against his, as if she could hold him next to her forever. He was headed for certain death.

"What do they do here?" Bobbien cackled loudly. "Can't leave these young uns alone. Do you not think of anything else?" she demanded. They turned but did not separate until V'sair saw what trailed behind the old woman. "Oh, like you what I found?" she asked.

A soft snort greeted them, and V'sair cried out with delight, "Hother!"

"Wandering around, getting attacked by wysbies, stupid stallius." Bobbien nodded. "Knew this would cure what ails you, young man." The stallius's hide was dotted with sting marks, and blood stained her white coat.

"Thank you. Thank you!" V'sair pressed his face against Hother, tears smarting his eyes. "The Elements have made it possible, Tulani. I have a job to do."

"Take me with you!" She ran to his side.

"No, it is not safe." He shook his head, and Bobbien agreed.

"Not your place, Tulani. Not your place." Her grandmother shook her head as well.

Tulani picked up one of the Fireblades and handed it

to V'sair, her face solemn. She turned to the old woman. "Have you any zandies left?"

"O' course. Let's make him an arsenal to take with him." Bobbien pulled several of the homemade grenades from her bag. "Better you should eat before you leave. Need your energy, I'm thinking."

They ate dried fruit—the Quyroos never ate meat—while they packed a double-sided pouch for V'sair to carry over the front of Hother. Together they put in as many grenades as they could.

Tulani walked him to the very edge of the tunnel. He touched her thin arms as he memorized her face. After kissing her quickly, he saluted her grandmother and said, "I will come back for you. You will be my queen someday."

Hopping onto Hother's back, he lit his Fireblade with his passion, and Tulani watched him ride off, afraid she never would see him again.

XXII

ZAYDEN KEPT HIS back to the wall, his Fireblade out but its glow extinguished for stealth. He heard Hilde's ragged breathing and the reassuring footfalls of the extra men.

"I will distract them," Hilde mouthed and pointed to the two guards outside the storeroom.

"Over my dead body," he whispered back.

"Then why did you let me come?" she demanded in the merest puff of air.

"So I could keep my eye on you." He motioned toward his last soldier and nodded for him to clear the next hall.

The young man put his sword away and walked into the lit corridor. "Which way to get something to eat?" he asked a group of Darracians guarding a doorway.

One pulled out his sword, and it hummed to life. "What are you doing here? It's off-limits!" he shouted.

"Sorry..." He raised both hands, his palms up. "Just got in from the Desa. Missed all the fun."

One of the two guards grinned. "Yeah, it was like picking off keewallas in the trees. The Quyroos just sat there."

"Too bad you weren't on patrol. I got this." The young solider reached down and retrieved a small pouch from deep in his pants pocket. "Got myself some crystals."

"Let me see!"

"No, they're mine. I earned them." He pulled back, the crystals encased in his fist. "Well, okay. I'll show you, but it's better when you come under the light."

"Stupid, stupid..." Zayden smiled as they took the bait. He pushed Hilde back and told her, "Wait and be still."

Resting their weapons against the wall, the Darracians moved closer to see the crystals, and Zayden shouted, "*Now!*"

His men leaped from the hallway. Zayden sliced deeply and took out the first guard, almost cleaving him in two. A few moments later, the second guard's head rolled to the floor, his eyes blinking in disbelief, his mouth moving wordlessly.

"The door!" Using his hilt, Zayden banged against the lock until it gave, and the door swung open to reveal a pitchblack room.

"Father?"

"Zayden!" King Drakko rose from the corner and stood as the group knelt at his feet. The king's braid looked bedraggled, and his eye was blackened.

He glanced at his niece, and she shook her head. "I

am loyal to you, Uncle. My father betrayed me more than he did you."

"Where is V'sair?"

"I'm sorry, Father. He is presumed dead, but no one is sure."

Zayden saw his father's eyes dull with grief as he asked quietly, "The queen lives?"

Zayden nodded. "She is held captive in the throne room. Communication has been shut down. Your two loyal generals are separated on either side of the castle. I…I don't see a solution, Father."

The king agreed darkly. "So all we have is Swart and Vekin. It doesn't look good, Zayden. I will need a Fireblade."

One of the men bowed, holding his weapon up as an offering. "Take mine, sire."

Another then knelt and said the same.

Drakko looked at each of them and took the first soldier's sword. "You will be rewarded."

"It is an honor to serve," the grizzled soldier responded.

"The best defense is an offense. I think, Zayden, that we should cut the Hydra's head off at the top," the king said as they set off for the throne room.

XXIII

TULANI LOOKED BLANKLY at her grandmother. "Is this all there is?"

"No, no, girl. This is just the beginning. Heard what he said, did you? He means to make you the queen. Sit there like a fool, will you?"

"But you said I should not go with him!"

"That I did. Certain death it would be. He is running like a keewalla without a head. Do you think I did not have a plan?"

"What plan?" Tulani demanded impatiently.

Bobbien knelt and placed her forehead to the floor. She turned her wizened face to her granddaughter. "Time is wasting, child. Kneel and appeal to the Element."

"The Element said the knowledge is within us."

"Then pray for enlightenment!"

Tulani got down, pressing her knees to the stone,

her forehead on the floor in silent appeal. "Oh, Great Sradda," she implored, "I don't even know what I'm praying for. I just want to keep V'sair safe."

The room turned red, and the orb appeared. "You are calling for help, perhaps?" it asked petulantly. Without waiting for a response, it laughed and said, "I am Ozre, Element of the earth. In what way can the land help you? Think, Tulani."

It rumbled, and the room fairly shook.

What can Ozre do? she wondered. She had learned it refused to force its will on all kind, but what other way could she harness the power to aide V'sair? *Think, she told herself. Think!*

"I don't know what to do," she said.

"I can't think for you, Tulani! Use your brain and think. I am Ozre. I am Ozre, Element of the land. I am the creator of the stars and planets. Through me, you can use the land to your advantage. Think, girl! I never had to spell it out for your grandmother," Ozre admonished.

"The belly of the beast!" Tulani looked up, taking in the polished walls of the interior of the volcano, her eyes shining. "Can you force an eruption?"

"To what purpose?"

"If Aqin erupts, the Quyroos will run down the sides of the volcano to the safety of the Plains of Dawid. Once they are there, I can speak to them—tell them of Staf Nuen— and perhaps they will storm the castle."

Bobbien got up slowly. "Only a high priestess can move the Quyroos. I have lost my status." "But I have not," Tulani said.

The room flashed with lightning, and a roar rolled up the hollow inside of the volcano, Ozre making good on its end of the job.

XXIV

V'SAIR HUGGED HIMSELF against the muscled neck of Hother, feeling safe. The cold night winds bit through his tunic, making him shiver uncontrollably. He pressed his knees into his stallius's heaving sides, urging the beast to go faster than he had ever demanded. Sweat lathered her neck, and he pressed a reassuring hand against her throat, begging the Elements to keep her safe.

As he burst through the treetops, he saw several guards but none that looked familiar. He knew he was fast becoming a noticeable target.

In the distance V'sair saw the dual suns rising to start a new day. The rays blinded him, hurting his eyes. He felt them water and wondered whether they were tears from the extreme light or tears for his family. As his vision cleared, he counted ten guards on stalliuses watching the skies for intruders. They were a ragtag bunch, not his father's Petrion soldiers.

One of them pointed at him, and he pulled Hother with all his might through the cluster of buildings toward the great sea. "Faster, Hoth. Faster, girl," he urged, watching their swords drawn and lit up with battle readiness.

They chased him through the openings between the buildings; they rode the clouds, their reflections dancing on the glass walls. He darted between two high-rises, their bulk shielding him from their view, and he knew he had to act now. After swooping under an awning, he eased backward, out of sight, and waited. As he pulled his Fireblade from his belt, he heard the reassuring hum and closed his eyes, briefly wondering why he ever had wanted this so badly.

Two guards barreled through, shouting noisily. As they passed, V'sair extended his arm as far as it could go, watching in amazement as the long reach of his blade sliced off the head of the first soldier and took the arm of the second one as they raced by. It had been a clean swipe, yet the impact almost unseated him. He righted himself as he heard the screams of the second soldier as he fell to the planet, his voice becoming fainter the farther he went.

V'sair pushed Hother to the fourth floor as he watched the reflection of the glass windows and spotted another group approach. Reaching into the pouch that Tulani had hung on Hother, he pulled out two zandy grenades and tried to remember how to activate them.

He had just one shot and knew he had to be higher, else it would fall to explode harmlessly in the Desa.

"Come on," he whispered to Hother, who strained to slowly move upward. He watched them skirt around the area as he eased the giant stallius as close to the wall of the building as he could. He knew they stood out like a beacon, he and his white beast. The suns moved over the land, chasing the shadows of darkness. Breathless, he waited until they were almost directly beneath him. With his teeth he pulled at a small clip, counted to five—lest they explode too late—and watched as the grenade descended. The blast's reverberation almost threw him off Hother. His fingernails ripped as he held on to the bridle while the shock waves rocked him in midair. His shoulder connected with the wall of the building, and for a moment, stars danced before his eyes, the wind knocked out of him. His field of vision narrowed for a second, and he took a huge breath to try to completely return to his senses. His arm ached from controlling his stallius, and his knees shook from the stress.

Man and beast below him flew apart, and the detail of guards met their Maker in seconds. Hands and legs pounded against the surfaces of the buildings, splashing bodily fluids everywhere. V'sair never would look at the skyscape again without thinking of the horror of this moment.

He regained control of Hother in time to see the last man coming at him, sword drawn, his face in a furious snarl. V'sair pulled out his Fireblade and, ready for battle, inched sideways to move into the open. The two men circled each other, the wings of their stalliuses creating eddies of wind that ruffled V'sair's hair.

"You killed my men," the commander shouted hatefully. "They're supposed to be my father's men!" V'sair called back.

"I will kill you and bring your head to Staf Nuen."

"You can try." V'sair laughed, baiting him into recklessness.

It worked, and the commander rushed in. V'sair caught him in the side, ripping a neat hole. The other man pulled up, the hooves of his stallius clipping V'sair's hand. The prince's knuckles erupted as if they were on fire, and his hand went completely numb. The precious Fireblade slipped from his hand, and Hother instinctively dove; V'sair saw the other warrior following him for the kill. Clamping his legs against her sides, he rolled, pulling his stallius with him, hoping Hother wouldn't get disoriented and plummet to the waves below them. Salty spray from the sea coated his face, and he knew if he didn't act quickly, he'd be swimming within seconds. He had to catch his Fireblade before it sank into the hungry waves. Reaching out, he stretched his fingers, and the hilt of his sword landed in his hand. He pushed Hother to turn to the left and came out of his barrel roll, slashing the belly of his opponent's stallius and watching blood pour from the widening slit. The stallius screamed in agony, its hooves lashing out in the throes of death. Man and beast turned headfirst to crash into the churning sea below them.

V'sair spun as Hother's hooves glanced off the waves, splashing him with water as she gathered momentum to head toward the rising suns and his destiny.

XXV

BOTH ENTRANCES TO the castle were destroyed, the gates hanging open and a detail of armed soldiers making it impossible to enter. V'sair scanned the fortress and remembered a service entrance he and his brother often had used to escape the confines of the castle.

He veered off, rethinking his strategy, hovering in the shadow of a hulking ship. His heart beat furiously in his chest, and he felt the heat of Rast and Nost burn through the layers of his clothes.

Hother whickered, and he shushed her, her great wings moving quietly as he backed off to find another way in.

As the sky lightened, he heard the loud screeches of herns before he saw them. A giant *V*, with hundreds of leathery-winged herns, flew directly toward him. His heart beat wildly as their razor-sharp beaks became visible, their cries rending the stillness of the morning. He had nowhere to hide; they would rip him to shreds. As the flap of their wings grew closer, V'sair circled in his spot, not knowing where to go. Two soldiers spotted him. He heard one of them shout and watched as they galloped toward him, their Fireblades blazing red in the morning light. To his back were the ship and a small group of guards; to his front were the herns; to his left, the soldiers racing toward him. Holding his breath, V'sair calmed himself. He kicked Hother gently into the oncoming flock of herns, their sharp beaks grazing him, the leathery wings feeling papery against his face. He screeched loudly, imitating their sound, relaxing when he realized that as long as he stayed calm, they ignored him. Their fetid smell, however, made him gag. Seconds later he heard the screams of the men as the birds raced in formation, their wild movements causing a frenzied attack. He watched in horror as the herns poked the men's eyes, stabbed and sawed, until each soldier had fallen from his stallius to the planet below.

An explosion startled V'sair. The flock dissipated, and he saw a great plume of smoke erupt from Aqin, leaving him perplexed as to what Ozre could be doing. He watched the sky darken over the Plains of Dawid. Then he heard the exclamations of more guards and a captain ordering them to find out what was going on below. Near the rear of the last donjon, a group hovered before the small entry to the kitchens of the palace. Several of the guards were shouting, and the group soon split up, leaving two men to watch the exit. It seemed it never got easy, V'sair thought as he swallowed hard. He counted patiently, watching the others become tiny dots on the horizon, then pulled out his Fireblade and closed his eyes.

"Great Sradda, I commend myself to thee," he whispered.

Putting the blade straight before him, he raced forward, the wind whistling in his ears as he swung the Fireblade in a swirling arc, and felt it bite deeply into the first man and just as quickly attacked the other.

One man's thighs gripped his stallius as his upper torso free-fell to the planet. The other held his belly together with his hands, shock on his face as he tried to stuff his intestines back into the growing cavity, the light fading from his eyes. V'sair turned, his stomach roiling. He looked at his bloodied hands and wondered why the Fireblade consumed him so. He decided he did not like this part, but he knew he had no choice. There was no glory in war, no romance in the blade. If he survived this, he couldn't wait to tell Emmicus his feelings had changed. He understood that the Fireblade existed to protect, not to oppress. His blade turned bluer than his eyes.

He rode into the deserted galleys, sickened by the bodies strewn across the floor. Food burned on the stoves, bread black and smoking in the many ovens. Quyroos had been cut down where they worked, hacked without mercy. He walked around spilled fruit that was mashed with the blood of the victims. It was a scene indelibly printed on V'sair's young brain; he doubted he'd ever be the same.

Stealthily he dismounted and tied up Hother in the

deserted kitchen as he spied the stiffening bodies of his servants. He bent and touched one of their necks, looking in hope for a pulse, but sadly confirmed the Quyroo was dead. As he took out his Fireblade, he heard the reassuring hum as it jumped to life. His arm tingled with the energy of the sword, and it enveloped him. Touching the blade to his forehead, he prayed for a second, then opened the doors that led to the palace.

XXVI

THE KING, ZAYDEN, and Hilde, along with their guards, ran through the corridors toward the throne room. Drakko cut down anyone who came into his path, his thoughts filled with worry for Reminda and V'sair. His head held high, he walked into the great room, which hushed as he entered.

Pacuto moved forward, raising his sword, but was stayed by Staf.

"You escaped my men?" Staf stood by the golden chair, his tip grazing Reminda's chin. Drakko's eyes found his wife and rested for a moment. Zayden stood to the left of him with Hilde behind him, hidden by his bulk.

Reminda gasped when she saw her husband, her relief warring with worry.

"As you see." Drakko held out his hands in a sarcastic gesture. Pacuto hissed with anger, and Staf held out his hand. "If you so desire my kingdom, come and take it from me, coward."

Beatha came forward, her hand on Staf's arm. "What are you waiting for? Kill him!"

Staf stepped down unhurriedly, his gaze never leaving his brother.

Spectators spread out, encircling the combatants. As the two brothers raised their swords, the battle began.

XXVII

TULANI RACED OUT of the volcano, her feet barely touching the ground. She heard Bobbien behind her, and as they neared the entrance, screams from the villages filled the air.

Her face drenched with sweat, she came outside to the sight of an inferno. Fire and black smoke belched from the crater of Aqin; streams of red lava slowly made their way down the wrinkled face of the volcano.

A sea of panicked Quyroos milled about in the great Plains of Dawid at the base of Aqin. *How can I get anything done with this rabble?* Tulani wondered forlornly as she looked at the swirling mass of crazed Quyroos fleeing the eruption. She raised her arms to the heavens, appealing for sanity to return. She prayed loudly so her voice could reach Ozre. If she could only harness a force of Quyroos to storm the castle, she thought, watching the way they were retreating from the volcano, perhaps they would overcome Staf and his minions. A blanket of black clouds covered the valley. The Quyroos watched the spectacle of nature as they screamed for mercy. Most thought this was the hour of their death; Aqin finally had decided to end their miserable existence.

All sound was muffled as the air took on an electric quality. Tulani's skin prickled with sensitivity. All eyes turned to the angry, spitting volcano. There was nowhere to run, and they knew they were doomed. A hush fell over the Plains of Dawid. She saw Tree People watching from the Desa as they hung from their perches in the forest. Tulani's voice rang out clear as a bell. She raised her hands to the heavens in supplication; she cried out for mercy. She stood on a small ledge, a halo of light surrounding her. Her red braids flared around her slim body as though they were a cloak. She saw the orb spinning before her hands, its mass growing until it spread over the entire Plains of Dawid, enveloping the population in a massive net of sparkling stars.

The Quyroos stood frozen, their faces paralyzed in a combination of fear mixed with wonder. The fire suddenly died, the lava turned to gray ash, and the volcano went silent. A trail of black smoke snaked across the clearing sky as the two suns burned away the black clouds. The volcano grew dark, as if an engine had been switched off, and all eyes turned to the young girl who appeared to control both the volcano and the spinning orb. She held out her palms, and the orb retracted into a small ball and came to rest in the cup of her hands. It grew smaller and smaller until it disappeared. One by one, Quyroos dropped to their knees and bowed to the new high priestess.

Tulani looked at the mass of people on their knees, their faces pressed to the red dirt as they waited for her to speak.

"Good Quyroos…" Her voice carried to the farthest fields, and Bobbien smiled with pride. Tulani turned to her grandmother and asked, "What should I do?"

Bobbien bent her head with respect. "Do what you must, child."

"I must save V'sair."

"Then ask for help."

Tulani turned to the people, who waited breathlessly for her to speak. "I am Tulani. I am Tulani!" she repeated. "I am Tulani, your high priestess, and I will lead you to freedom!"

A great cheer erupted, and four large male Quyroos climbed up the cliff and lifted her high over their heads to carry her into the frenzied crowd.

XXVIII

V'SAIR KEPT HIS back to the wall, his Fireblade close to his chest as he walked the corridors of the palace. Signs of the struggle were everywhere. Broken glass, bodies—results of the coup—littered each hallway. He turned a corner to find two guards patrolling, and raising his blade, he shouted as he moved in for the kill.

"Nooooo!" The younger soldier feinted left, while the older one deftly knocked V'sair's sword away, turning a deathblow into a minor gash.

"Your Highness…Prince V'sair," the Darracian panted as V'sair went after him with deadly force. "We are friends…" He barely could catch his breath.

"We are with Swart's forces," the older guard shouted from the floor, where he nursed the nick in his side. "Stop! We are here to help!"

Their words pierced the wall of anger, and V'sair slowed

his attack. He paused and looked into the worried face of the young soldier, who now allowed his sword to slide to the floor. "Please come with us. We must act swiftly."

V'sair bent over to help the older soldier. "Apologies," he murmured as he gestured to the gash in the Darracian's side. "Happens." The man shrugged. "Let's get you to Swart. He will be happy to see you."

General Swart indeed looked happy when V'sair was ushered in. He dipped low and said reverently, "Highness."

"Do you know where my parents are?"

"Captain Zayden and your father went to extract your mother from the throne room. One of my men reported that Vekin is making his way there as well. We've planned to mount an offensive to create a pincher, with the throne room in the center."

V'sair gripped his sword tightly, his face grim. "Let's do it now!"

XXIX

AIRBOATS STARTED TO rise, dotting the entire horizon with Quyroos—Bottom and Tree Dwellers alike—making unregistered flights to Cloud City. Nuen guards, outnumbered, were efficiently dispatched. Their bodies made a quick descent downward, their stalliuses now commanded by able-bodied Quyroos. Tulani stood in the first boat, her fist outstretched, her long red braids streaming around her, her eyes only on the castle in the clouds.

In the distance she saw a huge cruiser moving toward the same destination. The name was not visible, and she did not know its intentions.

XXX

REMINDA STOOD DEFIANTLY as the first exchange of swords rang in the room. Staf backed away, letting Drakko take the offensive, cleverly parrying his thrusts, his steps quick. Drakko was aggressive, his borrowed Fireblade red with angry intensity. The swords clashed, and Reminda realized that Drakko was furious, and Staf was letting that fury exhaust him. Drakko's green eyes narrowed with anger, and he slashed at his brother, who responded with the skill of a practiced fighter. Drakko aggressively went after Staf, who ended up with his back against a low table. He jumped up, with Drakko following him, and they moved down the length of the banquet table, knocking candles and food to the floor. This was an even match between two of the very best fighters in Darracia. Reminda prayed to the Elements for her husband to be victorious. A hot breath fanned her neck, and she spun to find her sister-in-law so close that they were almost touching.

Staf slipped near the end of the table, and Drakko moved in quickly for a fatal blow. Pacuto raced between them, raising his sword to prevent the king from killing his father. Zayden growled as he rushed forward to stop his cousin, revealing Hilde behind him.

"Hilde!" Pacuto shouted, and attacked Zayden with vicious hatred. If Drakko and Staf's fight looked like an elegant dance, Zayden and Pacuto's swordplay looked like a rampage.

Everyone moved out of the way as the blades rang with a rapid staccato.

"You see, my boy..." Staf's voice spat out the words. "He killed V'sair, and now he will kill your bastard."

"I will see you in hell!" Drakko's face was flushed with exertion, and he was momentarily distracted by Hilde's wild scream.

Pacuto had slashed Zayden and caught him in the face. Fluid dripped from his eye as he groaned and dropped to one knee. Zayden was bent in half, one hand holding his torn face, his eye destroyed. Pacuto laughed and quickly moved forward to finish the job.

Hilde rushed to Zayden, holding up her hand to stop her brother from delivering the final blow to her beloved.

"Traitorous whore!" Pacuto screamed in outrage and buried the blade in her chest.

White with shock, Hilde sighed, her knees buckling as she slid off the end of the sword. Zayden snarled as he staggered to his feet; he went after Pacuto as if a machine were moving his arm. Pacuto fought, but he was no match for Zayden's adrenaline-fueled rush of anger. He hacked Pacuto in the neck, and a gout of blood bathed them both so they looked as red as the Quyroos that began to fill the room.

Beatha screamed, grabbing Reminda by the hair and twisting her head so that the queen shouted with pain. They rolled onto the floor in a swirl of fabric, their gowns entwined. Small fists pummeled the countess, who ripped at the queen's head, tearing out tufts of hair.

V'sair entered to see an arena of bloodbath and heard Tulani shout over the din, "V'sair!"

She stood at the head of a mob of Quyroos that looked like a red tide of anger.

With relief the king stared at his son, who stood with his sword raised for battle, a look of triumph on his lean face. A scream split the air as the queen and countess rolled toward the roaring fire wall in a deadly embrace. Beatha stood, then dragged Reminda up and shoved her toward the raging inferno. As the queen fell backward, she looked at her son sadly.

Her small webbed hands grabbed Beatha's dress. The two women teetered for a moment as the countess's hands feverously tried to untangle Reminda from her. Their balance shifted, and V'sair watched in shock as his mother tumbled into the white-hot flames.

"Reminda!" the king shouted.

Staf took advantage of this moment to sink his Fireblade to the hilt inside the king's chest. "You are finished!" he shouted with triumph.

V'sair saw his father go down, the sword deep in his chest. Fury rolled through him as he leaped into the fray, his face a feral snarl filled with burning rage, to attack Staf. His uncle smiled, wiping the sword on his cape and expecting another quick victory.

Their blades sang with hatred, and V'sair's nimble feet soon made Staf fall backward in retreat. It was pandemonium—Quyroos cheering for the prince, and the sounds of General Swart's troops fighting with Staf Nuen's men on the other side of the room. A fierce battle raged; finally freed from their defensive positions, the king's men attacked together, attempting to squeeze out the Nuen rebellion. The halls were littered with heavy casualties.

Staf was surprised at his nephew's skill. He pressed forward, nicking him in the shoulder and unknowingly reopening the older wound. V'sair was tiring, but he refused to give in to his fatigue. He caught Staf's blade at the hilt, locking them together, their faces so close that their breaths mingled.

"I will kill you just as I destroyed your parents!" Staf spat.

"I think not!" V'sair spun, taking Staf completely by surprise, the blade catching him above his hip. It went in smoothly and appeared on the other side of Staf's back. He gasped as he staggered and slipped to the floor in a heap.

V'sair stood back, breathing heavily, and walked unevenly to his father's body. Tulani held a cloth to a bloody wound and shook her head slowly.

"Sire…" He fell to his knees, exhausted and heartbroken.

"You will make an excellent leader," Drakko said in the barest whisper.

"No, Dado." He pressed his hand over Tulani's, trying to stop the bleeding. "Tulani is a healer. She will help you."

"V'sair, it is over for me." He coughed, his eyes mere slits. "You must finish what I have started. Where is Zayden? Is he…" He placed a weak hand over his son's.

"I am here, Father." Zayden sat nearby, holding Hilde's still body, his cheek pierced and his free hand cupped over his destroyed eye.

"It is a rare privilege for a king to actually see… the next…You will be a great leader, my son, and I am proud of you both…" His voice trailed off, and his head rolled onto Tulani's lap. She reached down and gently closed his eyes.

A commotion erupted, followed by the wild screams of the masses of Quyroos in the room. A foot, small and webbed, followed by a blackened hand, reached out from the pit of the fireplace, seeking assistance. V'sair jumped up to pull his singed mother from the depths of the cavern.

"Mo'mo." He hugged her tightly. "You are whole!"

All eyes were on the tableau of the drama taking place in the center of the room. No one heard or recognized the chirp of an ancient communication device or the stealthy escape of Staf Nuen.

"Yes, Beatha has broken her neck. I fell into the exhaust damper. It saved me. Oh, Drakko…" She left her son to fall to her knees next to her husband.

V'sair saw Zayden; he bent down, gripped his

brother's elbow, and tried to help him stand. "I will get you help," he said.

"I will kill Staf Nuen!" Zayden exclaimed.

"It's too late." V'sair crouched down to look at his brother's face. "Our uncle is dead." "Where?"

V'sair pointed, then stood; the spot was empty.

Zayden staggered to his feet. "Where is he?"

"I got him. He was there!" V'sair's eyes scanned the room.

Generals Swart and Vekin barged into the throne room, their Fireblades bloodied. Taking in the body of Drakko, they fell to their knees before V'sair and murmured, "Your Majesty. Long live the king. Long live King V'sair!"

The crowd repeated the call, and V'sair bowed his head in acceptance.

Zayden walked to the wall of glass that heralded a new dawn. Both suns rose, filling the pewter sky with the colors of rose and cream. Blood stained his cheek, and he pulled out Hilde's ribbon from the inside of his armor. He held it to his cheek as he inhaled the last scents of his beloved. As he tied the ribbon clumsily around his muscled upper arm, he saw a destroyer quickly pull away from the castle. Its identity was emblazoned in bold paint—*The Grand Mestor*. It was the ship of Staf Nuen.

XXXI

V'SAIR STOOD IN his rooms as he looked out the vast window.

"She has gone?" It was his mother.

The king shrugged.

"She'll return."

He spun, his face tormented. "I wanted to marry her!"

"She loves you," Reminda said, putting a bandaged hand on his shoulder. "She has much to learn. She has just discovered herself."

"Tulani could learn everything she wants from here," V'sair responded petulantly.

"Yes." Reminda smiled. "You would think so, but you must trust that when she learns what she needs to, she will return."

V'sair sighed.

"You are feeling alone?"

"Dado and Emmicus are gone," he said sadly. "Tulani has left to find her soul."

"You found yours."

"But I have lost half of it. Zayden is leaving today."

"What? He has refused the office?" Reminda was shocked.

"He told me there cannot be two grand mestors. He will return when he can claim that title for himself alone." "Hilde." She shook her head sadly.

"I would say he is heartbroken, but he is Darracian."

V'sair looked at his mother. "Sadly you have given me a Plantan heart, and I am sorry to tell you it is making its presence known."

Reminda pressed her forehead against her son's. "Have faith in the Elements, Vsos. I am positive things will fall into place."

V'sair looked at the dual suns of Darracia and agreed.

"Sradda willing."

COLLISION

Book II

Michael Phillip Cash

Disclaimer

The characters and events portrayed in this book are fictitious. Any resemblance to real persons, living or dead, on Earth or Darracia, is coincidental and not intended by the author.

No part of this book may be reproduced, or stored in a retrieval system, or transmitted in any form or by any means, electronic or mechanical, including photocopying, recording, or otherwise, without the express written permission of the publisher.

Published in the United States by Red Feather Publishing
New York • Los Angeles • Las Vegas All rights reserved.
ISBN-10: 1-947118-75-7
ISBN-13: 978-1-947118-75-1

col·li·sion *noun* \kəˈliZHən\

1. an instance of one moving object or person striking violently against another. When you're drowning, you don't say "I would be incredibly pleased if someone would have the foresight to notice me drowning and come and help me." You just scream.

—John Lennon

I

THE SHORES OF Fon Reni were fine black sand dotted with purple sea glass that littered the barren beach. Stars littered the velvet sky; here and there a shooting cosmic spray spread across the inky darkness, illuminating the still night. It was quiet here, the distant planet devoid of life, save the lonely inhabitants who lived on the beach, footprints washed away by the icy seas.

He had constructed a crude hut for his guest using the fronds on the leafy trees that populated the jungles. Zayden slept under the night stars, enjoying the peaceful freedom of the beach. Living on what he hunted, he reveled in the quiet of Fon Reni, knowing it was far from Darracia, his troubles, and the memories. He was tired, exhausted by grief, angry with his lack of solution.

Staf Nuen had disappeared. It was as though he had never existed. Zayden had spent almost a year tracking him, coming up with nothing but dead ends. He had traveled from one end of the solar system to the other, living by his wits, surviving hand to mouth, always just missing him. He must have gotten close, because he was jumped outside a graphen den on the planet Venturian.

He woke up disoriented, shamefaced, with his new-found friend, Denita, and with a colorful tattoo on his biceps. He watched the ripples rise from the dark sand, the heat sucking the air from his lungs. It was as hot as a furnace. He wore just his trousers, naked from the waist up, so he could see the stupid tattoo taking up most of his shoulder. The bruises on his torso had faded a bit, but his face still looked as battered as an old suitcase. Sweat evaporated as soon as it appeared, and he let the hot air roast him. He heard the foliage rustle behind him, made a face, then laughed softly at the curse he heard muttered behind the screen of the dense brush.

There were fourteen planets in his solar system, Darracia being his native one. He had left it in search of his uncle Staf Nuen, who had killed his father, King Drakko, leaving his legitimate half brother, V'sair, the reigning king. V'sair pleaded with him to stay as his advisor, Zayden remembered, rubbing the still-raw scar that bisected his once-handsome face. The new king had appointed him grand mestor, Zayden thought with chagrin. Imagine that, the bastard of King Drakko was offered the highest position in the land.

He drew aimlessly in the dark sand with a broken stick. He didn't want it. He didn't want any part of it until he could bring Staf Nuen to justice. It was because of his uncle's overthrow that his beloved Hilde was slain, killed by her psychotic brother when she protected Zayden from the deathblow of a Fireblade. Clenching his hands into useless fists, he relived the last moments of her life. The empty socket where his amber eye used to be throbbed as though a thousand pickaxes were stabbing it. Pressing deeply with his palms, he covered his eyes, trying to blot out the images imprinted on his brain: blood, blood, and more blood, coupled with Hilde's dying gasp as she collapsed into his arms, a sword robbing him of his future with the only woman he ever felt he could love.

He glanced at his discarded Fireblade, thrown negligently on the sandy ground. He hadn't used it since that day, preferring the heavy pistol strapped to the side of his leg. Darracians disdained guns. Swords were for warriors, guns for cowards, he had been taught. His people valued the skill one developed with a blade, never respecting those beings who just aimed and fired. Guns were illegal at home, the punishment fierce if one was caught with such a firearm. His father had taught him it was dishonorable; if a warrior fought in combat, he must be engaged with his opponent, feel the heat of battle. Guns made warfare impersonal; there was no honor to kill without knowing the skill of your enemy. It showed lack of respect for the ideals of battle. That was why only a small part of the population knew how to fight with the Fireblade—it kept violence at a minimum. Darracian warriors were taught to uphold justice, never kill for personal gain, and until his uncle had tried to overthrow the government, Darracia had been a relatively mild place to live. He had picked up the gun on the lawless space station Pagil 7, far from the rules of Darracia.

After V'sair had rocked the foundation of the beliefs about the Fireblade, Zayden didn't want it anymore. It seemed that Darracians had gotten it all wrong. Chanters from all over his former home were meeting, trying to make sense out of the Sradda Doctriness. There were forums and debates; all the schools were rereading and trying to find new ways to interpret the messages of the Elements. Well, he didn't give a crap about all that religious stuff. His faith died when Hilde perished. He didn't know why he hadn't jettisoned the Fireblade from his portal as he traveled through deep space. He shrugged his broad shoulders, thinking perhaps because it was presented to him by his late father when he achieved his highest honors, and he was a sentimental fool, after all. He felt naked without it. He eyed his sword with resentment. Denita should never have taken it from the thug who tried to kill him. She should have left both him and the Fireblade to rot on the filthy streets of Venturian. Zayden sighed gustily. So here he sat, on the desolate beach of Fon Reni, reliving his nightmare and waiting for a sign— a signal for him to find Staf Nuen and kill him with his bare hands.

He watched the progress of the silver crabs as they clawed their way up the dark sand of the beach. The tiny feet worked in unison, scrabbling through dense patches of seaweed. There were hundreds of them. He tapped his stick thoughtfully. Well, he wouldn't have to work very hard for their dinner tonight. Pushing himself onto his feet, he stretched widely, feeling his cramped muscles expand and his bones crack. His head still ached where he'd been beaten, and his ribs reminded him they weren't all that healed after all. He grabbed a rush basket and then began to pluck the crabs from the ground until his container was a swirling mass of nervous creatures trying to escape. He placed them over the fire he had built earlier, in an old helmet he used as a pot. Soon, he heard the crackle and hiss of their bursting shells, their color changing to an appetizing light green. He thought to call out that dinner was ready, but shrugged instead, plopping down on the sand to eat alone. That's how he wanted to eat, by himself. His guest was nothing more than an encumbrance. He sneered at the dense forest behind him. Carefully, he pulled a cooked crab out of his makeshift pot, singeing his fingers, catching the green juice of the dripping crustacean with his tongue.

The fire warmed him against the stiff ocean breeze, and memories of camping trips with his father and V'sair came rushing back like a tidal wave. They had stayed here, the three of them, on this very beach. V'sair was so young, his royal braid barely touching his shoulder. No servants were allowed, and though his father's elite guards hovered in the sky above, they spent a sun-filled week on Fon Reni that became a yearly ritual. They returned V'sair, to his mother's horror, a lovely shade of brown, his light-tannish-blue skin burned and toughened by the strong rays of both suns. It was a special spot for Zayden. Here he was just Drakko's son and V'sair's older brother, not the illegitimate offspring of the king and his laundress.

He had loved his father, as well as his royal younger brother, despite the differences in their stations, even though it appeared that he was the only one troubled by it. He was older by a good fifteen years, and he didn't begrudge his younger sibling his inheritance; however, sometimes he admitted to himself that he felt invisible. It was funny, he mused, V'sair envied Zayden's Darracian strength, and he valued what V'sair took most for granted, his assured place in Darracian hierarchy. Oh, V'sair always treated him with respect, had offered him the position of grand mestor, but Zayden knew what the others felt. He was seen as an interloper, barely tolerated despite the fact that he was one of the army's fiercest warriors.

He constantly pushed himself to be faster with his Fireblade, the hardest rider when it came to his stallius, as well as the best jolter in the tournaments. He lived by his warrior's creed, happy to make his father proud. He enjoyed showing them all his royal placement was earned with dedication and hard work. But somehow the dynamics of the Fireblade had changed now. It was not about brute strength and chivalry, so where did it leave him? He reached over to grab his sword and heard it hum to life, great red streaks lighting with energy. He knew now it was the wrong color. It was the shade of anger, not strength. Once, it had been the true blue of justice and a force to be reckoned with. His had always been the blue of a pure heart, even though he never realized what it meant. Now it blazed red, like his enemy's. The Fireblade was about something else now, and he didn't have the patience to try to understand. He was too tired.

Angry and tired.

He threw the shells of his crab onto a neat pile, sucking the meat from the tiny claws. He should eat all of them, he thought with a mean chuckle. She had missed their nightly progress; Denita never learned. He eyed the last few crabs and groaned. Last time she had walked in the shallow waters, she had cut her foot. No, it wasn't worth it—he'd have to nurse her again and hear her complaints. She could be an ornery pain in the ass. Better leave her enough to satisfy her hunger. He tried to remember Hilde's soft laughter, and Denita's velvet voice smothered the ladylike sound. Instead he pulled a frayed black ribbon from a pouch and held it to his nose. Her scent was gone. Just like Hilde. Gone forever. None of that mattered now anyway. The one he wanted more than life was taken from him this last year, killed by the hand of her brother, Pacuto. Zayden could not rest until he brought her traitorous father to justice.

The four moons lit the beach, bathing him in their glow. He watched phosphorus mengles dance under the waves, their multicolored poison glowing iridescently under the swirling sea. Swimming was out of the question. One sting from their tails and he would sink to the bottom of the water, never to be seen again. He drank deeply from a flask, swallowing the burn of the liquor, his eye never leaving the horizon of the endless ocean. Then what would his guest do, he thought contemptuously. He needed this complication the way one needed a headache. She would do nothing but slow him down, and although they had a common hatred for Staf Nuen, Zayden had parked himself here hoping she'd lose interest. Denita had howled with outrage when he landed, screaming for him to proceed to Planta and find his uncle. He didn't need her or anyone else. He didn't want her or anyone else, for that matter.

He eyed the circular mark on his upper bicep. It didn't hurt anymore, and he supposed Reminda would know someone who could get rid of it. As much as he hated it, he thought he'd keep it now. It was just another scar, like his ruined face, marked on this journey for revenge. Taking a faded patch from his pocket, he covered the empty place where his eye used to be. A comet streaked across the sky. He searched his memory for its name and came up with nothing. Due to his fight patterns, he knew every celestial event in the sky. Hearing about this one must have escaped him. He watched its progress, its feathered tail stretched out for miles, curving toward the west. Comets always meant something. Emmicus, his old tutor, always said that. Something was going to happen, he thought, wiping the back of his hand against his mouth. The salt and sand burned against his lips. He scanned the stygian sky. Yes, something was coming. He just wasn't sure of when or what.

II
—

V'SAIR, THE YOUNG king of Darracia, stared pensively out of the window wall from his private chamber. It was the place he loved most in his castle, where he had spent many peaceful hours studying with his navigator, Emmicus. Leaning his head against the cool glass, he looked down on the Desa below, wondering where Tulani was now.

Aqin, the ancient volcano, was dormant again, and Quyroos were stubbornly rebuilding their homes on its craggy surface. A light mist created a wall of clouds that obscured the landscape. The air felt thick, the city strangely silent. The dense fog muted the sounds of traffic. The city of Syos looked peaceful, the forest of the Desa, not so much, and V'sair, not at all.

Nothing had worked right since he was crowned. His father had been the driving force for tolerance of the

Quyroos. Without him, getting everybody to the Moon Council had been almost impossible. First there had been several months of mourning. So many had been killed. Barely a clan on Darracia had not suffered. Those who sided with his uncle languished in prison, cutting his armed forces in half. In the spirit of equality, he had invited the Quyroos to join up. He was unprepared for the blatant hostility between the two species. While his father sought to usher in an age of peace and understanding, V'sair was bequeathed a planet divided by prejudice and distrust. He wanted to change things, to bring the equality and peace he knew deep in his heart was the right way for his home.

General Swart accused him of rushing these new laws. The older man was insecure with so small a fighting force. They had argued about importing large cannon. Swart wanted to modernize the army; V'sair would not have it. Swart had taken his place as V'sair's grand mestor, his advisor, and though he was loyal unto death, he was no friend to his late father's policies. He wanted to build up the army and go after the prince's nefarious uncle Staf Nuen. Eliminate the threat of invasion, then fix the problems at home, he had urged the young king.

While V'sair knew his uncle was still out there, planning something, the pressing problems of unrest lay heavy on his young shoulders. He missed his father's quiet strength; he missed his brother's support; he missed Tulani's unconditional love. He was bereft.

His heart melted when he thought of Tulani. They had known each other forever, but he realized what she meant to him only when they learned the secrets of the Fireblade together. When his cousin had threatened her with bodily harm, he discovered he was capable of a killing rage that filled him with white-hot lava. His heart and mind knew Tulani, and he felt connected to her in a way he had never experienced before. When the good general had brought up a marriage alliance with a princess of another planet, V'sair silenced his grand mestor with royal finality. He wanted no one but the Quyroo high priestess. Tulani was as much a part of him as his arm or eyes. He would wait forever until they could find peace in each other's arms.

The warm, wet tongue of Felise bathed his hand. Twining his fingers in the curly black hair on the top of her head, he looked down, a smile tugging at his lips at her mournful eyes. His mother had gifted him with a newborn jast mere days after his father was murdered. His pet was a mess, nervous to be separated from her litter, her clumsy paws tracking in the red dust that always drifted onto the balconies. Felise rubbed her wiry whiskers against his palm, demanding attention in her selfish way. She panted, leaping onto her hind legs, her front paws resting easily on his shoulders, and a laugh escaped his lips. She was not tiny anymore, and a rather big nuisance as well, because while his pet was really still an infant, she had grown to almost half her adult size, and an awesome size it was too.

He heard the door open and knew it was his mother from her light footsteps. Felise drooled sloppily as she greeted the queen.

"Walk with me, Vsos." She came up behind him and rested her hand on his back. He directed Felise to sit with a stern stare and heard his mother chuckle. "Silly beast," she said fondly, patting her head.

"It's cold outside," he responded, looking straight ahead.

"I don't care. The fresh air will do you good. I heard that it has stopped raining." He caught her intense gaze. "You are not eating enough, Vsos."

The king shrugged. "I am not hungry."

"I think Felise is eating enough for both of you." She smiled and scratched the giant animal beneath the soft curls of her chin. She turned and rested her hand in the crook of V'sair's elbow. Her white hair was threaded with black strands now. She had aged since losing her husband. Lines had formed around her iridescent eyes, bracketed her oncelush lips, giving her the appearance of a constant frown.

"Tulani would not know you, my son."

"Doesn't make a difference, since she won't come here."

The portal swooshed open, and they stepped onto the balcony connected to the room. They heard the giant jast follow them, her paws clicking on the wet tiled floor. Two Quyroo guards stood on either side of them, their impassive faces glued to the horizon. The interminable rain had ceased, but it was still overcast; weak sunlight fought to peek through the clouds.

"You have to allow her time."

"Time for what?" V'sair answered hotly. "Anything she can do there"—he pointed a long bluish finger down at the forests—"can be done from here." His eyes blazed with anger.

"She feels she is doing you more good down there"—Reminda gestured to the dark planet—"than here. She is the best ambassador you could have."

V'sair clicked impatiently with his tongue. "I have shuttles full of willing Quyroos that desire to be ambassadors. We could unite this planet if she were queen!"

"Yes." Reminda placed a thoughtful finger next to her temple. "Consider her place, V'sair. You above anyone else should be able to commiserate with her feelings. She is neither Darracian nor Quyroo."

"She is full-blooded Quyroo!" V'sair shot back, interrupting her.

"True," Reminda said reasonably, "but taken to live among us at three years of age. She can't be seen as one of them until she is accepted by them. Tulani understood for this to succeed, she must gain their confidence and then take her place by your side. Vsos, I don't understand; usually you are the most amiable of creatures."

"This is harder than I thought." V'sair pulled her by her hand to walk the parapets, far from the guards. "I don't know if I can do this anymore. I don't know if I want to do this."

"V'sair, this is your destiny," Reminda told him urgently. "Even Ozre told you that. I…I never expected this to be thrust on you so early. Your father and I still had so much work to do, but"—she shrugged, her eyes glittering with unshed tears—"this is what it is, and we have to make do with what we have."

"It is a test, but for what I don't know," V'sair told her absently. "I just wish Tulani were here with me, Mo'mo. She is my rock."

"She needs to finish what she has started. Being a priestess is complicated. She must learn how to use her power."

"Pah!" V'sair clicked his tongue. "If I were not king and she not a daughter of Nost, we could be together. This life you chose for me has become a burden. I wish Dado was here."

Reminda sighed, eyeing her son sadly. "We did not expect you to have to take the throne until you were much older. Your father had plans; he wanted to teach you many things."

"I don't know how to do this. The Quyroos are unhappy; the Darracians are unhappy; I am unhappy. This is hard, Mo'mo. I don't know how to make them get along."

"Patience. You have never learned patience."

V'sair rested his hands on the terrace wall, his face scanning the vast city spread out before him. "First Zayden runs off to slay his dragon, when I need him here. Then Tulani discovers she must learn about her Desa and make the Quyroos love her, before she can commit. What about me?" he demanded, turning to face his mother. "I need their help." "Well, at least you have me," she told him with a smile and a quick shrug.

"Oh aye, I am sorry, Mo'mo. I am being unreasonable." He looked at her sheepishly, a lock of white hair falling over his blue eyes. "It's just that...it..."

He looked so young; Reminda's heart softened. She reached out to push his hair from his eyes, thought better of it, and smiled gently. "Dado is gone. Emmicus as well. I know it's hard, Vsos, but everybody's life has been changed. The New Doctrines have shaken Darracian society to its core. You have to give everything time."

The whole of Darracia had been turned upside down, Reminda thought ruefully. Such a lot of nonsense simply because V'sair had shown them that the Fireblade could be earned and used by all. Darracians were not special, their superiority not guaranteed, and the whole species now had to relearn to fire their blades to the blue of courage and justice, rather than the red of anger and intolerance. Schools had shut down, chanters met for conferences, creating new interpretations and criteria so that all the inhabitants of this planet could share its bounty to live as equals with the same opportunities.

But there was opposition. Many clans stayed away from court, keeping their Darracian sons and daughters from mixing with the Quyroos who now were finding new positions other than the serving class. Why, just the other day, she had heard that a wealthy merchant had disowned his daughter for marrying a Quyroo communications officer. These new customs were going to take time. She looked at the fine lines of worry on her son's face. Both she and Drakko had wanted to bring about the changes slowly, not thrust them on her teenage son. And, she wondered angrily, where were the Elements? Why did they topple the old beliefs and then simply go silent? It made no sense.

"Have you asked the Elements for guidance?"

V'sair turned to look at the city again, his eyes distant.

He shrugged. "Yes, of course. They never tell you anything." He added sarcastically, "They wait for you to have the *illumination*."

"So, did you?" his mother asked.

"Yes, yes, Mother. I understand that we all have to look inside of ourselves to find our strength."

"And…"

"Well, I've done that already," he added indignantly.

"That's very nice, but what about Zayden and Tulani?"

V'sair didn't answer for a moment. He sighed and looked at his mother, his face relaxing. "I know, Mo'mo. Just because I have found myself, I have to allow the others to catch up to me. I didn't say I have to like it."

Reminda smiled and squeezed his arm. "I know it feels like forever, but it will really be a very short part of your life, this waiting. What is it, V'sair?" Reminda saw his lips turn down in a thoughtful frown.

"Ozre."

"Go on."

"I am concerned. I have not heard from him in months."

"Perhaps you are not praying hard enough?"

V'sair gave her a sidelong look. "Me? Oh, I pray hard enough."

"Maybe you are praying for the wrong things?" his mother asked gently.

V'sair didn't answer, his eyes searching the Desa. The red canopy of trees shielded the Desa floor from prying eyes; he could see nothing through the tangled forest. The wet treetops glittered as if they were dusted with rubies. Still, he watched, wishing he could see

Tulani and know that she was ready to join him. His fisted palm absently pounded the balustrade. Felise jumped up, pushing next to him. V'sair grinned, knowing the jast was watching him; he let himself lean into her strong shoulder.

From the rear, they looked as if they were two friends looking out on the city. Reminda smiled at his shortened white braid. It was what marked him as a Darracian royal. It would take a while until it grew back. His cousin Pacuto had hacked it off in a fight.

"Get down, you pestilent beast." His mother playfully hit Felise on her back. "You spoil her, Vsos. She shouldn't be out here."

"She was your idea."

"I thought you might need a friend," Reminda told him, then added softly, "I know I did."

"You miss him, Mo'mo."

"You have no idea, Vsos. It's like there is a great hole inside of me." She grew quiet, examining the dark plains of her son's face. He was all sharp angles; the sweet softness of youth had disappeared with his lost innocence. He was not the same since his father's murder. None of them were. His boyhood had flown with the destruction of her dreams. "Such is life, Vsos. We are born, we serve, and then our anima leaves." "Our anima?"

"Your soul."

"A rather empty existence, don't you think?"

"I would give up ten lifetimes to have shared what I did with your father, Vsos. I discarded everything I knew for him—my home, my family." She turned to face him.

"And he gave me you. And you gave me Tulani." She looked out at the Desa, her iridescent eyes narrowing. "Now if only she would finish what she needs to do, come back here, and give me some grandchildren."

"Yes," V'sair agreed. "If only."

"Have you thought about the coronation?" Reminda asked briskly, trying to change the mood. She observed her son's strong shoulders, the light growth of a white beard on his chin. He was no longer a pliable child. This topic was a sore spot. V'sair first refused the ceremony due to the depth of mourning in the court. Many times General Swart had brought it up, but V'sair clearly wasn't interested. Reminda knew it was something he must do, but now her son could not be forced.

"It feels strange, Mother. I don't know if I am ready for it."

"Your father would have wanted you to be crowned," she told him. "This is our way; you were born to be his successor," she added fiercely.

"It doesn't feel right." V'sair looked back at the dormant volcano, his eyes distant.

"He is not coming back, Vsos. You must declare your place."

"I will consider it, Mo'mo," he responded forlornly. They stood together watching the day wane and the four moons of Darracia climb the horizon. Gresh chirped their mournful love call nearby, while they both sat in comfortable silence.

"Are you hungry yet?" Reminda asked, ever the mother.

"I suppose," V'sair answered, distracted by a

spinning luminescence in the growing twilight. Felise barked loudly at it, racing down the balcony, chasing the blazing light. He followed the comet's arc. "Fon Reni," he said softly. A thought struck him, and he suddenly knew where his half brother had gone. His blue eyes lit up for the first time in weeks.

"What is it?" Reminda asked.

"That's where my brother is," he remarked with wonder as he watched the comet's tail light up the night sky. "He must be there. It is where I would go if I could. That's where he's staying. He went to Fon Reni—he loves it there."

"Will you go to him?"

"No." V'sair shook his head. "I can't leave here."

"Surely, for a few days…"

"No, Mo'mo." He sighed heavily. "There is too much unrest. There was an incident…"

"Oh." Reminda raised a delicate eyebrow. "I hadn't heard."

"I just got the report. General Swart captured a group of malcontents."

"Go on," Reminda urged.

"They were plotting an assassination. I didn't want you to know."

Reminda gasped, her face paling.

"Oh, Mo'mo. There was no reason to alarm you. We have it all under control. It's just the…the people are so very unhappy." V'sair looked miserable.

Oh Drakko, Reminda thought sadly, *what have we bequeathed to our son? Why couldn't we just run away and make a life for ourselves? Why did we decide to take on the world and change it?*

"Please don't worry. It's been handled." V'sair gave his mother a lopsided grin. "You know it comes with the job description. Besides, if Zayden is there, he wants to be alone. He is working things out, and once he finds what he needs, he will come home."

"You are so sure?" Reminda knew she was going to try to find a way to contact Zayden. His brother needed him now. Enough of his self-pity, she needed him to protect her son, his king.

"I know Zayden. He loves Fon Reni. You never saw that side of him when we were there. Fon Reni is his spot. You understand?" V'sair asked.

Reminda nodded her head. "Yes."

"If he is there, he will find his peace."

"What if he doesn't?"

"He will not return until he does," V'sair told her with finality. His breath caught in his chest, and he touched the area over his heart. "He will be coming home, I think. No…I know. He will be coming soon."

"You see. I told you things will fall into place." Reminda didn't know if she was assuring her son or herself.

"Soon," V'sair answered her absently. "Yes, soon."

They entered the castle, walking arm in arm to the throne room, Felise trailing after them. The fire blazed, its incandescence throwing sparks behind the giant fire screen he had installed after his mother and aunt had rolled into the blaze. It heated the room mightily, but a dart of apprehension curled up V'sair's spine, making him shiver involuntarily.

"What is it?" his mother asked anxiously, her concerned eyes searching his face.

"I don't know. I felt something, just for a minute."

"What?" she asked, her voice a mere whisper over the soft music playing in the room.

V'sair's eyes scanned the many groups clustered in the room. It was a court still in mourning. So many of them had lost members of their families when his uncle engineered a coup taking over the planet and killing his father. No one wore anything but white, the official color of mourning. Even the armed forces still wore the badge of white on their sleeves to mark that the year had not ended. Though Quyroos were invited, they rarely came to his court. The Darracians barely tolerated them. Old wounds healed slowly. "A feeling, Mo'mo. Just a feeling." He narrowed his gaze.

"As though someone just danced on my grave."

"Stop!" Reminda took his hands. "Don't even think like that. Come," she snapped at the musician, "play something lively. This court has had enough sadness." She held up her webbed hand to stop him. "No, wait, we have mourned enough. It is time to cast off our whites." She motioned to her new serving girl. "Come, Tosha. Attend me. I will change." She looked hard at her son. "It's time to move forward with your father's plans. I will be right back. Do not speak of graves to me again, my son."

The flutist looked at the king, who nodded his

head, and the music took on a light, playful sound. Conversations picked up, and Reminda smiled.

"You will excuse me, Your Majesty." She curtsied solemnly.

V'sair bowed deeply. "As you wish, Mother." He watched her leave the room, followed by a group of chattering females excited to wear colors once again.

He looked at the thinned lips and impatient glare of General Swart, took a deep breath, and tried to dispel his unease. He strolled over to his throne and sat down. Felise flopped at his feet, her cheeks resting on his thigh while he absently stroked her head. For his mother's sake, he would not mention it again, but while they could get rid of the mourning white, no amount of color was going to make this feeling of foreboding go away.

III

TULANI ROLLED ON the floor, her arms crusted with dirt and a bit of red mud. She was in a circle, naked save for her loincloth, which was torn and matted with dried blood. A steady drizzle had turned the red dust to a viscous mud that coated everything. It was twice as hard to fight in the slippery muck, and Tulani had the wounds to prove its danger. Long scratches grazed her arms, and her braids lay tangled on her back. She wished for a moment she had allowed Bobbien to tie them into a knot on her head.

Both her and her opponent's bodies were slick with sweat, as well as the moisture from the incessant rain. The fire turned their skin orange. She hefted the long pole she held in her hands, brandishing it again at the man who thought to conquer her. Seren lunged, and Tulani whacked him mightily on the shins. It would leave a bad bruise there. She smiled, thinking he would curse her mightily tomorrow. Several of the elders crowed, while many females clanged the bells they held over their heads.

This was not a fair fight, but it never was. Most marriages were arranged by the eldest member of a clan. Tulani had no clan; her parents were dead, murdered by Staf Nuen's son, leaving Tulani and her grandmother alone. Bobbien would never give Tulani away. She wanted her granddaughter to choose her own mate. Seren, son of the wealthiest Quyroo clan, had decided he wanted Tulani. They had met before the Quyroo League, and Tulani had insisted on her right of a Vorged, a battle until one combatant surrendered to the will of the other. She was in the seventh hour of the battle. Seren was as strong as he was stubborn, and no matter how she managed to clobber his thick head with her pole, he lumbered on, getting up, steely determination in his starshaped eyes.

Sighing inwardly, she wondered where this desire to live here and study with Bobbien came from when her heart yearned for V'sair. The king was angry with her. She had told him she needed time. Trust between her and the Quyroos had to be forged. V'sair and his family's dreams of a peaceful planet would be nothing but a mirage in the distance if she couldn't get the support of her species. They simply would not trust her. Building their faith in her as a medicine woman as well as their greatest representative was an uphill battle fraught with enemies at every corner. Why couldn't they see her intent? She had only their best interests at heart. She could be their greatest advocate, she thought angrily.

She was still an outcast. Despite how many babies she delivered safely, bones she set to be perfect once more, or purges she created to banish illness, they treated her with mistrust and contempt. She had returned to the volcano, but Ozre also remained elusive. She tried to organize the Quyroos, show them how to use the Darracian system she knew so well to achieve equality, but they failed to follow her once the volcano ceased its eruption. Now she stayed with Bobbien, going from tree to tree, learning her birthright, studying the plants and their uses in healing. She should have slipped something into this big lummox's drink earlier, and maybe this battle would be over.

"I will have you, Tulani," he told her through gritted teeth. "I will have you or die trying."

"You know I love another," Tulani taunted back.

"Who said anything about love?"

They circled each other, their breaths ragged, chests heaving with effort. Seren bared his white teeth, his huge chest glistening with sweat. His discarded Darracian uniform lay in a damp heap on the Desa floor. He was the first to join the Darracian Army, despite his father's anger. He had more ambition than the whole Quyroo League. Only those close to the fire stay warm, he told his father. He wanted to be in the center of the blaze. He was learning things, meeting the right contacts. When Darracia changed, he expected to be front and center. Seren knew that having Tulani as his mate would ensure promotion within that army. If V'sair wanted to see the girl, he would have to keep Seren at his side. He looked at her long legs and trim figure. If anybody was going to enjoy her beautiful body, it was going to be him and him alone. She was a Quyroo and belonged with him, not a half-breed mongrel.

"You need protection, Tulani," Seren sneered. "I am here to take care of you."

Tulani laughed. "I can take care of myself!"

She charged at him, her pole slamming the side of his head, then poked him deeply in the stomach. Seren attacked her by grabbing her by the upper forearms and squeezing until her world appeared to narrow into a twirling tunnel. He banged her in the head with his forehead; stars floated before her eyes. She felt her weapon going slack in her hands and would have lost it if not for the shout that pulled her back. Bobbien was screaming for her to kick straight ahead. He was just out of her reach, so she tossed the pole, swinging back and forth, building momentum, waiting for the moment Seren's guard went down.

She went slightly slack, let her eyes roll, and watched Seren's face light up with triumph. He brought her toward him, his lips pursed for a victory kiss, when she lashed out, connecting mightily with his manhood. Seren screamed, his eyes closed with pain. Tulani jumped free, grabbed her pole, and smashed it against his head, smiling satisfactorily as the giant went facedown into the mud. Seren moaned as he rolled onto his side, his face contorted with pain mixed with hatred. Tulani put her small foot at the base of his spine, forcing him to go onto his stomach.

"I hope minKays are satisfied?" She addressed the Quyroo League respectfully, using their title with an elegant bow. They were observing from a low-hanging branch. Most were smiling, but for a large Quyroo on the end, Seren's father, Jokin.

Seren's forearms shook with weakness as he tried to push himself off the ground. Tulani slammed him hard in the shoulder, grimacing with triumph when Seren's breath escaped in a gusty exhalation. She then pushed hard, watching with a satisfied smile as Seren fell face forward onto the red dirt floor.

"You won nothing, Tulani. I will have you yet," he growled through gritted teeth.

The head of the council grunted as he slid off the tree, approached Tulani, and raised her hand to the cries of the female Quyroos. "She has proven she needs no protector."

The other older Quyroos in the league agreed with nods, save Seren's sire, Jokin, who angrily shook his red fist. "It is unseemly for a maiden to be free. Even Darracians protect the females. What is this world coming to?" he spat at his defeated son, who hung his head shamefully.

"I am not a timid maiden," Tulani shouted back, fighting the chills from the colder air on her wet skin. Water ran in rivulets down her long arms and legs to pool on the red Desa floor. "I will not be owned, not by Quyroo or Darracian. I am the high priestess."

"One trick does not a priestess make," Jokin snapped back. He hated Tulani and her prince. He still blamed them for his brother Jonis's death. Jonis had gone to the Cloud City for peace talks, against his wishes, and was the first to be beheaded by Staf Nuen, the king's traitorous brother. He trusted no one. "Make the rain stop, Tulani," he shouted. "Make it stop rotting the randam crystals." He stalked closer to her, his face drenched from the moisture, water dripping from his nose and chin. "This is punishment from the Elements, the time of rain."

A grumble of assent went through the crowd. "Yes, High Priestess, knower of all things *Dar-ra-c-ian*," he added with a sneer, "use your magic to make the suns shine again and the fruit plentiful."

It was true; since the day she had made Aqin stop its eruption, Ozre, the Element that enabled her, had disappeared. Tulani and her people had stormed the castle, helping the Darracians loyal to the king crush the rebels. The king had died that day, leaving Syos with the future of a new king with bright promise. But the improvements came slowly, if at all. The Quyroos grew impatient. Tulani attempted to rally them, teach them how to appeal to King V'sair for new laws. There were some strides in the right direction, but with each policy came unprecedented problems that overwhelmed the ill-prepared government. The Moon Council deadlocked, and not even the hopeful ideals of the young king could break the stubborn ways of both species. Fewer and fewer Quyroos showed up to Tulani's meetings. Soon, nobody came, and Tulani felt their hostility at her uselessness. Ozre never answered her pleas, leaving her to face the Quyroos afterward alone and powerless. The rain started to fall then.

At first it was a gentle mist, which grew as each day passed. Torrential downpours followed, loosening rocks, uprooting trees, creating muddy quagmires that slowed growth as well as trade. Food was becoming scarce, and if not for the supplies sent by Syos, many Quyroos would have starved. The issues were overwhelming for the immature government. Many of the newly appointed commissioners were uneducated in running these programs. There was corruption, for sure; the Quyroos were disappointed, for the promised change was not coming fast enough. The Bottom Dwellers who had abandoned their homes on the volcano in the interest of peace slowly returned, making new illegal settlements. This angered the Darracians. The king dismissed his entire Moon Council, dismayed by the violent shouting, the inability to get anything accomplished. Both V'sair and Tulani were locked in a struggle beyond their capabilities to fix.

The rain tapered off, and this silenced the crowd. They were unsure of her.

Tulani scanned the horizon, her eyes searching for a ball of familiar light, when she saw a great comet streak across the black sky. "Ozre…" she whispered, until she realized it was not the Element but simply a racing comet.

Masses of Quyroos fell to their knees, their eyes wide in their startled red faces. "It's a sign."

"It's the end of days," another moaned.

Babies cried; there were shouts of dire warnings.

"Make it do something, Priestess!" Seren called out. "Prove you have the power."

Tulani slapped his head with the stick, silencing him but not the malice she saw in his lean face.

She watched the comet rocket toward Fon Reni, wondering if V'sair saw the comet as well and felt the same sense of doom. A light rain began to fall again, hushing the crowd, and soon the ruts of the planet's surface ran with a red rain the color of blood.

IV

STAF NUEN SAT comfortably in the plush chair, smoking the pipe his host had offered him. Smoke swirled around his head, stinging his yellowed eyes, a side effect from indulging in graphen. He liked it better than krayum, the heady liquor he drank at home. It left him relaxed, did not affect his reflexes, and he could smoke himself sick, and no one would ever know. He glanced out at the reflective walls of the fortress. He was the guest of King Lothen of Planta, Reminda's younger brother.

Lothen came into the room, a squire divesting him of his armor. He threw himself into a chair opposite Staf, bare chested. A servant draped a robe over his blue, well-muscled shoulders. He adjusted the golden rings he wore on his upper arms. He had at least four on each of his biceps, curling snakes that signified great victories. There was a fortune of randam crystals embedded in the metal.

Lothen shook his head like a wild stallius, freeing his shoulder-length ivory hair from a rawhide. Just like every other male here, he had shaved the sides of his head, leaving only the hair covering the top of his crown to cascade down the center of his back. For battle, they tied it in topknots on their heads. Orange tattoos covered his face in a swirling pattern. Staf knew each design was different, almost like a fingerprint. All Plantans had it done as they entered puberty. It was a mark of beauty, but Staf found it oddly distracting. Large silver hoops danced in his ears, and while the older man knew Lothen was considered handsome, he thought his feral grin off-putting. He had an oily laugh, his glittering lapis eyes darting constantly around the room. Two females prepared dishes in the background. Staf lazily rose, hand clasping the king, who bade him to reseat himself. Staf eyed the king's long, pointed fingernails with distaste.

"I see you have taken advantage of my hospitality." Lothen nodded as a servant brought him a large clear goblet. A silver fish swam in circles inside the glass. A similar goblet was brought to Staf. "You are not repulsed by our Plantan habits?" the king asked silkily.

"I have seen Reminda drink this way for many years."

They clinked their glasses, gulped rapidly, swallowed the fish whole. It squirmed down Staf's windpipe, so he belched loudly, helping to squeeze it into his stomach.

Lothen laughed loudly.

"The trick is to get it down smoothly, my lord."

"Reminda may have taught me many things, sire, but not that quaint custom."

"I barely remember my sister." Lothen frowned. "She was stolen by your brother when I was a child. We were peaceful people back then."

Staf grunted, "I don't remember you being peaceful. Your people started raiding ships. That's why my father sent us here, to negotiate."

"History is written one way and remembered another. Darracians don't negotiate; they take what they want, using their precious Fireblade as justification." Lothen laughed heartily. "Oh, don't get all high-and-mighty, my lord Nuen. How will you use your special sword now; how will you explain its extraordinary power?" He stood up. "You don't need a Fireblade to feel superior. The right warrior can use any tool to achieve what he needs. Darracians don't hold a monopoly on anything but arrogance!" Lothen shot back. "Yes," and went on, his forked tongue slipping out in his rage, "we were peaceful until your brother came to steal what didn't belong to him. We are docile no longer." He slammed his glass down on the side table.

"A tragedy." Staf covered the rim of his cup when a servant came to pour some more liquid. Lothen held his goblet up for a refill. Staf was in no position to debate with the leader. If Lothen chose to remember history his way, who was he to argue with him? Staf mentally shrugged. If he wanted to use the excuse of Darracian interference, and fail to remember that Planta served as the aggressor, he wasn't going to argue.

"You don't like it?" Lothen sneered, leaning forward, his eyes watchful.

"Much as I appreciate Your Majesty's delicious libation, I must decline. I want to be able to function tonight."

"Ha," the young king roared. "You like Naje?"

"She is entertaining."

"She is wild."

Staf dipped his head. The female had kept him busy his whole time on Planta. She was a slave, similar in build to his native Quyroos, her almond-colored skin smooth as silk. A wealth of black hair flowed around her slender form. She was a prize, captured on one of the many raids from the neighboring planet Venturian. Lothen had given him the woman soon after he arrived. He had come alone, bankrupt, deserted by his forces, the wound in his side half healed. It pained him still, and only the deep massage from Naje eased its torment. He felt a sense of peace around her that he had never known before.

She was a quiet person, watchful, understood when to talk and when he desired silence. When his dreams chased sleep, she was able to calm him as no other. Her supple arms embraced him; her hushed voice lulled him back into blissful sleep. She was not as young as he first thought, and he knew she had suffered before her capture as well as after. She ran his household on the tiny island on Planta with cool efficiency, and he knew wherever he went, Naje was going with him. She had made a home for him when he felt homeless.

After the battle for Darracia, he had escaped on his ship, only to face a mutiny when he ordered them to regroup and attack. Set adrift in a small craft, he looked for a place to land. They had expected him to die from blood loss, those sniveling cowards. His men had crawled back, asking forgiveness from his nephew, who embraced them by giving away much of his territory. Staf had lost everything—his home, his wife, his children. His oldest and youngest children had been killed. His remaining three daughters lived on Darracia still; however, he hadn't had communication with them since he escaped. For all he knew, they were dead as well. It was all gone, everything except his ambition. He considered throwing himself on V'sair's mercy but knew as long as Zayden lived, he was a marked man.

The king's bastard had followed him, from planet to planet, with a determination of a hunting jast. Time after time, Staf outwitted him, always a step ahead of the young warrior.

Staf had settled for a season on that icy cesspit called Venturian. He had accomplices there, allies who, for a price, supported him, and he stayed waiting, biding time until he could figure out where he could go. He created a new business, selling stolen items to passing criminals who stopped there. Lothen heard about him and reached out to him, offering a safe haven. Staf refused based on the long-term history of their two planets. He had made himself a base of sorts, but Zayden followed him there. The hirelings he had employed to protect him attacked his brother's bastard, leaving him for dead. Well, Staf thought ruefully, you get what you pay for—the job was ill done. Zayden lived. His bastard of a nephew disappeared into the stews of Venturian, and no amount of bribery could find him. Zayden was on Venturian, waiting for the opportunity to attack. There was not enough money on Venturian to protect him from Zayden's hatred. Staf's time there was done. He had to move on and find a new host. Staf left Venturian under the protection of Lothen, king of Planta and Reminda's younger brother.

Planta was a water planet with one small island, where the crowded population lived in a jumble of homes built in layers on top of each other. While some found the pastel colors appealing, to Staf it was a dirty place, made seedy by the lack of uniformity. It was a hodgepodge of edifices, a dilapidated, faded city. The castle was more of a fortress, built hanging over a buttress above the filthy seawater. It smelled there; the air was polluted and foul. The linens were damp with mildew, and everything had a patina of bronze, slimy mold. Much as he hated it here, he had nowhere else to go. Bina, the small moon orbiting Planta, was completely uninhabitable, mined for graphen by slaves from all over the galaxy. That left Ablas, in the far end of the solar system, which was colder than hell and about as hospitable.

He picked up the long pipe that was attached to the hanging bottle from the ceiling. A manservant dropped a blossom into the bulb, lit it with a long taper, and Staf inhaled deeply, letting the smoke envelop his airways. It was getting to the point where he needed to have the pipe in his hands all day long.

"Graphen can take over your life." Lothen sucked deeply on his own pipe, closing his eyes as the vapors filled his lungs. He released it, and Staf watched through slit lids as the smoke escaped from the gills that ran alongside the king's ribs. He had never seen Reminda's gills. They had been hidden under her clothing. He wondered briefly if V'sair had them as well, then shrugged, giving himself up to the enticing visions that followed a deep inhale.

They sat in silence, the king of the Plantans and the political rebel Staf Nuen. They were an unlikely couple, enemies their entire lives, their two governments never having found a common ground. Once, many years ago, Planta had been a peaceful planet, a land filled with fishermen and abundance. Changing circumstances had caused Reminda's father to reconsider his strategies, developing a reputation for cunning and deceit. It all started with subtle climate changes. They didn't feel it at first, but slowly resources grew tight. His home's natural commodities waning, the land and oceans became over-extended. The old king started attacking convoys that traveled nearby to make up the shortages. The people became lazy, stopped creating products.

Soon, the Plantans had forgotten how to produce for themselves. It was cheaper and easier to steal. Overpopulation and pollution continued to strip Planta of its bounty. The lush gardens, famous throughout the galaxy, withered and died. The sea became a filthy swamp, the arable land reduced to one small part of an island in a sea of poison. The planet could not support the growing populations of Plantans, its resources stretched to their limits. It became known as a lawless sector of space, and many were afraid to travel there. The Plantan raiders showed little mercy and attacked without discrimination.

Talks and treaties were rebuked, and when the Darracians had approached them fifty years ago, sending a young prince to initiate peace talks, Drakko was taken prisoner. Wounded in a fray, he was nursed by the king's daughter, Reminda, who had fallen in love with him. Drakko made a daring escape and took Reminda with him. No amount of peace talks could repair the damage. Reminda's father went on a rampage, making this end of the solar system a very dangerous place. It became too risky to travel in the area. Trade routes dried up, and the neighboring cold planet of Venturian sunk into poverty. The Plantans didn't care. They raided Venturian, enslaving its inhabitants, transforming the thriving society into a dismal, barren wasteland, the most important export the slaves they plundered from the population.

Venturian was a freezing rock of a planet that had a highly successful trade from its vast and varied wildlife. Trappers first settled there, drawn by the great beasts that supplied delicious meat as well as warm furs. Rudimentary settlements grew into sizable towns. It was an uncivilized place, on the western edge of the solar system, a wild frontier, barely governed. It was a freewheeling territory, the last civilized outpost before deep space thrust a traveler into nothingness. The Plantan raids destroyed all that. Stores and businesses closed. Law enforcement was crushed by the raiders.

Vast fish farms failed, and the lively planet became a devastated way station filled with criminals who traded on violence and fear. The sprawling villages had turned into garbage heaps, filled with cheap bars and a frightened populace. Soon it was depleted to an empty shell, leaving only the rejects or infirm to live off the discarded leavings of the raiders.

Eventually, the old Plantan leader died, and his son Lothen became king. The new king didn't remember the old ways, their religion. He respected nothing. He felt confined by the restrictions of the Elements and their forced morality. Abandoning antiquated beliefs, he ordered them to rip out the Temple of the Elements. It was forbidden to mention the Sradda Doctrines. They didn't need them anymore; the Elements had abandoned them and the surrounding planets, allowing a new religion that encouraged the idea of taking what belonged to others without consequence or conscience. The ideology took root, growing in the dead soil. The cult of Geva changed the buried heart of Planta from the sweet land of peace and plenty to a place filled with hatred and greed. Dancing naked around a caldron, the Plantans paid homage to their new goddess, Geva, by sacrificing whatever she asked for. Geva was a greedy goddess, one who demanded constant loyalty, but in return, she opened the door to a new way to see things, one where Plantan needs were the only ones that mattered. She urged her followers to mow down anything in their path to prosperity. A fickle entity, she punished when ignored and rewarded the wicked path Lothen led his people.

This opened a gateway for unimaginable carnage, a total disregard for goodness. It was a new age, a dark time, a time of stealing what you wanted at the expense of your neighbor, and only the strongest survived.

Plantans didn't need the restrictions or moral code of the Elements anymore. They were raiders, pirates, and thieves under the protection of Geva's dark heart. Everything was acquired by trickery or stealth. The Plantan Navy attacked ships passing through wider and wider quadrants of the solar system. They were a fearsome and lawless group. Now, far gone with decay, Planta, too, was a dying planet. Years of abuse had taken their toll. Lothen needed a plan; his advisors warned him they had barely a year left before they must find an alternative place to live. The toxic sea was slowly poisoning the atmosphere. Venturian was out of the question; starved to a useless ball of ice, the warmth of the two suns barely touching it, it made for an unwelcome home with its year-round winter. They had to find a new home.

The two leaders sat in silence for a long while, the whisper of the servants as they moved around the room the only sound. Night gulls called. Staf opened his eyes to stare out the windows to watch them dive into the restless sea, then resurface with fish speared on their swordlike beaks. He needed to resurface. He had to shake off this lethargy to dive back into the sea and spear that little fish, his nephew. Zayden was near; Staf felt his skin tingle with anticipation. *Let him come for me,* he thought boldly. *I will take care of him and then his slimy little brother.* He needed a faster ship than the little craft he was using. A fearsome army at his command could turn the entire solar system around. He enjoyed watching Lothen plunder any Darracian convoy stupid enough to wander into their airspace. The Plantans' ruthless tactics ensured they were the power in this end of the quadrant. Not even the Elements could stop them. As much as he liked it here, felt at home, he was nothing more than a guest. Lothen was popular with his own species. There was no future for him here on this dying planet. Sooner than later, he would have to find a new place to stay. Staf longed to go home to take Darracia from his alien of a nephew. He was full-blooded Darracian and considered himself its rightful leader.

"You are thinking about your home?" Lothen asked silkily.

Staf stared at the younger man, hating him for having his own throne, even if it was withering. He wanted one too. "I am always thinking of my home."

"Reminda is a traitor to Planta."

"She is a devious insect who controlled my brother," Staf replied with venom.

"You brother was a fool. You know, Staf, I have a proposition. Time is running out for me here. Planta cannot continue to sustain us for much longer. I need to find a new place for my people."

"What about Venturian?" Staf growled, his bloodshot eyes narrow.

Lothen glanced up and motioned for all his servants to leave the room. Staf's sullen Venturian slave left with a lingering glare at her master, who laughed at her rebelliousness.

"She is hot-tempered, that one." Lothen poured another drink.

"She is a challenge; it pleases me." Staf sucked on the pipe, his breath hitching on the inhalation. The room took on a pink, hazy glow, and Lothen wavered in the smoke. "Together we could use my fleet to attack Darracia." "Darracia?" Staf sat up, intrigued.

"Yes, it would be perfect. My army is unstoppable. We are seasoned soldiers when it comes to invasion. We have practiced on Venturian for years."

"Darracians are not Venturians. They will fight and may defeat you," Staf stated.

Lothen shrugged. "Think you your nephew will lead the Darracians against me? I have the power of Geva here!" Lothen laughed as he pointed to his hairless blue chest.

"We are known to be excellent warriors." Staf blew pale smoke through his nose, feeling the sting.

"Darracian, Plantan, what difference does it make? I need a new home, and so do you, my friend."

"There can be only one leader," Staf stated, his eyes glittering with purpose. He sat up straighter, the ache in his side gone.

"My people will not answer to you." Lothen watched the spray swirl above the filthy ocean. "You need me." He paused as if an idea had just come to him. "I have an idea. Your heir is dead. Make me your successor, and I will aid you with my armies. We will get rid of the Darracian ruling class, supplant it with a new one, loyal to you. I will have my men marry their daughters, take their property. What have your Elements ever done for you, given you false hope with your fire sword? We shall create a new world order. A world order loyal to Geva."

"A world order loyal to you." Staf stood, slightly unsteadily. "I do not know this…this Geva. I don't know of its power. What of the Elements? They will not stand for it. Ozre chose his side."

"They will be loyal to whom I direct them to be. They are not Darracians. As for Ozre, surely you don't believe in fairy tales?"

"You believe in Geva? Is it not a fairy tale too?"

"She. Geva, goddess of power. Someday, when you are ready, I will show you Geva, and you will feel the might of her will."

Staf stood up, weaving, pausing to consider how to say what he felt. "I don't see her might on this dying planet. Perhaps she will change her doctrine when you need her the most?"

Lothen jumped up to angrily pace the room. "You believed in your Fireblade…Can you say for sure, without a doubt, that the Elements really exist? Have you faced them?" he demanded.

Staf considered the question, choosing his words carefully. "For years we were taught to practice our skills until the night we became one with the Fireblade."

"We do not have a Fireblade. Plantans don't need them."

Staf acknowledged this with a nod. "A Darracian male is taught, well, was taught, that our strength is enhanced by the will of the Fireblade, and only because of our superiority, we are able to maintain the balance of power."

"You believe that, my lord. We don't have a Fireblade, yet we have the totality of power. Perhaps Geva does not believe in toys but in the power of real men."

Staf closed his eyes in thought. "V'sair should not have been able to harness the power." He opened his eyes and realized he was talking to another blood relative of his nephew. "Yet he surprised us all with great skill. It is said he looked into his own heart and found the strength to command the Fireblade."

"Strength is developed, not given by imagined beings."

"The Elements are real."

"It is your belief. The Elements are not real here on Planta; the only thing that matters is me and what I think."

"And what do you think, Your Majesty?"

"I think that the combined forces of Staf Nuen and a Plantan Army can teach young V'sair that merely closing one's eyes and wishing for power is a dream."

"Then let it be his nightmare." Staf puffed on his pipe. "Your men will be loyal to you in a fight for a distant planet?"

"And to you as well, my liege."

"You would call me your liege?" Staf pressed his face close to Lothen, their breaths intermingling, the fumes of Lothen's drink making Staf dizzy.

"I would call you Father if you made me your heir…" Lothen whispered. "Do it, Staf. Do it," he wheedled. "Why stop at Darracia? We can rule the solar system. With Darracian riches, Quyroo and Venturian slaves, by Geva's heart, we can control the entire galaxy."

Staf wheeled away, light-headed. It was the answer to

his dreams. Plantan might, with his leadership—V'sair wouldn't stand a chance. He would crush him. Staf made a fist and pressed it against the window, trying hard to conceal his growing excitement. The universe was within his grasp.

"What of the Elements? They will stop us."

"If they are real, then Geva will destroy them," Lothen told him passionately.

"Perhaps," Staf told him impatiently, wondering if indeed the Elements were nothing more than a chimera, as Lothen indicated. "Maybe Geva is not real as well?"

"Give me time to prove she is not only real but more powerful than anything in this universe."

Staf slid back into the comfort of the chair, picking up the pipe once more. He clicked the pipe against his teeth, deep in thought. "You would let me do what I wanted?"

"That is usually what a vassal does with his liege."

"Why? Here you are king, leader of many people. Why would you subjugate yourself to me?"

"You know how they think. If we work together, I won't have to be confined to this part of the system. Planta is withering." Lothen stood up. "We've exhausted our food supply; the fuel is gone from the ocean. We are running out of options."

"Why does not your Geva act to save you and your planet?"

"Perhaps her plan was to unite us, my lord Nuen. Who knows the mysteries of a goddess?"

"You would not be king there for a long time."

"I am known for my patience." Lothen laughed, his

forked tongue visible. "I am prepared to do this with or without you."

"Yes?" Staf raised his dark brow.

"I have an ally."

"Who?" Staf demanded. "Who did you find to betray Darracia and why?"

"Someone very close to the throne, to your nephew, the king." Lothen's voice was soft and menacing. "I have spies planted there, both Quyroo as well as Darracian."

"Why would two opposing forces help you?" Staf asked.

"When you promise them their heart's desire, you have no need to search for allies."

"In the same way you promise me?" Staf asked quietly.

"Surely it is not the same, my lord Nuen. We are cut from the same cloth. I could never betray you," Lothen said with a slick smile. He slapped Staf on the back and laughed. "The weather is changing here. I don't know how long this planet will survive. I can be your grand mestor." He called loudly for the servants to return with fresh goblets. "Let's drink on it."

A new libation was brought over, this time with a bloodred fish swimming furiously in it. Staf looked at the creature and realized it had human head, chest, and arms but a fishlike tail. He could hear the sound of its screams.

"The Talis. They live deep in our oceans and are quite a nuisance. A sacrifice on the altar of your success."

A keening wail rent the air behind him, and the king spun, sloshing his drink.

A female servant covered her eyes as she screamed,

pointing to the night sky. "An omen, sire, surely 'tis the end of the world."

The king and Staf edged close to the window, spying a careening comet spinning wildly across the vast sky, its reflection lighting the waves.

"A portent of doom?" Lothen watched the jagged trail of the comet streaking across the horizon.

"A sign of change. Change for the better." Staf held up his glass, laughing at the horror on the creature's face as he downed his drink in one giant gulp. He felt the being slide down his gullet as he smacked his lips with appreciation.

"To Geva!"

"To our partnership, with Geva at the spearhead!" the king agreed.

"Death to all who defy us." Staf watched with fascination as the king devoured the helpless sea creature.

V
—

ZAYDEN BENT OVER the chassis of his ship and blew gently against the sand that layered the engine. The ship had been made especially for him, the curved chassis white with green and blue racing stripes. It was a sweet goer with plenty of muscle that got him in more than a little trouble with its speed. Wiping his greasy hands on a torn piece of material, he jumped into the bucket seat and tried to turn over the turbo. He heard the squeal and grind of the sand against his gears and winced as it stalled once again. Cursing, he swung out of his cockpit and searched the sky angrily. He had waited too long. His engine was pitted with rust, his gears dried, the thrusters clogged with the ever-present sand that covered the beaches where he had landed. He hadn't cared back then. It had only been a week, and he was careless. He had landed here so he could regroup, think of how he was going to proceed.

He had Denita with him, and he needed to figure out what to do with her. Going back to Venturian was out of the question. Together, they had watched her home burn. Though she had marked him with a tattoo, she was the one who was really marked. By helping him, she had given up any chance of being safe there, and while she thought herself to be tough, he refused to leave her to their brutality. He would take her home; Reminda would know what to do with her. Then he would go after Staf and kill him. He could never rest until the deed was done and both his father and Hilde were avenged.

It had been a long journey so far, and the older man eluded him everywhere. He had followed Staf to Venturian, an icy shit hole in the back end of the solar system, to wander the shadowy brothels and graphen dens where some went in but never came out. Venturian was a tough place to be asking questions. The population was as unhelpful as they were unfriendly. He combed the gritty stores and dens, asking too many questions. He drew all the wrong attention, and it didn't take long before he knew he was being tailed. He dodged in and out of the freezing doorways, trying to lose his pursuers, but they remained hot on his trail. It had swelled to a group, and he realized he was vastly outnumbered. He needed to get back to the harbor, to the safety of his ship. He withdrew his pistol, ducking in and out of the winding streets, and saw they were coming from two different directions. He was in big trouble. He feinted left, but ran to the right into a deserted alleyway, panicking when he realized this one was a dead end. Doors slammed shut; it seemed the citizens of Venturian had a laissez-faire attitude toward crime, especially when it wasn't happening to them. They were on him in an instant, the pistol snatched from his hands, but not before he got off a shot and heard a howl of pain. A two-by-four hit him in the stomach, followed by someone kicking his head, hard, really hard. Before his eyes rolled backward, he heard a female shout and the sizzle of another gun. Something the size of a Darracian hit the back of his head, and then nothing until he woke in a run-down room in the rear of a graphen den.

He ached everywhere, his skull and ribs most of all. Sounds were muffled, and he saw everything in a distorted lens. He knew there was a woman taking care of him with the efficiency of a competent nurse, but everything else moved in slow motion. Smoke filled his head, and he burned with fever. Cool hands had soothed him. He had a faint memory of searing pain in his shoulder coupled with whispered words that he was marked. He woke with a throat so dry it hurt to swallow. Iron bands constricted his rib cage. His head ached with the intensity of a thousand banging drums. Soft fingers brushed his hair back, and a wavering vision of a beautiful, black-haired, sloe-eyed female with skin the color of caramel appeared in his line of sight. She held his head up for a drink, a smile on her wide carmine-colored mouth.

"Slowly, Warrior." She pulled the cup away from

his dehydrated lips. She had a deep voice that reminded Zayden of liquid mercury, both soft and smoky.

"Where am I?" The words came out in a croak. "This is my den."

Zayden attempted to rise.

"Stay still. You are safe, for now."

His shoulder ached as though acid had drenched it. He raised an unsteady hand to touch it, and she caught it within her own.

"Don't touch it."

"What…was I shot?"

"By me." She smiled down at him. "My needle. I have branded you." She ran her hands down his gray, pebbled chest possessively. "I saved you, and you belong to me."

"I don't think so." Zayden groaned from his gut as he rose, attempting to get off the pallet. "What is your name?"

"Denita." She turned her back and went to her cooking fire to fill a plate from a bubbling pot. "You will be hungry, I am thinking. Darracians are meat eaters, yes?" She ladled an overfilled spoon into a crude bowl, and Zayden's stomach growled loudly in the tiny room.

Sick as he was, he still noticed her tight-fitting black jumpsuit that hugged every curve. She wore high black boots that ended at the middle of her long thighs. She had a great pair of legs; Zayden eyed them with admiration. Though he wasn't interested, he still enjoyed looking at an attractive woman, and she was attractive. They were in close quarters, clearly in the rear of a noisy graphen den. It was dingy, a beaded curtain the only privacy from the patrons in the next room. Drafts blew through the chinks in the walls; his skin contracted with cold. He shivered involuntarily, and Denita threw a wrap around his wide shoulders, caressing him possessively until he shook her off. Denita had a pallet, two mismatched chairs, and a table that listed with a broken leg. Zayden walked unsteadily to the table and sat down heavily on the chair, his head feeling miles above his body. The girl dropped the bowl before him. Zayden pushed his snarled hair from his face. Denita stood behind him, stroking his head lovingly.

"Stop that." He slapped at her weakly.

"You didn't mind last night," she told him seductively, taking a brush and beginning to comb through his tangled locks. "Oh, it is a mess. I am going to braid it."

He felt her tugging on his scalp and moved his head away.

She tapped him on the shoulder with the brush. "Don't make me hurt you. Otherwise I'll just cut all your hair off. You'll feel better after you eat. You've been out of it for a couple of days."

Zayden knew the days were longer than on his native Darracia, this planet being so far from the suns.

"How many?" His voice was a rusty scrape.

She looked at him with a question in her eyes, which he noticed were a rich dark-brown framed by two dense rows of mink-colored lashes.

"Days, how many days have I been here?"

She shrugged. "Oh, I found you four days ago. You

were trying to attack a group of robbers. One slightly broken Darracian against fifteen thugs. No matter how talented you are, the odds were not in your favor."

"Why did you help me?" Zayden shoveled a spoonful of potted meat into his mouth. It was delicious, and he was ravenous.

Denita observed him with a possessive smile. She filled a glass with a white liquid and put it on the table. "Drink it. It will help."

Zayden took a gulp and recoiled at the overly sweet taste.

"It is good for you."

"I don't want it." He pushed it away, slightly nauseated.

"But you will drink it." Denita pushed it back and finished, "My warrior."

"Stop saying that. I'm not your warrior." He touched his cheek, wincing at its tenderness. His hand moved up, and he realized his patch was missing. "Where is it?" he demanded.

"You don't need it with me. I have seen far more of you than that." Denita laughed as she threw his frayed patch onto the table.

Zayden hastily put it on, feeling his shoulder pull. Looking down, he saw a strange blue circle within a black circle covering most of his shoulder. He touched it lightly.

"It tells everyone you are mine. I saved you, and now you belong to me."

"I belong to no one."

"You owe me, Darracian. A life for a life." She swiftly rolled her sleeve up, showing him a white bandage.

Deftly she removed it, revealing a long gash. "This is the price I paid. We are hardly even." Turning, she left him to eat alone. He heard her commanding voice rapping out orders in the next room.

Suddenly weary, he staggered to the lumpy cot, and his head hit the spare pillow to fall deeply into a healing sleep.

He awoke to silence, the rich time before the suns rose, when dew graced the ground, coating the grass like sugarspun crystals, untouched by the filthy rabble inhabiting the planet. Zayden flexed his legs, feeling stronger than he had, and rolled to his feet. The room was empty, the wind barely moving the ragged curtains. He looked around, spied his pistol on the table, rolled upward to snatch it, and put it in the back of his pants. He staggered up, finding the place he needed, his body's urges making themselves known.

"Ah, so you've finally passed water. Is it still bloody?"

Zayden felt his face heat up. "It's no business of yours." He pushed himself into the small kitchen, weaving just a bit.

"Sit down, you big lunk. You are going to ruin all my handiwork." She plunked another bowl of something steaming onto the crude table. "Was me that fought off those hired baboons and sewed up your cuts. Around here that deserves a bit of gratitude. I own you, Warrior."

Zayden laughed. "You can't own a dead man. I died a year ago."

"You mean Hilde?"

Zayden stalked to her and grabbed her arm, surprised

by the strength in her corded muscles. "How do you know about Hilde?" he demanded, his teeth bared.

"Settle down before you fall down. You talked is all." She shrugged out of his grip as he sat heavily onto the chair. "She's dead. I'm not. So accept your new reality."

"By the great Sradda, you will not tell me what to do!" Zayden shouted, but the fight was leaving him.

"There are no Elements here, Warrior. They left us to the Plantans years ago. On Venturian, we only have our wits, and this." She reached down and held up a Fireblade in her strong hand.

"Where did you get that?"

"I took it off a dead man. The one who had taken it from you." She threw it to him, and he deftly caught it. "Now you will teach me how to use the Fireblade."

Zayden shook his head. "I cannot teach you. It has no power." He tucked it into the loop of his pants.

"It does so…"

Zayden dropped his spoon, his amber eye narrowed. "How could you know?"

"I'll show you." Denita held out a calloused hand.

"When you hold it with both hands…"

"You had a flame?" Zayden asked quietly.

"Well, it was weak, but I am sure if you showed me how to--"

"What color was it?" Zayden demanded.

"What difference does it make? Relax, Warrior, I think it was a light blue; I admit it was weak."

"Don't touch it. It's forbidden. Don't ever touch it ever again." Zayden stared at her hard. She was younger than he first thought, but years of living in this hellhole had hardened her. He thought her to be a few years younger than he. "Why do you want to learn?" The room became so still, the air seemed to solidify.

Denita spoke almost in a whisper. "The Plantans have something of mine, and I have to get it back."

"What?"

"None of your business."

"Fine…Thanks for all you've done." He picked his jacket off the back of a chair, sliding his arm painfully into it.

"You can't leave. You owe me."

"Give me your address, and I'll have my people send you something."

"Oh, very funny, Your Highness."

Zayden turned and grabbed her wrist, his knuckles white. "What do you mean by that?" he asked, a fine white line rimming his lips.

"Nothing." Denita pulled away, her mouth thin with hatred. "You're hurting me. I don't want your money. I want your help."

Zayden shrugged. "I left my ship at the harbor. It's probably on its way to Pagil 7 in a million little pieces. Besides, I don't know Planta or its terrain. I don't even know what you're so hot to find. You don't even know me."

"I know enough. When you walk around Venturian asking questions, everybody is aware of you. Just get me to Planta, and I'll do the rest, Zayden."

"How do you know my name?" he demanded.

"Everybody on Venturian knows your name. They

also know that I am the only one willing to help you. If not for me, you'd be nothing but fertilizer."

"Whatever." Zayden shrugged. "I will not help you. I am looking for Staf Nuen."

"So am I," Denita told him with finality.

Zayden's knees shook, so he sat down, abashed at his weakness. "Not gonna happen, sweetheart."

"We'll see about that, *sweetheart*," Denita called back nastily as she left the room and their debate.

Zayden's lips split into a grin in spite of himself. She was as ornery as the horned toads of Fon Reni, but he had to admit she had a great little…He stopped to wonder how she had gotten the flame to turn blue.

The attack came the next morning without warning. Plantan raids were ruthless, as well as indiscriminate. The cries of the locals mixed with the blades of the invaders. He heard Denita's defiant voice fill the small den.

"He's not here, I tell you." A scabbard screamed as a blade was raised. Zayden grabbed his Fireblade from the floor next to his cot, feeling the flame of it come to life. He hadn't touched it as a weapon for almost a year but instinctively reached for it when he heard Denita's arguing. Looking at it with loathing, he looped it in his pants and took out his pistol. Hiding behind the beads, he saw Denita surrounded; a small nick in her neck dripped red with blood. His head heated up with rage, his amber eye glazed with hate.

"Even if he was here, I wouldn't let you have him!" she shouted.

A great sword arc upward, Zayden cursed loudly,

bursting through the curtain, firing off two rapid rounds, taking out both the man holding a knife to Denita's throat, and the other one by the door. Denita withdrew a small, wickedlooking blade from a sheath attached to the boot by her calf and gut stabbed the last raider.

"Why did you do that! I was fine without your help!" Denita spun on him.

"Yeah…I can see just how fine." He touched the droplet of blood dripping down her long neck.

She recoiled, her back ramrod straight, looking like a proper little soldier. "You've ruined everything. I had it under control."

"A regular general," Zayden said sarcastically.

Denita touched her neck, cursing at the pain. "We have to get out of here," she said urgently. "There'll be more coming now."

Zayden ripped a piece of his shirt and with an intimate gesture dabbed her neck. She pulled away, and Zayden grabbed her arm, forcing her to bare her neck. Their eyes locked. Her skin was soft, and he touched a rough knuckle to the vulnerable underside of her chin. She moved her face higher. It almost felt like an offer, he thought. She moistened her lips, her lovely lashed eyes wide in her small face. They stared at each other in silence, until she hissed in pain.

Zayden muttered softly, "Well, I have nowhere to go." "Your ship," she told him, her lips inches from his own.

Zayden looked down at her. Time seemed frozen, when he suddenly threw the scrap of cloth in a corner, angry at himself for caring. Feelings were for others, not him.

"My ship is gone and of no use," he said flatly.

"No, no, it is safe. It was missing a binding plug and a masen board. I had them replaced." She grabbed his hand. They stopped at the door; the icy streets were striated with blood. Still warm, it made a miasma of steam and filled the air with an iron-like odor. Venturians were murdered as they stood; screams pierced the air. Smoke swirled around them, obliterating the shabby storefronts. Zayden coughed, his ribs protesting mightily. Fires dotted the street where Plantans had thrown lit torches onto the wooden roofs.

Zayden hung on the door, breathless, his head wound weeping, falling to his knees in the icy slush. *Where are the Elements now?* he demanded. How could they stand by and watch beings mowed down, letting them be plundered by tribes that knew no mercy?

"Move, Warrior!" Denita placed a shoulder under his arm. "This way."

He turned to watch her home go up in a blaze, falling when an explosion rent the air. Her home went up in a fireball, raining debris over their heads. Ducking his aching head, he watched burnt pieces of flesh splatter the icy, rutted lanes.

"The graphen." Denita smiled, her face lit up by the flames. "It's highly unstable. I hope those bastards were still inside."

He pointed to smoking flesh. "Looks like your wishes came true."

"If only…" she replied harshly.

"Well, this bastard is ready to go," Zayden told her, holding her by the elbow. "Which way, Denita?"

"Follow me."

They sprinted through the back alley, slipping in the freezing mud. Zayden panted as they weaved between the burning buildings. All around him, he could hear cries for mercy, and the sounds of rampage. The Plantans pushed in doorways, carrying whatever they could on their backs, including the young women of the colony. Zayden gripped his sidearm, turning to enter the fray, when he felt Denita tug his arm.

"This is not your fight."

"It seldom is," Zayden responded. "They are carrion."

"They have my sister. I need you," Denita implored him.

He looked at the carnage. His amber eye narrowed as he turned to help the victims.

"You won't make a difference here! They do this all the time. Look, do you want me to beg?" she demanded. They stood frozen, eyes locked, and Zayden swore he saw all the way to her soul. It was just as bleak as his own.

Denita pushed him into a small building. Zayden gasped when he recognized a familiar outline underneath a tarpaulin. Sweat glistened off her almond-colored skin.

"Warrior, help me," she urged him.

With his good arm, Zayden pulled the heavy material off the dulled surface of his ship, his ribs screaming in protest.

"You didn't wax it?"

"Idiot. Get us out of here."

"Hop in."

He climbed up, hauling himself in as the door burst open, revealing a group of Plantan warriors with blood-lust in their eyes, swords and spears held high. Punching the thrusters, he gave a satisfied grin when they roared to life, and without regard for his sore shoulder, he shoved it to the maximum level, praying to all the Elements that he wouldn't stall.

A huge Plantan jumped onto his wing, and Zayden cried out to Denita, "Buckle up, buttercup!"

The engines squealed with power, and he felt the giddiness that always preceded the burst of speed his ship was capable of. They shot out of the building with dizzying speed, the warrior peeled off by the force of gravity.

His ship picked up momentum as it left the embattled planet but did not escape notice of a Plantan hunting party. His left arm almost useless, Zayden swerved his ship toward the blazing suns, hoping his maneuver would blind his pursuers. He felt the jolt as one of the heat seekers grazed the wing of his small ship, making it go into a wild spin. Denita pounded on the glass that separated their compartments with her fists.

"Not now, sweetheart," he yelled sarcastically, "I'm sort of busy!" Gritting his teeth, he grabbed the wheel, sparks of pain flashing behind his eyes from his busted ribs. His hand went numb, but he held on, pressing for as much power to go to his tiny engines. He loved his ship. It had been a gift from his father for his captaincy. It was compact and the fastest on Darracia. The engine screamed in the void of space, zipping under the startled pirates to escape into the darkness beyond the atmosphere.

"You okay there, Denita?" No answer.

"Denita?" He painfully shifted in his seat and saw a fine line of blood from a hairline cut. "Shit."

He needed a place to think. He needed to heal his wounds. He turned his ship and headed to Fon Reni.

◆

The brush swayed, and Denita stood in her torn black jumpsuit proudly holding a dead pozin in her hand. It had been a dicey few hours after he landed, according to him, crashed as far as she was concerned. Denita suffered a concussion; she had never belted herself in, as there had not been time. Her head connected hard with the dashboard, and she missed the entirety of their daring escape. After they landed, Zayden pulled her from the ship painfully, stripped out of his shirt, and doused it with cold seawater to place on her head. It took a few hours, but she returned to him, angrily cursing that he didn't land on Planta.

"Where is this place?" she spit, mobile once again.

"Fon Reni."

"Fon Reni? Fon Reni!" she shouted. "You take me to a resort when we can avenge my family!" She paced the indigo beach shakily. "Take me to Planta, now!"

"No can do, General." Zayden didn't look up from the small fire he was building. "I would remove the boots before you burn your feet through them. The sand doesn't react well to the material of your soles," he explained calmly.

"Don't tell me what to do, and don't call me general," she grumbled.

They barely talked for the rest of the day. Denita had taken herself off to explore the dense forest of swaying palms, and he had removed his shoes and rolled up his pants to enjoy the gleam of the suns bouncing off the golden ocean. "She's back." He smirked hearing her stomping through the brush madder than a wet gresh.

She eyed the pile of discarded crab. "You ate already," she accused him with disgust, laying her catch beside the fire. She stared at the ribbed muscles of his chest, gleaming in the firelight. He had the rough, pebbled skin of the Darracians; she saw that his chest was a lighter gray than the rest of him, with big purple bruises covering half his torso. She knew he was still in considerable pain. His shoulders gleamed in the firelight. The shadows played off the sculpted angles of his lean face.

"Didn't you hear the dinner bell?" Zayden looked up innocently. "You snooze, you lose."

"I wasn't sleeping. Unlike some, I was checking this place out for a way to get off. And I trapped a pozin as well." She kicked it toward him with the toe of her boot.

Zayden held up his index finger. "One, we are alone. My family owns the rights to Fon Reni, and no one can come here without permission. Two"—he touched the next finger—"pozin are foul, nasty rodents that have a scent sac that makes them inedible."

"You could have left me some crabs. Who is your family?"

Zayden ignored her question and simply said, "Look in the basket." He pointed to the container with a small wave of dismissal.

Denita walked over to him and leaned against the side of his ship. "We go to Planta?" she asked hopefully.

"No. We are going home."

"I don't have a home."

"But I do."

VI

TULANI RACED THROUGH the treetops, her arms grabbing one branch after another effortlessly. Her upper torso had developed, and she wasn't the soft cloud dweller anymore. She grabbed the slippery vines with her calloused hands, but still worried she would slide down and find herself on the wet Desa floor if she wasn't careful.

"Wait up, you keewalla!" Bobbien called from behind her.

She was faster than her grandmother and smiled, her white teeth gleaming in the darkness. Her hair bounced against her back, her braids thick and numerous. "Faster, Greanam. I want to get out of here. It's pouring."

It had started raining in the last moon phase and never stopped. It was a steady downpour; the randam crystals rotted on the bark. Flowers failed to bloom, and fruits were scarce. This was unprecedented, and the Quyroos complained but failed to see the impending disaster. Food stores were running low. Even the wysbies had disappeared, their wings too fragile to fly in the downpours.

She was headed for Aqin, their home. They had moved into the vast chambers to be closer to Ozre. Tulani had so much to learn, but try as she might, the Element was elusive. Bobbien used the time to teach her about the herbs and medicines of the forest, but Tulani was miserable. She missed V'sair and felt she could not return until she understood her role in this world. No longer a servant, not quite a healer, a half-fast high priestess, she was floundering in her own insecurities. She needed to make a connection to her people. She knew her role was to serve as conduit to the king, but she felt as removed from them as she did when she lived in Syos, the city of the clouds.

"Just go to V'sair if you are unhappy here," Bobbien told her, clearly out of patience for her lovesick sighs. "I am tired of seeing Seren's nasty face stalking you."

The big Quyroo hadn't given up and frequently could be found just watching their home. She would often catch a glimpse of him hiding in the treetops, his narrowed eyes cold.

"I am not afraid of that one." She dismissed Seren with a disinterested shrug. "I can't leave, Greanam. V'sair wants me as his queen. I don't want to be an ornament; I want to make a difference. I fear I know nothing. I need to be able to help. I want to make a difference."

"Yes, I do agree, child. Time—you need time to learn to use the Elements to achieve greatness, I think. Yes, you do."

"But the Quyroos still don't accept me."

"They are leery of you, they are," Bobbien said with a sage nod. "Don't trust you, don't trust nobody, the Quyroos. You understand why, don't you?"

Tulani thrust out her lower lip. "It's all so exhausting. We are caught in this terrible limbo. V'sair strives to make peace; Darracians act superior; the Quyroos don't trust them." She plopped down next to her grandmother. "Some mountains are too hard to climb."

"Defeatist talk!" Bobbien yelled at her, her red face turning an unbecoming shade of magenta. "Remember you not Ozre telling you to look inside your heart?"

"I have, and all I see is love for V'sair."

"Then go and live only for your love!" Bobbien got up to angrily ready their next meal. She threw ingredients around like a mad chef, and Tulani bit back a smile. "Whiney, whiney," said her grandmother. "You think everything should come in a snap?" She held up her hand and snapped her long fingers impatiently. "You have just learned of our healing ways, crammed years of training into mere months. If you want to be accepted by your people, you have to become one of them."

"I am Quyroo," Tulani told her defensively.

"Physically, yes, but up here"—she pointed to her temple—"I think not. Do not blame others for your lack of success. Search your mind to see what more you can do."

"Did Ozre tell you that?"

"He didn't have to," Bobbien replied curtly, then turned back to pound some forest edibles into a pulp.

So they settled in the caves, gathering the roots, making potions. Tulani studied the Quyroos and slowly began to see their way of thinking. Every night she threw herself onto the cold stone floor, called for Ozre, but heard nothing. "Why have you deserted me, Ozre," she cried out. "I need your guidance."

The echoes of her pleas were her only response.

VII

"HIGHNESS, WE MUST schedule the coronation," General Swart stated from his seat on the Orbitus Chamber, a group that met daily with the king.

"I am still in mourning, General. It is out of the question," V'sair answered absently, his gaze on the condensation coating the wall of windows. "It's filthy out there today," he added to no one in particular.

"A strange occurrence, for sure." Brault, the chanter, added with his querulous voice. "The weather is strange. We have not seen Rast or Nost for months. Rain, rain, rain, it's making the whole Desa run red like blood."

"Enough, Chanter Brault," V'sair said curtly. He didn't like the man. He had been appointed to the head of the Temple of the Elements, and V'sair hadn't warmed to him. It had been a fair appointment; he was chosen by a group of lesser chanters. Due to his seniority, it was a given that he should lead the temple. Short and dumpy, he had a long, thin nose and beady eyes that seemed too close together.

Chanters shaved their heads when they took their religious orders in order to be able to hear the Elements better. He wore the maroon robes of high office, with a golden breastplate signifying he was the most high warrior for the Elements. V'sair thought him an ugly little man, whose wrinkled and faded skin gave him the appearance of something that lived underground to tunnel in the soil. He was small-minded, hated the Quyroos, and basically made life in the Orbitus Chamber very difficult for V'sair.

But it was true—the weather had changed. It was a few degrees colder, and they'd had unexplained record rainfalls. V'sair had appointed a committee to study the problem. He had yet to hear anything from them.

V'sair fiddled with a pen. "Enough about the weather." He glanced up at a map of the Desa that hung suspended in midair. He motioned with his hands, and the images changed, from topical, to bird's-eye, to frontal. V'sair studied the screens, searching every face for the familiar one so dear to him. He saw panicked people, filthy and shocked, their homes destroyed. "How many people were hurt?" There had been a major mudslide with many casualties. V'sair wanted to organize relief efforts.

"The coronation, sire," Swart appealed.

"Will wait. What happened on the hills of Aqin?"

"It's all this rain. The Bottom Dwellers have been

flooded out of the illegal settlements. We have set up refugee camps in the Plains of Dawid."

"How do you expect me to think about things like coronations when my people suffer?" V'sair rounded on General Swart.

"How can you call them your people when you haven't been properly crowned!" Swart stood angrily. "Perhaps all this is a sign from the Elements."

"What kind of sign?" V'sair's back went rigid as he inquired quietly.

"I meant nothing, Your Highness. I am only looking for the good of the monarchy." Swart leaned closer to V'sair.

"Walk with me, sire."

V'sair stood and strolled the chamber next to his grand mestor, their footsteps echoing off the slick floor.

The general waited until they had passed a distance to give them privacy. "I have information." "Yes?" V'sair looked at him intently.

"The interrogations of the assassins have been troubling." Swart frowned.

"What have you discovered?"

Swart looked around the room, his eyes darting to every dark corner. "I am taking every precaution for your safety. But, sire, I am not happy...I feel that we are missing something."

"What, General? You did an excellent job. You intercepted them before anything happened." V'sair placed his hand on the general's stooped shoulders. "I know I am a sore trial to you, my lord general, but, like my father before me, I trust you with my life."

"Thank you, Your Majesty."

"You used to call me V'sair."

"I am worried, my…V'sair. Although they have talked, I suspect they know someone close to you is involved. I am nervous."

V'sair shrugged his shoulders. "I feel secure in your hands. But please, General, make sure my mother is safe."

"I have doubled the guards on you both."

V'sair placed a trusting hand on his shoulder. "I knew I could depend on you."

"But, sire, I would feel better if we had the coronation. It would give you legitimacy as the king. Besides, all the people love the pageantry."

"Well then use funds for all this pageantry to get supplies to the ones suffering down there." He pointed a finger to the grayness outside. He watched the general shake his head and go back to the large stone conference table where the rest of his council argued. Walking slowly to the window, he was oblivious to the discussions taking place behind him. He glanced through the gloom, wondering if Tulani was safe, warm, dry, and safe.

He didn't want to be crowned. It felt so final, as though his father was really gone. He stared at his reflection in the window, and the room receded as mist hovered, changing shapes over his head. It spangled the air, filling it with the smell of ozone, and his hair went static, rising off his scalp. All sound receded as he watched the image of his father materialize in the window. The face floated, becoming fuzzy, indistinct. It became more clear as a familiar body took shape next to V'sair. The reflection smiled sweetly, the eyes lit with incandescence. Drakko was healthy and whole, taller than V'sair. The boy rubbed his eyes, afraid to blink lest the apparition disappear. He glanced to his advisors, noting them locked in heated comments, then looked back at the specter. A smile spread across his father's generous mouth. He nodded to his son, and V'sair felt tears sting behind his eyes. Pressure landed on the young man's shoulders; V'sair touched the spot, knowing without a doubt his father had just squeezed him affectionately. Strong hands reached up, lifting the crown from his own dark head to hold it over V'sair's blond one. The jewels sparkled with the reflection of the waning light, and he watched in wonder as his father placed it on his head. Though he knew nothing graced his pate, he felt the crown's heavy weight resting there. Their eyes met to make a peaceful communion. Drakko pointed back to the council and shook his head with sorrow, letting V'sair know he was not happy with the discord. He watched those eyes rest on each of the Orbitus representatives, and while he frowned, V'sair couldn't read his father's thoughts. Then the lips moved with a soft whisper, and V'sair distinctly heard his father say, "Reminda." The shimmering reflection winked, dissolving into nothing.

V'sair touched his head, then the corner of his eye, wiping a crystal tear that had gathered there. Beyond speech, he cleared his throat noisily. Turning slowly, he looked at his councilors arguing over petty nonsense. He tried to figure out what his father was trying to tell him, but the whole thing was a muddle, from the councilors to the wet planet surface. Great Sradda, he wished Zayden were here to help him. He had to take command; the apparition, his father, had indicated it. Taking a deep breath, V'sair made a decision.

"General, arrange for my coronation for the first moon phase. We will do it in the temple. I want representatives from the Quyroos equally present. In fact, I will have one from the Quyroo League crown me."

"Out of the question!" Brault fumed.

"That's my job.

That is our custom!"

"We will circumvent the custom." V'sair turned his back. "That is all for today. Send in my mother."

Swart grumbled as he stuffed his notes into a briefcase. "Now he wants the coronation and within weeks. How am I supposed to get this done so quickly?"

Chanter Brault nodded, his face gray with indignation, and whispered, "I knew nothing good would come from the Plantan influence. A Quyroo crown him, indeed!" They walked out of the room, Brault tense with anger.

Reminda floated in, her face serene. "You asked for me?"

V'sair took her hand and kissed it. "Yes, Mo'mo. I have decided to go ahead with the coronation. You must find Tulani. I want her by my side."

"I will do my best, sire." She smiled and bowed her head.

VIII

V'SAIR STALKED TO the temple, walking purposefully down the long aisle to come close to the altar. It was a high-ceilinged room, the walls made of clear quartz, polished to a sparkling shine. Fossils of tiny prehistoric insects were frozen in the depths of the rock walls, testifying to both its age and majesty. It was a cool room, and when filled with Darracians, the walls reflected the array of colors adorning its inhabitants. Today it was empty, so the sleek ice-looking walls mirrored his bleak mood.

The altar stood before him on a high platform, completely carved from clear, solid rock. The legs were a bas-relief of his ancestors holding aloft a giant beam for the grand chanter to sing the Songs of Sradda, the prayers of his people. Behind the religious leader was a wide block of wall, polished so that it mirrored the service taking place. It had cracked sometime when Aqin erupted, and as a result, the light refracted, allowing for one person to be multiplied into a hundred. V'sair looked up, seeing his face split in two, imitating his own internal schism.

He slid into his place, a pew just like the rest, nothing decorating it to make it special. Ornamentation could distract the pious from their sole purpose of communing with the Elements. A great pit with the eternal flame of the Elements burned bright, its orange and blue flames creating a show of dancer-like movements on the smooth surface. The shadows were compact and small, and as they traveled toward the rear of the temple, they stretched to become distorted images on the wall that seemed somehow threatening. The vast chamber echoed with the hiss and crackle of the flame. His father had stripped religious houses of all ostentatiousness, insisting that in the temple, all Darracians would be heard by the Elements equally.

He bowed, placing his head in his hands, praying for guidance. Positioning his fingers in the appropriate spot over his heart, he cleared his mind, letting his cares fall away so he could devote himself to finding solutions. V'sair concentrated on calling out to the Elements, picturing them, recalling the sound of Ozre's voice, feeling nothing, with the exception of his own desperation. He was missing something, his answer just out of his reach. It was as if it were one giant puzzle and the center was missing. The comet, Ozre, the non-stop rain—the solution was hovering before him in a jumble of answers that he could not sort out. He heard the echo of his whispers bounce off the polished clear walls, but no response was returned.

Chanter Brault gripped the chalice in his pudgy fingers. His lips thinned with rage, his eyes darting through the empty chapel. Weak sunlight filtered in from the tall, narrow windows, and he asked for a sign. It had been a close call, but nobody had talked. He was safe, and yet, the king was alone. Could he not finish the plan and kill him in the Temple of the Elements? Wind chimes called the faithful to prayer; the window of time would soon be lost. Brault reached under his robe to touch the hilt of his Fireblade, unused since he had been elevated to the temple. It was purely ceremonial now, and he wondered briefly, if he activated the flame, would it burn the red of his youth, or the new blue flame of Darracian justice?

He withdrew it, his eyes widening as it jumped to life, bathing his face vermillion, and he suddenly realized he didn't care about the color anymore. He had heard that the prisoners had died, taking with them the secret of his role in the overthrow, as well as the instigator of the assassination. He walked toward the chapel, his Fireblade humming at his side, just beneath his robe. Trembling with excitement, he thought it was almost too easy.

As if the king heard him, he looked up, his face innocent in its youth, and he smiled at the chanter. "Have you come to lead me to the Elements?" V'sair asked.

Brault's clammy hand gripped his weapon, his insides turning to jelly, feeling the fire of purpose die along with his courage. Blood would be on his hands;

they would know that it was he who did the deed, and perhaps the guards would overwhelm them. How would the new social order they had planned survive without his guidance? No, let someone else rid the Darracians of V'sair's liberal ideas. But then, if he rid the planet of this half-breed, he would be hailed a hero. Lothen might give him a title, some territory of his own...

Wiping a nervous hand across a sweat-dotted head, he looked at the altar and shuddered, thinking he had seen a movement. It couldn't be, he thought wildly, a trick of light, nothing more, but the image returned, and he found himself staring into the eyes of Drakko, V'sair's dead father. Gasping, he coughed, his eyes bulging from his gray face, now a pasty shade of green.

"Are you well?" V'sair stood to hold out a hand to help the older man.

Brault backed away with a slight bow, sliding his blade into his holster behind his back and then smiling with uncertainty. "Together we shall ask for guidance." Falling to his knees, he heard the door open and knew that V'sair's royal guards were taking seats in the rear. "Oh, Great Sradda, giver of life, I commend myself to thee..." He began the Songs of Sradda, his mind feverously working on a different solution.

Brault had lost his nerve, losing his chance to ignite the coup. He watched the king sideways, lost his prayer, his face illuminated by the great Fires of the Elements, and wondered what he had just witnessed. Never a warrior, he had chosen religion because he was afraid of fighting other Darracians. Only because of his well-placed family was he able to advance through the temple hierarchy. There were no such things as ghosts—it was his imagination, nothing more. He smiled to himself. He had made the right decision. If V'sair and Swart survived this, he would be their religious lodestone. If Lothen succeeded, then he would be seen as a great ally. Leave his holy hands clean. Let them find someone who had no need to wonder of ghosts or devils, to take the chance with their souls.

He knew there were other rebels out there, operating within unknown cells. To protect them from being discovered, only one person knew all the members of each group. That man was now dead, and Brault had no idea who else was involved. He just knew he had to sit tight. Help was on the way. Let Lothen or one of the others take the glory; he would be fine taking a backseat until it was safe.

"Oh Great Sradda"—his voice soared to the roof of the great temple—"show me the way to your light!" Who knew which way it was going to go? "Spare me to be useful to the victor, whomever he may be." Brault smiled at the king's bowed head.

IX

REMINDA'S BARE FEET slapped on the cold stone of the volcano. She was alone, her guards unhappily waiting outside. She secured her wrap around her small shoulders. Aqin was damp as well as cold. The rain dripped along the inside walls of a dead volcano whose fire had been extinguished.

The cavern was empty. Reminda seated herself with a sigh, hoping Tulani and Bobbien would return some-time soon. She eyed the small altar, then walked over and kneeled to place her tattooed forehead against the cold stone.

"Oh, great Ozre, I commend myself to thee. Return and speak." She paused, taking a deep breath. "I beg of thee..." she added in a whisper.

The cavern filled with wind, racing in a circular movement, lifting anything not attached to the floor.

Reminda held her dress down; it billowed beneath her palms. The wind was fierce, and the fabric ripped.

"You are angry with us?" she yelled, her blue eyes wide.

"Not angry, disappointed." The response filled the room, and a ball of light appeared in the center of the small tornado.

"So am I!" Reminda replied indignantly.

Ozre's laughter echoed off the walls. "Are you now?"

The gusts died, and the ball of light came close to Reminda's face. It hung inches from her, and she saw into the bright red core.

"You accuse your son of not having patience; we think the apple does not fall far from the tree."

"Perhaps," Reminda replied, exasperated. "That is not important! Why have you deserted us? V'sair is floundering, Tulani is lost, Zayden is wallowing, and I…"

"Yes?" the light said softly.

"You are the Element, Ozre. You know what I am."

"So you say…"

"Why?" Reminda implored.

"Why?" Ozre repeating, sounding exactly like her.

"Stop repeating everything I say!" Reminda demanded. "You upended our world, threw us head over heels by indicating all we believed in was not the truth."

"V'sair made that discovery, not us."

"But all of Darracia is reeling from this revelation. The roots for all their doctrine are based on their superiority, and the blinders have been removed for them to find that strength is drawn from our inner values."

"Isn't that what you wanted?" Ozre asked.

"Yes, yes, Drakko and I wanted V'sair to be supported as the king because he earned it through his strength of character."

"Then my job is finished," the Element said with finality.

"How can you say that?" Reminda held out her hand. "He is struggling."

"No one said it was going to be easy," Ozre said reasonably.

"Well, yes, but…"

"It has not turned out precisely the way you expected," the ball purred as it caressed her head.

Reminda sighed, tears glistening in her eyes.

"There are other Elements, my dear, other Elements to fulfill your hopes. But they can help only when you reach out for them."

"I am reaching! How can I find Ereth?"

"Reach higher, deeper. I can't believe Ereth has been sending all of you signs; he is there for you. You are all so steeped in grief and unhappiness you cannot see what is right in front of your eyes."

Reminda's heart cracked within her chest as she fell to her knees; her pride evaporated like the morning dew. She felt the warmth of Ozre envelop her, and a knowing heat filled her body. Taking deep, absorbing breaths, she let the feeling of peace wash over her, her soul lifting up.

"I can feel you now, Ozre. Why?" she asked softly.

"This I can help you with, my dear. You are finally asking the right questions. I am the Element of earth."

The voice reverberated in her head, and she listened, tears running down her cheeks.

"I am the Element of truth, the direct path of mind

to heart. You know me, Reminda. You and the others have just lost your way."

"Sometimes when you are distracted by nonsense…"

A new voice spoke, and Reminda gasped, her hands over her mouth with joy. She rose slowly, turning to see her husband inside the shimmering ball of Ozre, young and handsome, his gaping wound gone.

"Drakko…" she whispered.

"I never left you, my love. I am right beside you." His voice filled her with serene joy, warming her to her cold feet.

"Drakko, beloved," she whispered.

"When your grief abates, you will see me and finish the work we set out to do."

She felt his voice like a warm balm to her soul.

"I miss you…" Words were inadequate, so she thought it instead, and her dead husband smiled.

The ball of light expanded, and she felt its comfort invade her body. She covered herself with both arms, trying to hold on to the feeling, as his voice vibrated inside of her.

"I am always with you, my life. I would never leave you or my sons. You have let emotions cloud reason, and because of this, you are all failing in your missions."

Reminda gasped as his hands covered her heart; closing her eyes, she relaxed into his embrace. For a second, she could smell him; she inhaled, trying to attach him to her.

Drakko chuckled. "You don't have to do that. Strip your fears. Wash away doubt, and open your mind to see things as they really should be. Tell our son I understand how he feels and he is on the right path. I support his decisions. When I was in the physical, I thought I knew everything, but now I really do, and he is on the right track. Tell him not to ignore his heart, that the Elements are with him. If he opens his eyes, he will see the answers right before him. Know that I love you, Reminda, and you have always been the best part of me…" His voice started to fade.

"Noooo…don't leave," she wailed.

"I must. You have work to do yet, and then you will understand. Search your heart, and you will feel me."

The ball winked and disappeared, leaving Reminda in total darkness.

The queen sank to the floor, her face wet with tears. Curled into a tight ball, she felt her heart expand. He was not gone, just in a place where she could not see him. If she did what she had to do, then they would be united. She felt lighter than she had in a year; the grief had lifted. She saw a mountain to climb in her head; now she knew what she had to do. Caught up in her own thoughts, she didn't hear Tulani enter the cave, her braids hanging limply from the rain.

Tulani fell to her knees. "Highness." She bowed her head reverently.

Reminda looked up, her face serene, holding out her arms. "Tulani, I have missed you."

The girl needed no more invitation. She rushed into the queen's embrace as if Reminda were her long-lost mother.

X

NAJE CRUSHED THE magon beetles to make a paste for Lord Nuen's wound. He was bound to be irritable tonight; she knew he hated drinking with Lothen. They were leaving tonight on Lothen's lead ship, traveling to Darracia. In the privacy of their rooms, he complained about the climate, the food, the customs. She knew he missed his home, perhaps even what was left of his family. They didn't share much. Glancing at the floor, she spied a box of graphen packets sticking out. Cursing softly, she kicked at it gently, pushing it in so it wouldn't be seen. She planned on taking them on board the ship, and that was definitely against the law. Pausing, she reached down, took a few of them, and slid them underneath her shirt, next to her breast. Dangerous, yes, but necessary, and at least she was armed somewhat. If she threw them against a wall with force, they would explode, giving her some sort of security.

She parted the curtains to look at the dying light, wondering if her sister knew she was relatively safe. Poor Denita, how would she manage without her? Denita was the youngest, though she was not a child, but she knew nothing of graphen or the business of a den. The graphen den did not belong to her. Denita was always the protected one. They had wanted a better life for her; Naje had been saving to get her off the planet and into an academy. Anything but staying on the cesspit they called home. After their parents died in the Fever of '27, she sold their butcher stalls. They had been one of the numerous purveyors of different meats on Venturian. Denita moved into the back of her sister's den. It wasn't what anybody wanted. It was a dirty trade, and she wasn't proud of it.

The business had been purchased by her husband, Racin, killed, like her dreams, by his dependence on the drug, leaving her a poor widow running a vice-infested store. Did she miss him, she wondered, cocking her head, her dark hair falling to the side of her face. She supposed not. They had married young, before they really knew each other. She had wanted to get away from the meat stalls, her overbearing father, and escape to start her life. Well, the graphen den was no escape, especially when Racin started using. He became addicted so quickly, so thoroughly, that soon he was smoking more than they could afford. Oh, she could have left him, but for what, to go home and tell her father he was right? Instead, she ran the shop, widowed young and cutting the graphen to make it stretch. She almost welcomed the invaders when they took her away.

Slicing some fruit, she knew it would refresh Nuen and perhaps put him in a better mood. He thought he was tough, Lord Nuen. Cried like a baby when she didn't give him graphen. She had this forbidden stash of it hidden away. Highly unstable, it was not allowed on anything except for transport vehicles; certainly they'd kill her if they knew she had some on a royal barge. She could blow them all to Venturian and back with the amount she had.

Staf was easy to handle now that she knew his inner demons. Compared to the animals she handled in the graphen den, he was putty in her hands. As long as she anticipated his needs, he was relatively easy. She played up her hatred in front of Lothen, though. She would die before submitting to him again. The Planta leader was vicious, cunning and without a soul. She hated him and would have killed him if she could have found a way. He was as ruthless as he was deceitful, and she knew nobody should turn their back on him.

The door slid open, and Staf entered without a word. He grunted some sort of greeting as he threw himself into his chair. Naje reached forward wordlessly to remove his boots and smiled slyly at his sigh of relief. Staf rolled his head back on the cushion, his eyes bleary.

"Your head aches, my lord?"

She placed her cool hands on his temples and kneaded them. His eyes were too yellow, and if he didn't stop, he would soon be too far gone with graphen. Though he was relaxed, his sharp eyes observed her.

"I don't know why I like you."

"Don't you?" she asked, and smiled at Staf.

"I was married to a princess. Beatha was granddaughter to a king."

"You can call a hag a beautiful." Naje shrugged. "But at the end of the day, she is still a hag."

Staf laughed, grabbed her hand, and kissed her wrist.

"Indeed, she was a hag." He pulled her onto his lap.

"I am not a princess." Naje eyed him, pulling away.

Staf hugged her against him. "But you are beautiful." He kissed her full on the mouth, smiling with triumph as her lips softened. "So beautiful."

"But, alas"—she raised herself, holding his head with both her hands—"still a slave."

"You are mine," Staf whispered possessively, and the discussion was finished.

♦

Mere hours later Staf found himself on the bridge of Lothen's light cruiser. The Plantan leader had three ships under his command as he embarked on the two-day journey to Darracia. Naje watched Planta shrink as they ate up the miles to deeper space. She was happy to see the back end of it. It was a filthy place, the sea a churning mass of acid, the landmass a tiny wasteland. It rivaled Venturian for its lack of charm, and although a better climate, the recent global warming from the pollution had made going outside impossible.

The ships flew in a defensive formation, the king in the lead vessel. They were by no means large or considered capable of intergalactic travel, but they were able to land stealthily on the sea, surprising and then destroying their victims before they had a chance to retaliate. The ships were triangular, with easy maneuverability. They were known to zip in, create panic, steal what they needed, and take what they wanted. The Plantans painted the bows of their ships with fantastical creatures with frightening expressions. With mostly a male crew, Lothen balked when Staf insisted on taking Naje.

"She is a slave, my lord. You will get another," Lothen told him.

"I don't want another," Staf replied with finality.

He kept her in his quarters, away from the bloodthirsty crew. Naje happily complied. She was there when Staf swaggered in, high from graphen, furious with Lothen for encouraging its use. Already, she had seen the Darracian's hands shaking when he needed the drug, and although she warned him with long looks, he ignored her pleas. She shouldn't care, she knew, but oddly enough, she liked him. He had an aura of power; as opposed to the waste of a male she had had for a husband, she felt that with Staf she had a future, if he didn't kill himself with graphen first. As long as she kept him under control, he'd be fine. She shrugged. If he needed the drug, she would get it for him, but on her terms and in the dose that would keep him under her thumb and useful.

"What is the matter, my lord?" she asked as he stared sullenly out the portal into deep space.

"Geva. What do you know of their Geva?"

"I know nothing." She kneeled and took hold of his face as he reclined on his chair. "And neither do you!" she said urgently.

"She is foul and evil. Please," Naje begged him, "do not go to her altar."

Staf sighed as he looked bleakly out the window.

"Staf," she whispered, "she will steal your soul…"

XI

"I CAN ARRANGE for a transport to take you to the surface, Your Majesty." The stable master followed V'sair as he leaped into Hother's saddle.

"No. I told you, I am going riding." V'sair dismissed him, turning his mount toward the openings. It was still pouring. He didn't care. His mother had gone down to the surface hours ago; he was going after her. He was sick of Syos and all of its inhabitants. He had just come from another meeting with Chanter Brault, and their heated argument frustrated V'sair. It had started innocently enough, first with a service in the temple, followed by a discussion in the chanter's office. He respected the counselor about as much as the chanter liked V'sair. He missed the steady influence of Emmicus. Something in the older man's eyes made him uneasy, and V'sair was beginning to have a decided lack of trust in him.

It was the same old thing as far as the young king was concerned. The chanter was white with rage over the idea of a Quyroo crowning him. V'sair was tired of it all. Nothing was smooth. Even the relationship with his father's most loyal servant, General Swart, felt strained. He knew the old man meant well; it was just that his ideas were antiquated. He was clinging to the obsolete notion of the Fireblade and Darracian strength. Sometimes it was too hard to keep swimming against the tide. He missed Tulani and her comforting arms with an intenseness that bordered on pain.

He turned to the four guards saddling their stalliuses behind him. "No! You are to stay here," he ordered them.

"Sorry, Highness." One of them bowed his head respectfully. "We've been ordered to stay close to you by General Swart."

"It's fine. I will be fine, and I dismiss you."

"He will have our heads." The soldier shrugged, his eyes forlorn. "We will keep a distance," he offered, his palm up.

V'sair gave in as ungraciously as any twenty-year-old feeling burdened by unwanted watchdogs. "If you must." He wheeled out of the stables quickly, smiling at his deft maneuvering, thinking he had lost them for a minute. The sky was deserted, the weather making most travel impossible. He heard the labored breathing of their mounts when they tried to make up the growing distance, Hother easily outdistancing them as she ate up the miles.

The rain stopped and the sky brightened, the dual

rays of Rast and Nost creating a halo of light. A rainbow sprang up over Syos, painting the horizon a multicolored hue that framed the dormant volcano. He guided Hother toward the Desa. Brilliant sunlight blinded him momentarily; he heard the whickers of several stalliuses behind him. They said they would keep their distance, he thought with fury. He spun, rigid with anger, to come face-to-face with General Vekin, his father's other trusted advisor. The older man had never recovered from the battle for Darracia. His left arm hung uselessly at his side. He had lost three of his sons, leaving him without an heir. A fog of sadness surrounded him. His voice, raspy from a wound to his throat, stopped V'sair's progress to escape.

"Relax, Highness." The older man halted him with a raised hand. "Cannot you spare some conversation for an old friend?" He paused and gazed at the young man. "We used to be good friends, V'sair."

V'sair tapped his pommel and sidled up next to the wizened man. He smiled warmly to the wrinkled face, fond memories of playing soldier with the general reminding him of the relationship.

General Vekin motioned for his own men to leave. "Give us space." He motioned for them to fly in a formation a bit away from them.

Together they began a leisurely flight, their stalliuses gliding together in a ballet of synchronization. They floated through the pink and orange clouds, above the condensation, so that they heard the muffled sounds of the Desa beneath them. Hanging in suspension, they galloped over the Hixom Sea, watching the flying fish jump into the wet atmosphere.

"This weather seems to be here for good," the general observed.

"It makes the Desa bloom." V'sair pointed to the lush red foliage populating the hills. It appeared even denser than his last visit. Tulani was down there somewhere.

"You always find the good in everything, V'sair," Vekin stated kindly, then sighed.

"What troubles you, General?"

"I have news." The general reached into his tunic and pulled out a white paper.

V'sair reached across to take the paper. He read it quickly, then crumbled it into a tight ball, his mouth down turned into a narrow white line. "I am not surprised," he said through gritted teeth.

"I don't know how much time you have, but you must act quickly." General Vekin grabbed his arm.

"You are with me?" V'sair looked him full in the face.

"You had to ask?" The general's stallius moved restlessly as she neighed.

"I have to get my mother. I will be back very soon."

Vekin wheeled his mount toward the castle gleaming in the suns, the polished surface blinding his eyes. "I will mobilize."

V'sair held out his hand, clasping the general's in a firm embrace. "I will never forget this."

Vekin nodded and turned to the castle.

XII

V'SAIR URGED HOTHER downward toward the hills leading to the hulking great outline of Aqin. It was raining in earnest, and he was soaked, the chill creeping under his tunic to settle in his bones.

He landed hard in the mud, Hother skidding, coming to rest up to her knees in the soft earth of the planet. She looked like a different animal, her white coat speckled red, like a wild hybrid stallius. After jumping off, he sank deeply to his thighs. Rain dripped off the canopy of leaves to run in icy tracks under the back of his shirt. His white hair was plastered to his forehead; his clothes stuck to him like a second skin. He looked around to get his bearings, unsure because of the dense gloom. The Desa was hushed, the rain pattered on the leaves, and V'sair heard nothing, not a bird, frog, or keewalla monkey. Wrapping the reins around his hand, he whispered for

Hother to follow him up the steep incline toward the secret entrance Bobbien had taught him to use.

If it was quiet before, it became deathly still, not a breeze, as if the entire world was holding its breath. Even the gentle whine of insects ceased. V'sair turned his head, trying to figure out what he was hearing. A roar as loud as a thousand cannon rent the air, getting closer. V'sair spun, his feet stuck in the mud, only to lose his balance and fall hard on his elbows. In the distance he saw a rushing wall of water, as if the bowels of the earth had opened. It was a swirling mass, its sound magnified by the echoing wall of the canyon until it deafened him. V'sair opened his mouth in a soundless scream; he pulled at his feet, which uselessly sank, trapped in muddy shackles.

He looked around wildly, knowing there was no escape. Turning, he slapped Hother hard on the butt. She reared, her eyes rolling, but wouldn't leave. "I will weigh you down, you stupid beast!" He grabbed a stick and whipped her flank, watching with relief as she opened her vast wings to lift off above the impending disaster. He pointed upward, and his mount obeyed. V'sair watched sadly as his only avenue of escape floated upward.

The water shook the ground, and the spray splashed his face. Licking his lips, he realized it was salty, and he wondered where the seawater was coming from. Turning to meet his destiny, ready to accept fate head-on, he stared boldly at the churning mass of gray seawater barreling through the Desa, flattening everything in its path save the oldest and strongest of the trees. Taking a deep breath, he parted his mouth to meet the Great Sradda with a song on his lips, when he was grabbed under the armpits and lifted violently, his feet sucked out of the thick mud painfully. Airborne, he tried to turn his head but saw only that it was a Quyroo male and he was being propelled through the tangle of vines at a dizzying speed.

"Who are you?" he called out, watching the force of water travel on a destructive path toward the volcano. He heard only labored breathing and knew he had been snatched from impending death by this savior.

The Quyroo slowed, coming to rest in the lee of a tree that was so tall it grazed the clouds. V'sair looked up, seeing Hother circling above them, a smile splitting his face. He started to laugh and heard the Quyroo laugh right along with him, their bodies shaking with relief. He felt the weight of the branch dip and knew another Quyroo had joined them.

"This is getting to be too much, my lord," a familiar voice told him.

"Bobbien!" he shouted with joy. He turned to identify the man holding him. "Do I know you?" "Your Majesty." The officer bowed.

"I do not think we have met." V'sair studied his handsome face. He was big, his royal infantry uniform stretched across impossibly large shoulders.

"I am Seren." The huge Quyroo nodded.

"I have to get to the volcano—my mother is there." V'sair reached out for a vine to leave.

The native shook his head. "I am sorry, my lord. There is no way to get there until the water recedes.

This area is my responsibility. General Vekin asked me to watch out for you. I saw you and the stallius on the mountain ridge struggling with the mud."

"No." V'sair tried to free himself of the iron grip. The talon-like hands held fast. "My mother…"

"I am sorry, Your Majesty. We have to wait for the water to leave before we can examine the volcano entrance. It is unsafe. Those are my orders."

"You think I don't want to go there?" Bobbien demanded, grabbing the front of his tunic, her face pink with fear. "Tulani is down there too," she choked out, her voice thick. "Watch, watch. The water is leaving." She pointed with her staff.

XIII

DENITA FUMED ANGRILY as Zayden's capable hands belted her properly into her seat. "Let me out of here, you oversized ape. I should have let you die back there!" she spit angrily.

Zayden cinched the belt tighter, laughing when Denita turned as red as a Quyroo. He chucked her under the chin, which only inflamed her. "I'm taking you to my stepmother."

"Over my dead body."

"That could be arranged," Zayden replied as he jumped into his seat. The engines roared to life, and once again he heard Denita pounding the glass partition. "What…What…? I can't hear you." He chuckled, placing his headset over his ears. He did hear her curses and took off steeply, knowing she was pressed uncomfortably in her seat. That ought to shut her up, he thought, hearing the screams change to retching. *Not a great flyer, our Denita.* He smiled as he steered his compact ship toward the rising suns of Darracia.

They drifted through the nebula, Zayden enjoying the peace of the void of space. It was a small ship and made a lot of people nervous—not much metal separated a passenger from the nothingness of the outside. Zayden felt lighter for the first time in a while. Much to his relief, Denita's screams had died down to sullen silence. He admitted he felt a bit bad for her. He was an independent person and understood her need to control her own life, but he was going to go after Staf, and he couldn't do it with an encumbrance. He knew he could really dump her anywhere. She was a big girl; it was also clear she could fend for herself. If only he didn't feel so responsible for her.

"Look, General. I'll spring your sister. What's her name?" The silence had finally gotten to him, and he threw out a peace offering.

"I don't need your help, Warrior. When I get the chance, I'm going to finish what the Plantans started!" she shouted, her face a mask of rage.

He looked at her indulgently and replied, "You're kind of cute when you're mad."

She sputtered furiously, "I don't need your stinking Fireblade—I'm going to kill you with these!" She held up her clenched hands, her face a grimace.

"Get in line, General," he replied as he swung left, heading toward the haven of home.

◆

They observed a few convoys, mostly truckers hauling products from one end of the solar system to the other. Many of the planets had to rely on these outsourced vendors. Most of the societies weren't rich enough for more than just the wealthy to have ships. On Darracia, only the richest had ships that could travel outside the atmosphere of their own home, let alone travel to other planets. Zayden lazed the day away, making notes on weather conditions, and pulled into Pagil 7 to refuel. It was a rowdy space station owned by a bigshot company outside their solar system. He remembered that his father had negotiated rates with them, and though he felt a lump in his throat, it didn't pack the punch it had when he thought about him before. In fact, he realized with surprise, he hadn't thought about Hilde for a few days either. He looked back at Denita's angry face, asked if she wanted to grab a bite, and told her it wouldn't have to be silver crab.

They disembarked; Zayden lifted Denita from her seat, marveling at her tiny waist. A mechanic rushed past him, pushing the big Darracian. Zayden grabbed Denita close to him to prevent them both from falling. The world narrowed to the two of them as her hands gripped his shoulders tightly. Denita's tongue touched her lips, her eyes holding Zayden's in a lock more powerful than a force field. Her long-lashed eyes closed for an instant, and he leaned forward to caress her lips with his own, lightly grazing her. Denita grabbed his braid to pull his face close to kiss him with a desperation born from loneliness. Zayden's hard body wrapped naturally around her softer one. Their skin melted together as though it had familiar memories matching up like puzzle pieces cut exclusively for the other.

The sound of the bustling terminal coupled with the cry of "Get a room already!" broke the mood, and Zayden felt his face heat with embarrassment. He lowered her to the floor, took her hand, and said, "I'm sorry. I didn't mean to do that."

Denita looked him hard in the face and replied, "Well, I did."

The restaurant was typical spaceport food—greasy mystery products from all ends of the galaxy and just about as old. Zayden approached her with a tray laden with an array of products, but they picked over the disgusting containers and smelly wrapping, hardly eating at all.

"The food here is prehistoric." Zayden hit the table with stale bread, watching bugs march fearlessly across the surface to feast on his crumbs.

Denita's face curled into a disgusted frown, and he marveled at her tiny nose, thinking it made her adorable. She wasn't a bad-looking female, he mused. In fact—he watched her intently—she was rather beautiful.

He sipped his steaming chay, while Denita drank the beverage native to her home, a white, overly sweet liquid that made his bile rise.

Denita watched his stern face softening and figured she might have a shot at making him take her. "You have to take me with you," she informed him over the din of the place. "It's not safe. I can't worry about you and do what needs to be done. Look," he said with a conciliatory smile, "you're going to like Reminda. She's a great lady, and besides, how many of your friends can say they hung out with a queen?"

"I don't have any friends. You need me." She pounded the table, her brown eyes imploring him. She had a white mustache rimming her lips, and Zayden's own eye caressed her face. Reaching out, he wiped her top lip with a gentle finger.

"I wish I could, but it's just not safe. I will bring your sister back to you. I promise."

He purchased her a change of clothing and arranged for them both to be able to bathe. Her boots were shot from the sand of Fon Reni, so he replaced them too. He left her at the female spa while he went to the baths for a cleanup as well. He didn't want to deliver a ragamuffin to his stepmother, and he wondered why it suddenly mattered so much. Zayden's fingers touched the tattoo embedded in his shoulder. The swirls beckoned him with the same hypnotic effect as the desire in Denita's eyes. Closing his eye, he pictured her creamy caramel skin, accepting the responsibility to keep her safe. He would never let a female put herself in harm's way again. He allowed himself to be shaved and his hair trimmed, and enjoyed the steaming water more than he had expected.

Denita gave herself up to the fancy, high-priced attendants. She had never been so pampered in all her life.

Venturian was so cold that rarely did one get a

chance to bathe more than one part of the body. Hair was washed monthly, the cost of heating water too dear.

The perfumed water coated her skin, making it feel and look like a golden pelt. Her hair floated silkily, and when they came to take her out, she refused the first time, enjoying the cocooning warmth of the steaming bath. She sat in the pool, listening to the piped-in music, wondering how she was ever going to return to Venturian. Cupping her hands, she poured a waterfall of soapy liquid over her head, inhaling the flowery essence, thinking of Zayden's soft lips and the way his hands had felt as he held her against him. Her skin tingled with desire, yet she was angry at Zayden. There was no way she was going to let him go to Planta without her. She realized with a start that she couldn't live if something happened to him.

They met outside the spa, and Zayden blinked, his amber eye wide with surprise. Denita's hair framed her café au lait face, feathered in a new style. He had thought her hair black but now realized there was a symphony of browns and golds streaking through the wavy locks. She wore a tight gray pantsuit that emphasized her coltish legs.

"Denita, you look…good." Zayden swallowed.

Denita stared at his wide shoulders encased in a darkblue tunic. He was so tall, his powerful tail peeking through the back of his pants. Denita reached up to touch his scarred face. Zayden pulled away, but she placed her palm gently on the ruined skin, her fingers leaving a trail of gentleness in their wake. Zayden closed his eye, and when he opened it, it was to see Denita's face close to his own. Her lips pressed against his, and he felt her lips moving.

"You are mine, Warrior, and don't you forget it."

He grabbed her hand, walking briskly to his ship. He had to get her to Reminda, and fast.

XIV

STAF'S YELLOWED EYES observed the large screen in Lothen's bridge. The Plantan leader sat in his chair, his long legs stretched out before him. They didn't allow graphen on the ship, yet Naje had managed to smuggle some on board, and he smoked it alone in his quarters. He smiled thinking of her seductive smile and sultry eyes.

"We will be passing the space station momentarily." Lothen pointed to a huge doughnut-shaped wheel rotating in a circle.

"It's a dump." Staf laughed. "Don't drink the chay. I hear it's made from recycled piss."

"Everything is recycled. I wouldn't eat anything there," Lothen agreed.

This, coming from a being who ate live species

from his planet, made Staf laugh with abandon. Lothen watched him coolly.

"We amuse you, my lord?"

"More than you realize," Staf acknowledged.

"Perhaps you will share what humors you?" Lothen asked in the deathly silence of the bridge.

The station was surrounded by docked ships. Staf had been watching as some attached themselves for a landing and others departed in many different ways. It was an important way station, and he and his brother had argued over it for years. He had wanted a piece of the profits. It bordered Darracian territory. Drakko wouldn't hear of it. He didn't want the responsibility; his brother only worried about the Quyroos and their issues. He never saw the bigger picture. A small craft detached from the landing bay, its tight lines and green and blue stripes unmistakable. Staf leaned forward, his hands gripping a rail, a growl erupting from his throat.

"Look." Staf pointed to a small ship leaving the spaceport. "It cannot be…"

Lothen sat forward to observe. "What is it, my lord?"

"Zayden! I would know his ship anywhere."

"Who?"

"The king's bastard, Zayden of Darracia. Get him!" he ordered, superseding Lothen's authority.

The helmsman glanced in question to the king, who nodded in assent. "Follow them. Now!"

◆

Zayden looked up and did a double take when he realized a painted Plantan cruiser was bearing down on him at a dangerous speed. Flipping his switches to fire up his turbos, he called back to Denita, "Hang on! This may get bumpy." Pressing the throttle to the max, he felt his spine press back into the curve of his seat as the ship jumped into its hyperspeed. The stars elongated into white strips as he zipped into a vortex of speed, hoping to escape the murderous intent of the enemy ship.

Glancing backward, he realized the Plantans had not only followed him but were fast eating up the distance to his ship. With more powerful engines, they overpowered him, and his craft lurched as a powerful tractor beam attached itself, then started to pull them into its gaping maw.

Zayden wondered why the Plantans had targeted him. While they were lifelong enemies, they seldom bothered with small recreational craft, waiting to attack the fatter pickings of the large cargo ships. Well, he thought with chagrin, V'sair would just have to pay the ransom. Then he would be free once more to resume his search for Staf.

The ship was sucked into a landing bay, and once he saw Plantans surround his ship, he knew the atmosphere had been normalized. He pressed the mechanism to open the glass hood, unstrapped himself, and climbed onto the wing of his ship.

"What do you want from me?" Zayden demanded.

"That depends," came the gravelly baritone he knew so well. "That depends on how much you are willing to take."

A shot rang out, and Zayden heard a scream, but as he tumbled from his ship, he didn't remember if it was Hilde's or Denita's.

XV

"I HAVE MISSED you so, child." Reminda held Tulani's face in her hands and kissed both her cheeks.

"Oh, Your Majesty, me too!" Tulani replied, her eyes glistening with tears. "I think I am ready to join you. Maybe I can accomplish more from Syos than I can from here." She paused, her face horror-struck as if a thought had just occurred to her. "I mean, that is, if you still want me?"

"Want you?" Reminda smiled. "Silly girl. If V'sair doesn't marry you, I will!" Reminda laughed at the absurdity.

"I cannot break the barriers here; they will not accept me as one of their own."

"I understand more than you realize, Tulani," Reminda said sympathetically. The rain battered against the walls of the volcano, and she shivered. Turning her head toward a sound, she asked, "What is that?"

Tulani stood, looking at the mouth of the tunnel. "I don't know. It sounds like a mudslide." She pressed her ear to the wall, but did not feel the heat of Ozre, or recognize the new sound.

"Oh heavenly Sradda!" Reminda's eyes widened in her pale face. "Look!"

A wall of water was rushing through the corridors of the volcano, bright green with ocean foam. Uprooted red trees floated in eddies of the whirlpools. There was no other escape; they were trapped, Tulani thought wildly. The safety of Aqin had turned into a prison. Tulani raced to a forest of stalagmites to climb to safety. She reached out to Reminda.

"Hurry! Get as high as you can go!" she called out over the deafening sound of rushing water.

Reminda's personal guard swirled in, reaching out to cling to anything that would hold them. She heard their helpless shouts and watched them tumble out of view. Tulani grabbed Reminda's wrist, and using her Quyroo strength, she hauled her up, almost losing her as the water gushed through the cavern in a violent wave.

"Hold on," she cried out as she climbed up the stalagmite, her fingernails tearing as she scraped them against the hard surface. Reminda's face was white as fallen snow, her hand just as cold. She shook her, urging, "Stay with me, Your Highness…Reminda!"

She pulled her up so they were face-to-face, clinging to the structure. The queen's eyes had narrowed to slits, a cut high on her cheek, blood flowing freely. As their feet dangled, the water surged higher, until they were covered to their chins. Water invaded their mouths; they both retched and choked, pushing up their chins to escape the rising tide. Reminda slipped under the foamy seawater. Tulani scrambled to get her back, but the queen disappeared under the swirling mass of violent waves.

"Oh no," she wailed, holding tight to her stalagmite, her skin rubbed raw by the abrasive surface. Sobs racked her body, and she pressed her face into the damp rock, angry. She cursed the Elements, she cursed Ozre, and she cried for her lost friend. The air was sucked out of the room as she inched higher to the ceiling, the water dangerously close to her mouth. Light-headed and weak with grief, she held on to the structure, her body wrapped so tightly she shivered with numbing cold. A webbed hand grabbed her arm, and Tulani screamed as if a thousand wysbies had stung her. The manicured fingers squeezed her encouragingly, and she turned around, reaching down to press her shoulder into the queen's armpit.

"Oh, my lady, are you all right?"

"Did you forget," Reminda choked out between spasms of coughing, "did you forget I yet have my gills?"

"Gills?" Tulani asked stupidly, her long lashes crusted with the salt from the ocean water.

"I am Plantan. We have gills. However, life in the clouds has weakened them. What's happening?" Reminda gasped.

"I don't know. Great, sweet Sradda, preserve us. Ozre, Ozre save us!" Tulani's voice echoed off the wet wall of the cavern.

"Courage, child" reverberated inside her head. The

water tickled the lower lip of her mouth; she gagged on the saltiness of it. Their heads were pressed to the ceiling of the chamber, the sound of their ragged breaths echoing above the waterline. The entire room was phosphorus from the minerals in the water.

"Oh Ozre, why have you forsaken me?" she asked.

The water began to recede with a great sucking sound. It pulled, dragging both Reminda and Tulani. Their arms ached from holding on, yet they stayed glued to the safety of their perches. Debris banged into them, injuring and ripping skin. Reminda heard her ribs crack, yet Tulani's soft prayers kept her holding on, despite the pain.

Soon, only the damp sound of dripping water filled the small space. They heard the tide being pulled out of the cave, and Ozre's bright light lit up their space. Tulani and the queen dropped, exhausted, to the soaking floor, their breathing harsh in the cold air.

"Do you hear me now?" Ozre demanded and disappeared, leaving them in pitch darkness.

◆

They heard V'sair's cries before they saw him. He was running into the cave, Bobbien right behind him, and a passel of Quyroo guards following. He paused at the mouth of the room, his clothes sopping wet, to double over, his hands on his knees, while he caught his breath, relief evident on his young face. Standing, he held out his arms, and both women wordlessly ran to his embrace. "You are unharmed?" he asked quietly after kissing each of their heads.

Tulani nodded but kept her face buried in his shoulder. Tears filled her eyes at his familiar smell, the warmth of his arms, the concern in his voice. *I am home,* she thought, and didn't realize she had spoken aloud until V'sair answered her, his voice a rumble in his chest. "Finally."

Bobbien went to aid a groaning soldier, motioning for the other Quyroos to help.

V'sair looked at his mother. "Are you all right?"

"I will need Bobbien to tape my ribs—no, stop, Vsos. It is nothing I can't handle. Let her see to my men first."

"Have you any idea what this was about?" V'sair asked.

Reminda looked around. "Yes…no, I am not sure. I have to think about it a bit. But let's go home—we have much to discuss."

Tulani looked at V'sair with wonder. He kissed her gently on her lips.

"I have missed you." His voice bounced off the walls of the cavern.

Tulani opened her mouth to answer him, but another gaze caught her attention. Seren stared at her, his star-shaped eyes menacing with hatred. Tulani shuddered, burying her face in V'sair's shoulder.

"You are safe, my love."

Tulani whispered that she hoped so.

XVI

A DEVIL WAS jumping from one end of Zayden's skull to the other. He heard a moan, wincing at its depths of agony, then caught his breath when he realized it came from him.

A familiar, cool hand pressed on his clammy forehead, and he heard Denita whisper, "Don't show you are awake, yet. I hear them coming."

Zayden explored their surroundings through a slit lid. He didn't need his eye to know that they were in the bowels of a ship, the great hum of randam crystals loud in their ears. Still, he glanced around, puzzled.

"It's Plantans," Denita informed him, reading his thoughts. "Shhhhh…"

He heard the door slide open, followed by the sound of booted feet.

Denita felt him tense; she reached around to press down on his shoulders, reminding him to stay quiet.

"Is he up yet?" The hated voice filled the room.

Zayden swallowed the bile that rose to the back of his throat. His body vibrated with anger, but he held himself still.

"Not yet, my lord." Zayden heard Denita's humble voice. Humble? What had they done to her—she was afraid of nothing. She squeezed him reassuringly, and he wondered what her game was.

A hand pressed down on his chest, testing his response, but he looked inward, willing himself not to move a muscle. They moved upward to clutch his face, roughly turning it as if to observe his injury. He bit back a groan, keeping silent.

"I don't like it, Staf. He's been out too long." It was a new voice, but Zayden dared not glimpse at the speaker.

"It is a serious wound, sire," Denita offered, bowing her head. "I am not a healer. His eyes move but do not open. Perhaps your bullet struck true, and he will sleep forever?"

"It is a graze only." Staf dismissed her explanation. "I know of a healer on board. She understands the ways of these things."

Zayden heard them leave, and waited a few minutes until Denita's voice cut through the pain.

"They are gone, Warrior. You can get up now."

"Some warrior I turned out to be. I couldn't even keep you safe," Zayden replied as he eased into a seated position. Black dots swam before his eyes, and he wondered if he was about to pass out again.

Denita's heart did a little flip-flop when she realized he meant to protect her, not bully her. Oh why, why, why did she not trust others' intentions? she thought ruefully.

"Oh, your nose is bleeding again!" He felt tender hands cup the bottom of his head and lean him backward to slow the bleeding. "You are a proper mess, Zayden." She chuckled. "No, don't get up yet, you dummy."

"Yes, sir, General, sir!" He gave her a half-fast salute, which pained his forehead. "Ow…ow…ow…" His eyes were closed, and he was startled when he felt her soft lips caress his.

"Better?"

Despite the pain, Zayden reached out to pull her closer to kiss her fully on the lips, their arms entwined. Denita rested her forehead against his, then kissed him again.

"Oh, this is nice!" A voice interrupted them, pulling them apart, Denita's face lighting up with joy. "Just what are your intentions with my sister?" the stunning woman demanded from the doorway.

"Naje!" Denita ran to her sister, grabbing her around the waist, tears of happiness springing to her brown eyes.

Naje hugged her fiercely, her gimlet eyes watching Zayden, who observed with a reddening face. Closing the door, she held her sister at arm's length, asking, "What are you doing here, and with a Darracian?" She glanced at the long, messy braid dangling down his back. "And a royal one at that?"

"Royal? Zayden?"

"Hardly royal." Zayden stood painfully, gripping the cot as the room spun.

"Sit…Zayden, is it?" she examined the bloody crease above his ear. "Are you Drakko's get? Oh, don't tighten up on me, you numskull. Even out in Venturian we've heard about you."

"Drakko?"

"This is the king of the Darracians' firstborn, not the prince, Denita. This is his natural son. Hold still. This is going to sting a bit."

She poured something sharp smelling over the wound near his ear, and Zayden arched with a hiss; his eyes rolled backward, and he fell forward. The women caught him with easy hands and slid him back onto the cot. Naje checked his pulse, gave a satisfied nod, and sat down on the side of the bed.

"He's out," Naje said to her little sister. "Now tell me what's going on."

Denita explained her past few weeks and then asked her sister to relay what had happened to her.

"You don't seem like a prisoner to me," Denita accused Naje, who then covered her hand affectionately.

"I would have gotten word to you if I could, Denita. Make no mistake." She got up to wrap a bandage around Zayden's head. "I am a slave here. I have no rights, but Staf has been good to me."

"You are still a slave!"

"Was I not a slave to my husband, Racin? Do you think I loved him or that horrible graphen den? Do you think I liked peddling death?"

"You are still a slave…" Denita repeated. "But no matter. I am here, and we escape together."

"You will have to. Staf means to kill you both." Naje stood. "I cannot let that happen. Do you love him?"

Denita shrugged. "What is love?"

"If you have to ask, then I have my answer," Naje told her sister. "I will let Staf kill this one and let you go," she told her matter-of-factly.

Denita grabbed her arm. "No! I...You can't. He...I won't let him die."

"So the cold Venturian heart can speak. Yes, Sister. I will have to think of something to save both you and your fallen hero."

She exited quickly, leaving Denita to wonder what else her cold Venturian heart would have to say.

◆

"I have waited so long for this. Why does not the bastard wake?" Staf demanded as he sucked the smoke from the ever-present graphen pipe.

Naje shrugged. "Why have you this need for revenge?"

She came close, wrapping her arms around his midsection.

He was mean and arbitrary, and Naje did not understand why she was drawn to him. She worried her bottom lip. "Can't you forget? There are places, my lord... There are places we can go to forget."

"What are you talking about?"

Naje pressed herself against him, holding both him and her secret close, and whispered against the back of his strong shoulder, "I am a slave to the Plantans." She rested her chin against him, trying to see his reaction, but his face was elusive. She watched the muscles tighten under his beard.

She heard a soft reply: "You are not a slave to me."

Emboldened, she went on, "As long as I am near a Plantan, I will be seen as a slave."

"You are my woman. You will be my consort."

"But not your queen." She moved away to turn and look him full in the face. "I have no future. I see no future for me. You will contract a royal marriage. Lothen will see you married to one of his pig-faced daughters. I will die alone."

Staf grabbed her by both arms. "Stop this talk! Stop it instantly!"

"I may be Lothen's slave," Naje hissed, "but I will not be yours!" She yanked free and ran from the room, leaving Staf with his graphen and his thoughts.

XVII

"I DON'T QUITE understand what Ozre was telling me," Reminda told her son from the confines of her room. "I have searched my mind but cannot find an answer."

"But he did communicate with you?" V'sair asked, filling a glass with liquid for her to drink.

"Yes." She paused, biting her lip. "It has something to do with Ereth, but what exactly, I just don't know."

V'sair nodded. "That flood was deliberate. Do you think the Elements are angry with us?"

"If they were, neither Tulani nor I would have survived. The Elements are never vengeful. You know that."

"But what could the flood signify?"

"I feel like I know; I just can't put my finger on it. If they meant to frighten me, they succeeded." Taking a shaky breath, she added, "I did not realize how long I haven't really used my gills. I have gotten lazy in the clouds."

"What use have you or anybody else for gills when you make your home in Syos? It makes no sense. I watched the whole flood from Hother's back, unable to do anything. If not for Bobbien and that captain, Seren, surely I would have perished trying to get to you."

"They have my eternal gratitude for keeping you from harm," Reminda said quietly.

"I have the bruises to show for it." V'sair smiled.

"Bobbien said only their strongest warrior was able to contain you." She motioned for him to sit beside her. "So, Tulani is finally here."

"Just in time for the coronation," he agreed. "I will make it a wedding ceremony?"

Reminda nodded regally. "It is time for you to start your dynasty. I just wish Zayden was here."

V'sair kissed his mother's forehead. "I must go, Mother. General Swart is waiting for me."

V'sair took the steps from his mother's apartments two at a time. She would be moving now, he knew. These would be Tulani's quarters within a few short weeks.

Both Swart and Vekin were waiting in his own chambers when he got there.

"You have told him?" V'sair asked the old man.

Vekin nodded but Swart spoke. "I cannot believe it. How could he betray us?" He had seen the message revealing Chanter Brault as a traitor. It detailed a coming invasion, a Plantan invasion, engineered by both his uncles. Their unlikely alliance was as disturbing as their plans to replace Staf Nuen on the throne by getting rid of V'sair.

"The problem is, we don't know how deep-rooted is this decay."

"I want to arrest him!" Swart slammed his fist against the wall. "I will flay him alive!"

"Think, General—if we arrest him, we will never know who else is a part of this. We must see this thing through.

What have you done, General Vekin?"

Vekin stood painfully, snapping his gnarled fingers so that a three-dimensional map sprang up to rotate in midair.

"We don't know where the attack will be, so I have spread our forces throughout the four continents. Division one is hidden on the lee side of Aqin." All three of them walked around the map, studying the placement of the troop. He indicated the slope of the great volcano and continued, "I have placed a regiment facing Hixom Sea. The third division, run by Seren, the new commander, is hidden in wait in the eastern provinces, and lastly, I have left the elite guards within the castle."

"Seren?" Swart asked.

"It's the new Quyroo infantry that we've created. I've given him a brevet command for his bravery in the flood. I've removed all Darracian commanders from the Quyroo forces, consolidating them into one huge fighting unit. Rather than facing the infighting within the ranks, we are keeping the two groups separate."

"Do you think that's wise?" V'sair asked, looking at a list of each unit and its commander.

Vekin shrugged. "I'd rather they fight the enemy than each other."

"A recipe for disaster!" Swart argued. "As it is, we are

spread too thin. You can't expect swords and spears to beat their guns! I wish I had cannon!"

"May I remind you, General, it was the Quyroos that stormed the castle and made it possible for us to put down the rebellion, without the aid of gunpowder. I know my uncle; he would never use cowardly means to retake Darracia. He will never be able to keep it that way. Besides, there is no missile or ammunition capable of penetrating our dense rocks." V'sair's blue eyes bore into General Swart.

"That may be so, Your Highness. You know my thoughts on the matter."

"I will go over the battle plans with each individual commander, but I fear to bring them together until we root out the traitors," Vekin added. "I know they are waiting.

Waiting for a signal."

V'sair sighed. "As long as we remain a planet divided, there will not be peace within."

"As long as your uncle is on the loose, there will be no peace anywhere," Swart told him grimly.

◆

V'sair knocked gently on the door to Tulani's quarters. He was admitted by Bobbien, who smiled and said, "I go to your lady mother now. I must then return to the Desa. I have work to do, you know." She pressed her hand flat on his chest. "Are we friends again, Your Highness?"

"Don't ever do that to me again!" he told her sternly.

"You could have told Seren to let me go. I know a Quyroo will listen to a high priestess over a king."

"Things have changed in the Desa. I don't know if anyone hears me anymore. Besides, I changed your diapers, quite a few times." She chuckled. "You may be king, but to me, well, it is different."

"Greanam!" Tulani hissed. "Some respect for the king, if you please." She reached out to pull him deeper into the room, her lips moist and inviting. V'sair needed no more invitation.

They heard Bobbien's boisterous laughter all the way down the halls.

V'sair embraced Tulani, his lips kissing her temple, her cheek, then finally her lips. She moaned with pleasure, pulling his shirt free so their skin could touch. She ran her hand nimbly up his strong back. V'sair gasped with pleasure as their skin molded. He pushed his face into the soft skin of her neck and inhaled her fresh scent. Tears leaked from the corners of her eyes, and V'sair stopped to push her chin up.

"Tears?"

"I am happy...I feel whole once more." It was hard to speak with the king nuzzling her neck. She felt her skin come alive, tingling from head to toe, and wanted nothing more than to touch him all over.

He hugged her tightly. "I know. I know." Their lips met again for a soul-searing kiss that seemed to last forever. They parted for a second, their breathing harsh. "I have to stop, or I won't be able to..."

"I don't know if I want you to stop," Tulani whispered, her eyes bright pools of longing in her face.

"I have to go—there is a battle looming."

"A battle?"

"Yes. Staf is planning an invasion." He pulled her deeper into the room, his lips close to her ear. "There is a traitor." "Who?" Tulani searched his face.

"Chanter Brault."

"The chanter!" Tulani whispered. "Have you arrested him?"

V'sair pressed his fingers over her sensitive lips. "Not yet. We are waiting to flush out his accomplices. We are not sure where or when the invasion starts, but we are mobilizing."

"I am scared."

V'sair cupped her face. "One last battle and then we will be divided no more, not Darracian, not Quyroo. You and I"—he kissed her deeply—"will unite the planet and bring forth an age of peace and prosperity."

"But the battle-"

"Will be over and the threat gone. We will prevail, Tulani." He kissed her thoroughly, leaving her knees weak, her heart beating a frantic tattoo. She watched his broad shoulders longingly as he left the room.

She touched her bee-stung lips, the taste of him lingering.

"How do you know?" she managed to ask the empty room after he left.

XVIII

STAF WATCHED DARRACIA fill the screen as they entered the planet's atmosphere.

"We arrive," he said with satisfaction.

Lothen stood impatiently. "We have hours yet. I am waiting to hear from my contact. It is time to introduce you to Geva."

It had been cold between the two leaders since they captured Zayden. Lothen simmered about the remark Staf had made. Plantans had an excess of pride that rankled him. They walked together toward a room beyond Lothen's quarters.

It was larger than Staf expected. A caldron stood in the front, bloodstains dripping down its sides. Lothen motioned for Staf to stand next to him. Covering his face with his webbed hands, Lothen called out with weird clicks of his tongue, sounding much like the giant fish that swam in the Hixom Sea. The room was freezing, the frost clouding before their lips. A keening wail sounding like one hundred voices answered Lothen's call, filling the room so loudly that Staf covered his ears. Lights flashed; electric charges similar to jagged lightning sparked around the room, followed by kettle-like clanging so loud it hurt Staf's ears. It vibrated through his entire body, thumping in time to his startled heart. Staf was afraid he'd never hear again.

Lothen pulled out an X-shaped dagger and slit his palm from one end to another. His eyes were so glazed they appeared white. He held his hand in the air, cocked his head, and turned to Staf. Swiftly, without warning, he grabbed Staf's palm, slicing quickly, opening it as well. Staf hissed with pain, and would have slapped him, but the Plantan pressed their palms together. Instantly, they sizzled, and the room filled with the odor of burned flesh. A charge coursed between their bodies, sending them into a vortex of exquisite pain. Staf saw himself from outside his body, levitating, hand pressed to hand, as they began to spin in a dizzying circle. The room erupted into a kaleidoscope of neon colors, the light penetrating his retina to stain his brain. He heard wild laughter, wondered whose it was, and considered that this far exceeded any graphen vision he'd experienced. As they slowed, a black cloud gathered above them to settle over their heads, lazily changing into the shape of a woman, her head covered with a nest of squirming snakes. She had bottomless black pits for eyes, and a mouth with hundreds of sharp, pointed teeth. Staf closed his eyes from the pain of the scorched palms. He expected the vision to disappear when he reopened them. He heard her laughter first; it was an evil thing, raking through his head, clutching his heart. Staf's knees weakened, and his legs would have buckled if Lothen had not held him up.

"He is one of us, Geva." Lothen spoke triumphantly.

"Staf Nuen," she said, her voice a nasal whine. "We have waited for you to join our legions."

He felt the hot gaze of the monster on his face.

"You are a welcome addition to our army," she added. "The dark forces have been waiting for you."

Staf was speechless. He stared openmouthed, no words coming out.

"Kiss him, Lothen. Give him the kiss of Geva." The thing glowed red, the snakes on her head hissing and spitting.

Lothen grabbed his face, kissing him full on the lips. Staf felt his breath sucked out of his mouth, his body emptying completely. His knew his blood was gone, his bones so brittle that if touched, they would turn to dust. His head was hollow, his skin a dry shell covering his depleted body. From sightless eyes, he watched Geva grow until she took up the entire room. Lothen still held his face, his palms caressing his numb cheeks, an evil smile on his face. Taking a deep breath, Staf felt himself fill up with the fetid air and knew he was back, but something was different.

"You and I are one," Lothen told him. "Your soul belongs to Geva. We will rule the galaxy in her name."

He released Staf, whose boneless body weakly leaned against a wall.

Lothen turned to the revolting creature. "Thy will is done." He knelt reverently. Glancing up at Staf, he said plainly, "Kneel. Kneel to your new goddess and know in her hands is your destiny."

XIX

"WHAT HAPPENED?" ZAYDEN groaned as he sat up. "Did I pass out?"

"Like a little girl." Denita rolled her eyes. "You better?"

Zayden got up slowly and rolled off the cot to examine the door for a way out.

"Yes, we have to get out of here."

"My sister is going to get us out."

"How do you know?" Zayden walked the perimeters of the room, looking for escape routes.

"She's my sister; she is eminently resourceful," Denita told him, as if that would be enough.

Zayden hauled himself up to open a vent. It was stuck fast. He searched the room, looking for something to pry it open.

"What do you need?" Denita asked.

"Something sharp," Zayden said absently.

The door rattled, then opened, Naje framed in the hallway, her face tense with fear. "This way…" she urged.

They raced through the corridors, toward a landing bay, through the lower decks of the ship.

"You have but a small window of time," Naje told them breathlessly over her shoulder. "Leave Darracia. Go back toward Venturian. Forget this place."

Zayden shook his head. "I can't. My family is here. It is my home. I have to help them."

"He may have to, but you don't." She locked her gaze with her sister's. "They will be destroyed."

Zayden shook his head. "The rocks of Darracia are too thick. Nothing will affect them. Your artillery is useless."

"It's not my artillery; this is not my fight. Lothen will call on Geva, and she will crush Darracia." They hid in a hallway, watching guards patrol.

"Geva?" Zayden asked.

"The opposite of your Elements. She is the essence of evil." She looked at Denita. "He goes to certain death if he returns to the planet surface. You could stay here with me."

"Nothing is for certain." Denita touched her arm. "You would choose slavery?"

Naje placed her hands on her abdomen. "I choose Staf Nuen."

"I don't understand you!"

"Shush! They will hear you."

"Come with us," Denita pleaded.

"I cannot." Naje shook her head. "Whatever the outcome, my fate is tied to Staf Nuen." She kissed her sister on the cheek, then pointed to the door to the landing bay.

XX

LOTHEN'S EYES GLEAMED with icy resolution. He stood on the deck of the ship, Staf next to him, and gave the command for the three ships to begin their invasion. His communication officer interrupted his thought.

"Highness…"

"Yes?"

"It is the holy man, Brault." He pressed his earpiece tightly to the side of his head, listening through the static. "He is afraid they've been found out. They have captured some spies…The first cell is dead. Every member."

"Just the first cell?"

The officer typed in a response. "He says he never met the others. He can't swear that they are all in position."

Lothen grunted, then nodded to the navigator to begin their descent.

The three triangular ships began slowly descending

onto the choppy surface of the water. Plantan strategy was to land on the Hixom Sea and bombard the city of Syos as well as the Desa. The population would gladly give up their weak king in order to have peace. He would install his puppet, Staf Nuen, on the throne, load him up with graphen, and strip Darracia of its resources. A smile of malice split Lothen's face.

"Do you give warning?" Staf asked.

"What would be the fun in that?" Lothen laughed.

"The Elements may react."

"Let them try. That is why I have Geva! Let's say hello to our new friends. On my command, begin the bombardment."

"You mean to bomb? I thought this would be a raid," Staf asked Lothen. "Darracia can withstand any siege—the city walls are impenetrable. Gunpower means nothing to us."

"I don't remember discussing strategies with you, my lord Nuen," he answered frostily.

"We never talked using guns. You said it would be like your raids on Venturian." Staf's face was red with anger.

Lothen stood with both hands reaching the ceiling. "Geva! Silence this fool!"

Staf choked, grabbing his neck, the veins popping from lack of breath. His feet left the floor as he was held up like a wet puppy to be shaken ruthlessly. Lothen snapped his webbed fingers, and Staf collapsed to his knees, breathing hard. "The Elements...the Elements do not allow..."

"To hell with your Elements! You have sold your

soul to Geva; to you, the Elements do not exist," Lothen shouted, his mouth foaming. He came close to Staf, taking his shirt in both hands. "Are you with me or against me?" he asked with a lethalness that chilled Staf.

Staf swallowed. "With you."

Lothen turned to his gunner and screamed, "Prepare to fire."

The orders were echoed, guns were aimed at the castle, and Lothen, calm once more, told his gunner, "Commence to fire."

XXI

V'SAIR HEARD ABOUT the formation of three Plantan ships landing on the Hixom Sea. He raced to the Orbitus Chamber and met up with both Vekin and Swart, his hands on his hips, deep in thought. "Did they ask permission to land?"

The room had been turned into a command center. Uniformed officers rushed in and out of the chamber, relaying messages to the various commanders. Giant screens floated in the air, static interfering with transmissions. V'sair saw Seren's worried face, explosions rocking the ground underneath him.

"What's going on?" V'sair demanded.

"They've fired on us," Vekin responded, then turned to give instructions to an aide.

"Fired on us? They are using guns?" V'sair asked incredulously.

"We have had no communication with them," Swart added.

"Have you tracked their radio signals?"

"They are trading dialogue with—"

The walls of the palace shook as a salvo blasted against its surface but did little damage.

"What are they using?" V'sair watched the missiles hit the surrounding buildings, but the red rock was dense— strong enough to withstand their firepower.

"It's old but can be quite lethal for the Desa, and our population," Vekin told him. "I will have two battalions head toward them."

"With what?" Swart yelled. "We will be obliterated. We are no match to their guns."

"The stone walls of Darracia will withstand their ammunition," V'sair said with finality.

"Our skin will not deflect their bullets!"

"It is the Desa I am worried about. Can we evacuate the Quyroos?" V'sair asked urgently.

Vekin shook his head. "Not enough time. I have sent soldiers in to guide them as deep into the Desa as they can go. Many of the older ones are stubborn and won't leave. You know how they are."

"It is their home. Bombardment is unprecedented," V'sair replied. "This is an abomination."

Swart growled, "I told you we should have bought the cannon the Pagilans offered to sell us."

V'sair ignored the older man, then glanced at the giant screen, feeling his mother's presence before she said anything. They stood together in mute horror, watching the enemy ships lob bombs into the vulnerable forests.

"Have you tried talking to them?" she asked quietly.

V'sair shook his head. The screens lit up with Quyroos running wildly from their burning homes, scrambling through the trees to escape.

"Return all the shuttles to the Desa to evacuate as many as you can," V'sair ordered.

"Sire, you may as well paint a target on their backs. The shuttles will just condense people into obvious groups for them to shoot."

"We have to do something."

"Let me go down there and speak to him," Reminda told him, her hand on his arm in appeal.

"No, Mother." He winced as another shot echoed off the strong rock wall of his fortress. He watched a spray of sparks ricochet. "It is too dangerous."

"He is my brother."

"You hardly know him."

"He is still my brother."

"I can't allow it," V'sair told her with finality.

The room was filling up with additional members of the high command. V'sair could hear his experts rapping out orders. The latest battle for Darracia had begun in earnest.

Swart came over to him and said quietly, "It is time for us to take Brault in."

"We still don't know who he is associated with."

"It hardly matters now." Swart shook his head. "He is an enemy that must be contained."

V'sair nodded in agreement and watched Swart direct his men to take the chanter into custody.

◆

Tulani looked on in wide-eyed shock as fires ripped through the Desa. Felise whimpered beside her, resting her paws on the balustrade.

"You shouldn't be out here." V'sair rested his hand on the small of her back. She turned to face him, grim faced. "Have you heard from Bobbien?"

She shook her head, a silver tear tracking down her red cheeks.

"I am sure she's fine," V'sair assured her. "I have sent my personal guard to find her."

"She is hiding from the flames. If I know her, she went inland, deep into the Desa. How many Quyroos have been killed?" she asked thickly.

"We don't have any numbers yet." He paused. "If I had known they were going to bomb, we would have evacuated the population earlier."

"Nobody expected it. I shall go down to help."

"Afterward, Tulani. We will both go down to help."

XXII

SIRENS ERUPTED ALL over the ship. Lothen turned toward his communication officer with a question on his face. "What's going on?"

"The prisoners have escaped." He held his device close to his ear, nodded, and added, "They are heading to the landing bay."

Staf grabbed his Fireblade from his side and responded, "I will kill the devil's whelp, once and for all." He stormed out of the room to finish his fight with Zayden.

Zayden, Denita, and Naje stood in the corridor, waiting for an opportunity to reach the escape door. Naje turned to her sister and said, "This is where we part." They embraced. She turned to Zayden. "Take care of her, Warrior, or I will find you."

Zayden smiled, taking Denita's hand, ready to sprint

toward his ship. He spun, coming face-to-face with his uncle, Fireblade drawn.

Zayden backed off, raising his pistol.

"You would fight me like a coward?" Staf asked silkily.

Zayden held the gun, Staf in his sights.

"Pull the trigger, Zayden!" Denita screamed.

Naje withdrew a volatile packet of graphen from under her shirt. She watched Zayden raise his weapon and yelled, "No!" throwing the small explosive to smash against the wall next to him. Upon impact, it exploded, tossing Zayden like a rag doll to land in a heap on the floor.

Staf shook his head, dazed from the explosion, saw Zayden prone on the ground, and stalked over to fillet him with his angry blade.

"Why did you do that?" Staf turned on her. "I had him." As he raised his sword for the kill, she stilled his arm. "Leave him." She gestured to the dying man. "He is finished. Blinded. See?" She pointed to Zayden's bloody face.

"Let him suffer."

"I have to finish this!" Staf shook himself free.

"Lothen will steal the throne. I know him. You must go to the deck, before he takes your birthright." She placed his palm on her abdomen. "Your son's birthright."

Staf looked down at her, his yellow eyes brightening. "You are sure?"

Naje shook her head. "Yes."

He grabbed her hand. "Come with me."

Naje put her arm through his and began walking toward the deck. Discreetly, she made eye contact with

Denita, hidden in the shadows. She mouthed, "He lives. Get to safety."

Rolling her eyes, she motioned to the escape route, Zayden's ship just past the door.

Denita watched in mute shock as her sister hustled out of the area, Staf Nuen's arm around her. Getting on her knees, she surveyed the wreck of a man and pulled him unsteadily to his feet. "Let's get out of here."

Somehow, Denita pushed and prodded Zayden into the backseat. Fingers fumbling, she belted him in. She took his face between her palms, surveying the damage. He was a bloody mess. She tried lifting his eyelid, but it was glued tight with blood. Zayden brushed her hands away with a deep moan. After sliding down the skin of the ship, she ran to a console with a board full of switches. She considered their colors and chose what she thought would be the correct control, watching in awe as the rear cargo doors parted. A blast of cold, wet air hit her in the face, and she saw they were hovering over the choppy gray sea. She hoisted herself into Zayden's bucket seat, looked at all the switches, shrugged, then started flipping everything into the on position. The radio blasted, lights blinked, and the pretty little craft jumped up to do a little spin, making her dizzy. She heard sirens and once again looked at the door in time to see a group of Plantans burst through, guns drawn and aimed at her.

"Here goes nothing!" she told no one in particular as she punched the throttle and backed into them, spilling them like toy soldiers. There were screams and a few shots.

Ducking instinctively, she twisted the knob in the other direction, projecting out of the Plantan ship like a shot. Soaring over the water, she felt the engines stall, and, cursing, she heard Zayden's weak voice.

"Use the red handle."

Looking back, she saw his bloody face—his good eye was closed, his breathing raspy.

"What?"

"The red is up; blue is down…Get it?" He turned white; his head rolled to the side.

She pushed the red throttle, smiling as the ship took off almost perpendicular to the raging sea. In the distance, she saw the walls of a beautiful city under bombardment but still amazingly whole. She knew she couldn't fly into the line of fire, so using the wheel, she turned sharply toward a giant volcano rising from a smoking red forest.

XXIII

THE BATTLE RAGED. By nightfall, many buildings were pitted by the attack but standing as strong and as solid as they had in the morning. Using ships, the Darracians sent their whole first division to attempt to board the enemy in the Hixom Sea. V'sair watched in horror as they were picked off to drown, their boats never even getting close to the alien vessels. Parts of the Desa burned; the beaches were littered with Seren's soldiers, killed in the second attempt to repel the invasion.

"This is getting nowhere." V'sair turned to his staff. "They are destroying the Desa. I will go and talk to them."

"They will kill you, and where would we be!" Swart growled. "Syos is safe."

"But the Desa is not," V'sair said miserably.

"Look." Vekin pointed to a screen showing a slender body picking her way through the carnage to reach the sea. V'sair looked at one of the many screens and realized his mother was on the beach.

"Mother," V'sair whispered despairingly, turning to follow her.

"V'sair, wait." Vekin stopped him. "Let her do this. Perhaps she can talk some sense into them. They are her species, after all."

"She is unprotected." V'sair shook his head. "Prepare Hother."

"You cannot leave, sire!" Vekin held his arm.

"This is madness. I should be there. I must be the one to negotiate with them."

"You can't negotiate with the devil!" Swart yelled. "That fat bag of wind Brault hasn't talked! We don't know who the other traitors are!"

"It doesn't matter anymore. All is lost. At least if I go to them, perhaps I can make things easier for Darracia and my people."

"You go to certain death," Vekin told him.

"In life nothing is certain except for death." V'sair ran to the stables.

◆

Reminda slid down the embankment, her white hair a beacon to her brother, who watched with interest as she approached the sandy beach.

Lothen sent a small craft for his sister and waited for her in his quarters. It was quiet now. They didn't know that he had used up most of his firepower. He was running low on ammunition. The damn city remained as upright and whole as when he started. He looked upward, calling out to Geva, his eyes hot pits of coal.

"Geva," he demanded, "does the Element have more power than you! Make these bastards fall." He pounded his chest. "My time has come! It is our covenant. Forsake not your most cherished follower."

The air around him churned, enveloping him in a gray mist, followed by a foul odor. "You dare question my power?" He heard Geva's voice fill the room. Pressure grew, and Lothen fell to his knees as if he had been slammed to the floor. "I lust for blood. Bring me blood, and I will bring you Darracia!"

"Geva commanded." Lothen bowed his head. "And I obey." He rose to look at the bombarded city in the sky, the black skyline of the burning forest. "So, Geva says it won't be long now. They have lost; we have conquered them." He didn't even think he needed his puppet, Staf Nuen, anymore. He had watched Staf preening over the slave, calling her his queen. It disgusted him, but what did he expect—the man was a graphen addict and in the thrall of the Venturian slave. He would make a gift to Geva of that one.

The door opened, and he saw his sister pushed in. He bowed with a sneer. "Ah, the mighty Reminda. Your son is not man enough to do his work."

Reminda walked in, furious. "He is ten times the man you are. He wouldn't kill innocents!"

Lothen grabbed her by her forearms, his face purple with rage. "There are no innocents!"

"Why are you doing this?"

"Oh, high-and-mighty Reminda, the good and generous queen. When did you think of anybody but your precious Drakko or Darracia? Did you ever think to do something for your homeland?"

"I asked…We tried…"

"Not hard enough."

"Father put a price on my head. What did you expect me to do?" Reminda spat. "What did you expect me to do?"

"I know what I am going to do." He pressed his intercom and threw her toward two guards who entered. "My sister wants a new career. Put her in a pod. She goes to Bina to work in the mines."

Lothen stalked past her white face, turning to sneer before he left, "Now I go to finish your son."

♦

V'sair rode Hother to the banks of the great ocean, his army below, his cavalry behind him. Dressed all in blue, with the flag of Darracia held by Swart's grandson, his standard-bearer, he approached the ships bobbing on the water. The sea had turned an odd shade of purple, swirling foam covering the choppy waves. He realized with a start, his two uncles stood united on the enemy ship, looking to overtake his home.

"Lothen?" he called out, his voice ringing through the fog.

"Here." A tall man with a war knot of ivory hair

moved in front. "Greetings, Nephew." He bowed, a mocking glint in his blue eyes. "I bring you tidings from your home planet."

"Darracia is my home planet." V'sair nodded in acknowledgement. "Where is my mother?"

"She is safe."

"I didn't ask you that! Where is she?"

"It is of no consequence. We have won. Your Elements have changed sides. Geva is the new religion here."

"What do you want from us?" V'sair called out.

Lothen laughed, smiling as a stallius cantered toward the king. "Took you long enough." He spoke to the Quyroo riding toward the king, his voice carrying over the distance.

"I was detained; forgive me, sire." Seren jumped off his stallius to kneel toward the ship. He pointed a gun at V'sair's heart. "You are invited to join your uncles on the ship, V'sair," he sneered.

Fireblades were drawn as two Darracian soldiers jumped from their mounts.

"Do anything, and your king dies." Seren turned to V'sair. "They have your mother. King Lothen has told me to tell you that if you do anything, she will die, and die painfully."

"Seren! Why? We gave you a command of your own." Seren walked over to V'sair. "You poached on the Quyroo preserve. Tulani will never be yours."

V'sair slid off Hother and gave the reins to his standardbearer. "Take her." He followed Seren to the launch to take him to the Plantan ship.

XXIV

THE SMALL CRAFT careened over the smoking forest, bumping into trees. With each thump, she heard Zayden groan painfully.

Denita scanned for a patch of meadow or grass to attempt a landing. It was all just one jumble of red; she could barely distinguish anything in the gloom. The ship lurched, the wing clipped by an outcropping of rocks, sending it into a spin. Bile rose to the back of Denita's throat when they rotated upside down to hang suspended for a minute before the engines died and they began to spiral down. Locking her arms rigidly, she wrestled with the wheel, trying to right the craft, but it wouldn't budge

The monochromatic wall of trees sped past her, tears gathering in her eyes at her and Zayden's helplessness. Something grabbed the ship, halting it in a springlike motion, and it bounced nauseatingly in a trap, rocking as if in a cradle.

The motion slowed, the ship still bouncing, her stomach rushing up to meet her gullet. Zayden was ominously quiet. Denita unbuckled herself to check on Zayden. Fumbling with his latch, she tried to lift it, but it was stuck fast. On her knees, she pounded with her fists, but it was immovable.

She felt a hot hand touch her shoulder, and she screamed, turning to see a wizened creature curiously looking at her. Naked from the waist up, she was wrinkled and red, with star-shaped eyes examining her.

"Bobbien help?" she asked in a musical voice.

Denita opened her mouth, but no sounds came out. The odd creature looked in the backseat and spied the injured Darracian.

"Oh my, Zayden. What have you done to yourself?" Bobbien climbed onto the craft, making it feel even more unstable. She considered Denita's white face. "Don't look down, dearie. It's a long trip."

Denita turned to gaze at the drop, swallowing compulsively.

"I told you not to look down," Bobbien admonished.

"Help me."

Her long red fingers were able to loosen the glass hatch, and she watched, slack-jawed, as the old woman pulled Zayden from the wreckage with unbelievable strength.

"Come!" She held out a hand to the younger girl. "Follow me. I fix him, no?"

Denita reached out and let this alien creature guide her to safety.

XXV

SEREN HUSTLED V'SAIR into the knee-deep water to board the skiff sent out to them. They climbed in, and V'sair turned to the Quyroo. "Not two days ago, you saved my life."

"I had to. I was being watched. Bobbien was right behind me."

"I don't understand…" V'sair said quietly.

"There is nothing to understand. As long as you are king, the most I can hope is to serve you, rise to some inconsequential post in the army. Lothen made me a better offer."

"But he is Plantan."

"So are you," Seren responded, then looked to the red stone city floating in the clouds above them.

Seren pushed V'sair none too gently as they boarded the painted Plantan vessel. It bobbed in the unsteady water, and V'sair reached out to hold a rail. Seren shoved him hard in the shoulder, directing him to Lothen's quarters. Inside, Staf stood next to Lothen, a dark-eyed woman next to him. The room was icy cold; V'sair shivered in spite of himself. Lothen drank from a clear goblet—a small red fish swam inside. V'sair heard faint mewing, but could not find its source.

"So, now you have both my mother and me. What do you want, ransom? Crystals?" V'sair asked.

Staf stepped forward. "Your reign is finally over. You and that Plantan whore can orbit the planet for the rest of your miserable lives. Now Darracia will have justice."

"You will never rule Darracia. Ozre will stop you," V'sair replied defiantly.

Lothen eased his lanky frame from his chair, taking his goblet with him. He walked close to V'sair, towering over him. He raised his glass with a salute, and V'sair watched in horror as he downed a small humanoid creature.

"Delicious…Would you like some?" Lothen asked with his basilisk stare. "You are Plantan—you might like it."

"Half Plantan," V'sair said distastefully. "I prefer Darracian customs."

"You are a rare mixture, a regular ambassador for all species." Lothen walked around the room. "Your mother is Plantan; your father Darracian; you love a Quyroo." He stopped and grabbed V'sair by his chin. "I know everything about you, Nephew; you sip from every flower, taking only what you want. Do you have gills, V'sair?"

"No," V'sair answered curtly. "This is no business of yours."

Lothen grabbed his hand. "No gills, no webs between your fingers, yet you are shaped like us." He pulled the sleeve up his arm roughly to examine the bluish skin.

V'sair pulled away. "I am Darracian in body and anima. If this is your idea of what makes a Plantan, I am happy to say the only thing I have in common with you is my mother.

Where is she?" he demanded.

"She is no longer your concern."

"If you have harmed her, I will kill you."

Lothen laughed. Staf shifted from one foot to the other impatiently. "Kill him and get it over with."

Lothen ignored him, walking over to consider V'sair again.

"I just want to know if you are more Plantan than Darracian." His uncle circled him, watching the younger man. He touched the white braid, and V'sair defiantly pulled away. "You are not in a position to be arrogant. Try it," Lothen commanded as he brought another goblet with a fish swimming frantically around in a circle.

V'sair realized the mewing sound was coming from its frightened mouth.

His uncle held the glass to his lips, forcing V'sair to drink. "Try it, V'sair. You might like it, and us. Try it and we can talk about a proposition," his oily voice wheedled.

V'sair looked away, his eyes scanning his ruined forests through the portholes.

"What!" Staf interrupted. "You didn't say anything about this!"

"I don't remember that I have to report to you.

Meanwhile, I see two kings here, not three."

Staf stalked over to him and put his face very close to Lothen's. "This was not our deal."

Lothen touched the older man's neck and replied, "Don't let me call on Geva." He turned to Seren. "Take them out of here and lock them up."

Seren paused, looking at both men. Lothen laughed, reaching out to touch the Quyroo on the shoulder. "Oh, don't worry, Seren. Both the Desa and Tulani are yours."

Seren grabbed Staf, and another guard used his gun to push them out the door.

"Come sit by me, Nephew." Lothen eyed his sister's son with interest. "They say you are the new Darracia. Why?"

V'sair looked out the ports of the room. "What does it matter now that you will destroy it?"

"I have no need to do that. I merely need a new place to make my home."

"You came with Nuen."

"He is a graphen addict. Oh yes, he is far gone and useless. We could do great things together."

"Your Geva and the Elements will not coexist together. They are fundamentally different."

"Yes, V'sair, you are right." He spun and shouted to the room, "Do you hear that, Geva? You can't coexist with Darracia's precious Elements. What do you think of that!"

The air rippled around them, almost gelling. V'sair felt the oxygen being sucked out of his lungs. A small whirlpool started over Lothen's head, filling the room with rushing air. It swirled around the room, caressing him with its slimy heat, then narrowed to a long, thin stream to fly out the window. Once outside, it grew into a huge black cloud, filling the sky to skirt through the buildings. It looked like a living thing, expanding and contracting, covering whole areas, obliterating the skyline, and taking a leisurely route to the volcano. The giant mass settled on the beach. V'sair watched his soldiers look up as it blanketed them like a black blizzard. There were muffled shouts, followed by blood-curdling screams, and then a stillness that screamed louder than sound.

The dense thing lifted, leaving the beach strewn with bodies, their gray faces bleached white and bloodless. V'sair gripped the back of a chair, then turned to his uncle. "You are despicable, pure evil."

Lothen bowed his head, a smirk on his lips, as if V'sair had bestowed a compliment. "Thank you. I do try my best."

V'sair turned to attack, and Lothen froze him with his next sentence. "Try it, and Geva will smother your city in the clouds. Oh, look. She engages with your Ozre."

They turned to see fire spitting from the roof of Aqin, the sky darkening with the ash spewing out of its cone. The vaporous being moved aggressively toward the volcano, and V'sair watched in astonishment as it expanded to cover the entirety of the huge mountain. The atmosphere clouded with sulfuric fumes, while a battle raged behind the screen of the entity that cocooned the majestic volcano. An explosion rent the air, rocks flying, huge plumes of fire, and for a minute V'sair felt the relief of knowing Ozre had overcome the enemy. A second explosion, followed by the racket of thousands of rocks hitting the walls of the volcano, deafened the air, echoing back at them.

Lothen laughed like a wild thing. "You think Ozre will triumph over Geva? Watch, V'sair, and understand you never stood a chance."

The sky slowly cleared to reveal Aqin hollowed out, broken like a weak tooth, reduced to a great pile of rubble. Shaken to his knees, V'sair sank onto a chair, turned to his uncle, and said in the barest whisper, "Do what you want to me, but leave the people alone."

Lothen threw back his head, roaring with laughter that shook the very rafters of the ship.

"I will not help you," V'sair told Lothen in a low voice.

"Then you will die." Lothen walked out of the silent room.

♦

Naje waited until they stepped out of an elevator before she flicked two graphen packets behind her, shoving Staf before her so they wouldn't get caught in the explosion. Seren flew backward into the lift, the wind knocked out of him, losing consciousness when a guard fell on top of him. Staf stumbled, and Naje grabbed his hand, but not before relieving a dead guard of his firearms.

She threw one to Staf, who deftly caught it. "I will not use this!"

"Oh, grow up!" she shouted back. Turning, she fired on three Plantans running toward them, their guns drawn. "Let's get off this ship."

"I will not run. I was promised the throne."

"Lothen's forked tongue talks two ways. We have to get out of here!"

They ran to the pod level, squeezed into the tiny escape vehicle, and Naje ejected them out of their enemies' clutches and into the unknown.

XXVI

BOBBIEN COVERED THE young Darracian's eye with the sap of the caylet tree, but held little hope. He was awake but not speaking. She liked the girl and her devotion, but the hulking young man was shriveling up. She had no time for his self-pity.

Bobbien had set up a base of sorts under the low-hanging trees of the eastern provinces. They were surrounded by the muddy quicksand, and if a body didn't know its way, it would be swallowed by one of the many sinkholes and end up roasting in the thermal springs underneath. She glanced up sadly at the ruined face of Aqin. So many dead, so many, she thought sadly. This was indeed a dark day for Darracia and its people. Soon, the Quyroos would find her, and she would help them. They would be rebels, for she knew V'sair was gone. Perhaps this one, Drakko's other son, would lead them to victory. When he woke up to stop feeling sorry for himself and realized he could do everything he needed to without his sight, he would be their savior. Yes, Bobbien thought, he would lead them to victory against the advancing evil.

♦

Reminda looked out the tiny pod window and watched the stars speed by. She was no longer shackled; she didn't need to be. She was a prisoner, programed to meet up with a prison ship where she would be transported to land in Bina. She would be destined to live on the cliffs, her name forgotten, only a number to identify her when death claimed her. Her only comfort was that then, and only then, she would be joined to Drakko forever. She only hoped it would not be too long.

♦

Staf and Naje flew toward a new unknown, homeless, friendless, and without any idea of how or when they would come back. But the one thing they both knew with certainty was they would return to destroy Lothen and take the throne.

♦

V'sair walked toward the metal cage, his hands tied behind his back. Seren stood by the control device, a giant bruise covering half his face.

Lothen stood on the highest point of the ship, a

speaker in his hand. "Behold, Darracia, your king will be dead.

Long live Lothen!"

The air was still. Crowds of Quyroos watched silently from the treetops, their red faces barely distinguishable from the foliage.

Darracians lined up on the balustrades; Generals Swart and Vekin, broken old men, watched helplessly as their king was escorted to his destiny. V'sair looked for the face he wanted imprinted on his final memory. When he saw her stricken look, their eyes locked, and for a second, no one existed but them. Tulani shook her head, her hands covering her mouth in mute shock.

V'sair walked to the golden cage, stepped inside, and held out his tied hands. "Surely I don't need to go to my death shackled. One prison is enough?"

Lothen looked at his nephew. "Your bravery does you credit. Untie him!"

"But sire!" Seren interrupted.

Lothen turned a fierce glare on the Quyroo. "I said untie him, else you will join him in his watery death."

The ropes were cut away, and V'sair solemnly stepped into the stark jail. The door clanged loudly behind him, and he faced outward toward his home, seeing only Tulani. His lips formed the words "I love you."

The nasal whine of the winch echoed over the water as V'sair was lowered into the lapping waves. He refused to look down. Soon the icy water chilled his body as it closed over his legs, his waist, and finally his head.

Tulani's wail of horror carried long after the water covered his hair.

Automatically he held his breath, his eyes closed, waiting for the last bubble to escape so he would sink into nothingness. His head got light, his arms floating within the cage, his body weightless. V'sair's breath hitched, and he released a final exhalation, feeling his lungs fill with water, and a peacefulness surrounded him. He heard music, ethereal and beautiful, angels singing. It was a holy choir, and in his mind's eye, he saw a white light coming closer. It split into two globes of light, one with a red center, the other blue. Reaching for it, he felt the last of his air escape and then nothing more.

The cage sank slowly to rest on the deep ocean floor. The young king lay in the ripples and eddies, small fish swimming around him. His tunic lifted, billowing out in the gentle wave of the water. The two orbs hovered over him, expanding to surround him, caress him, invade his still form. V'sair's body became incandescent, the inner lights of the blue and red balls shining from his chest. A pulse started in his neck, his heart warming to the light of the orbs. The tight skin of his sides split. One, two, three slits appeared, opening like gentle flowers, bubbles of air filling the young king. Slowly the tiny gills struggled to move. Unused, underdeveloped, they worked hard to breathe, and then they did. V'sair's eyes popped open.

RISEN

Book III

Michael Phillip Cash

Disclaimer

The characters and events portrayed in this book are fictitious. Any resemblance to real persons, living or dead, on Earth or Darracia, is coincidental and not intended by the author.

No part of this book may be reproduced, or stored in a retrieval system, or transmitted in any form or by any means, electronic or mechanical, including photocopying, recording, or otherwise, without the express written permission of the publisher.

Published in the United States by Red Feather Publishing

New York • Los Angeles • Las Vegas All rights reserved.

ISBN-10: 1-947118-76-5

ISBN-13: 978-1-947118-76-8

To Kevin

I am thankful that in a troubled world no calamity can prevent the return of spring.

—Helen Keller

ris·en *verb* \rīz/en\

1. to get up after falling or being thrown down
The greater the obstacle, the more glory in
overcoming it.

—Molière

I

V'SAIR BECAME AWARE of a cushion supporting him first. He was weightless, his mind in the hazy netherworld between lilac-colored dreams and sepia reality. His arms rose, as if supported by marionette's strings. He was wet but didn't notice it. He saw the dull sheen of the bars of the cage imprisoning him but couldn't seem to care. Eyes sliding shut, the siren of sleep called him; the air escaped from his body in a long hiss. Sounds mutated to become soft music, and he relaxed, drifting in peaceful solitude. Closing his eyes, he let go of life, allowing a final stream of bubbles to escape his lax lips. He floated in an abyss, his senses dulled, his mind lethargic. His skin pebbled as the water grew colder, wrapping a vise around his chest. His body numb, his legs heavy, he spiraled downward, enveloped by lassitude.

With detached calm, he observed two burly males,

their skin tinted an opalescent blue a bit lighter than his own, using their combined strength to pull the golden bars apart. They were trying to get to him, he thought indifferently, watching as if he were a spectator in some drama. The water swirled, buffeting him gently as it was stirred by a being next to him. A female swam close to him; he felt her cool hands grab his chin. Lips covered his, a soft kiss, blowing gently, his nostrils flaring in indignation at the interruption. His eyes opened wide to see her face close to his, fine green hair creating a swirling cocoon, wrapping around his chilled body. The tendrils caressed his skin, warming him, awakening him in a sensual dance.

V 'sair arched painfully as his skin tore, five gills ripping into each of his sides to undulate, forcing seawater into his starved lungs. His chest expanded, salty fluid invading his insides. His body filled, choking him, making him gag. Rolling violently, he struggled like a hooked trout, only to feel iron hands pull him through the small opening, abrading his sensitive skin against the rough metal, then steadying him in a viselike embrace. Both his arms and legs were straightened by another pair of hands. V'sair kicked back wildly. A scream rose to explode from his throat in a giant silver bubble that escaped, rising before him like liquid mercury. Firm fingers grabbed his thrashing head, holding it still, until he exhausted himself. The hands held him until his eyes opened to find a light-blue face with huge, clear eyes studying him.

She was distinctly female. Four large males surrounded

him, holding his weak body. The girl's small mouth opened as she communicated, but all V'sair heard were garbled clicks, followed by a whine, not unlike the string instruments played in his court. She was almost a comical creature, with two holes where the nose should be, a high, intelligent forehead, and those unearthly clear eyes that studied him intently. A webbed hand slapped his face, the water cushioning the blow, but it did get his attention. She resembled his mother slightly. Reminda had more defined features—a larger nose and, of course, her beautiful orange facial tattoos. He looked wildly around, taking in the five creatures. They were all kicking easily, while he worked hard to float. Certainly he saw differences from his Plantan ancestors, but where had they come from? He watched the blue-tinged face with bulbous eyes, swimming gracefully before him. She studied him intently. He saw her irises were a light blue; they were not clear at all. The sounds came to him, and it occurred to his dazed brain that she was speaking to him. He forced himself to concentrate, but the lack of air muddied his mind. He realized with a start that he was indeed breathing, water trickling in through his chest to be expelled though his lips. Scrambling, he ripped at his shirt, and the female brushed his hands away to help him lift the garment. V'sair's eyes widened at tiny, raw gills working hard on each side of his chest. He was familiar with gills; his mother had them. He touched the top one. The sensitive flesh trembled when he ran the pad of his fingertip over it. His mouth opened in shock as well as awe. It appeared as though he had been surgically cut, but he knew that was not true. They were tender. His whole body was sore. Tiny bubbles escaped. He looked up to see the creature smile with a nod. He depressed the gill, feeling himself choke as though he was being smothered. The female spoke again, but he shook his head. He didn't understand her. She pulled his hand away, slapping his wrist lightly, then shook her finger at him. Clearly, he was being told to leave his newly formed gills alone.

She swam around him, her body long, her webbed feet so like his mother's. She was young, perhaps his own age, maybe younger. V'sair stared at her, feeling a familiarity nagging at his brain. He shook his head as if to clear his fogged mind.

The female took his hand, coming alongside of him horizontally, then hooked his fingertips to urge him to follow. He barrel rolled, unused to the currents of water streaming around them. Two of the males steadied him and, with a nod, showed him the direction they would be swimming. They made no eye contact with him but took their commands from the girl. Her hair floated around her like seaweed, shrimp and other small creatures nesting in its glorious depths. He reached out to take a small urchin, staring with wonder, but the girl plucked it from his fingers, letting it scuttle away on a wall of multicolored coral.

V 'sair turned to consider his surroundings. He was well and truly deep in the Hixom Sea, either dead or learning how to use his inborn skill to breathe underwater. Fluid burned in his nose, his eyes winced, and he looked up to find her laughing at his discomfort.

He realized he was instinctively scissoring his legs, the motion keeping his floating feet off the murky ocean floor. His eyes adjusted to the darkness, and he glanced around, taking in rainbow-hued coral, teeming with tiny creatures in a multitude of pastel shades. The water had settled, and the sand was a pale pink, littered with orange starfish. He bent to pick one up and was snatched backward by one of the burly males swimming next to him. The girl shook her finger with admonishment. She swam downward, reaching for a long branch of coral discarded on the floor. She tapped the starfish, which reared inward, revealing a circular mouth filled with snapping teeth. It snatched the coral from her hands, crushing it in its tiny jaws, reducing it to pink dust. The girl motioned for him to follow, and he realized with a start she was naked, save a small covering on her loins, not unlike the red seaweed that washed up on the shores of the beach. Clumsily, he surged forward, his movements awkward, with the gentle help of the four males surrounding him. They swam for hours, it seemed. V'sair's heart beat tiredly in his chest; his arms moved with leaden determination. Though he breathed the seawater, it irritated his chest, and he felt the need to cough every so often, pausing to hack uselessly.

He heard nothing except for his own pulse, beating wildly in his head—a steady tattoo that became a song of survival. By all rights, he should have been dead, and worry for his mother, Tulani, and his home weighed heavily in his chest. He paused to glance up at the distant surface. Crouching, he made to surge upward but was caught easily by one of the guards. V'sair struggled in the tight grip, fighting a losing battle. Taking a woven strand of some sort of hemp, one of the men tied it to his waist, imprisoning V'sair. Wearily, he stared at the smudged light just over the surface of the water, but the tug of the tether held him fast, propelling him swiftly along the ocean floor.

He glanced at his saviors. They were mythical creatures, he laughed to himself, spotted only by drunken Darracians. There were stories about beasts that swam deep in the sea, but no evidence had ever been found. For years, he had been teased about his resemblance to the legendary beings. Nobody really believed they existed. The likeness was nothing short of astonishing. V'sair paddled his feet furiously to keep up with the group. Every so often, he slowed enough to be dragged along while he caught his breath. Breathing was hard, and his legs burned. Several times his eyes drifted shut with exhaustion, but still they traveled along the rugged ocean floor. It was a cornucopia of life-forms, multihued creatures he could never have imagined. Strange, long eels, yellow and black with neon-green eyes. Giant clamshells rippled the water as they opened, revealing purple-fleshed tongues that reached out to ensnare hard-shelled lobsters daring to climb the scalloped-shaped shells. He saw schools of large fish with tufts of brown hair that surrounded their pointed faces, looking like old monkeys.

His group froze, one of the male swimmers protectively pulling the female next to him. His tired mind registered they were armed with long spears, with deadly sickleshaped blades mounted on the top. A huge gray beast with a white belly lumbered by. Its skin sparkled like mica as it moved in the darkness of the water. He could see the frightened faces of the group. They barely breathed, and he held his breath as well. He was dragged behind a wall of gently swaying fronds, camouflaging them from the giant predator. It had an enormous maw for a mouth, a pointed snout with two pulsing nostrils, large enough to put his fist inside. A platter-sized eye—its black pupil took up the whole mass—turned its dead stare on them. The female froze, her hand gripping the young king's forearm, holding him still. The monster opened its mouth, revealing rows and rows of razor teeth the size of his forearm. They gleamed in the murky depths, small fish swimming innocently around the white sentinels as though it was a form of coral. The beast sniffed; the eyes rolled back, turning white. One of the guards slowly raised his spear, aiming for the great eye, his bulging muscles quivering with intensity. The fish thrashed its tail, creating a tsunami of small waves, turning its great head to swim on in indifference to the tasty morsels it had just passed up.

The girl smiled, her small mouth exposing pointed white teeth. She said something to V'sair, and while he didn't understand her language, he comprehended she wanted him to hurry.

They swam down a ravine, the water becoming denser, the currents colder. V'sair couldn't stop the shivers running down his body. His legs cramped, paralyzing him, forcing him to curl into a tiny ball. Impatient hands grabbed him underneath his armpits, and he allowed them to take over, his body too tired to try. His head sagged, his chin resting on his chest, until they rounded the last hill to swim into a clearing with a large underwater volcano. V'sair forced himself to look, swallowing seawater that sent him into a coughing fit, snapping the last thread to his new reality. His last sight was of a vast underwater city, peopled by a busy population of this fish species.

II

"HE SMELLS!" COSFAR said with disgust. "He smells, and his odor will give us away to the Plantans."

The handsome Quyroo walked next to Bobbien, his fist in the air. He was the de facto leader in the bush, taking control when Lothen and the Plantan ship bombed their homes.

"I say we give him up to the Plantans, trade him for some of ours," he wheedled. He was tall, with an imposing air of leadership. He ran a hand through the tangle of his braids, leaving them disordered, making him lose his look of authority.

Bobbien chuckled, then shook her staff at him, the dried gourds at the top making a rattling noise. "Enough, Cosfar. He is injured. He needs time to heal."

"He is Darracian. Let him heal with his own kind," the Quyroo spat, his braids shaking as he shook his head in anger. He liked to use his superior height to intimidate the older woman.

"Throw him in prison, they will," Bobbien responded, brushing his concerns away with her hand.

"Who cares? They did nothing for us when the Plantans destroyed the Desa." Cosfar followed her, leaning too close when he spoke. She stopped, using her staff to create a boundary of personal space between them.

He was popular; Bobbien just didn't know why. He did have a winning way with the elders, as well as the young females. Bobbien didn't trust him or his sleazy ways. He was always taking credit for things. When she ran the risk of finding food supplies, he claimed it was he who found them. He challenged everything she suggested, making creation of any rules to bring order to the growing encampment impossible. The group had grown, spreading under the last of the great Desa to hide from the invaders. She found herself too often squaring off with him. Whether it was regarding medicine, sanitation, or dispensing of food, it seemed all they did was lock horns with each other. She had known his parents and remembered thinking he was a petulant child when he was young.

Bobbien thought before answering him. Anything she told him would be spread in the camps later. "Unprepared they were." She looked at him hard and stressed. "They have never been attacked with cannon before."

"Look you, Bobbien." Cosfar pointed to Syos, the red rock city in the clouds. "Their home survives. Life goes on for the Darracians." He pounded his chest indignantly. "Only the Quyroo homes were destroyed. Life is as it was for them."

"Not quite, Cosfar," Bobbien interrupted him. "See the city?" She pointed her long red arm upward.

It was clear things had changed. The city in the clouds no longer teemed with Darracians. Syos was deserted, the fine red walls of the city pockmarked and dull from the attack. There was a seedy air of decay about the buildings. Repairs had never been made; it seemed Plantans only understood destruction. Few patrols dotted the sky. She could tell their resources were strapped. The Plantan population was aggressive but small. Yet they had managed a total take-over by breaking the backs of many of the noble houses. Lothen understood that he had to divide and conquer, and that was exactly what he did. Tree Dwellers fell back into the forests with the Bottom Dwellers. Former enemies became allies. Darracians were alone with the intruders. The people of the earth were not wanted in the new society. They were disappearing. It was as though the population in the Desa had never existed. Bobbien's eyes narrowed as she stared at the defeated city. It hovered closer to the planet, the randam crystals used as a power source to keep it floating running low. Many of the valuable trees had been destroyed in the invasion, leaving the crystals to rot. There was a limited work force trying to harvest them. It was a skill only known by the Quyroos, and the stupid Plantans had eliminated the hunters. The lights dimmed on the city towers and walls, leaving a fuzzy outline of where once stood a beautiful civilization.

"Now they have total control of the randam crystals,

and we are left to rot in the swamp. They are making slaves of our people. I have heard of transports," Cosfar stated angrily. "Transports?" Bobbien asked.

"Any Quyroos captured are being transported out to only Sradda knows where."

"Most of those left are hiding in the eastern provinces. Find us, they won't." She shrugged, letting him know the conversation was finished.

Cosfar nodded. "That is true," he conceded. "How long, do you think, before they figure out how to get through the quicksand to get to us?"

She turned patiently to explain it to him slowly, as though he were a dull-witted child.

"Travel through the Deep Fells, they won't. The rain has made it impossible."

"But Bobbien," Cosfar continued, "not even the wysbies will stop them. They don't like Plantan blood. The time of rains has taken out all natural predators. The herns have become extinct. They have murdered them all."

"Given time, extinct the Plantans will be." Bobbien smiled, though in her heart, all she cared about was Tulani. She hadn't heard from her granddaughter since V'sair was thrown into the Hixom Sea.

She had traveled to the Plains of Dawid, disguised in voluminous robes, and visited the new marketplace set up by that bully Seren, but could find no information about the girl. It was a raw place, with its lack of regulations coupled with rampant shortages that made prices skyrocket. Food was at a premium. Medicines, other vital goods were becoming scarce, and a valuable trading commody. Stalls were set up, mostly by displaced Darracians, the Quyroo population inexplicably getting thinner and thinner. The Quyroos were disappearing and not all to the eastern provinces. The new town was rife with rumors, but sources were unreliable. Bobbien was a concrete kind of person. Until she saw it with her own eyes, she didn't accept anything she heard. But not finding Tulani weighed heavily on her heart. She had to get Zayden moving. He was their last hope.

"Meanwhile, the problem of this big Darracian is on my shoulders, Bobbien. He is a nuisance." Cosfar began his nagging again.

Bobbien wanted to argue but knew this was an argument she would lose.

They both turned to observe Zayden propped up against a tree, his hair a matted tangle in his face, several bottles of roothes (homemade alcohol) discarded around him. He was filthy, with muddied clothes and a dirty face. He did smell. He was unwashed, unkempt, and so drunk he couldn't even sit upright. Singing a foul song, he raised his unshaven face to the wet sky, letting his voice carry to the outer reaches of the camp, disturbing everyone's peace.

After the Plantans attacked, every Quyroo took to the treetops to escape deep into the red forests of the Desa. The bombs had rained down on them, indiscriminately hitting homes, hospitals, and schools, killing a large part of the population. Bobbien had set up a base camp deep in the swamps, where no Darracian had ever traveled. It was cold there, the dual rays of the suns prevented from warming the land by the overgrown tropical trees. The ground was a red, soupy mess, filled with snakes, rodents, and nasty predators that attacked without warning. It was not a safe place. No one ventured there, but the Quyroos knew it was their only salvation. It was unmapped, unexplored, and barely reachable. The population had been sorely compromised, but every day new groups found their way in. Some were wounded, many burned and close to death. Bobbien had her hands full. She worked hard to heal as many as she could, appealing to Ozre to help her do what she was trained to do.

Bobbien turned to see Cosfar's flinty gaze watching Denita intently. He rubbed his hands together with a laugh. "What does she see in him, I ask you?" he demanded.

Bobbien shrugged. "Who understands other species? Loves him, she does."

"He is half a man," Cosfar sneered.

"Indeed, Cosfar, but it is the important half that counts!" Bobbien laughed at his reddening face. "Sometimes, my friend, half is enough."

"This conversation is not finished, Bobbien." Cosfar had lost patience.

"It's done when I say it done!" Bobbien retorted.

Cosfar snapped his jaw shut, grinding his teeth. He stalked off in the direction of the new office he had created for himself.

Rude bastard, Bobbien thought with distaste.

She better get Zayden on his feet. That power-hungry Quyroo was trouble, she knew. She smelled a lot more than Zayden's dirty laundry in the air. A storm much larger than their blasted weather was brewing. She considered the hulking Darracian. She had insisted he stay under the great janjan tree, the dripping leaves creating a noisy umbrella against the weather. She heard the message. When would he realize the Elements were trying to contact him? It was there, right in front of him, all around him, but he might as well have been deaf too. When was he going to realize the pattern, she wondered.

She had no time for Zayden and his pity. He would not see again; that she knew for sure. The girl who had crashlanded with him had coddled him, and that was a problem too. The high priestess barely had enough time to eat with all the sick and wounded. Zayden came far down on her list.

Oh, he was very ill in the beginning! She bathed his eye with caylet tea. The Hallis tree was deep in the Desa, and she had risked much to gather the leaves. Twice she was almost caught, but she liked him. He was at heart a good person and had great potential. If she was ever going to see her granddaughter again, she had to make him realize his capabilities. Bobbien knew leadership was in his blood. He alone could rally the Quyroos to repel the invasion. It was his birthright. While Cosfar had his bullying ways, she understood that he was not a born leader. He would crumble like melted sugar when challenged. Bobbien knew his type.

Ozre, Ereth, Ine, she appealed silently. *Tired these old bones are getting. Great Sradda willing, make the man better. Make him see what the rain is doing. I am weary.*

Silence answered her, and Bobbien realized if Zayden

were to recover, it was up to them both to make it happen. A crowd of children had gathered around him, a group of young boys, four or five of them, and threw leaves at the drunken man. They giggled as he blindly waved his flailing hands. One of them picked up a rock, and Bobbien started purposefully toward him. She noticed Zayden had cocked his head in her direction, a small clicking sound reaching her ears. Bobbien smiled.

Zayden chose that moment to let loose a great belch, followed by lyrics so foul the crowd dispersed—mothers covering the ears of the young. Bobbien shrugged, and her face colored with embarrassment. But she knew she had to get this great, lumbering Darracian sober again, or she would lose all her newfound credibility. Still, she did hear the clicks. Perhaps the janjan tree had done its work. Standing in the lee side of a broken trunk, she picked up a handful of pebbles. Using her thumb, she flicked them to land nearby. He was oblivious at first, but then she noticed a shift. His back grew rigid, and he appeared to sit up straighter, his head cocked as if he was suddenly aware of the noise. *Yes, yes*, she thought, throwing the pebbles around his form. She watched his great head follow the movement. The rain changed to a downpour, and she smiled, knowing the leafy fronds would be pitter-pattering all around him. Standing taller, she winced at the cracking in her knees, kneaded the chink in her back.

"Elements! Take over for me, huh?" She laughed.

She walked through the crowds of Quyroos sitting on the ground, toward the hut she shared with the Venturian female. The female was loyal to Zayden; Bobbien would give her that. Most girls would have run in the opposite direction saddled with a drunken cripple. Denita was on her knees, reaching under a cot to grab a bunch of roots and vegetables that Zayden had kicked around earlier. Bobbien bent to help her. Denita herself had just gotten over a bout of hufen. She had been one of the first cases, her stomach rejecting any food. Bobbien worried for the girl, who had no immunity to this planet's diseases, but she survived. Denita hid her illness from Zayden, sitting as quiet as a ghost in the hut so he wouldn't think her sick. So absorbed in his own troubles, Zayden remained remote. Bobbien wanted to shake him senseless.

"I would make him retrieve them," Bobbien told Denita as she crouched down to help.

Denita paused to give her a sideways look. "He didn't mean to; he is tired of this kind of food. Darracians eat meat."

"Spoil him, you do, Denita. He's never going to get better if you don't make him help himself."

"Easy for you to say. How am I supposed to make him see again?" Denita asked angrily.

"Believe in the Elements, do you?" Bobbien asked softly.

"There are no Elements on Venturian." The girl shrugged indifferently. She held a fruit in her palm, squeezing it gently. Bobbien laid a long-fingered red hand on top of the girl's.

"Everywhere are the Elements," Bobbien told her, holding her arms outstretched.

"If they are everywhere, how could they let a man

like Zayden be blinded? How could they leave your granddaughter a prisoner, or worse, perhaps?"

"Aye, it looks grim, but..." Bobbien stood to go to the crude window to look out on their small camp. "There is a reason for all this. The Elements are not arbitrary. We have to find their reason."

"Is there a reason for your Reminda to have been killed?" "You don't know if she is dead," Bobbien argued.

"Then where is she? How could they have let the boy king drown? He was beloved by all. The Elements don't exist. The only one you can depend on is yourself."

Bobbien turned on her. "So if that is true, then why don't you make Zayden see that depend on himself he must?"

"How? He is blind!"

"Only in his eyes," Bobbien told her cryptically. "A minor inconvenience." She left the hut and Denita to shoulder her way through the crowd to the infirmary.

"A minor inconvenience," Denita repeated bitterly.

III

NAJE PLACED A hand on the wide swell of her belly, the child heavy in her womb. She looked out of the window of the palace, thinking how things had changed in so many ways in the past few months. The dual rays of the suns broke through the watery clouds. The Desa, so famed in the solar system for its vibrant red color, was a dull, matted brown. The lush forest looked like it had been clipped by a blade, the broken stumps giving it a desolate air. Naje looked across the vast horizon, searching for life. There used to be herns, gulls, and other waterfowl. The sky was still, the air turgid, a miasma of death hanging over the newly exposed hills and valleys. When she arrived here, it was a planet in transition. The small Plantan force took control with a vengeance. The planet's economy tanked with the loss of all the crystals during the invasion. The castle lurched; Naje grabbed the wall to steady herself. The great building groaned, the lights dimming for a minute, then righted itself. The city in the clouds was in trouble, the randam crystals that kept it flying high in the stratosphere not doing their job. Supplies were stretched beyond their capacity. Her long nails tapped the wall, and Naje again wondered if she had done the right thing returning to Darracia when Lothen went after them so many months ago.

Halfway to Venturian, Lothen's forces had intercepted them with a peace offering. Sweet words, promises of grandeur seduced them back into the Plantan fold. Staf Nuen, it seemed, was needed. Lothen stormed the castle after destroying the Desa, leaving the red forests of Darracia a smoking ruin. The Moon Council was imprisoned, and the leaders were replaced by Lothen's commanders. All of the Darracian nobility were ordered to the castle, but they too stayed away. Only with force, Lothen was able to bring them to his court, but they refused to bow to his rule. The Plantan population was limited; there were not enough of them to keep the planet running smoothly. They were actually the minority. It was as though they had captured a treasure ship but did not have the reserves to operate it. They needed the Darracian populace to cooperate. Lothen supplanted the Elements with the might of Geva, showing them a firestorm of her capabilities. He built impressive altars to her power but found few converts. Geva was a demanding goddess, her punishments cruel. There was nothing more than fear to motivate followers. He broke down the population one group at a time.

The deportation of the rebellious Quyroos made the Darracians scared as well as submissive. Lothen used the vast resources of Quyroo slaves, exporting them to Bina to mine graphen for trade outside of their solar system. But he could not conquer by suppressing both species. The Plantan king realized the might of the Darracians would expand his empire. He needed to persuade them to join his army. The combined power of the Darracians, their Fireblades, and his Plantan warriors would soon control the entire solar system. There were thousands of trained warriors that would enhance his army by morphing it into an unstoppable force. He needed them not as a conquered people but as the machine to mow down any opposition. The Quyroos were expendable, a perfect commodity to use to build a financial empire in the production of graphen. Once a species started using the drug, it was an unending source for income. No matter what he tried—coercion or brute force—Lothen couldn't break through the hard castle walls or Darracian hearts. Certainly Geva did her dirty work, but Lothen needed a populace that supported his visions of grandeur, not one that was frightened into subjugation. A conquered species would ferment into rebellion. He had to turn them into a supportive population to build his far-reaching empire.

Lothen needed a representative, one of their own, to calm their fears so they would join up to do his bidding. He had Seren, the Quyroo commander, keeping law and order on the planet surface. Malcontents were shipped out; only those who helped harvest randam crystals were allowed to stay in the new holding camps they created. If they thought they had been oppressed in the past, the future for any Quyroo looked bleak indeed. They were herded into huge camps where their every movements could be watched. All their freedoms were curtailed. Faced with being sent to certain death on Bina, many were relieved to be able to stay on Darracia, even if they were little more than slaves.

The Darracians were necessary as his army. Strong, fearless, and stupid, they would make an unstoppable fighting force. The myth of that damnable Fireblade could be molded to turn his armed forces into a celestial fighting machine to conquer the whole solar system. He had to find someone to make the Darracians listen to him. He needed Staf Nuen. Lothen had raced after their escape pod himself, leaving the planet in a hurricane of turmoil. He knew he had botched that part of his invasion. He expected to seduce his nephew V'sair into joining him. V'sair's bravery both surprised and irritated him. The young king's death was a waste.

Losing Staf Nuen to his own ego was also not wise. He knew he better use more finesse in his politicking; otherwise his entire enterprise was in jeopardy. Naje could be the key to that success. He understood Naje, had used her well. Smiling, he remembered hot, sultry nights with her, before he gave her to Staf. He had seen her with her defenses down, her desires naked in her eyes. He shouldn't have given her away so quickly; she had uses still.

He had caught up with their escape pod and, with

his oily charm, induced them to allow him to board in order to speak with them. Staf was more than useless, an addict. Lothen could see the growing tension between the two lovers. The older man's shaggy head lolled against his seat. Naje paced the pod with a restlessness born from someone used to action. Lothen and Naje sized each other up in the small confines of the vessel.

"Come back with us," he said in a sibilant whisper.

Staf tried to unhook his seat belt. "Not on your life, you fucking flounder!" he shouted, drool spilling from his slack lips.

Naje sneered at his face, disgust written all over her caramel features. It had not been an easy flight. Staf refused to shoot guns at the enemy. He was old, so he insisted on the honor of fighting with Fireblades. Naje turned away from both men, staring at the void of space before them. Its emptiness filled her with gloom. Instead of fighting the enemy, Staf fought her. She wanted to head for Chal Mala, where a criminal overlord controlled that territory on the most outer planet of the solar system. If they offered support, perhaps the aging leader would make a new home base for them. Everyone traded information. She knew how to spin a story to make them both valuable. She had heard of this overlord. He was power hungry. She had planned to entice him into attacking Lothen. Instead, Staf had insisted they go back to Venturian. What was he thinking? She cursed. Didn't he know one must never go back? What did that icy rock have to offer? Did he expect to become a shopkeeper or meat-stall owner? Maybe he wanted her to start over, breaking her back in the graphen dens again. What future was there for her child, kicking furiously in her womb? She spun to look at the two males in the tight quarters. Staf's eyes rolled in his head, then narrowed to yellow slits. He loosed one arm, waving it at Lothen.

"You think you have me, my lord?" he growled. "I can fillet you like a slimy fish. You're scum, coming in and destroying the Desa. What were you thinking?"

Lothen smiled, his forked tongue flickering. "Oh, Your Grace?" He bowed respectfully. "I lost my head. See, I need your courage and brilliance to help me guide the people of your planet. My inexperience interfered."

"Naje!" Staf yelled, fumbling with his seat belt holding him captive. "Release me now so I may talk to this puppy."

He screamed her name when she failed to respond. She stalked over to him, unlatched the buckle, and watched him slide out of the deep chair to weave over to Lothen.

"You thought yourself too smart." He pointed a gloved finger to his head. "You need me, Lothen. You can't control the Darracians without one who unnderstands them," he slurred.

"Staf!" She tried to make him stop. "He's-"

"You think to tell me what to do?" He rounded on her. "I am king! You know nothing of kingship. You are a woman, not even royal at that."

"Your Majesty." Lothen's words slithered in the small room. "Forgive me; I got caught up in the heat of battle.

Surely you must sympathize." Lothen's voice was

smooth, but his eyes never left Naje. They followed her around the confined space, saying, "See, girl, look what you left me for."

Naje understood. She watched Staf strut around the room, directing her once again like a slave. "Get our things, Naje. We return home." He looked out the porthole.

"It's in the other direction, my lord," Naje told him sarcastically.

"No matter." He dismissed her. "We are allies once again?" He held out his arm to Lothen, who took it in his tight grasp.

"We were never enemies, Your Highness. We had a miscommunication only."

"Naje, what say you?" Staf called out, his face alert once again.

Naje wavered for a minute. Just how much was he aware of, after all, she wondered.

"Do we return to take our rightful place? You will be a queen," he stated baldly, challenging the other man in the room.

Lothen wondered who really held the power here: Naje, with her hard heart and cool head, or Staf, with the heat of his Fireblade and its mythical powers. Naje nodded to Staf, who grunted.

"So we return."

The one who held the power was Naje, the woman, Lothen realized, observing her silently. Staf blustered, ordered, but ultimately let the woman decide. He may bully her, make her appear subservient, but Lothen watched their dynamics. Staf was an empty bag of wind, filled by Naje's quiet influence. Promises were made, and Lothen now understood the way to Staf was through Naje. She would be queen, he assured them both; however, Staf had to take one of Lothen's daughters as second wife, he argued. Lothen remembered Naje's hunger, her desire for her own power. He understood what she both needed and wanted to hear.

Later, they stood together in his own royal quarters, negotiating. Staf Nuen slept in a gray fog of graphen in another room.

"Why should we stay, my lord?" Naje stood tall, her caramel skin glowing in the early stages of her secret pregnancy.

Lothen walked over to Naje, taking her chin into his long bluish fingers. "You liked me once." His fingers caressed the soft skin of her arm. Lothen narrowed his smoky eyes, his lips touching the nape of her neck. He wrapped his muscled arms around her body.

Naje pulled away, her face disgusted. "You used me."

"We all use each other," he said as he poured himself a drink. "Nuen is an addict. Make it easy for me, and I will see you properly rewarded." He held out the drink, watching her intently.

"How do I know I can trust you?" Naje came closer to take the drink he offered. She put it to her plush lips but did not drink. "You threw me away. I have made the most of my new situation. I don't need you anymore."

"With him?" Lothen laughed. "Nuen is useless."

Naje watched him carefully. "I like him. He makes me feel like a woman." She thought for a minute, choosing her words carefully. "He needs me," she said with an indifferent shrug.

"You compare him to me?" Lothen lifted his brow. He pulled her against him so she could feel his turgid flesh. He rested his hips against hers, brushing lightly, his lips grazing her lower cheek, his forked tongue flicking her earlobe. His breath tickled her, sending shivers of pleasure up her spine.

"You are breeding," he whispered intimately.

Naje spun away. "No!" She covered her belly protectively.

"Yes, I can tell. Your son will be king of Darracia." He walked up to pull her against him. He pressed himself intimately into her, letting her remember his arousal. Naje stood rigid but took a sip of his liquor, allowing it to warm her insides. She leaned her head backward, closing her eyes.

"You would let that happen? How can I trust you?" she asked quietly.

Lothen swallowed the bitter liquor in one gulp, laughing. "Oh, I think you can, Naje. In fact, I know you can." He spun her around to face him, placing his mouth over hers possessively. Naje tore her face from his, but Lothen touched her cheek gently, his eyes burning bright with passion. "Naje," he whispered.

It didn't take much after that. They returned to Darracia, landing triumphantly and with great fanfare. They stepped onto the smoking ramparts of the castle, Staf promising safety and peace. Was he not of the Darracian royal family? Staf invited the families back, doling out titles, knowing just what the noble class must hear. Using family ties, old friendships, he reassured them that life would slowly go back to normal. He promised them anything they wanted just to return and support the new regime. Warily, the ruling families appeared at court. They admired Staf Nuen's Venturian woman. She charmed them with her beauty and devotion. Naje created a group of ladies that surrounded her, and together with Lothen's silent support, she selected couples of Plantan warriors and Darracian maidens. Soon, most of the major houses had foreign masters ruling them. Many of the Darracian sons were given high posts in the new army Staf formed under the guidance of the Plantan conquerors. Rebels found themselves quickly dispatched to transports to die in the graphen mines. Darracia was a changing planet.

Naje sat with Staf Nuen now, doling out enough graphen to make him pliable to work with Lothen. She was respected now, necessary to defuse the situation when Staf grew difficult. Naje understood how to spin the words into a shimmering net of compliance so Staf went along with every plan. He sat on the king's throne, urging Darracians to embrace the Plantan invaders. Though these proud species were defeated, the actions allowed the illusion of freedom to fool them into compliance. The rape of Darracia had begun.

Quyroos retreated to the forbidden eastern provinces, where no one ventured safely. The ones that had stayed behind were exported to the mines on Bina to die on the high cliffs. The court became a dangerous place, where a loose tongue could cost a family its fortune as well as its home. Anyone who objected to the new rules disappeared the next day, along with their entire families. Staf sat on the throne, Naje next to him, and Lothen's pig-faced daughter to his left, the blue-skinned girl now in the early stages of pregnancy. Naje hated the girl, seeing her as a rival for Staf's attentions. He was easily persuaded, and if not for her careful regulation of graphen, who knew who would control his mind?

That was the key to her compliance. She was the sole distributor of graphen on Darracia, the new drug of choice. All vendors had to go through her to get orders. It made her rich beyond her wildest dreams. Krayum, the distilled liquor, was outlawed, and if one wanted a narcotic, they had to buy directly from Naje. She had security, money, status, and finally power.

Naje narrowed her cocoa eyes to scan the hostile audience. They bowed to her now, the flowers of Darracian nobility. Of her sister, she thought not at all. She had enabled her to escape. More than that, she had closed her heart. She had to worry about herself and her little one now. She laughed, looking at the smiling faces of the conquered. Lothen had cut them off at the head, these cloud people who thought themselves the most superior in the solar system. Who was superior now, she wanted to ask them. The Quyroo slaves left to service the ruling class were under the iron thumb of Seren, the native turncoat who basked in Lothen's goodwill. He ruled his nether kingdom on the murky red soil of the planet, keeping the randam coming to power Syos, the Cloud City. The Quyroo commander had the girl,

Tulani. Naje had heard of her beauty but had never seen her. It was said she would be imprisoned until she willingly submitted to her captors.

Stupid girl, Naje thought bitterly, looking at the angry gray faces of the Darracians. Submission was easy. She laughed inwardly. Appearances were everything. Once one gave the illusion of subservience, gaining trust, nothing mattered. Naje smiled, her white teeth stark in her caramel face. She understood the secret and kept it close to her brittle heart. Protect yourself; do what you must. Success means nothing without survival. She caressed the infant, the heir, under her skin. She possessed the future of Darracia in her growing womb.

IV

DENITA WATCHED ZAYDEN from the window of the hut. She placed the food on a heavy leaf, then picked her way through the muddy red soil to where he sat under the janjan tree. The wide leaves protected them from the worst of the weather, but she shivered. She moved close to his bulk, hoping he'd warm her. Placing her cold hands underneath his tunic, she warmed them against his hot flesh.

Closing her eyes, she leaned her face against him, remembering the safety she once felt in his arms. "Go away," he told her tonelessly.

Denita ignored him. "I brought you food."

"Take it away. Give it away. I want to die."

Denita crawled in front of him so that she faced him. "Why? Do you think yourself half a man?"

Zayden laughed, "Half? I am nothing, not a shell. Save yourself, because there is nothing left here for you."

"I don't believe that," Denita told him, her lips close to his ear.

"I am dead."

"You told me that once before, Warrior, and we both learned that was untrue."

Zayden sighed, turning his face away. She could have been a tree or a rock, the way he shut her out.

Denita touched his face and ran her hands through his disordered curls. The tattoo she had made on his bicep gleamed wetly in the firelight. She traced it with her fingertip.

"You are mine, Warrior. Nothing will change that."

V

THE TRIP TO Bina had taken forever. Tied to a metal bench with other prisoners, Reminda at first refused to eat. She wanted to die. She must have gotten close, because she remembered little of the journey. Feverous, she lay in her own waste, her face against the cold wall of the ship, her hands clenched in shackled fists. The Plantan guards forced food though her resisting mouth, beating her until she automatically opened her lips, her eyes swollen shut. It was cold. Her blue skin grew pale, and she wished for the Elements to take her to peace. She tried to call her husband's name; nothing but garbled nonsense filled her ears. Her gills grew infected, pus gathering in the folds, making breathing difficult. She wheezed, trying to become smaller so she could slip away to the warmth of Drakko's arms. Her dreams were of darkness, of murky water, the pressure of the weight of it, squeezing what was left in her lungs to bubble out in a shallow exhale. Everything hurt—her arms, her legs, her head.

She became aware of a softness, a hand brushing back the tangles of her white hair, the gentle pressure of fingers parting her lips to dribble fluid onto her parched tongue. She rejected it, but he persisted, caressing her face to urge her with soothing words to drink.

"My queen, my queen." She heard the voice filling the corners of her brain, refusing to let her hide. "You must drink, please, my queen…" Sometimes it was playful, reverent, others insistent, with a forced cheerfulness that made her want to strike the speaker with impatience. The murkiness parted, and she saw her head was in the lap of a giant Darracian, his gray face kind, his fingers tracing her face. He had a vicious slash down one side of his face. Reminda tried to rise, but he held her down, relief evident on his face. He had bright-green eyes, so reminiscent of her husband's that her breath caught, and he asked her, "Are you all right, Your Highness?"

Reminda rose slowly, her breath hissing in pain as her scabbed gills tore.

"Easy, my lady." He helped her up to rest against his huge chest comfortably.

It was presumptuous of him, yet Reminda found she didn't have the energy to mind.

"Do I know you?" she asked with as much dignity as she could muster in her weakened state.

"I'm not sure." He smiled, revealing rows of pointed Darracian teeth. "The guards have been kind enough to allow me to take care of you." He ducked his head. "They feared you were dying."

She realized he was older than she first thought. He had a Darracian royal braid, and she blinked in recognition.

"Colonel Brend?"

He nodded, adjusting her so she folded into the wall of his chest. His large hand reached over to pull her face inward, his fingers forcing her eyes to close. She heard his voice, suppressed in anger, muffled by the wall of muscle she was leaning on.

"What'd ye want now! She's still out, you great bastard."

Reminda went limp against him to give truth to his exclamation. She felt a baton prod her, and steeled herself not to respond to the shock that followed contact with her tender skin. Instead, she felt her protector shove the baton away from her. It sizzled when it made contact with his skin. The air filled with the smell of scorched flesh.

"You've done enough. If you expect her to live to Bina, you better start listening to me."

Though his large hand covered her ears, she heard a smattering of the response. Words like *royal* and *Lothen* filtered through the barrier, and the sting of the electric shock did not come. Reminda let out a gusty exhale as the echo of the guard's feet moved in another direction. She lifted her head to study her guardian once again.

"I do know you," she said quietly.

"I am honored."

"You are Swart's son."

Brend bowed his head. He saw her look at his royal braid, a question in her blue eyes.

"My mother was"—he touched his braid—"Princess Pavia."

"Drakko's great-aunt."

"I was in your husband's honor guard." His eyes grew dark. "I now am yours."

"Your hand?" She looked at the burnt skin.

He waved it negligently. "It is nothing. I've had worse." He smiled gently.

Reminda had a vague memory of this man, always in her husband's great shadow. Drakko had hundreds of cousins. Most of the Darracian nobility was connected through marriage. Reminda hardly noticed anyone, as Drakko eclipsed everyone in her eyes. The man was a few years her junior. Reminda lowered her eyes, suddenly uncomfortable in his arms. Sensing her shyness, Brend propped her against the bulkhead, turning to the next prisoner to say something. She felt the air change around them, heard the chains clanking against the metal with purpose as a murmur of excitement changed the texture of the air. Whispers filled the confined space, mixed with fumbling, until a small feast was lowered to the floor next to her. Reminda's blue eyes widened with question.

"We are all your honor guard now, Your Highness."

In the darkness, she made out the eager faces of Darracian soldiers, their hands clasped, with smiles lighting the gloomy darkness.

"We have prayed for your recovery." With clumsy hands, Brend unwrapped small portions of stale food that had been hidden in anticipation of her awakening.

"I can't take this." Reminda shook her head. "You all need your sustenance to survive."

"We cannot survive without you, my lady." The soldier next to Reminda bowed his head. "Please eat the food."

Reminda heard the soft words of the guards whispering back to her like a hushed prayer. "Please…please…" echoed off a hundred lips. She didn't need to see their satisfied smiles when she chose life and began to eat.

VI

STAF NUEN PACED the Orbitus Chamber, the conference table empty. Weak rays of light filtered through the gloom. He stopped to stare at the destroyed forests of the Desa, angry with both Lothen and Geva for the wasteful destruction. The ceaseless rains continued making the roads impassable. Work crews were inexplicably getting thinner and thinner. The door opened. His adjunct, a narrow-chested Plantan boy, entered, his Darracian armor swimming on his thin form. *We are arming children*, Nuen thought with disgust.

"Your Majesty," the boy said, interrupting Staf's musings. "Your Majesty, Commander Seren to see you."

"Seren?"

"'Commander of the Desa' is his title, sir."

"What Desa? There's nothing left," Staf grumbled. "What does he want?"

The youngster cleared his throat. "I, ahem, I didn't ask."

Staf rounded on him, walking forcefully to backhand him mightily. The young man fell to his knees, cowering on the floor. "Next time ask. Send him!"

Seren was ushered in to stand tall before his Darracian liege. They eyed each other casually, two stalliuses measuring the opposition. Staf broke contact first to walk back to the window. He gazed at the darkening sky. "Commander Seren?"

"Your Majesty." Seren bowed deeply, so deeply it bordered mocking.

The air barely stirred. Staf rested his gloved hand against his thin lips, his yellowed eyes narrowed. "Who gave you, a lowly Quyroo, the Desa?"

"Your Majesty knows; it was Lothen."

"And why did Lothen give you the Desa?"

Seren had an idea of where this was going but wavered on how to answer the king. He didn't like Nuen. He had killed his uncle Jonis, who was head of the Quyroo League when he overthrew Drakko, the last king. He had a blood feud to settle with him. Yet, for all his sins, Nuen loved Darracia, and the planet was in trouble.

"For services rendered," at last he responded to Staf.

Staf turned to look at him, his face set like iron. "Services for whom?"

Seren shifted uncomfortably. He understood what Staf was going to say. There would be no help from his quarter. "Today, the Office of Justice slid onto the Hills of Terun." He moved closer to Staf. "Look, you."

He pointed out into the cloudy gloom. "The Secondus Residential Building is hovering over the Hixom Sea."

"So…?"

"So, your city in the clouds is falling. It's falling on my…I mean, on the Desa."

Staf shrugged indifferently; Seren went on.

"Lothen is a madman. He is transporting all my… the Quyroos. If I don't have a work force, we cannot find the crystals."

"Take it up with Lothen."

"I have. He says I must make do with what I have."

The building shifted, gears moaning. Both men rolled onto the balls of their feet as the building leveled. Staf used his tail to gain balance.

Seren walked close to Staf. "You see? The crystals are failing. I can't find enough to replace them."

Staf reached into his pocket to take out a graphen blossom with a pipe. He stuffed the pipe and lit it, his eyes never leaving Seren. "You made your bargain with the devil. Now abide by it."

Seren threw up his hands in frustration. "Why did you come back here?"

"Not to help Quyroo scum like you," Staf told him.

"You are allowing them to destroy our home!"

Staf turned to stare out the window bleakly, wondering why indeed he had come home.

VII

FOOD WAS SHOVED through the cell door to splash against the wall. Tulani eyed the mess with disgust.

"Eat it, you red keewalla," the guard said, sneering. He pushed his baton through the cell bars, catching Tulani under her chin to hold her face flush to the iron. The rusty residue ground into her cheek, scraping her sensitive skin. Pinpricks of electricity needled her skin. Gritting her teeth, she refused to show pain, and the guard laughed, leaning close to her.

Her red braids hung in a tangled mess down her back. Her clothing was in tatters. She had been in this filthy cell for weeks. Half starved, her bones accenting her thin cheeks, she closed her eyes forlornly.

"I can make it easier for you here, girl." He licked his blue lips with a reptilian tongue. "I can come to you tonight with food." He reached in to caress her chest.

Tulani turned to memorize his face, knowing when she got out she would kill this person.

"I would rather lie with a jast," she said through gritted teeth. Despite the dryness in her mouth, she found enough moisture to spit in his face.

Her jailor jerked the cudgel to glance off her cheek, her jaw cracking from the blow. He wiped his face, his eyes never leaving hers. "I will make you pay tonight. Even a jast won't want you when I get finished with you."

He stormed off, leaving Tulani to slide down the cell wall to the floor.

Seren had put her there when she refused to cooperate. She remembered that fateful day when she watched V'sair fall to his death in the Hixom Sea. Tulani stood on the ramparts of the great castle wall, screaming, her heart broken. They had hauled her in after they surrendered, and she'd sat in silent grief, mute with shock at the mindless violence when Reminda's brother, Lothen, took control of the planet. The Desa smoked, violated from the constant bombardment, the high tree homes of her species destroyed. The vast population of the Quyroos, both Tree Dwellers and Bottom Dwellers, lay either dead or scattered on the smoking planet. The gaping hole of Aqin—a raw, weeping wound—silently cried at the loss of Ozre. The volcano was leveled, its walls blown apart by Geva, the evil goddess worshipped by Lothen and the Plantan invaders. Tulani stared at the colorless sky, her home ruined, her people systematically enslaved, the Darracians powerless to fight the new ruling class of the planet.

Swart and Vekin, along with any Darracian with

a pretense of rebellion, were deported to the graphen mines, to die on the high cliffs. Transports left daily. She watched them herd captured Quyroos onto the huge ships to be sent to certain death on Bina.

She was sent to the surface of the planet with a mixed group of captives to be deported on the next transport. They waited in the Plains of Dawid, which had been transformed into a crude marketplace. Rutted streets were flanked by makeshift stalls. Shopkeepers had come up with inventive ways to keep the ever-present rain off their products. Many had used the wide leaves from the janjan tree woven together as a covering, bringing a pang of homesickness to Tulani. Others used hammered metal, the constant rain adding to the deafening noise. Tulani's head ached from it. Her feet sunk into the loamy soil, up to her ankles. Soon her dress was plastered to her body, her skirt heavy with water. The fine mist created a hazy blur of the planet's surface. Everything was wet, the wreckage of the rotted trees giving off an offensive smell of decay. It was crowded. Plantans, Darracians, and other species packed together in a teeming maze of streets. Most of the Plantans were armed, and the Darracians had the bleak-eyed, worried stares of the conquered. Now they knew what it felt like to be insecure in their own home. Confidence belonged to those who felt safe. Strangely, confidence, too, belonged to those who didn't care. She understood that feeling well.

She scanned the crowds, looking for a familiar face. No one knew yet if her grandmother had survived. There was nothing to live for anyway, and Tulani wished for death. Her eyes were hollow, especially after she watched the invaders kill V'sair's jast, roasting him whole in the fireplace in the throne room. They were barbarians, with no respect for life except their own. In fact, she observed them fighting among themselves, murdering with abandon in duels over loot. She had always known prejudice, had seen unfairness in the way the Darracians treated Quyroos, but this took suppression to a whole new level. She was in a line, waiting to be stamped, then loaded, when a hand pulled her out of the formation, throwing her onto the wet red ground.

"You there!" A Plantan official stomped over. "What do you think you're doing? She's scheduled for the next deportation to Bina."

"She's mine." A hated voice filled her ears. Tulani stood to get back into the line. Seren put his foot on her thigh, his hand imprisoning hers. "I have been searching for you and that disgusting hag, your grandmother."

"I belong to no one," she told Seren. "Bobbien lives?" she added, hope lighting both her heart and star-shaped eyes.

"You belong to me, Tulani." Seren gripped her wrist. "The king is dead, and your grandmother is missing. You've led me on quite a chase," he sneered, his red face dripping with moisture. He wiped at it with his other hand. "You'll be coming with me now, Darracian slattern."

Tulani resisted against his hand. "You're hurting me."

Seren laughed. "Get used to it."

He pulled her toward his stallius tethered to a post nearby.

It was white, as pure as the color of V'sair's hair. Tulani's eyes filled as she whispered, "Hother." Her heart broke.

"Yes, like Hother, you will be mine as well." Seren dragged her.

"Hey, Quyroo! You can't just take one of them like that!"

Seren spun, pulling Tulani as he approached the Plantan guard. "Do you know who I am? Do you? Do you? I am Seren, the district commander of the Desa." Seren pulled out his sword, menacing the other man. The Fireblade was a dull orange, humming deeply. He raised his arm to attack, when a shout stopped him.

Lothen, king of the Plantans, rode up on a black stallius.

He was surrounded by his elite guards.

"Seren, my good friend, what goes on here? Ah, you desire this female?" Lothen had seen the Quyroo commander stalk over to the transport line. He was a hothead but a necessary hothead. He helped fight the Quyroo rebels and organize the work gangs on the planet. With his network of informants, he brought vital information, squashing rebellion before it took root. There was a strong cell of fighters that evaded them. Well-coordinated skirmishes destroyed two supply trains, taking out boxes of the vital randam crystals. Stocks were running low, and already the great city in the cloud's lights were dimmed. Due to the destruction, the interruption of war, everything was limited. It seemed the only thing this world had in abundance was the graphen that Naje imported. Though he made a small tax from Naje's hoard, the power for everything was the crystal. He had been too hasty in his attack, destroying many trees. He needed Seren to organize the harvesting of the crystals. Without the crystals, the city would fall, along with his power.

Seren spun, his rage subsiding. "This is Tulani. This man was disrespectful." He pointed to the guard who had challenged him.

"The girl you were searching for? Well, you must take her." Lothen needed Seren quiet. He was rounding up Quyroos for him daily to ship out to replace the ones dying on Bina. He also ran the work groups searching for the crystals. Seren ruled the ground with ruthless coercion, keeping the supply to the minimum he could survive with. His attack had destroyed most of the trees that produced the sap that kept the city floating in the clouds. He needed the experts to search out the surviving trees to find the valuable commodity. Seren saved the hardest workers from the transports by offering them and their families a home in hastily made internment camps as long as they hunted out the crystals. Many jumped at the chance to keep their clans together. Bina was certain death. Hope remained still on Darracia.

Lothen turned to the guard. "We do not treat our treasured allies like this." He reached for his gun and blasted the guard's head off. He bowed his head to Seren. "I will never forget your role in the invasion. Take your prize and celebrate."

Seren saluted the king with his sword. After dragging her to his new home, he proudly showed her his domicile. He had commandeered the old council building, furnishing it with whatever his men could steal. He had turned a cellar into a prison, threatening Tulani she would rot there if she didn't cooperate.

At first, he locked her in a chamber, sending servants, former daughters of noble Darracians, to bathe and dress her. The large clothing swallowed her lithe form. Tulani stared out of the barred window, allowing them to comb and braid her long red hair. The food they brought in lay untouched.

Seren arrived at dusk, slapping his gloves in the darkened room. "Tulani!" he barked.

Tulani sat in the dark shadows, ignoring his call. He called her again, walking in to light the many tapers so the gloom dissipated.

Seren pulled her into his rough embrace. Tulani turned her face, her gaze distant. With rough fingers, he gripped her chin, bruising her tender flesh to press his mouth against hers. Tulani tasted blood. Her eyes stared at Seren with hatred. Seren backed his face away to examine her. Tulani wiped her lips disgustedly with her wrist.

"Am I not good enough for the high priestess? I am an important man now." Seren paced the room. "Tulani, join me as my woman. I am hoarding the crystals. Lothen will have to grant me a higher office."

"You are allowing them to transport our people."

"Only the weak, the injured. I am keeping the strongest here. I am building an army, an empire."

"You disgust me." Tulani eyed him with distaste. "V'sair was good to you. You turned on him."

"Crumbs!" He grabbed Tulani by her thin shoulders. "He gave us crumbs. I am no man's servant. V'sair was ineffectual. He couldn't get the planet united. What did he do for us?" Seren tossed her into a chair, imprisoning her there. Tulani covered her ears, and he used his large hands to hold hers in her lap, forcing her to hear. "He did nothing for us!"

"He was a good man!" Tulani shouted, her face red, her cheeks wet with tears.

"He was a boy! Now you will see what a man can achieve."

"You are not a man but a coward," Tulani told him quietly, her face impassive.

He grabbed her, pressing his lips against hers. "You will feel a man, Great Sradda willing."

Tulani ignored him. Seren shook her, her braids falling around her body like a cape. He grabbed a hank of her hair, violently grinding his lips against hers. This time Tulani bit his lip, drawing blood. Seren backhanded her so that she fell against the hard-packed walls of the earthen room. He stalked over to her, lifted her by her hair, and slapped her again.

"Like your men blue better?"

"You're not a man," Tulani said through gritted teeth. Her nose bled freely, her eyes bright in her face. "You are a beast. I don't couple with animals."

Seren roared, coming at her with both hands raised, when his father, Jokin, burst into the room.

"Stop, you fool!" He banded his arms around his son's chest. "She is worthless to us dead."

Seren screamed with rage, but his father held fast.

"Think, Son; you now have power. What would a leader do?" He shook him. "What would a leader do?

Nuen rejected you. You need Lothen. We need Lothen. Think! Use her to your advantage; you could smoke out her grandmother and make a present of her to Lothen. Forget about Staf Nuen.

Lothen, for all his sins, has been better to you."

"Bobbien?" Seren asked, his breathing ragged.

"She's been succoring the Quyroo. She has created a camp where they are mobilizing, trying to build a force to eventually attack us. Think what it would do for you in the Plantans' eyes if you present Bobbien's head on a platter. You will have single-handedly stopped the rebellions."

Seren had calmed enough, so his father let him go.

"Send her to the cellar. Keep her there and let the word get out. They will mount an attack to rescue her, and then we strike."

"No!" Tulani raced to the door, but Jokin took his staff and hit her on the back of her skull, knocking her senseless. She slid to the floor, her eyes rolling back in her head.

"Yes, we will stamp out the rebels and make a gift of them to Lothen. You might rise to grand mestor."

"Lothen is grand mestor. He has brought back Staf Nuen as king."

"Staf Nuen is dying. They are killing him with graphen. Lothen will be king by the next moon phase, as soon as he assimilates his kinsmen into the Darracian culture."

"There is no room for the Quyroos."

Jokin kicked Tulani's silent form with his foot. "It is time for you to mate. Mate with a Plantan and dilute your Quyroo blood. In a few generations, there will be no Quyroos left but for the museum. Don't waste your seed on one such as this. She will get you nowhere."

Seren grunted in agreement. Tulani was not appealing lying on the floor, her face bloodied. His father had a point. Tulani had been important when V'sair sat on the throne, but V'sair was dead and buried in the Hixom Sea. It was time for him to find a new way to climb a ladder to the city in the clouds.

"Take her downstairs," he told a passing guard. "Lock her up. Keep her there until I tell you otherwise."

The withered old Darracian lifted the girl by her arms to drag her downstairs.

"Bait," his father said as he nodded.

"Yes, bait. Let's see what she attracts."

VIII

V'SAIR CAME AWAKE with a violent start, rising off a soft pallet. He took a deep breath, his nostrils flaring, as he gasped, realizing he was not underwater but in a warm, dry chamber. It was made from red granite, not unlike his home in the clouds. He looked around curiously, noticing there were no windows. The surface of the wall was rough and unfinished, carved from solid rock. It had a high ceiling, and strange violet shadows danced along its surface, undulating like the waves of the ocean. It was quiet. V'sair touched his ears, wondering if they were affected. They felt clogged, as if fluid was stuck inside. Shakily, he rose, the room spinning, his fingers lightly gripping the soft quilt. He picked it up, and holding it, he recognized it was made from the skin of a great fish. It had been treated, softened, but it was fashioned into a blanket. He wobbled over to a small table that had a plate of food. Small bits of fish were cut up and served with stewed red seaweed. V'sair's mouth watered, and he grabbed the food and shoved it into his mouth. He enjoyed the savory flavor as the food hit his empty belly.

A tall glass of liquid was next to the plate. It was faintly alcoholic, like a fermented beverage—sour but satisfying. He gulped it down, his thirst quenched. V'sair's strength slowly returned to his young body, his reserves replenished. The door opened, revealing a tall, blue-skinned man with masses of white hair. They looked so much alike that V'sair blinked and put the cup back on the table, leaving a small amount in the bottom.

"You must finish that, young sir!" the man said in a friendly way, gesturing to the drink. "You need the fluids." He was dressed in pants made from the same iridescent skin as the blanket, but his blue chest was bare. He was older, perhaps Drakko's age. The hair receded on his forehead at each of his temples, and V'sair's hand automatically went to his own head.

"It's uncanny, it is." The man smiled, revealing pointy white teeth. "Let me see. We share white hair, blue skin, and a forked tongue."

V'sair shook his head and displayed his Darracian tongue. "Who are you?"

The older man smiled kindly. "Ah, but you do have gills, too." He gestured to V'sair's chest with a webbed hand.

V'sair raised his shirt to watch his newly formed gills struggle with weakness.

"They are underdeveloped, but that will change the longer you stay here." The older man nodded.

"I cannot stay here," V'sair stated firmly.

The man shook his head, but his face remained friendly. "You will get used to them," he responded heartily.

"I cannot stay here. I have to go back to my home, sir. Please, where am I?"

"Oh no, no, young man." He smiled sadly. "I am Ovie, by the way." He took V'sair's wrist between his thumb and forefinger, encircling it. "Now do that to me. That is our greeting. You cannot leave here. You have seen us. You will give us away."

V'sair lightly circled the older man's wrist, politely returning the greeting. "You have my word that I won't reveal your presence, but I have to go home," V'sair informed him, his voice more forceful.

"No! Your home is here now. You will not leave here. Once you have seen us, it is, I fear, impossible. You will get used to us. There is great unrest on the surface anyway, now. It is not safe for either of us," Ovie replied with agitation.

"You don't understand." V'sair came to face him. "I am the king of Darracia. I have to go and save my people."

"You are king of nothing. The Plantans have destroyed your home. You have no home."

"You are Plantan," V'sair shot back.

"Oh no, no, no. We are descendants of the same species that peopled Planta eons ago. We call ourselves Welks. We are very different from them. While the Plantans developed outside the ocean, we have stayed underneath. We don't choose to mix with the species above ground. You'll see. You'll be happy here. We live in a peaceful society here. The Elements have made it so. Here Ereth answers our prayers." "Ereth?" V'sair asked.

"Yes, come. I will show you."

They left the chamber, walking through a passage-way made out of the same rough-hewn rock. V'sair's eyes adjusted to the gloomy interior. He paused to examine the wall, noticing its craggy surface was dotted with fossilized crustaceans. His long blue fingers glided over the pitted surface.

"We are underwater?"

"Yes," the older man acknowledged.

"Where?"

"We are deep under the Hixom Sea. We have been here longer than you."

"You never go above?"

"It is against the law. We have avoided your species for eons."

"Why?"

Ovie considered the best way to answer the stranger. "Because we don't trust you."

Mildly insulted, V'sair could find nothing to say in response to that. Ovie must have felt his embarrassment and shrugged.

"It's nothing personal, you understand. It's just that you are…your species is so destructive. Come. The hour grows late. We are having an assembly to introduce you later today."

Without another word, V'sair considered what Ovie

had said, silently following him. Perhaps his species was too destructive.

They entered a huge cave, deep-purple shadows painting the vast room. V'sair found it hard to believe he was underwater; it seemed the chamber went up endlessly. A giant waterfall taking up the entire right side of the cavern filled the room with a deafening roar. Water droplets misted the area, and soon V'sair's pale hair hung in a damp rattail against his wet back.

"Where is this place?" he shouted, but his voice was lost in the ceaseless pounding of the water. Licking his lips, he realized it was seawater. The entire right side of the room was a crystal wall, revealing the ocean floor. Cut into the rock, it served as a vast window to the ocean. V'sair's jaw dropped when Ovie waved his hand and lights backlit the area, revealing a multitude of fish—some the size of buildings— swimming lazily behind the polished quartz. V'sair walked over and placed his hand on the wall, his face in awe. Silently he stood, gazing at the bottom of the sea, the creatures on the other side ignorant of their observer.

"Humbling, isn't it?" Ovie commented with a wry smile. "Takes my breath away every time. Ah…" He smiled, his face lighting with pleasure, as the female who had rescued V'sair swam over to touch the glass over Ovie's hand on the other side. "My daughter, Hennith."

V'sair watched her float nearby, her webbed hand placed directly over his on the other side of the glass. "She is the girl who saved me." She swam backward with a smile on her lips. A pink turtle floated by, and the girl mounted it like a stallius to ride in lazy circles.

"Yes, she was out on patrol. Usually we allow nature to take its natural path."

"I don't understand."

"We rarely rescue your kind or the red ones." "The Quyroos," V'sair supplied.

"They're never happy here and want to return to land. We can't allow that."

"I don't understand why." V'sair turned to face him.

"You are destroyers. You don't give back to the planet. Take, take, take—always making changes. Why wasn't the land good enough for you? Instead you had to build cities in the sky. Taking crystals, making everyone work for them, always improving…"

"Improving is a good thing," V'sair said indignantly.

"To what purpose? Can one simply exist? Look." Ovie drew closer. "See my daughter? She swims every day. She protects the ocean floor and our creatures. We take only what we need to survive. We replenish what we take. We live alongside all the creatures in this great sea, not oppressing or trying to change them."

"Darracians don't do that!"

"Oh, I beg to differ, young sir." He held up his webbed hand. "One, you suppress the Quyroos. Two, you take the crystals to fly your home, making a separation between species. Three, you create differences by claiming only some have the power to operate the Fireblade."

"That is not my belief. I learned the Fireblade is lit by the soul of its owner, and anyone can operate it."

"To what end? What is the importance of the weapon?"

"You have blades!" V'sair accused. "I saw the spears."

"Yes, because we have to protect ourselves from the likes of you!" Ovie spat.

The waterfall froze midair, and the room vibrated with intensity. Colors flashed around V'sair as a great rumbling rocked the floor.

"Enough!" a booming voice declared. "You see! You see what is happening? He is here less than a day, and you are bickering, fighting like the landwalkers."

Ovie fell to his knees before the back wall. The rocks squirmed, undulating as a roar shook the room. Small boulders bounced off the cliff, falling like gravel to land around the two men. V'sair dodged the rocks nimbly. His eyes scanned the giant wall; he stood stock-still realizing it went upward for several stories and was quite alive. He walked over to touch the red wall, communing with the being living in it. His eyes scanned up in disbelief.

"Ereth?"

IX

THE RAIN TURNED the Desa floor into a red quag-
mire impenetrable for the Plantans to pursue the escaping Quyroos. The hidden camp swelled as more Quyroos
arrived daily. Sanitation became a problem. Bobbien
could barely keep up with the influx of refugees. Tales
of mass transportation of the species were told in the
hushed, makeshift city of earthen huts. The rest that
stayed were in internment camps, forced to hunt for
crystals demanded by the conquerors. Thousands of
crude homes were created, side by side, small cooking
fires outside adding to the murky, wet haze. The air
quality was poor, laden with moisture, combining with
the smoke to turn the pure air into a smoggy mess. Mold
coated every surface; food rotted on the vines. Her people were starving, and she could find no answers in the
prayers she voiced each night.

"Ozre, Ozre, why have you forsaken us?" She held great hanks of her long braids in her hands as she cried on her knees. She worried about the growing multitude of her people. She worried about Tulani. She worried so hard that she felt her heart beating with fear every minute of the day. They were disorganized. The joke was to put two Quyroos in a council, and nothing would get accomplished. All they did was argue.

Her back ached from the long hours she worked treating the outbreak of hufen just this week. Poor sanitation coupled with lack of fresh water made for a bad recipe of communicable disease. She hoped that Tulani was still in the castle, warm and dry. She traveled weekly to the marketplace in the Plains of Dawid for information about Tulani, but thus far, there had been nothing. Not a word about her granddaughter alive—or dead. The rain poured daily, making travel next to impossible. If only the incessant rain would cease. If only the growing population of displaced Quyroos could organize themselves into a fighting machine. If only Denita would stop babying that great hulk of a warrior so he could lead her people to victory. *If only*, she thought, looking out the door where the girl sat next to the broken soldier that held the dreams of the future in his useless hands.

Denita sat beside Zayden silently while he slept. She watched the rise and fall of his filthy tunic, his eyes closed, his face devoid of the new lines she had noticed fanning from his amber eye.

He had been so silent today; she feared he was dead. A plate sat between them, his forgotten meal destroyed by the hungry bugs eating it. She had protected it for the longest time, giving up when he failed to answer her questions. How long could he mourn, she wondered. Blind, almost always drunk, she knew his life was over. His humor and kind gallantry had fled when he lost his sight.

"I told you to go away." His raspy voice broke the stillness of the evening.

Denita ignored him, moving her behind, settling in.

"I said I don't want you here!"

Denita held still, breathing lightly, thinking she would fool him into believing he was alone once again.

"Denita!" he shouted angrily. "I know you are here. I can hear you breathing." He turned to face her, his blind eye blazing with heat.

"You don't know that." She got up, stealthily moved before him, and stared at his sightless face sadly. She was inches from him but held herself as still as she could.

Zayden grabbed her wrist and twisted it in a merciless grip.

"You see me?" Denita gasped through clenched teeth.

"Stop it, Zayden; you are hurting me."

"I told you to leave me alone." He stood, dragging her upward. Slightly dizzy, he leaned heavily against a broken tree.

"You there!" Cosfar stomped toward them. "You are hurting the female."

He came in on Zayden's left. The big Darracian cocked his head, listening intently. Raising his leg, he expertly kicked the Quyroo in the stomach, sending him sprawling backward into a well of mud. It splashed them both, coating them with the red substance.

"You can see?" Denita asked wondrously, the pain of his grasp forgotten, her free hand traveling to touch his scarred cheek.

Zayden expertly knocked the hand away before it even touched him.

"Don't be a fool. Your sister blinded me." He held her by the shoulders, shaking the helpless girl.

"She was protecting you."

"She destroyed me!" he roared. "I am useless to everybody now!"

Denita escaped his merciless hold and cupped his face with both her hands. "You are not useless to me, Warrior." She kissed him softly.

Zayden's cheeks were wet, and she brushed away the tears tracking down his face. He staggered away from her, tripping over a protruding root. He fell face first into the dirt, and his arms sank into the mud to his elbows. Cosfar hooted with laughter.

"Denita, leave this beast and come with me. I will show you how a real man takes care of his female." Cosfar rose, grabbing Denita's arm in a viselike grip.

"Leave me alone." Denita struggled with the big Quyroo.

"How long has it been for you?" Cosfar encased her in his arms, putting his mouth over hers. He ground his lips against her mouth, cutting off her curses.

Zayden's head turned to Denita's direction. "Denita?" he growled. The muffled cries were his only answer.

"You can't see me!" Cosfar yelled. "Slink off into the forest, and stop being a drain on us."

Zayden cocked his head, listening for Denita. He turned his head slowly, clicking his tongue against the roof of his mouth. His head did a slow scan, stopping directly in the line of sight of the couple. Zayden's amber eye glowed with heat. With a roar, he launched himself at them and collided with Cosfar with a resounding smash. His balled fist found Cosfar's face, his pebbled knuckles making painful contact with his nemesis's nose.

Through the entire attack, Denita heard a steady clicking, wondering where it was coming from.

They scrabbled in the dirt, the thick mud coating their skin, blood dripping from both their faces. Cosfar gave as good as he got, making no concessions for Zayden's handicap. Truth be told, he wondered, what handicap?

Bobbien saw the fray and launched herself between the two combatants. Her strong arms pulled them apart. "Stop that, you big lug! Supposed to fight the Plantans, we are. Not each other." She pushed Cosfar out of the way. Zayden clicked, spinning to follow him. A smile split her face, her star-shaped eyes watching the blind warrior follow his target. "Figured it out, have you?"

Zayden paused, turning in Bobbien's direction. "What are you talking about?"

Cosfar cautiously approached the two of them.

"Think you I put you under that dripping janjan tree for no reason?" Bobbien demanded.

Denita came up, placing her arms around Zayden's heaving chest. "What did the tree do?"

"Nothing," Zayden answered. "The tree did nothing."

Bobbien laughed. "But the rain did its job, right, Zayden? The Elements have provided you a means to see." She nodded sagely.

"The rain?" Cosfar demanded.

Bobbien watched a grin grace the Darracian's face. "If you don't tell them, I will," she stated.

"Could it be true? Was it Ereth? Ereth is your Element of water?" Denita asked.

"Water is the birthplace of life. It makes the Desa grow." "Too much rain can destroy," Denita told her.

"The Elements would never destroy! Ereth gives life. Sometimes you don't need anything but faith," Bobbien said softly.

"It wasn't faith, Bobbien. The rain fell in an auditory pattern around me. If I listen just right, I can hear it dripping. When I click my tongue against the roof of my mouth, the sound reflects back its location. That's science, old woman." "If you say so, Zayden. Some may call it science. I choose not to."

"That was the strange sound I heard, those clicks," Denita interrupted.

"Like a whale or a bird, reflecting sound back is part of nature," Zayden spoke.

"Or a miracle," Bobbien added.

"He is still blind," Cosfar fumed. "He is of no use to us!"

"Says who? Have you forgotten the Elements?" Bobbien demanded. "Are your ears so full of anger and rain that you have lost your ability to believe? The minute you are challenged, you fold like wet laundry!"

"The Elements have deserted us!" Cosfar's face shook with rage.

A crowd developed, grumbling, calling for more to join them with Cosfar, Zayden, Bobbien, and Denita in the center. The rain dripped steadily, covering them all with moisture.

"Have they?" Bobbien returned menacingly. "Or have they put obstacles in our path to test the depths of our faith? Are you so sure they have left?" She held up her hands in the gloom "Let us rejoice! Spoken through this man, Ereth has. A miracle has happened. Close to death as it comes, he was, and Ereth has breathed life into him. Lead us to victory, he will." She grabbed Zayden's lax hand high, reaching with all her might to the tallest tree. "Unite, we shall! We shall unite to save our home!"

"Wait a second there, Bobbien. I'm blind. I can't..." Zayden whispered.

Cosfar took that opportunity to pick up a stick and swing it toward Zayden. Zayden pulled away from Bobbien, spinning, his tongue clicking furiously—one hand catching the weapon, the other bunched fist clipping Cosfar neatly on the jaw.

Zayden stood over the unconscious Quyroo as he finished his sentence with wonder: "See."

X

NAJE LAY ON the divan, her hands rubbing the protruding mound of her belly with oil. She wanted her figure to return as soon as possible after the birth. The door opened, and Staf Nuen entered, his glassy eyes yellow with graphen, his pitted face grim. He sat down heavily next to her on the couch, waving out her attendants. They were in the Ambros room, Reminda's former court. Naje had changed the room from the airy and light reception room into a dark, shadowy place. Heavy furniture filled the space, the light from the wall of windows covered by thick, dark drapes that trapped the air inside. She had always lived in a freezing home and vowed never to be cold again. The room was hot, fires built up beyond what Reminda used to have. Staf wiped the sheen of sweat that dotted his forehead. His tail drooped forlornly. "Leave us!" he called out to her attendants.

Naje rolled over, as if to sit up, but Staf stayed her with a hand to her shoulder.

"No, I have missed you." He leaned forward to wrap her in his arms. She slid out of his embrace easily.

"Shouldn't you be in temple with Lothen?" She pulled a graphen packet from her pocket. Flicking it with her forefinger, she walked to the table to pick up the ever-present pipe she kept in the room. She filled it expertly and brought it to him, presenting it with both hands.

"I didn't come here for graphen. I came here for you." He rose to press against her, nuzzling her neck. Naje winced at his clumsiness. Wrapping her in his arms, he embraced her stomach from behind. "How is my son?"

Naje turned to face him. "He would feel both safer and better if his father was with Lothen. Think, Staf. You allow Lothen to conspire with Geva!"

"Geva is a weak goddess." Staf dropped his arms, walked over to pour himself a glass of illegal krayum. He swallowed it, his throat burning from the heat of the liquor. Closing his eyes, he was transported in time to another meeting in the castle, when he plotted with his deceased wife, Beatha, to take the throne from his brother.

But he had the throne now. Staf Nuen was king. King of what, though? Lothen had destroyed Darracia. Transports had denuded the population of Quyroos. Darracians now filled the roles as servants. Plantans held every position of power. He had lured the nobility in, only to watch helplessly as Lothen raped the land, stole titles for his people, and married the Darracian females to his own limited supply of Plantans. Staf Nuen was king to a hostile population that was not even his own species.

"A weak goddess?" Naje rounded on him. "Stop speaking nonsense. She crushed your Elements."

"Element." Staf saluted her beautiful face. "Only Ozre was affected."

"What are you saying? Ozre is gone?"

"He has disappeared for now, but there are three Elements. Didn't you read the book I gave you?"

Naje made a face. "I do not like to read."

Staf stalked to her side. "You have the future king of Darracia in your body, and you don't even understand our culture!"

"What culture?" Naje shouted. "You are a conquered people. Soon the Quyroos will be extinct. The Darracians are the new subspecies, the servants. Why would anyone want to worship their gods—gods that deserted them and allowed them to be vanquished? Not me, Staf, not me!" She turned to leave him alone, another graphen packet on the table for him to use.

"They're not gone," Staf said as he picked up the graphen to spill the dried blossom into his pipe. He lit it thoughtfully, sucking deeply, letting the drug envelop him. "Just sleeping, but none of you listen to me."

XI

BY THE TIME the slave transport reached Bina, a communication system had been developed between the prisoners. Colonel Brend was the highest-ranking officer on the ship. His careful nursing had helped Reminda get better. She was still weak. The food rations were meager, but somehow she had enough for her body to regain its strength. The queen was quiet, watchful, her hooded eyes scanning the room. She said little, accepted no considerations for her status, and a quiet rapport between her and the colonel had developed. As they neared Bina, she hid her anxiety. He had become a solid wall from the ugliness of life, and Reminda was used to his calm resolution, making her feel protected and cherished. His deep commitment and quiet strength reminded her of Drakko. She found comfort when her weary eyes rested upon his large form. The guards were lax. When one of his men succumbed to fever, they switched his clothing.

Wrapping him in blankets, they called the jailors.

"The queen is dead. She has died from the fever."

"Uncover her."

"If I do," Brend told him, after a long bout of coughing, "it will contaminate the entire room. You will get the contagion."

The Plantan backed away. "Jettison her out of the rear hatch with the trash. Yes, yes, get rid of her quickly."

He had disguised Reminda, using bits and pieces from everyone's clothes. Her long white locks were cut close to her head with a contraband razor, dirt rubbed into her skin to hide the color. She disappeared into the role created for her—a young teen, a servant, one of the great unseen who traveled in the shadows. She was his squire, his younger cousin, he told the watchmen.

"Keep your face down," he told her, adjusting her shirt. He pulled a cap over her face, hiding the telltale tattoos. "I mean it. No matter what you hear, keep your face to the ground."

He placed her between two of the biggest Darracians as they exited the ship, getting her past the lazy guards and into one of the metal quarters set up for slaves.

"In a perfect world, my lady, you would be in an allfemale room." He made her a bed in the bunk above his and tucked her between the blankets when the lights were extinguished.

"You have a plan?" she whispered in the dark. "Colonel-"

"Shhhh." He rose to face her. He loomed above her

in the dark, like a great bat, his wide shoulders blocking out whatever weak moonlight reached the room. "I think for safety you must call me by my birth name."

"That is highly irregular, Colonel."

"These are irregular circumstances. Marek. Call me Marek."

"That is for your family, your wife…" she whispered back.

He shook his head. "I have no wife. I will call you Minda."

Reminda watched his lips as he spoke, the words clogged in her throat. It was not that she was a prude; she prided herself on being rather progressive. It just wasn't done, and on top of it, she was the queen. Instead she found her lips breathlessly saying his name, Marek, as though she couldn't help herself.

He nodded in assent. "It is for safety only, my la… Minda. We have a plan." He reached out to touch her hand. Her knuckles were white, gripping the filthy blankets tightly.

The lights in the room burst on, and several Plantan guards spilled in. They had batons that they slammed the bunks with, making a deafening racket. Reminda winced as they neared but slid down at the demands for them all to stand by their beds.

Marek stood slightly before her, his large bulk hiding her slight form.

"Stand, too, you Darracian slime!" a tall, blue-skinned man screamed. He was accompanied by a Venturian male, elevated from slave to housemaster. "This is Unis." The Plantan pointed to the Venturian.

"He is not your friend. You will obey him. He can make your life here easy or hard." He walked up and down the room, looking at each of the men. He stopped before Marek to stare at Reminda's downturned face. "What's wrong with him?" He placed his baton under Reminda's chin. Sparks flew, making her eyes water from the pain.

Marek placed a hand on the stick. "He is my squire, my cousin, a half-breed." "He looks…"

"Blue," Marek finished. "My aunt mated with a Plantan. I promised to keep him safe."

Their eyes locked as if they were taking each other's measure.

Marek shrugged. "He is simple. A blow to his head as a child. I promised."

"He will not last if he cannot keep up," the guard told him simply. He leaned forward. "Save his food for yourself, and dump him at the cliffs. You'll do better without excess weight."

Marek's gray eyes locked with the blue ones. "I made a promise."

"Oh, you and your Darracian code of honor. Let's see how strong you are to withstand the graphen mines. Let's see how long your ethics last there." He laughed as he walked out of the room. He stopped at the doorway to look back at Reminda once again as she stood behind the great bulk of her protector. He smirked, tapped the wall with the baton, hitting the lights to throw them into darkness once more.

TULANI RESTED HER head against the bars of the cell, the light from the four moons bathing her face. The cell was carved in the red rock of the planet and jutted out over the Hixom Sea. She watched the churning waves below her, the white froth swirling in anger, the water choppy. A light breeze blew in from the sea, and she licked her dry lips, tasting salt. She touched her face, realizing the salt was from the tears bathing her face. All was lost. V'sair, Reminda, Zayden were all dead. Life was over; she had no reason to live. She stared at the sky, the dim lights of Syos blurring in her eyes. She brushed at them, ashamed of her feelings, yet she was so alone. It was so quiet, the broken skyline of Aqin silent and dead, now that Geva had crushed the volcano. The raucous sounds of Quyroo encampments were still as a grave. Everyone was gone, silenced by the invasion, defeated by the parasites taking control of the once-beautiful planet. All the problems, the issues Darracians and Quyroos had fought over, paled in light of the conquerors. The differences that divided the planet seemed insignificant. If only they had worked together, united, and stopped fighting over petty nonsense. She looked sadly at the smoking Desa, with its uprooted trees, broken like weak twigs, thousand-year-old trunks snapped like saplings. It was all gone, and she would have the rest of her life to think how she could have played it differently, using her resources to bond V'sair and herself, rather than polarize them.

The old man shuffled by her cell. "You do not eat the food."

Tulani shrugged, her eyes glued to the horizon out the window.

"You are Bobbien's girl?"

Tulani sniffed loudly, then nodded.

"I always liked Bobbien," he offered as he picked up her plate to take it away. "She was nice for a Quyroo. My name is Kovo."

Tulani stiffened, then turned to see if he was baiting her. He had kind eyes. He was a very old Darracian, way too old for this kind of work.

"What do you mean by that?"

"If we understood what it meant to be a Quyroo, things might have been different, is all." He heard his name called, and she noticed his gray skin paled. "You'll only hurt yourself if you don't eat. I will leave this after all." He placed the food next to her on the ground. "Eat it, child. Eat it for Bobbien."

Kovo backed out of the cell without another word.

Tulani considered his words and took a piece of fruit to nibble while she stared absently at the silver surface of the sea. A ball of light spun across the top of the water. Tulani perked up, watching it zip in circles to come and rest on the waves.

"Ozre?" she whispered.

It grew larger, spreading out like a net of stars, blanketing the water. Tiny sparkling lights twinkled, reflected on her face. She pulled herself against the bars, hope blooming in her chest. She reached her hand through her cage as far as it could go. The small ball bounced on the waves, sending geysers into the tiny room. The seawater splashed Tulani, the fluid baptizing her, bringing the ghost of a smile to her face.

"Sweet Sradda," she prayed, her chest filling with excitement. "Water means life. The Trivium is whole. One without the other is not whole. Creator to Ozre to Ereth to Ine—one is powerless without the other. Without them we are nothing." She finished the prayer. The lights winked in agreement, then slowly sank. She watched the illuminated water slowly grow dark as the constellation of lights descended toward the ocean floor. Cocking her head, Tulani digested what she just had witnessed. The lights were blue.

The orbs were Ereth.

XIII

V'SAIR SANK TO his knees before the living rock. "I bow before the mighty Ereth."

The ground rumbled, but oddly, V'sair felt as safe as when he was in the volcano with Tulani and Ozre. He began the Songs of Sradda, the ancient prayer filling the giant space. His voice soared to the ceiling, his passion making him blind to all around him. At last, V'sair felt at peace. He was found, familiar, with something he understood. He sang the words his tutor Emmicus had pounded into his head, finding solace in their message. He ended his prayer with a sigh, relief filling him, waiting for direction to come to him. A net of blue light shimmered above the chamber, outside the glass wall. The balls of energy danced in the water in a synchronized ballet, a thing of beauty. Slowly, gracefully they descended into the giant vault, creating a spangled cloud around them. V'sair stood in wonder, noticing that both Ovie and his daughter, Hennith, were with him, their faces reflecting startled joy.

V'sair raised his arms, waiting to commune with Ereth, allowing him to invade his body. He was drenched; a fine mist surrounded each ball of rotating light. When the voice came, it vibrated inside the entire room.

"I am Ereth, Element of life, born of the water."

"Ereth, Ereth, I commend myself to thee," V'sair responded.

"Well, you should." Ereth laughed. "Took you long enough to notice me."

"Notice you? What do you mean?" V'sair questioned.

"The rains? I tried everything—floods, mists, clouds, torrential downpours—yet none of you reached out. Silly, silly creatures."

"We were preoccupied," V'sair explained.

"To quote my good friend Ozre, excuses…"

"Ozre, is he well? Oh, please say he is well. I saw Geva destroy him."

"Looks can be deceiving," Ereth told him cryptically.

"So," V'sair said simply.

"So," Ereth responded.

"I have found you."

"Yes, you have. What are you going to do now?"

"The Elements are the Trivium. The Elements are whole. Without them we are nothing." V'sair quoted the prayer. He turned to look at the others. "This is a sign. We have to go back."

"No!" Ovie yelled, moving close to the giant

mountain. "I see only one Element: ours, the Element of water. The Trivium is not whole!"

The room started to hum, the vibration coming from the hard rock under the soles of their bare feet. A spinning orb rocketed around the room; its color changed from white to red. Ovie ducked as it made to hit him.

"One does not have to see something to know of its existence!" The deep voice reverberated through the chamber.

"Ozre!" V'sair dropped to his knees, his arms spread in supplication. He could barely contain his joy, his relief.

"Ozre, does my mother live?" he asked.

"Yes, but we must act quickly."

The two Elements hung suspended, their brilliance lighting the chamber. The stone wall was nothing but rocks now, the Elements' power in the spinning orb.

"I don't understand." Ovie approached the ball. "We have heard of Ozre but were not sure of its existence."

"There are three Elements. Ozre, Ereth, and Ine. The Trivium is whole; one without the other is not whole." V'sair made the holy arc from his chest with his hands as he quoted the stanza of the song.

"One cannot exist without the other." The Elements responded to the prayer.

"Ozre, Ozre, light the path." V'sair paused thoughtfully. "Ozre, I thought Geva had destroyed you," he said, his voice ending on a broken whisper.

"Pah, parlor tricks. She is a sham and will disappear when we have united land, sea, and air."

Hennith walked up and placed her finger into the

center of Ozre's red depths. "Oh, Father," she said in shock. "He means to have us join the landwalkers."

"No, no, no." Ovie shook his head. "We do not go there."

V'sair turned to him. "But you must, because Lothen will poison this planet as he did his own. Your own future is compromised."

"We will outlast them," Ovie said firmly. "Welks always do. Your civilizations come and go. We shall be safe if we stay here, away from you and your segregations."

"Is that not segregation, too?" the red ball purred. "The Plantans are capable of coming here. Once they deplete the land, they will ruin the sea." Ozre's voice cut through the tense silence.

"I think he may be right, Father. I have watched them. They do not respect land, so why should they respect the sea?"

"I don't know what to do." He looked at the glowing blue ball. "Ereth, I don't know what to do."

"Nothing happens by chance. It is all preplanned. Eons ago, your ancestors were dropped here to thrive under the Hixom Sea. The Quyroos were given the land, and the Darracians the sky. What is so hard for you to understand? The Trivium is whole," Ereth said gravely.

"The Trivium has been out of balance for too long. The Trivium must be united. One without the other is not whole. One without the other is nothing." Ozre finished the thought.

"Where is Ine?" the girl asked but was ignored.

"Ovie, don't you see? You are the water. The Quyroos

are the land, and the Darracians are the air. If the planet is united, the Trivium will be united," V'sair said, his face filled with excitement. "You said this was preplanned?" He turned to the red ball. "All of this was supposed to happen?" His hair hung around his face, and to Ovie he looked like nothing more than a boy. Yet Ovie trusted him.

"Nothing happens by accident." Ozre spun around the room. "You have to learn."

"Learn what?" V'sair asked.

"V'sair, V'sair…" Ozre sighed. "If we tell you, what would be the fun for us in that? To learn, you must experience it and come to reason yourself. Don't you remember the Fireblade?"

All the death, the fighting, V'sair thought feverously.

"The purpose. It was all a waste!" he accused aloud.

"You told me he was bright," Ereth commented as he came to the spot next to Ozre.

"V'sair," Ozre said, "can't you do any better than that?" "I don't believe this," Ovie stated.

"I still don't see Ine," Hennith complained.

"You didn't see me, yet I am here," Ozre told her. "Think, V'sair."

"It's all for nothing." V'sair looked straight into the warm light of the orb. "All of it. It's all nonsense. Pride, feeling superior, different species. In the end, we are all the same. We build artificial differences and live and die from them."

"Bravo!" Ereth bounced around the room. "One cannot exist without the other."

"It's the basic tenet of our creed, and the chanters

have it all wrong," V'sair said in a shocked whisper. "No one species is better than the other."

"Ereth, what say you?" Ovie dropped to his knees, his hands clasped before the giant rock wall.

"I manifested in the rock, the waterfall, just as Ozre was in the volcano. We don't need to be represented thusly anymore. True belief makes it possible for you to look inside yourself, instead of at a prop, to understand the meaning of life."

"Is it all an illusion?" Ovie asked.

"If you accept the belief, the illusion is over," Ereth said gently.

"Like the Fireblade. We invested it with false powers," V'sair offered helpfully.

"Oh the power was there," Ozre responded, cruising over to V'sair. He glided along the young man's chest and came to rest above his heart. "The power was always there. You were just looking in the wrong place."

"We have no choice," Hennith said. "We have to leave here."

"The Elements have spoken," Ovie intoned.

"The Elements have made it so," V'sair finished.

The lights went out, sending them into complete darkness. Hennith started to say something, and V'sair silenced her. "Shhhh."

The air cooled, and V'sair saw his breath form in clouds before his mouth. Water dripped, pooling around his feet. He jumped back, losing his balance, bumping into Ovie. The older man steadied him as the Element relit the room with a blue glow. Their eyes were drawn to the hard-packed floor where the puddle of water swirled, bubbling violently. Ozre hovered over it, warming it with a red heat. V'sair saw an unmistakable shape forming. Pebbles molded, the dull red turning into the shining gold of fire. The rocky quartz buried in the ground melted into a cross-shaped hilt, and the clear handle filled with elements of the soil. V'sair stared in wonder at the stunning Fireblade. He had never seen one as beautiful in his life. Made from the same substance of the very planet, V'sair knew it was for him and the destiny of his home.

"Yes, V'sair." He heard his father's voice. "You are the new Darracia, my son. You have the heart and strength of a warrior but the soul of a leader. Go and fulfill the promise of your purpose. Make Darracia and her people whole."

V'sair kneeled, tears streaming from his eyes. At last, a Fireblade. Hewn from the red earth of Darracia, solely for him. He had achieved his own heart's desire. He was one with the Fireblade. He reached down his strong fingers, dug it out, held the glowing blade to his face. The heat warmed him, illuminating his face.

Ovie gasped; Hennith's eyes opened wide. The Fireblade's light grew until V'sair was completely encased. His skin turned golden; flames lit his eyes internally. V'sair, the heir to the Fireblade, was one with the sword as no one else before him. His core belief defined the Fireblade instead of the other way around. His destiny dazzled from the light of power shining from his chest.

THE MAUVE CLIFFS of Bina were a sight beyond any description. They jutted out into space, the craggy graphen bushes growing between the cracks in the rocks. The prisoners were lined up, waiting to be harnessed to the high cranes that rose a mile above the cliffs by slow-moving Plantan guards. Given a tasteless soup for breakfast, they marched for hours to roast in the thin air in the mountaintops of Bina. Quyroos had it the worst. Used to the moist, humid air of the Desa, many died where they waited, their lungs exhausted from weak air. Gasping, they would fall to the ground, trembling like fish out of water, until the lack of usable air finished them off. No one could help them; the guards wouldn't allow it. Reminda watched helplessly as a Darracian was thrown from the cliff for stopping to help a dying comrade. His screams went on forever, echoing back from the bottomless fall.

The harness hurt. She was tied into it and thrown over the cliff to free-fall for almost a half hour. Reminda was warned not to lose her collection sack, else she be released to fall to her doom. Marek nodded as she went over the cliff before him, and she felt his steady gaze watching her as she dropped. She tried hard not to be afraid, but fear lodged itself in her heart, and she was breathless for most of the drop, the lack of support leaving her disoriented. For a minute, she prayed the rope would break, allowing her to join Drakko and V'sair. But despite her loss, the spirit within her prevailed, and she held on to life as the rope slid through her fingers. Much as Reminda thought about death, she knew she had a job. Marek and the people on Bina needed her. She was the lodestone, the beacon of their hope, and she had to finish her purpose. The queen watched the rock speed past her. The screams of others as they descended filled the air. Buffeted by the hot, dry winds, she called out to the Elements to guide her. Abruptly, her rope ended, and Reminda smashed into the rock wall, scraping her arms raw. Marek was thrown a minute later, he was falling right behind her. Soon he was beside her, steadying her with soothing words. His entire cheek bled, and Reminda reached up to brush away the pebbles embedded in his gray skin. He hissed at the pain, and she shushed him.

They swung free, their legs dangling, the dual suns beating down without mercy. He squinted from the harsh rays of the suns. The sky was a pale green, the soil a crusty white—bone-dry dirt that sucked the moisture from their bones. The air was so thin, so lacking in moisture that their tongues felt thick, and it hurt to swallow.

Marek had a tube of water that he removed from his plaquette. "Drink it slow, and don't let the guards see it," he warned, handing it to Reminda.

"I can't take this. What about the others?"

"We are used to it," he said harshly. "Do not be foolish or brave. Your people need you, their queen, not a martyr."

Reminda bowed her head. "Never think that I Market touched her wrist, sending sparks where their skin touched. "I know, Minda. There is not a soldier here that wouldn't give his or her life for you. I would give my life for you."

Marek was abruptly pulled away to swing dangerously over the vast chasm. Reminda gasped with worry as he spun out into nothingness. He was warned by a staccato voice ordering him to do what he was supposed to do and not hang around. The Plantan guards never tired of this joke, and it had the same uproarious effect on them.

Marek swung forward and grabbed the teal-colored roots of a graphen bush. It had blue blossoms, giving off a sickly sweet smell. He plucked one, sticky white sap coating his fingers.

"Graphen." He showed her. "Put as many in your bag as you can. If you don't bring enough—arrrr!" He shoved her out of the way as a screaming Quyroo dropped heavily next to them. His line snapped, and his scream continued for a long time. Reminda's eyes followed his drop, the way down seemingly endless.

"Marek…" She touched his arm. "We have to get out of here."

"Of that I have no doubt. We are working on an uprising," he whispered back.

"How? You are unarmed," she told him.

Marek held up the blossom, twirling it in his fingers.

"Perhaps not, Your Majesty."

XV

ZAYDEN SAT IN the hut, while Bobbien placed a plate of steaming food before him. "Eat, eat, you must. Make up for all those starving days, you must." She smiled at him. He was clean-shaven, and she longed to tweak his cheek as she had done when he was a boy. He had bathed, found new clothes, and looked more like Drakko's son once again. Bobbien was happy. Her heart beat lightly once more in her chest. She had discovered on one of her forays into the marketplace that Tulani was in a cell under Seren's guard. She was on Darracia, and she was alive. Bobbien had a message from the castle, from the female Naje, and a plan had formed in her mind to rescue her granddaughter. Now she had to get Zayden well enough to do his part. He had worked with the elders of the community formulating a plan. The attack was planned for tomorrow.

The food smelled delicious. Zayden had a Quyroo nursemaid in his youth, and the vegetable mash brought back sentimental memories of his time in his father's royal nursery.

The odors wafted up, and saliva gathered in his mouth. He could smell the orange zacky roots mixed with nectar from the wysbie nests. Leaning down, he allowed the steam to bathe his face, his eyelids prickling with emotion. He knew the plate was a beautiful symphony of colors. He smelled the rich humus of the forest, the dense moisture of life. He didn't need his eyes to know it was filled with the yellows, greens, and reds of the Desa, savory with a wealth of flavors. He was hungry, he thought with surprise. His face moved up, reaching across the table to touch Denita's soft face. She gasped and pulled away, but he stayed her, the calloused pads of his fingers caressing her cheeks. With the barest touch, his fingers feathered across the planes and angles of her face.

He sat back abruptly, calling out, "Bobbien!"

"Aye." The older female lumbered by, her hands on her hips. Zayden reached up, his hands unerring, and clasped the fine bones of the old woman's wrists.

"You can see everything now; yep, you can," she told him with a nod.

Zayden sat back, pushing the plate away. "You are starving," he stated plainly.

"Aye," Bobbien responded. "We are."

"Why haven't you said anything?" He stood to pace the room, his tongue clicking so that he managed the small space expertly.

"We have." Bobbien was packing a small bag with birthing tools.

Zayden turned to face her, his head cocked. "When?"

"Too drunk, you were, to notice."

Denita rose to take his hand and kiss his palm. "You can see all this?"

He pulled her close, resting his chin on the top of her head. "One does not have to be blind not to see."

"But…" Denita was puzzled.

"Eyes are only one of the senses," Bobbien said. "Others, he has. Knows what must be done, he does. Don't waste the food, young uns." Bobbien walked out of the hut, leaving them, the sack thrown over her shoulder.

"Where are you going, Bobbien?" Zayden called out.

"You know we plan to attack tomorrow."

"I have a job that must be done. Be back by daylight, I will." She took her traveling staff and left the hut.

"Bobbien," Zayden said, "we go whether you are here or not."

Bobbien nodded, tucking her head under a robe. "Great Sradda willing," was her reply.

Denita reached up to cup his face in her hands. "I have missed you."

Zayden pulled away. "I am no good for you, Denita."

Denita crouched before him. "You think I care about a paltry thing like sight? I love you, Zayden. I love all of you."

"I am useless."

"You move as well as someone with full sight," Denita responded.

Zayden winced. "I have found a solution so I can

fight and do what my father would have expected. I can't do anything for you."

Denita sighed. "Zayden, I am broken. I may be able to see, but my heart is not like anyone else's. I will never be soft and sweet like some of the women here. I am not kind."

"Don't talk stupid. You are brave and loyal." He turned to her, taking her hand. "I would have died without you. Twice!"

"You could love someone like me?" she asked incredulously.

Zayden stroked her cheek. "You have to ask?" he whispered.

"So why do you hold yourself at a different standard? We are all broken in one way or another. You may not be able to see my face, but you can heal my heart."

"It…it doesn't bother you that I am blind?"

"Stupid, stupid warrior. I don't care. I don't care at all."

Zayden covered her mouth with his own. She smelled of sunshine and grass. He rubbed his cheek against her hair, releasing a perfume he identified only with Denita. He pulled her tightly against him, and his body tingled as she arched against him, her sighs filling him with excited joy. He held her hands high above them, palm to palm, his voice low.

"I love you, Denita. I think I have loved you from the minute I first met you."

"Well, why didn't you say so?" Denita kissed him tenderly, stroking the hair from his face.

"I say before the Elements, we are one. Say it with me, Denita," Zayden urged her.

He kissed her deeply, robbing her of breath, but she whispered, "You would make me your own?"

"I will never have my sight."

"But you will always have my heart." She gripped his hand and placed it on her chest, then moved her mouth to his palm and kissed it. "I love you, Zayden. We are one."

"We are one," he repeated the words, making her his wife.

Denita ripped at his shirt, freeing it from his pants, so that she could caress the hard planes of his chest.

He pulled her into the sleeping quarters, lay down beside her on the low cot, loving her with his hands, his skin, his senses, seeing her like no other woman. He knew her body as if it was part of his own, their skin becoming one. He covered her, thrilling in her cries of delight. Zayden smelled love, tasted love, felt love. He didn't need to see it to know it was there.

XVI

THE PAINS CAME with daybreak. Naje bent in half as her belly contracted. She thought it was early. She hadn't expected the child this soon. The midwife, an old Quyroo, rested her palms on her stomach, giving her a knowing look. Her cool hands stroked the woman's taut stomach, massaging the infant within.

"You came," Naje said. She was alone with the Quyroo. Naje had sent all of her women from the room.

"Asked, you did. There is a problem, my lady. The child is breech." Bobbien stood, her eyes locked on Naje's, making sure the pregnant woman understood.

Naje's face turned white. "You can help me?" she asked shrilly.

"Impossible, it is not. Just difficult." Bobbien held up her hands. "My hands are old. They are no longer nimble. Turn the child, we must. My granddaughter is imprisoned by Seren. She will be able to do it."

"I can't do that. Seren is overlord of the Desa. He answers only to Lothen."

"Then tell Lothen to turn the child." Bobbien began to pack her tools. "Help you, I cannot."

"No!" Naje held out a hand in supplication. "Don't leave me."

"Deliver your child, I will, but not before you give me back mine."

"I don't have any say on the planet. I don't know if I can get word to Seren."

"You got word to *me*." Bobbien walked toward the door.

"No, wait!" Naje called out to her. "I need you." She held out her caramel hand, imploring the older woman.

"Aye, you do." Bobbien pointed to her belly. "The child must be turned." She looked Naje directly in the eyes. "You will get my granddaughter released, or I will not help you."

Naje winced. There was a rush of fluid between her legs as the water protecting the baby gushed out.

"The child comes." Bobbien nodded knowingly, pushing her long braids from her face proudly.

Naje had contacted the old woman, afraid of the Plantan doctor. His cold blue hands repulsed her. He had forbidden her to eat certain fruits, be outside, and twice he had tried to bleed her, as was their custom. It was not right; Naje felt it in her heart it was not the right thing to do.

"It is early," Naje told her. "The child is a month too soon."

"I think not, my lady."

They heard a commotion outside the door. Naje gestured for the Quyroo to hide. She ducked into the closet, leaving the door slightly ajar so she could hear the conversation.

Lothen stalked into the room. "You asked for me? What do you want?"

"The future king begs to be born." Naje gingerly sat on the edge of the bed, her head bowed with another contraction.

"Why are you alone?" He paced the room impatiently.

"Where are your women?"

"I don't want them. You must do something for me, Lothen," she implored, her hands clasped.

"She is not alone." Staf Nuen walked in. "I am here." The two men stared at each other like feral jasts.

"I wasn't talking about you," Lothen sneered. "Where is the doctor?"

"I don't want the doctor. I will have a woman." "Who?" Staf demanded.

"I want the one called Tulani."

"No." Staf shook his head. "I will bring a Darracian healer."

"By Geva's heart, you will not," Naje hissed. She moaned, bending in half. "I want the Quyroo girl!" she wailed. Her hands went to her hair, pulled the long tresses free, and the black locks cascaded down her back. She looked wild, her eyes glazed white. Her voice took on a husky sound, filling the room, and the voice of Geva filled the chamber.

"She will have the girl, now!" she screamed, a blast of air rushing through the room, scattering papers and clothing.

Lothen stood, his blue face ashen. "By your command, my goddess." He bowed deeply, backing out of the door. "Thy will be done. Deliver the future king safely."

Lothen left the room to do Geva's bidding. Staf looked around suspiciously, then stalked out the door.

"Neatly done." The old Quyroo slid out from her hiding place.

"You will have your child, and I will have mine." Bobbien nodded regally.

XVII

"RELEASE TULANI!" SEREN crushed the note in his fist. "No!"

"You have no choice. You have been commanded."

"By whom, Staf Nuen? He is nothing." Seren wrote furiously at his desk. He handed it to a messenger at his door. "Give that to the king."

Jokin stalked to the door and snatched the note from the servant. "No! Wait here." He pushed him into the hall, turning to round on his son. "Fool! Have you no idea how the court works? What do you care for the girl? Make a trade." He poked him with a red finger.

"But she's our bait. How will we get Bobbien if we let her go?"

"We will follow her," Jokin responded. "She will lead us to them."

Tulani rubbed the raw skin of her wrists as she

was led to a shuttle to take her to the castle. It was a shorter trip, she noticed. The fortress hovered below the clouds, not far from the surface of the higher ground of the planet. Bright moonlight lit the night, and she raised her face to catch the light rain drenching them. It misted against her skin, making her close her eyes to revel in the clean feel of the water. It smelled like ozone, and she turned to see the hulking shadow of Aqin in the distance. The sky was dark, the faint outline of the cityscape blurred, the lights mere smudges in the night sky. She scanned the city, noticing that some of the important landmarks—buildings that were built when the city was first sent into the sky—were missing. She searched the floating edifices but couldn't find the outlines. Statues, signs, anything not associated with one of the larger structures were gone. The city looked deserted, and Tulani shivered, despite the warmth of the evening.

She traveled in a shuttle in such a state of disrepair that they stalled twice, falling rapidly into frightening tailspins. Finally, she was delivered, shaken, to the doors of the fortress. A Darracian servant informed her she was to follow him. The walked in sullen silence. The great halls were deserted. Rodents had left droppings on the once-pristine floors. Lights were dim, as if there was not enough power to go around. The busy noise that made Syos a grand capital was gone, leaving the city a weak shadow of itself. She recognized the way to the Ambros rooms, Reminda's old salon, and felt her heart contract with sorrow. Everyone was gone; the ghosts didn't even walk the halls.

The door opened, and her wrist was grabbed by a hooded servant. Tulani's breath hitched, the realization that the fingers were both dearly familiar and in a shade of red that made her feel faint with relief. Strong arms and Bobbien's ample chest surrounded the shocked girl—words too difficult to even utter. Tulani rested her head on her grandmother, so overcome that she gulped air, dry sobs racking her slender body. Bobbien patted her back with a familiarity that brought more tears to her eyes.

"Oh, Greanam, I thought I'd never see you again."

"Never say so, Tulani. Desert you, I never would. We will have a victory yet. Did he hurt you?" Bobbien searched the young face worriedly.

Tulani shook her head. "No. I think he was using me for bait to bring you in. What are you doing here? It is not safe." Tulani looked up, her star-shaped eyes shining. A feral scream rent the air, making Tulani jump. Bobbien turned to the divan to see Naje's face contorted with pain.

"I made a deal; your small hands, I have need of." She led the girl to the bed. "Help you, my granddaughter." She turned to Tulani. "The baby is breech. Turn it, you must." "How?"

"Inside," Bobbien said grimly.

Tulani shook her head. "I cannot." The woman on the bed was breathing in short pants. Sweat gleamed on her caramel face. Her almond eyes narrowed to slits.

"Help me, old woman!" she gasped between pains.

"Easy it is." Bobbien held up her hand, showing her the movements. "Like so..." She rotated her fingers on

Tulani's fist, showing her how to turn the child. Bobbien made her cleanse then oil her hands thoroughly.

"Why do you wait?" Naje wailed.

"You want to die from an infection? Do not you know even the most basic rules?" Bobbien asked.

"I. Don't. Care," Naje responded between grunts.

Tulani observed that she was beautiful despite the strain reddening her face. The veins stood out on her long neck as she groaned. They heard a knock at the door, followed by a harsh voice. Tulani froze, her face ashen, recognizing Staf Nuen's sinister voice.

"What is happening in there?" he shouted, frustrated with the lack of response. "Let me in. I want to see my son."

"Tell him, you cannot. She labors, and the child comes," Bobbien urged her granddaughter to speak. "Tulani, he knows you are here, but he cannot know that I am."

Tulani swallowed, repeating what her grandmother told her.

The door rattled, and this time Naje screamed, "Go away, you old fool! Leave me to woman's business!"

Tulani placed herself between the woman's legs. Concentrating, she reached into the tight flesh, feeling the contractions pulse against her hands. Bobbien wiped the woman's head, urging her to pant. Tulani felt a blockage, realizing with a start it was the smooth skin of the infant. Her fingers caressed the back of the child, finding a slippery place to squeeze her hands in the narrow opening to adjust the baby. Naje was cursing, her face mottled, blood pouring out of her. Tulani looked up in panic to see her grandmother's gentle eyes smiling.

"Normal, this is. Don't worry. Let the Elements guide your hand, girl."

Tulani bit her lip, relaxing her hands, moving them carefully to ease them between the baby and the woman's womb. She found an opening, slipped them to surround the baby, turned him ever so gently. Naje was shrieking like a banshee, her face mottled. Tulani looked worriedly at her grandmother, who smiled benignly.

"Good work, you do, young healer," Bobbien told her proudly.

"I see his head!" Tulani's face lit with relief. The baby's head crowned in the opening. "He is coming," she said with awe.

"Push now, my lady. Don't be afraid. Push!" Bobbien told Naje as she wiped her head.

Naje gritted her teeth, concentrating all her effort on pushing the baby out. She groaned a sound so deep, it came from the well of her womb.

"I have his head," Tulani shouted, her face filled with joy. This was beautiful, and it made her feel happy.

Another push, and the shoulders burst through, followed by the rush as the feet escaped.

"My son," Naje asked urgently, "is he well? I don't hear him."

Bobbien grabbed the child, slapped him heartily, and they heard the wails of life fill the room. Tulani's smile faded as Bobbien rested the infant on his mother's breast.

"Great Sradda, Greanam, did you see…"

"Quiet! Be still," Bobbien warned her as she finished the job, cleaning the new mother.

Naje looked up, her eyes filled with gratitude and just a bit of surprise.

"So, you were right, old woman. He was not early." She played thoughtfully with the child's tiny hand.

"Just as I thought."

Staf banged on the door. "Let me in, Naje! Now!"

"All right, you will be?" Bobbien asked, ignoring the racket.

Naje shrugged indifferently. "You had better leave. Take the girl and leave." She looked down at the infant, smiling.

"Swaddle him first, I think." Bobbien wrapped the baby tightly in blankets.

Bobbien turned, grabbed Tulani's hand as if she were a child, and escaped out of the chambers through the rear terrace. She reached into her bag and pulled out a large robe. "Now I will swaddle you," she said with a smile. "Put this on, girl," she said as she covered her own braids with the cowl-like hood. They jumped over the balustrade to leap down the many levels until they could descend to the vehicle station to fly home in a stolen shuttle.

Naje looked up as both Lothen and Staf entered the room, the baby wrapped tightly in swaddling.

"A son?" Staf asked.

Naje smiled, her carmine lips wide. "A son for Darracia."

Staf reached out to take his son's hand. The webbed fist grabbed the gray finger tightly. Staf growled in shock. Flicking back the blanket, he stared in horror at a blue infant with a shock of white hair. Lothen threw back his head and roared with laughter.

XVIII

ZAYDEN USED A long staff as a weapon as he stood in front of a group of Quyroos. A volunteer faced him, defensively backing up as Zayden lunged with the stick. He tapped him on the shoulder, despite the Quyroo's nimble feet. The observers clapped in wonder as Zayden showed them moves to protect themselves in an offense.

Anyone who didn't know him would think he was fully sighted. But for the quiet clicking of his tongue, he seemed a great warrior. Denita watched from under the janjan tree, proud of her man's fleet footwork.

Zayden invited three men up. The land was marshy, the light rain falling but ignored by the combatants. They had made a clearing, cutting the low-hanging branches, so they could practice fighting skills. Most were amazed with the blind warrior's skill. No matter how quiet they were, he heard them approach, using a stick to show the movements to dispatch an enemy. He placed himself in the middle, and they arranged an attack, surprised by his deft movements. They were dispatched without harm, and Zayden lined them up again for another go. This time, they managed to outwit his moves, and Zayden applauded their movements. His easy smile instilled confidence, and soon his group had swelled to hundreds. He worked with them all day, teaching them defensive movements.

Cosfar stormed over, his red face seething. "You play soldier with a blind man! To what purpose?"

Zayden reached down and took a cloth to wipe the perspiration running down his face and neck. "You have a problem, Cosfar?" he asked.

"Yes! This is madness. Madness. How do you expect them to go up against the Plantans tomorrow? With sticks?"

He gestured to the staff. "They have guns."

Zayden nodded. "You are right. So should we stay here like herns, waiting for them to find us and pick us off one by one?"

The crowd rumbled in agreement.

Cosfar turned. "You listen to a blind man. A Darracian? You would trust one such as him?"

He spun to hit Zayden, who bent backward, Cosfar's fist flying past him uselessly.

"He is not blind anymore," Denita called out. "He has sight." She ran to their small hut, then came back a minute later, her hands hidden behind her back.

"You lie," Cosfar hissed.

Denita called out, "Zayden!" and pitched something

at him. He caught it easily, his hand wrapping around the hilt of his Fireblade.

The small clearing got deathly quiet.

"Denita…" Zayden held out the sword for her. "Where did you get it?"

"I've always had it. It was on your ship. I never let it out of my sight." She had been saving it for the right time to give it back to him.

"I don't…I don't know…"

"Try, Zayden. Just try."

Holding the Fireblade with two hands, Zayden closed his eyes. His fingers gripped the hilt, and the sword leaped in his hands, the familiar hum singing out in triumph. He swallowed convulsively, sweat beading his brow. His muscled arms quivered, his knuckles white.

"Tell me the color," he whispered, then spoke loudly.

"Denita, tell me the color."

"Blue, my warrior. Your blade is bright blue with the color of justice." She turned to the crowd of Quyroos. "Will you follow him?"

"Aye!" a large male called out, raising his pike in the air.

"I will join him to defeat the Plantans."

"Me too!" Another jumped up. Soon the air was filled with the cries of the Quyroos, united in their support of a new leader.

"He is blind, you fools. He is blind!" Cosfar's shouts were smothered by the growing crowd surrounding Zayden.

"We march!" Zayden raised his shining blade into the air. "We march to retake our home."

His small army roared with approval, forming lines to follow the glowing beacon of justice to their destiny.

XIX

THE WEAK BOY was on his stomach, reaching under the bunk for the coins he had thrown there. Unis eyed him with a nasty smile. He had sent the others to race around the compound, leaving him time alone with the big Darracian's squire. There had been a showdown. It had been weeks in coming. Unis antagonized Marek, wanting to separate the protective Darracian from his little squire. The little one intrigued him, and Unis wanted to get to the bottom of those long-lashed eyes. He set Marek up for a fight, punishment being a run around the track of the compound for the whole night with the rest of the Darracians from his quarters. The entire barrack was sent out for the senseless exercise, save the young boy. Marek hesitated, not wanting to follow the orders, but Reminda urged him not to disobey. Unis threw contraband coins to roll on the floor, then ordered the weakling to retrieve them. Every time he bent over, Unis pressed his baton into the fleshy part of the boy's thigh, delighting in the squeak he made when it zapped him. Unis laughed, his head thrown back in mirth. He was so bored on Bina.

He rolled a handful of pebbles under the heating units, chuckling gleefully as Reminda crawled on all fours to retrieve them. Unis came so close that when Reminda turned to find him breathing heavily on the back of her neck, she could count the ugly pores on his rubbery nose.

He stared at her feminine face. "Who are you?" Unis whispered as he licked his lips, frozen with the realization that Reminda was not a boy.

She used this advantage to smile coyly, swallowing down bile, peeping up at him through softened eyes. Reaching out, she squeezed his upper arm and sighed dramatically.

"You are so very strong," she told him coyly.

Unis gulped. "You are female."

"Oh, please don't tell," came the sweet reply. She moved closer to his face and spoke in a seductive voice. "I just want to be close to you." She shivered, closing her eyes dreamily.

"I don't know. It's against the rules. I could get in trouble. I should report this." He looked out the window warily at the running males, gaging how much time he had.

"Can't it be our little secret? If you tell, they will move me to the women's side, and I'll never see you." Reminda moistened her lips, leaning forward to kiss him gently. She brushed her breast against his arm as she leaned in.

Unis reached over to grab her, but the loud squawk of his communication device made him jump back guiltily. His commander's tinny voice came through, slicing the tense air. "Unis!" he shouted. "Unis, report to me at once!"

Unis stood shakily, bumping into a chair. He stumbled out the door, leaving it wide open, allowing the freezing morning air to enter. The prisoners filed in, Marek's worried gaze finding Reminda with relief. She sat on the floor, a satisfied smile on her face.

"Are you well?" he asked, his face filled with concern.

Reminda reached behind her to take out a baton. "I think we have our catalyst," she told him with a smile.

Marek took the weapon, considering it thoughtfully. He looked up at Reminda.

"I distracted him, but he knows I am female. We must do it today."

Marek nodded grimly. "Yes, today."

XX

ZAYDEN'S FORCES SWELLED. Males and females with makeshift weapons marched through the eastern provinces, picking up more and more Quyroos as they traveled into the swampy fells, tramping with the single-minded purpose of taking out the oppressive rule. They used whatever tools they could find from the land. A young boy approached Zayden eagerly, pulling at his tunic.

"Are you the commander?" he asked.

Zayden kept walking. "Go back to your mother, little boy. Only adults can fight."

"I can help!"

Zayden nodded. "Of that I'm sure. Go back and watch the young uns, freeing up the elders."

The boy held up something in Zayden's line of vision. "What! Are you blind? Look. I have something that will help!"

Zayden paused, causing the whole crowd to slow, a hush falling over the mob.

The boy realized Zayden was indeed sightless. "I'm sorry, my lord," he said in a shocked whisper. He placed a stick with hollowed-out gourds attached with vines in Zayden's hand. "Look. I made this weapon. We." He gestured to a small tribe of children, each holding a handful of the slingshots. "You don't need skill. Look." He then amended his command. "I mean listen." The boy loaded the gourd with a rock. "Name a target."

Denita stepped forward. "Can you hit the wysbie nest on that tree?" The boy looked at her with apprehension. "Oh, they're gone," she said. "Can't you see the nest is empty? Unless it's too far?"

The boy spun the gourds in his agile hands, so fast they became an orange blur.

Zayden cocked his head, listening to the whir of the weapon, followed by the whistle of the small rock launched to bring down the nest. Zayden didn't need to hear the crowd's murmur of approval to know it hit the target true.

"How many of these do you have?"

"We have hundreds of them. We have been preparing for an attack."

Cosfar stomped over, his face a red mask of rage. "Stupid boy," he sneered. "They have no skill to lob mere rocks at the enemy. Go back to your mother and hide until it is over."

"No," Zayden told him. "Think, Cosfar, of the effect if hundreds of these missiles are launched at once."

"Don't forget the zandy grenades!" Denita held one of the homemade bombs in her hands.

"You will all die!" Cosfar warned. "You fight the Darracians as well as the Plantans!"

"Then either way we will die! Whether it is in battle or on a transport to Sradda knows where, we have no choice. I believe that when my kinsmen realize their freedom lies united with us, we will see a defection."

"You don't know that," Cosfar replied.

"That is true. One thing I do know is that the Elements taught us that only when they unite, they create the perfect balance of life." He raised his voice for all to hear. "My father, King Drakko, died for his belief that every member of this planet must be equal and deserves a voice. Maybe we have to follow the Elements' example and unite as well." Cosfar silently considered this idea.

"Who wants one of these?" Zayden held up the slingshot.

There was a chorus of ayes. Cosfar picked one up, tucked it in his loincloth. Denita looked at him in question.

He glanced at Zayden, admiration in his eyes, and said, "Perhaps I have been the one who was blind."

XXI

V'SAIR SET UP a command center in Ovie's living space. Ovie invited the clan leaders of each of the families to help formulate a plan to invade Darracia. They arrived, wet and exhausted, from a network of caves that ran under the seabed. At first, they refused to join him, but when Ovie recounted his experience with the Elements, they agreed but with many differences of opinion.

"This is foolhardy, V'sair." Ovie pointed to a map spread out across a table.

"I don't see another way. A frontal attack to take out the village on the Plains of Dawid."

"Just march out of the water and attack?" Pudar, an elder, asked. "No disrespect, young man, but they will wipe us out. I would rather take my chance staying down here until they all kill each other off. Aside from that," he added, "how will we prevent being mistaken for Plantans? The resemblance is remarkable."

V'sair nodded. "You don't have facial tattoos. All of them are marked at puberty. It's the lack of the design that gives you away as different."

"Still, it seems foolish to make war when they are not even aware of our existence." Another one of the elders spoke up. "They are strong, warlike; we are not."

There was a great murmuring of approval. V'sair ran a hand through his loose hair. He refused to braid it until he returned home.

The girl Hennith spoke up. "No, don't you see there are so many of us? Their forces are limited."

V'sair turned to her. "Exactly how many of your species are capable of fighting?"

"We number in the thousands. I have heard that there is a finite number of Plantans. The worry is of the Darracians.

They will sway any battle."

"It still doesn't matter how many we are. We won't be able to reach the city in the clouds," a tall male interrupted, his face worried.

One of the guards who had brought V'sair to this place spoke. "It won't be as hard as you think. The city is sliding onto the planet. They have used up all the randam and are running out of fuel."

"How could they use up the crystals?" Ovie asked, his face incredulous.

"When they bombed the Desa, the crystals rotted on the broken trees. They have decimated their work force.

V'sair is right. They are sucking the life from this planet, and we will be next."

"If we make a concerted attack from each of the shorelines, meeting together in the center, we would not only surprise them but overwhelm them with sheer numbers," V'sair said, a blue finger pointed out at the four entry points to land.

Ovie shook his head. "It could work. If we had muster support from the landwalkers, the Plantans would be easily overwhelmed."

A young guard burst into the room, breathlessly interrupting. "It has begun. The Quyroos are marching en masse from the eastern provinces, under the leadership of a Darracian."

"This is a sign from the Elements. Do you know who the leader is?" V'sair asked.

"I don't know him. They say he is blind," the guard answered.

"That's crazy, a blind leader," Pudar sputtered. Many agreed loudly.

"Perhaps the Elements are guiding them," Hennith offered.

"It doesn't matter." V'sair shrugged his shoulders as he rolled up the map, looking to Ovie for direction. "If they are heading west, then they are going to attack in the Plains of Dawid. What is our most direct route there?"

"We swim east," Ovie stated. He directed the biggest group to follow them. Three other groups were sent to various shores to meet in the center of the great landmass.

Armed with their spears, V'sair with his blade, they left to join the rebels heading for Plantan territory.

XXII

THE LINE MOVED painstakingly slow this morning as they reported to work. It was bitter cold, the coming dawn barely reaching the thin atmosphere of Bina. The bleak landscape blended with the colorless sky. Marek shifted from foot to foot in the cold, trying to block the worst of the winds from Reminda. The queen's eyes teared, making frozen tracks down her tattooed cheeks. Marek reminded her to keep her face down.

Harnesses were cinched, and soon Reminda was freefalling over the cliffs, her heart soaring, knowing that whatever the outcome, she was doing something to help the others.

She bounced painfully, feeling the descending drop as the next person came to hang suspended near her territory of bushes. She looked up to see Marek hurtling down, too close to the stone wall. An outcropping of rocks jutted away from the cliff, and Reminda watched in horror as he collided with the mass, a groan escaping his body. Several rocks came loose and fell downward, hitting workers on their way to oblivion. He flew past her, his eyes closed in pain, one leg a bloody mess.

Reminda spun herself in a circle, using her feet to propel away from the wall to try to reach him. The suns' rays began to burn through her hat to bake her head. Sweat drenched her body as the temperature radically changed. Her feet dangled, and no matter how hard she pushed herself away from the wall, she couldn't get her straps to lower her. A shout from above made her look up into the blinding rays of the suns.

"Hey, you!" a guard shouted, his hands resting on his gun a he looked down. "Start picking."

A hand touched her back, and she turned, relief warring with worry when she saw Marek painfully making his way up the rock wall. He waved to the guard, showing crushed blossoms in his big hands. The guard shrugged, walking away to check on the other side. Marek made eye contact with the men of their barracks. As planned, the soldiers clustered themselves so they all appeared to be picking blossoms. Reminda watched as they formed two layers. The ones closer to the rock wall chipped away at the surface, while a man behind them covered their bodies with their own as they picked the graphen.

"Are you all right?" she asked Marek.

"I was pushed," Marek responded.

"I thought so. Do you have it?" Marek nodded, showing her the handle of the baton.

"How long do they have to dig?" Reminda used her pickax to start scraping an opening in the rock face. It crumbled easily; her hands were soon coated with the mauve dust.

"Hard to say. Will you be able to climb up?" Marek studied her face intently.

Reminda looked at the vast wall rising above her. "I must. Great Sradda, give me strength."

"Tomo will be right behind you." He nodded to his next-in-command, who motioned back at him.

"I wish it were you." She placed her hand on his arm. "Will you be able to climb up with that leg?"

"This scratch?" he laughed. "Drakko would make fun of me."

The mention of her dead husband sobered them, and Reminda looked away.

The day wore on, and soon the entire cliff was honeycombed with small pockmarks that were methodically stuffed with crushed graphen blossoms. Every so often the Plantans would look down the cliff wall to see the Darracians and Quyroos working silently in the oppressive heat.

Reminda's tongue swelled in her mouth, the mauve dust clogging her nostrils. She rested her head against the warm stone, exhausted.

"It won't be long now, my lady." Marek came up behind her. He hefted her up from behind. His hands molded to her backside, and no matter how clinical he tried to be, Marek knew where his hands were. And her shaking body told him that Reminda was just as aware. "Start climbing," he ordered.

Reminda stretched her arms to grip small spaces so she could inch her way up. Her fingernails tore; her hands were scraped raw. She glanced down to see row after row of Darracians and Quyroos swinging to Marek. He used his baton's heated tip to light small rags. They stole looks at her progress, watching Tomo inch up silently behind her.

As planned, the small group of Quyroos started to chant the song, the signal that they all had to get ready. Reminda's hand fumbled with the crumbling edge of the cliff. Her arms shook with effort, and she was suddenly afraid she would not be able to make it. She felt a hand push her up so that she lifted over onto the top.

Tomo followed her up and screamed, "Now!" He ran forward, grabbed the guard's gun, and spun him so that he was launched over the side of the cliff. He aimed the gun at an armed Venturian running toward them, his weapon blasting away. Tomo shot him, then ran to hit the switches, reeling in all the harnessed men and women hanging off the side of the cliff.

Reminda was on the other side, going down the rows of winches, reversing the direction so the air filled with the whine of the machines.

The first explosion rumbled underneath them. Reminda worried that the graphen wasn't going to be dry enough to be an effectual explosive. The staccato of their homemade bombs going off rocked the mountain. Hordes of prisoners bounced onto the hilltop, screaming as they took off to attack the guard's quarters. For a minute, Reminda stared at the horizon, not knowing what to do, when Marek limped up to her. She smiled in relief. He smelled of graphen and looked slightly stoned from breathing all the smoke.

"We have to get out of here. The graphen veins run deep. Once a tree is lit, the flame will burn to the root. I'm not sure, but Bina could be doomed."

"Well, good riddance to that!" Reminda panted as they dodged the crowds.

Marek pulled Reminda along. It was bedlam. Prisoners stormed the guards, making short work of the opposition. Desolate, on the back side of the solar system, Bina was not considered a threat, and Lothen used a small command of barely a dozen men to control it.

Reminda gasped, hiding her face in Marek's strong shoulder, when a Darracian marched past them holding a pike with Unis's head decorating the top of it. Loaded onto the first batch of ships, Reminda watched Bina shrink as they headed back to Darracia, her home and her destiny. An explosion rocked the spaceship as Bina exploded into a million tiny pieces.

"What?" Reminda sat up straighter. "What happened?"

Marek looked down at her fondly, and he made a bold move and kissed the top of her head. "Just as I thought, the graphen roots ran deep. My guess is our small detonations caused a chain reaction."

"Look!" She pointed a long blue finger out the window at the floating rubble. "It's…"

"Gone," Marek finished grimly.

XXIII

"CERTAINLY WE SHOULD head to the Desa, Greanam," Tulani said breathlessly as they walked toward the marketplace on the Plains of Dawid. "Greanam!" She pulled at Bobbien's covered arm. "We go to certain death here."

"Cover your braids as I showed you, girl," Greanam admonished. "Don't walk so fast. A job, we have yet to do."

"What could we possibly do?" She looked around into the sea of Darracian faces. Hardly any Quyroos were left. You could count them on your hand.

Bobbien strategically placed her staff behind her so it looked like a Darracian tail. She had done the same for her granddaughter. They were draped in voluminous robes worn by Darracian healers. Cowls hid their faces and braids. They walked down the narrow lanes, hawkers calling out illegal items. This was not the home Tulani remembered. It looked lawless—the pinched, hungry faces of the Darracians testimony that it was not the same planet for them as well. No longer privileged, they scrambled on the surface trying to feed whatever family members they could. Tulani looked at their faces, seeing a princess here, a countess there, men noticeably missing. Clothes looked worn, colorless, frayed. Many children looked emaciated, as if hunger as well as fear were their companions.

"Ozre," she murmured, "what have you allowed?"

Her grandmother overheard her, said simply, "Only man allows. Elements are bystanders. A message, I must get to a few merchants. Watch for soldiers."

Bobbien walked through the maze as if she'd done it a thousand times. She stopped, pulled a stall merchant close, whispered a short message. Tulani stood behind her, her eyes scanning the marketplace for trouble.

She watched her grandmother lean in, her red fingers wrapping around the gray wrists. There were nods of understanding. Sometimes she heard a nervous gasp, but always the reaction was swift. The key people were chosen to get the message, and slowly, one by one, stalls shut down. Then the crowd dissipated, and Tulani yearned for the moment that she and her grandmother could melt into the red of the forest.

They emerged from a filthy alleyway to head for the forest, when a white stallius mounted by a Quyroo stood in their way. Tulani shuddered as she recognized both the animal and the man who rode it. The soldier was surrounded by warriors who blocked their path.

"Who are you?" the officer demanded.

Tulani felt her muscles quiver with fear, her jaw clench with hatred. Before she could answer, she was grabbed by strong hands on either side, and the cowl was ripped from her head. Bright sunlight blinded her, and she was held fast by her captors.

"Ah, Tulani." Seren laughed. "I have missed you. We never got to finish what we started. Take them!" he ordered, spinning quickly to gallop toward his command hut.

She was back in the prison in the basement. Bobbien was missing; Tulani worried mightily. The heavy metal door opened with a squeal, and the old Darracian servant Kovo unlocked the door. He motioned for her to follow him.

"Where are you taking me?" she asked in a hurried whisper.

"Seren wants you to watch what he does with your grandmother," he replied without looking at her face. His shoulders were bent, his steps heavy with defeat.

"Why do you help him?" Tulani demanded. "They are destroying the planet."

"What choice do I have?" the old man shot back. "If I don't cooperate, he will send both my wife and me to Bina. We are too old. Oh, how this place has changed," Kovo lamented. "Before the invasion, I was a distributor of machinery. I had wealth, status, and many Quyroo servants…" He grew quiet, shaking his head. "Oh, how the outlook has changed for me!"

"What do you mean?" Tulani looked at his face in the dark room.

"I was nice to my servants, but I never realized how hard they worked. When Drakko, you know, the last king, wanted them to join the Moon Council, I voted against it.

I didn't understand how it was for them. I didn't know." He shook his craggy head as he shuffled up another level of steps. "It is not fair."

"No," Tulani agreed quietly. "It is not."

"Everyone should be treated with dignity," Kovo stated.

"Yet you work for Seren. He is not a fair commander."

The Darracian shrugged, much like the Quyroo fashion. "One must eat."

Tulani touched his arm. "You can help me."

He shook his head. "I cannot."

Tulani followed him to the top floor and was led to a door at the end of a long hallway. She entered to find Bobbien strapped to a chair, her head hanging, her braids loosened, hiding her face. Her raspy breath filled the room.

"Greanam!" Tulani ran to her grandmother and fell to her knees. She touched her leg but got no response.

"She may be close to death." Seren laughed. "She was always a fool. She wouldn't tell me what she was doing in the marketplace."

Tulani touched Bobbien's cheek, relief filling her when the star-shaped eyes winked. Bobbien groaned long and loud, letting everyone in the room know she yet breathed. "Ah!" Seren smacked a whip against the palm of his hand. "She lives. What to do, what to do…Shall I hurt the granddaughter to make the old one talk, or hurt the elder to make you tell me what you were doing? So many choices, ha!"

"We were doing nothing!" Tulani shouted. "Nothing. How could you hurt Bobbien?" Tulani accused him, her face angry. "She set your arm when you were seven. What kind of monster have you become?"

Seren stalked over to her, grabbed a fistful of hair, and pulled Tulani across the floor. He leaned closer, his face inches from hers. "We can finish this once and for all between us, Tulani. Give me what I want, and I will let her go."

Tulani looked at the slack figure of her grandmother in the chair. She glanced out of the window to gaze at the city in the clouds, now listing so heavily to one side that it rested on part of the Desa, crushing whatever trees grew there. The dreams were dead. V'sair was gone. What did anything matter anymore? All she had was Bobbien, and she would do anything to protect her. She noticed it was so quiet outside the air was thick, as though a thunderstorm was coming.

Taking a deep breath, she looked up at Seren, her eyes filled with tears, and said, "Tell me what you want."

He leaned down to kiss her roughly, and then the door swung open, Kovo in the portal. He was holding Bobbien's walking stick. "Here, girl," he called out, throwing the stick to her. "Defend yourself! We march to take back Darracia! The species have united!" He let out a war whoop and ran from the house.

Tulani reached out and deftly caught the stick in her hands, her agile fingers wrapping around it.

Seren shouted, "What is the meaning—"

Tulani spun, her leg landing squarely in Seren's groin, bringing him to his knees. He screamed, fumbling with his holster to grab his gun. Tulani banged his hand with the stick; Seren howled with rage. He stood, then crouched low and ran to attack her. Tulani bashed him in the shoulder, knocking him sideways. He rolled to stand to come at her again, but Tulani leaped high, smacking him on the back of the head. Seren fell like a toppled tree, moving no more.

"Tulani!" Bobbien called, her voice weak. "Pull the hair from my eyes. I can't see."

"No time, Greanam." Tulani fumbled with the knots on the rope. "What do you know that I don't?"

"Has it started? We just had to last until Zayden hits the town. Rescue us, he will."

"Zayden? V'sair's brother?"

"Yes. Attacking at dawn, he is. He has rallied the Quyroos, and I have spoken with the Darracians. We will throw out this yoke of oppression together."

Bobbien stood, leaning heavily on Tulani. They heard fierce shouting from the open window. They both gazed out, welcoming the sight of a line of Quyroos walking toward them, the horizon filled with armed warriors.

"Let's get out of here," Tulani urged.

"Put Seren in a place where he'll do the least damage, we will." Bobbien smiled with a big grin.

XXIV

LOTHEN LOOKED HELPLESSLY over the balustrade, watching the city sink lower and lower. At this point even the broken contours of Aqin the volcano were higher. Syos hung lopsided; many of the buildings rocked drunkenly on the waves of the Hixom Sea. They were doomed. The planet had been stripped of its resources, just like Planta.

He saw a line of movement from the dark recesses of the red Desa. Like a writhing snake, it moved closer, the dual rays of Rast and Nost illuminating the morning horizon. It had stopped raining, the suns baking the forest so it steamed with heat. Lothen's narrowed eyes watched the small line cresting the final hilltop to the Plains of Dawid, realizing with horror that it was a mass of Quyroos, their marching feet beating in a strange rhythm, as if calling more to join their battalion. He counted rows of thousands of them armed with primitive weapons.

The sun splashed its brilliance onto the glistening gray water of the Hixom Sea. The dazzling rays pranced on the surface, illuminating a school of blue fish swimming close to the surface. Lothen leaned closer, his eyes starting out of his head when he realized they were not fish but hundreds of blue arms swimming above the waterline. He leaned over, seeing a synchronized swarm of Plantans swimming determinedly to the shoreline. He knew instinctively these were not his people, but who could they be? A lone white-haired head popped above the choppy waves to pause and stare right at him. His eyes locked with his nephew V'sair—alive and with an army swimming behind him.

Lothen turned to go inside and raced through the hallways, skidding on the slippery polished floors, rounding a corner to dash into the throne room. Staf Nuen sat dejectedly on the throne, his fist under his chin, his leg swung negligently over the arm of the chair. The court was empty. The wind whistled through the hollow room, blowing abandoned papers littering the floor. Lothen stooped to pick one up.

"What is the meaning of this?" He scanned the notice, crumbling it after reading the words.

"Primitive but effective, as you can see." Staf pointed to his vacant room. "A call to arms for all species. They mean to overthrow us."

"Nuen, Nuen!" Lothen screamed. "We are being

attacked. Call out the guards! Go out there and defend our home.”

Staf Nuen ignored him, his yellowed eyes slivered in the dark room.

“Staf!” Lothen grabbed him.

Staf turned slowly, his face feral in the darkness. “I don't care.”

“Raise the army. For your son!”

This time Staf Nuen threw back his head to laugh, the bitter sounds bouncing off the walls to echo in the empty room. Staf Nuen laughed like a madman, spittle foaming at his mouth. Lothen backed out of the room.

Lothen walked purposefully to his staff headquarters, coming into a near-deserted chamber. Three Plantan commanders sat at the command table, talking quietly.

“An invasion! A revolution!” Lothen announced, banging his fist on the table.

“We have heard of it.” One of his generals stood, twisting his arm ring nervously.

“Where are your men?” He glanced around the table, noting not a single newly appointed Darracian was there. “Where?” he screamed, the veins sticking out on his blue neck. His white war knot listed to one side, making him appear as off-balance as he sounded.

“They have deserted. The Darracians are missing. Many of our Plantan warriors have gone missing.”

Lothen pulled out his sword, menacing it before their frightened faces. “I expect every able-bodied male—Plantan, Darracian, or Quyroo—to be behind me on those beaches within the hour!”

"Sire, the Quyroos are near extinct, and we have deported them all." A lone general stood, shifting from one foot to the other.

Lothen struck off his head with a single blow. It landed with a bloody thud on the conference table to roll into the center, the surprised, sightless eyes still fluttering.

"Are there any questions?" Lothen asked with menace.

The remaining males jumped up and rushed out of the room. Lothen approached the dead man. Reaching down, he ripped off one of the bracelets adorning the man's upper arm. He worked it up his forearm to his bicep. Flexing his arm, he watched the bracelet mold to the muscle and bone of his own arm, the metal snake undulating in its new home.

Lothen ran to the stables, saddled his black stallius himself to leap out of the low fortress and land on the planet. There were no guards, not a single one. He galloped over the spongy ground toward the Plains of Dawid. The humidity bathed his skin with a sheen of perspiration. He wiped his damp palms down the material of his pants. The tightly woven streets of the marketplace were eerily silent. He walked the stallius though the rutted lanes, the wind picking up to whistle down the narrow alleyways. The animal balked, neighing, her eyes rolling in her skull. She pranced, nearly unseating him. Lothen tugged on the reins, his spurred feet digging holes into her dark sides. Her coat frothed pink where he jabbed her.

He pulled the reins, making his way toward Seren's compound. It had been looted. Clothes lay discarded in the dirt square; broken plates, items from the house were strewn haphazardly around. A door hung drunkenly on its side, half-opened. Lothen dismounted and tied his stallius's reins to a post. Taking out his pistol, he walked into the darkened interior. It was deathly quiet, the bang of a loose shutter making Lothen jump. He heard a whimper and walked cautiously toward a pantry door. One hand on the doorknob, he swung it open to find Seren bound and gagged on the floor. His pants had been pulled down around his legs, leaving his red backside exposed for all and sundry.

Lothen pulled him out with an ungentle tug, then sliced off the shackles.

"Pull your pants up!" he commanded. Seren's red face grew pinker as he hastily complied. "Where are your men?"

"Deserted." He cleared his throat.

"Did they do that to you?"

"No, it was Tulani and her grandmother," he replied shamefacedly.

Lothen slammed into the commander's head with his gun. "A girl and an old woman! Where are your men?" he demanded.

"They have run. It is the warrior Zayden. They have heard of him, and he is on the way here!" Sweat shone on his frightened face. The Quyroo shook with terror.

"Get your guns, and muster up whoever you can!" Lothen shoved him away. "We fight. Move to the beach."

XXV

THE SUNS BEAT down to bake the red sands into a pale pink. The heat shimmered so that the distance looked as smudged as a watercolor. Lothen sat on his black stallius, Seren to the right of him on Hother. Both animals snorted, pawing the loose sand. Seren worked hard to control his beast, crushing the wings that threatened to spread against his command. He thought briefly of sending the animal back to the stables for another mount but lacked even one servant to do his bidding. Every man was armed and ready for the impending battle.

The wind picked up, whipping the gray sea into a frenzy of foam. The sky darkened, and Lothen spread his hands wide while balancing himself on the stallius. "Geva, great goddess of destruction, you must wipe out the Quyroos once and for all." He looked dusted in gold, his blue skin iridescent with sweat. His arms were covered from shoulder to elbow with snake rings, each a clear message to his enemies of past victories.

The wind screamed, sending sand and rocks flying. A cloud shaped itself in the sky. The oncoming Quyroos slowed, suddenly fearful of the fury of the wind. They paused, cowering on the uppermost ridge before the descent into the Plains of Dawid. The whole valley spread before them in a great, dusty pink bowl, the wind gusting to swirl great gouts of sand into tornadoes dancing along the great open space.

Zayden yelled over the howling wind, "What's the matter with them? Denita, be my eyes."

Denita squinted through the growing darkness. "Lothen has conjured something up, Zayden. Something evil."

"There is no such thing as evil," Zayden scoffed. "Move forward." He motioned with his arm but felt Denita pull his elbow back.

"They are frightened!" she yelled over the growing noise. They held their spot, buffeted by the warm winds, their clothes plastered to their bodies, in a standoff.

Zayden heard Lothen praying to his dark deity.

"Kill them, Geva!" he commanded.

Clouds roiled in the sky, turning day into the darkest night. A dark ball of energy spun across the sky, whizzing past the Quyroos' heads, making them cringe with fear as they dropped to the ground. A fetid smell followed the ball in a trail of cosmic refuse.

"Tell me what you see!" Zayden shouted to Denita.

"Lothen and his army are between us and the sea. His forces are surprisingly small. If we can get our people to rush down the hill, I think we can take them. Oh…" She stopped talking.

"What?" Zayden reached out to grab her arm. "Something is happening."

"I don't know if this is good or bad…Oh no. There are reinforcements coming from the water. A whole army of Plantans is swimming to the shore. Zayden," she said, her voice full of despair, "we are lost. We are a lost cause."

"Shit," Zayden cursed. "Think, think, think…" He hit his forehead with the palm of his hand.

"Hold on!" Denita stopped him. "Lothen…oh, Zayden…Lothen is moving to attack his own people. They are different somehow."

"What is different?" Zayden urged, grasping for anything. "Tell me what you see. Leave out no detail."

"The tattoos, Zayden. They don't have them. They don't have those war rings on their arms either. They are slighter.

I have never seen Plantans without tattoos on their faces." "They have no tattoos?" Zayden asked in a rush.

Denita shook her head, replying, "I mean, no, and they don't wear their hair in war knots either."

"I don't know who they are, but they are not Plantan."

He stood, turning to be seen by his troops. He could sense a difference. More fighters had joined the ranks. His army had increased, picking up new members from all over Darracia. He needed to coalesce them into a cohesive fighting force. They were untrained, unprepared, and probably doomed. The one thing they were, he realized with a smile, was united.

"There is a battle going on down there. Are we going

to sit here like a target or go down and kick some Plantan ass?" Zayden shouted, standing his full seven-foot height. There were murmurs, a few cheers. He spun around, clicking his tongue to locate his troops. "I may be just a king's bastard, and a blind one at that, but I am willing to go down there and show Lothen and his army what we are made of." The voices stilled, his soldiers watching his every move. Zayden filled his chest and spoke as loud as his voice would carry. "The time has come for us to change or die. All men and women, no matter their species or color, should have the same rights as everyone else. I declare this day that I will take my father, King Drakko's, dream and turn it to reality. As the Elements are the Trivium, so are the species of Darracia. One is not whole without the other. The Trivium is whole, and so are our people. Be they gray, red, or blue— one is not whole without the other. I declare for one and all that the species of Darracia are whole and equal or nothing at all!"

Noise of hundreds of shouts erupted, filling the bowlshaped meadow with the cheers of Zayden's army.

Denita spun slowly, gasping, breathless. "We have doubled, my warrior. There are hundreds of fighters together on this hill. I see equal parts Darracians and Quyroos."

He scanned the crowd, clicking his tongue to gage the size of his fighting force, knowing by the noise it had swelled and had more than just the lithe forms of Quyroos. Darracians had joined the ranks. Finally, they were one. The planet was whole, as his father had wished. He had fulfilled his destiny.

He turned to Denita and held her by her shoulders. "This is where we part. Stay here." He pulled her close, then kissed her full on her lips, leaving her breathless.

"But I am your eyes!" she protested.

"More importantly, you are my heart, and I will keep you safe." He kissed her again and told her, "I will come back for you."

He shouted for his men to follow him, and Denita watched him run forward, knowing he had just told her a lie. She followed him stealthily down the hill.

XXVI

LIKE A MAGNET, V'sair's blue eyes caught and held his uncle's gaze. V'sair stood tall in the water, raising his sword as a beacon for his troops to follow. Their wet skin glistened as though they were covered in diamonds. The army of sickle-shaped spears followed his lead, looking like a sheet of steel. Their feet marched in tandem, the steady thrum of the footsteps echoing off the back wall of the landmass. V'sair's eyes caught the ragtag line of Quyroo and Darracian warriors in readiness on the crests of the hills surrounding the Plains of Dawid. He knew at this moment a full brigade of his fighters was making its way from the other shorelines, crushing any opposition. He paused, sucking in his breath, a broad smile lighting his face when he realized it was his brother who stood proudly on the ridge.

"Brother-in-arms," he said quietly, then saluted him

with his sword. He frowned when there was no return, but the large field became deathly quiet.

Restive stalliuses whinnied, and V'sair recognized a familiar sound. Hother took that moment to scream wildly, raising herself onto her hind legs to try to unseat Seren. She pranced toward the water, shaking Seren from her back like an unwanted parasite. He fell onto the red sand hard on his shoulder, watching helplessly as the stallius opened her wings to glide to her beloved master. V'sair reached for her, hugged her muscled neck, inhaling the familiar scent of his mount. Tears prickled the backs of his eyelids, but he drew a deep breath, blocking out emotions.

V'sair blew gently into her nose and, in a fluid motion, pulled himself onto her back, lifted his sword to the heavens, and cried out, "For Drakko, for equality, for Darracia!"

A loud cheer deafened the field, marrying the two forces. With a unified war cry, they took off at the same time with the sole purpose of destroying their invaders. The blue tide of fighters raced across the beach toward the incoming gray-and-red mass of warriors descending the hill.

V'sair galloped Hother across the beach, his sword gilded by the suns, Lothen and his black stallius in his line of sight. Sand sprayed behind him, creating a sparkling aura around both V'sair and his stallius. He looked like an avenging spirit, his mount's wings spread in stunning white glory, his face against the creamy coat of the stallius, his white hair entwined with her mane.

Lothen pulled his reins up, making his mount open its wingspan to fly above the bloody fray. V'sair mirrored his movements, and they met, their swords clashing in a tremendous explosion of energy. V'sair's arm shivered from the blow, but he swung around to raise the weapon again for another swipe at his uncle.

They danced in the sky, nicking flesh, hitting bone—equal to the task for defending their territory. Although Lothen had experience, V'sair had agility and youth. V'sair spun to his left, knowing Lothen tried to put him in a position where the suns' dual glare blinded him. V'sair danced Hother in a tight circle. Hother bit the other stallius, making Lothen's animal rear up in anger, frothing at the bit. Lothen held tight, slashing V'sair, opening his forearm wrist to elbow. Blood dripped to leave a trail on the water, falling in tiny ripples on the foaming surface. V'sair stabbed Lothen's thigh, the hiss of pain letting him know he had struck true.

Staf Nuen watched the battle from the listing balcony of the grounded castle. Observing the aerial ballet of Lothen and his nephew V'sair, a smile tugged at his lips. He saw V'sair get in a successful jab at Lothen and whispered, "You should be proud of your son, Brother. Tire him, V'sair," he advised to the vacant space. "If you let him exhaust himself, you may yet win." While he was twenty stories up, just this morning the randam had expired, settling the fortress in a muddy lake known for its murky depths. The first two levels sunk below the waterline; the next level filled fast. He felt a presence behind him and turned to see Naje holding her infant.

"You are king still?" she asked, her face white with worry. "Does it matter?" He turned back to look at the carnage. The flower of Darracian warriors was gone—people he'd trained with, soldiers with both honor and merit. All that was left was this fighting force of old men and little boys who had joined to Zayden and his red troops. "It has all been for nothing."

"What?" Naje stalked to him. "Your son!" She gestured the wrapped infant in her arms.

"Lothen's son. This is no boy of mine. I killed my son with greed and stupidity. Drakko was right."

"What are you talking about?" she demanded. "Is that the graphen talking?"

Staf shook his head. "I wanted to be king because I thought I knew better. I wanted to suppress the Quyroos for all the wrong reasons. No species is better than the others. Emmicus was right. The Trivium is whole; one cannot exist without the other."

"You babble. Who is Emmicus?" Naje asked accusingly.

"A very wise man. Darracia cannot stand without the unity of its species." He paused. "I was wrong about everything." He turned his face away.

"That's it?" she shrieked. "That's all you are going to do? I will never forgive you."

He turned to look at her, assessing her coldly. "It's not your forgiveness I am looking for." He turned to stare at the horizon. "I must forgive myself, and I'll never be able to. All is lost," he mumbled. Wearily, he climbed to balance himself upon the balustrade. He looked down into the swirling depths of the lake. "It was all for nothing. I was wrong, all wrong," he said in a shocked whisper. He had been so filled with his own sense of rightness, and he now realized he was empty. There was indeed nothing else. He pitched forward, feeling at peace, allowing himself the last feeling of complete freedom before the water engulfed him, pulling Staf Nuen into obscurity and oblivion.

Naje cursed, watching in helpless horror. She shouted, "Nooooo!" as Staf threw himself out of the fortress. She leaned over, watching his cape spread out like a giant bat, his face staring up, his worry erased. "Old fool," she cursed him.

She ran from the room and shoved items in a sack. The baby cried, hungry, his pinched little face blue with rage. She shushed him, rocking him against her full breasts until he quieted.

"Come, Loki. I will save us. I have always depended upon myself." She kissed the white, downy head, satisfied as her son's eyes slid shut. "It appears that I will continue to do so."

Throwing a dark cape over her head, she raced to the exit and was swallowed by the yawning forest outside the castle door.

XXVII

THE TWO LEADERS of the land clashed overhead, their swords ringing in the valley below them. V'sair called out to his Darracian ancestors with the ancient war cry, causing great cheers on the ground below. The battle raged, hand to hand, with fierce fighting, leaving a swath of destruction below. Zayden created a line of soldiers on the top of the hill, armed with the small slingshots. He led the charge down the incline, then stopped his warriors at the base in a coordinated move. Plantan warriors took this as cowardice and moved forward with confidence.

Zayden clicked his tongue, gaging the approaching enemy. Then he screamed, "Turn!"

The Quyroos and Darracian soldiers turned to climb up the hill, the Plantans screaming with victory behind them. As they landed on the first terraced area, Zayden's soldiers threw themselves face first on the floor, leaving the oncoming enemy exposed to the line of marksmen above them. Round after round of deadly missiles were loosed, catching the attackers unprepared. The gourds sang as they were loaded then launched in an unending barrage of shrapnel.

Zayden cocked his head, listening to the thuds of the rock missiles as they found their marks on the enemies' torsos. His sonar working, he fielded a blow meant to take off his head by ducking and stabbing his attacker. He paused, the noise of the battle receding, when he zeroed in on his brother V'sair's war cry.

"V'sair." He looked upward, seeing nothing but knowing from the change in the air currents that his brother was flying on Hother above him. He waved, his back unguarded, a target for a Plantan sergeant who stood, taking aim with a gun. He shot at Zayden, the whistling bullet heading toward him.

Denita screamed, "Zayden, duck!" Looking around, she spied a pistol in the dead hands of a soldier, took aim, and shot the enemy in the heart.

Zayden dropped to the ground, the bullet tearing at his shoulder, ripping his tunic. He stood, furious, then marched while screaming, "Denita, I told you to stay back!"

She ran and threw herself at him so they tumbled onto the ground, their legs entangling. "Why?" She kissed his cheek, filthy with the grime of battle. "Why, my heart? Where you go, I go."

"It's not safe." They rolled into a ravine, the sounds of the fight dying off. "You are female," he said as if that explained everything.

"A female is just as good a fighter as a male, any male, be he Quyroo, Darracian, or Plantan!" Denita answered hotly.

Zayden shook his head. "I know. I know. You are right. But, Denita, you are *my* female."

"If you plan on equality, my love, it has to be equality for all," she whispered. "Besides, did you think I could not shoot?"

"I know you can shoot. I have to go back."

This time when he stood to assess the battle, his woman was beside him, protecting his back.

Lothen stared in disbelief as the bulk of his army was cut down by makeshift soldiers without real weapons. V'sair used that moment to rush at him. But Lothen moved, and the stallius took the hit, screaming in pain. The animal spiraled down to the planet, taking Lothen with it. V'sair followed relentlessly.

Lothen's eyes scanned the beach for Seren, for help, angry with his failure to not only hold on to his mount but the ineffectual command of the landed forces. He aimed the dying stallius away from the thick of the fighting and landed with a hard crash. He spied his erstwhile commander near the waterline on the beach. He was holding on to a girl, a Quyroo, while battling with an older woman. The old Quyroo used a stick against his sword and looked to be tiring. He ducked into the bushes, lost in the confusion on the ground.

V'sair lost Lothen when he landed, his eyes searching the bloody beach. He glanced downward to see a woman used as a shield by Seren. He redirected Hother to move in to help the woman, his mount's hooves grazing the choppy seas. He landed on the beach and noticed the fighting had tapered off. He leaped off his stallius and ran to block Bobbien, saving her from a thrust that would have taken off her head.

"V'sair!" Tulani screamed. "V'sair!"

"You hide behind a woman?" V'sair taunted the Quyroo commander.

"I will kill her before I let you have her again." He backed into the water, holding Tulani, his sword resting on her thin neck.

V'sair could see her pulse beating, the resignation in her eyes. He rushed after them, the water reaching his hips. Seren nicked her; the blood welled to drip into the small swells of the sea.

"I will finish the job, V'sair. Come closer. I'd like nothing better!" Seren snarled.

V'sair's breath caught in his throat as the snout of the giant beast he'd seen under the water arced its vast head above the waterline, its nostrils flaring with the scent of Tulani's blood. It moved its bulky head back and forth, exposing rows of gigantic white teeth. Opening its jaws, it rose from the water and snapped off Seren's head.

"Tulani, jump!" V'sair screamed, propelling himself toward her, his hands outreached to grab her.

There was a crunch as Seren's head was snapped from his torso, and a great sucking sound of the pull from the great fish as it tried to grab Tulani. Tulani floundered, her arms flailing as she slipped in the oily water, slick with the fresh gouts of blood shooting from Seren's corpse.

V'sair used his gills, diving deeply, wrapping his arms around her body, placing his mouth over hers to give the breath of life. He felt her go limp in his arms, whether from fear or because she had fainted, but the swells of waves from the furious fish buffeted them both toward the shoreline. They emerged—V'sair holding Tulani in his arms—to walk slowly toward the war-torn beach littered with the dead and dying. The battle was over, he thought with exhaustion, his glassy eyes taking in the carnage. A force of nature plowed into him, wrapping great arms around both V'sair and Tulani.

V'sair looked up to find himself in the crushing embrace of his half brother.

Zayden sniffed the air and said, "You smell like fish, Brother. And you, Tulani, smell like sunshine."

V'sair took in his brother's weary face, seeing new lines and scars. "Are you hurt?"

"It's a long story, and now is not the time." Zayden smiled. He clicked, getting his bearings. "Sounds like something still going on that way." He pointed to a ridge on the left. "See you after the battle." He dashed off, screaming for his warriors to follow him into the fray. V'sair observed a cocoa-skinned girl devotedly following his brother's moves, covering his back.

V'sair kissed Tulani on her lips. "Have you heard anything from my mother?" he asked hopefully.

Tulani shook her head that she hadn't. Salt crusted her lashes; her eyes were giant pools of shock.

"I will see you later. I know I saw Bobbien. Find her. Get to the castle. I will meet you there," he told her. "Go. I have to finish this." He scanned the beach, looking for Lothen.

Lothen stood on a rock watching the destruction of his army. Holding out his arms, he summoned Geva again. This time the sky darkened, and lightning flashed, stilling the last combatants. Lothen walked out of his hiding place to scream, "Make them pay, Geva!"

Like a plague, Geva swarmed the remaining soldiers, a dark mist descending to choke the life from them. V'sair felt the thickness in the air, the foul evil of Lothen's goddess, despair filling him with dread. He was tired. He had fought and thought victory was in his hands. He watched the black cloud move toward his brother, still fighting high on the final ridge. Slowly it moved, leaving corpses in its wake.

V'sair screamed out, "Ozre, Ereth, and Ine, I commend myself to thee. Great Sradda, what more do you expect from us? After this, you would let them win?"

He fell to his knees and buried his head in the pink sand. A great rumble shook him so that he fell over. He heard startled cries as the water in the Hixom Sea boiled, turning the gray water white with foam. An explosion rent the air, and the water parted to reveal a huge volcano rising from the seabed. It roared to life as it got bigger, blotting out the entire horizon. The ground shook with a massive earthquake, and the top of the volcano opened, erupting and spewing forth a fierce display of fire. The fighting on the beach ground to a halt, all eyes on the raging inferno that was blazing to massive proportions. V'sair looked up, wonder replacing despair, as multicolored orbs of light raced out of the cone of the volcano. Green, blue, and red orbs flew into the sky, surrounding the dark cloud, reining it in like a net. The black cloud slipped through an opening to move across the large sky. The three orbs raced, getting there before Geva. It was as though they could anticipate her every move. Geva thinned, hoping to escape by dissipating enough she would be too big to contain. The balls of light exploded into a thousand small beams of brightness. They spread out across the sky, filling the horizon, trapping the smoky blackness that was the essence of Lothen's goddess. It struggled against the confines but was no match for the speed and dexterity of the glowing spirals of bright light. They bounced, attacked, and confined Geva, smothering the blackness with light.

Lothen yelled, "Geva!" He watched miserably as the black cloud got smaller, finally disappearing into a small puff of smoke. The orbs turned to him, spun toward his direction, and filled the Plantan king until he was lifted high, his body rigid. He spun in a vortex of color, his white hair burning brightly, until he was dropped into the fuming cone of the volcano, his screams echoing for a full minute afterward. The orbs spread out, pulsing high above the Plains of Dawid, a rainbow of colors reflecting from their depths. The green light bounced forward, taking precedence and sweeping across the land, touching the sand and leaving a lighted path. The lights then gravitated together, forming a single large ball of green, blue, and red. They floated above the Plains of Dawid like a new sun.

"The Trivium is whole. One is not whole without the other." V'sair stood, intoning the prayer.

Ozre dipped. "The land will grow…"

Ereth's blue light nodded. "Water is life…"

The green in Ine raced again in a great circle around the bowl-like structure of the meadow, each revolution making her go faster and faster, until all one saw was a shadow of her color. She exploded into dazzling green sparks that filled the space, then landed gracefully on the ground.

V'sair walked over to touch the tiny light in his hand. It glowed, pulsing with life. "Ine is the seed," he said in awe.

The large green orb went back to rest between the others. Her voice became the soft music of a mother's call. "Ine is the seed to make the Desa grow again."

The three orbs bounced to rise above the volcano. All eyes were drawn to a row of ships moving into the atmosphere. They were the Plantan ships used to transport the Darracians to Bina.

V'sair sighed. "Oh no, not again." He felt his brother behind him.

"Tell me what you see, V'sair."

V'sair turned, realizing his brother was blind. He momentarily felt great sorrow for him but knew they must press on.. "I'm not sure." He shrugged. "Ships. Another invasion."

Tulani came to his other side. "I told you to find Bobbien and return to the castle."

"I have found Bobbien." V'sair turned to see the old Quyroo behind him, a smile on her face.

"I will never be parted from you again." She took his hand. "We are one, forever, V'sair. In the sky or on the land, we will never be parted again."

Raising her hand, he brushed her bruised knuckles with a kiss.

Zayden mobilized his troops on the ridge, weapons ready. The entire crest was lined with V'sair's Welks, Quyroos, and Darracians standing tall, ready to defend their home. The new volcano smoked lazily from its home in the ocean, filling the sky with the charred odor of fire.

"You should be farther back, Your Highness," Zayden advised his king. "I will meet the enemy on your behalf."

"Only a grand mestor can tell me that."

Zayden bowed his head. "I am blind, Brother. I am crippled. You will need someone who is not handicapped."

"I need you, Brother." V'sair turned to face him, knowing Zayden could sense how important he was to him. "Your blindness is a handicap only if you make it one. To me, I see my brother. The only ones I see crippled are the victims who tangled with you. You are the warrior our father expected."

Zayden's eyes misted. "Then as your grand mestor, I advise you to remove yourself."

"As your brother only, I respectfully refuse. We meet our destiny together." They turned to face the lead ship, now lowering itself slowly onto the pink soil.

The lead ship's thruster blew the sand in swirling circles as it placed itself on the pink beach, the doors opening. A large Darracian stepped out, his eyes scanning the surroundings, his hands wrapped around a baton of sorts as a weapon. Both V'sair and Zayden readied their swords as the large male turned, holding out his hand to help another from inside the ship. A small boy descended shakily, his head covered with a cowl. He had a decidly feminine grace about his movements. On the last step, the smaller one removed the head covering, revealing spiked white hair, and with a gasp, the realization of her identity shocked the crowd. Her worried eyes moved wildly about, then came to rest on her son.

"V'sair!" she called, tripping quickly down the ramp.

V'sair dropped his sword and shouted with joy as he raced to the steps of the ship.

He looked older, bloodied by battle—like a warrior king. Pride filled her chest.

They met at the bottom of the craft in a loving embrace. It was so silent; only the wind made noise. V'sair was shocked at her fragility as well as surprised by the possessive glare of the draconian Darracian assisting her down.

"It is over, Mo'mo. Darracian is whole," he assured her.

Reminda looked to the clouds, seeing only sky, not a building on the horizon. Syos was gone.

"Dado's dream has come true. All Darracians are equal, be they called Quyroo or Welk; no one will live above or below. They will share in the bounty of the land equally."

"The Elements have spoken." Bobbien came forward to embrace her friend. "The Elements have made it so."

EPILOGUE

TULANI AND V'SAIR were both crowned and married in a beautiful celebration. They rebuilt the royal city on the Plains of Dawid. Land, sea, and air lived together in harmony. It was an age of growth. The arts flourished, and Darracia became an epicenter of culture for the galaxy. V'sair and Tulani were sought out to help with other planets, advising them how to end disputes. Their family grew and, with the first child born just a year later, the succession was assured. Cawa was beautiful and smart, the perfect heir for her parents. They even found the perfect babysitter in Bobbien who was now living a few floors above them in the castle. She was more than willing to teach her new granddaughter the ways of her people.

Zayden's sight never came back. As he was the respected grand mestor and the father of a growing brood, it made no difference. Denita worked to find ways to compensate him, winning the Galacial Prize for Health and Science, and was celebrated all over the galaxy. They had six sons, each as different and diverse as the solar system. From the army to medicine, each one embraced a profession that brought grace and honor to the family.

Reminda lived in a compound not far from all her grandchildren. She had a noted salon that people longed to join to sit at her table and discuss how to make society better. She championed prisoners everywhere, working hard to find punishments that were more humane. Marek never left her side, and once V'sair got used to his presence, they found that second chances are the sweet aperitif to life.

There was peace and prosperity in the land, even in the Deep Fells, where a young, blue-skinned boy climbed among the trees in the new forest growing alongside the seedlings of peace.

About the Author

Born and raised on Long Island, Michael has always had a fascination with the paranormal, fantasy, and science fiction. After earning a degree in English and an MBA, he worked various jobs before settling into being a full-time author. He currently resides on Long Island with his wife and children.